P9-BYD-463

FUTURE WAR

EDITED BY
JACK DANN & GARDNER DOZOIS

ACE BOOKS, NEW YORK

This book is an Ace original edition,
and has never been previously published.

FUTURE WAR

An Ace Book / published by arrangement with
the editors

PRINTING HISTORY
Ace edition / August 1999

All rights reserved.
Copyright © 1999 by Jack Dann & Gardner Dozois.
Cover art by Chris Moore/Bernstein & Andriulli.
This book may not be reproduced in whole or in part,
by mimeograph or any other means, without permission.
For information address: The Berkley Publishing Group,
a division of Penguin Putnam Inc.,
375 Hudson Street, New York, New York 10014.

The Penguin Putnam Inc. World Wide Web site address is
http://www.penguinputnam.com

Check out the ACE Science Fiction & Fantasy newsletter
and much more on the Internet at Club PPI!

ISBN: 0-441-00639-6

ACE®
Ace Books are published
by The Berkley Publishing Group,
a division of Penguin Putnam Inc.,
375 Hudson Street, New York, New York 10014.
ACE and the "A" design are trademarks
belonging to Penguin Putnam Inc.

PRINTED IN THE UNITED STATES OF AMERICA

10 9 8 7 6 5 4 3 2 1

CONTENTS

PREFACE

That there will probably always be war is a conclusion with which your editors have to reluctantly agree, although, unlike some others, who seem almost to relish the prospect gloatingly, we take no pleasure in that predication. Still, a realistic appraisal of human nature and the often bitter lessons of history lead one almost inevitably to the conclusion that as long as human beings are still *human beings* as we understand them, war, of one sort or another, on one scale or another, in one arena or another, will probably be part of the human condition. (Some science fiction speculates that you could eliminate war by changing human nature *itself*, by, say, regimentation and control of the brain and the emotions by nanotechnology, or by eliminating human aggression through biological or chemical means; but, in almost every such scenario we know of, the cure seems almost worse than the disease.)

If war will probably always be part of the human condition, at least until war manages to wipe the human race out of existence, then the future will have war. And that's the unsettling but all-too-probable scenario that we deal with in this anthology, which features stories that examine the ultra high-tech battle-fields of the future—on Earth, in space, behind the front lines after the concept of "front line" itself has become meaning-less and *every* place in the world is itself a battlefield. These stories give us a powerful, and sometimes harrowing, look at what future war and future combat might *really* be like to those who live through it—and those (probably the more numerous) who do not.

Over the millennia, the human race has turned an enormous amount of its scientific ingenuity into inventing ever more effective and devastating ways for people to kill each other, to give one army a technological edge over another, to win wars at *any* price, even at the price of the destruction of life on Earth. And we're pretty sure that you ain't seen *nothing* yet. Just as people peering into the upcoming century from the end of the nineteenth century couldn't possibly have imagined the horrors

and complexities and sinister wonders of technological warfare
that awaited humanity in the twentieth century, so we too lack
the ability to see the as-yet-unimaginable weapons and technolo-
gies that lie ahead in the twenty-first century and beyond, things
that would seem just as bizarre and impossible to us as the
atomic bomb or a Stealth fighter or a cruise missile or a nuclear
submarine (or a radar set, or a laser bombsight, or a computer, or
a microchip) would have seemed to somebody back in 1899.

The ten science fiction writers in this book, daring and expert
dreamers, take their best shot at it, coming up with some of the
strangest, most imaginative, most mind-bending—and frightening—concepts of recent years, including some stuff that we
sincerely hope doesn't come to pass, for the sake of all those who
will have to live in that new century . . .

So quickly, before one of those future wars comes along to
interrupt you, while you still have the chance, open up this
anthology and enjoy the vivid entertainment, slambang action,
and sometimes-disturbing visions of the stories that wait within—and keep your fingers crossed that all of this stuff remains
science fiction!

SECOND VARIETY

Philip K. Dick

A dedicated investigator of the elusive nature of reality, an intrepid explorer of alternate states of consciousness, a wickedly effective and acidulous satirist, the late Philip K. Dick wrote some of the most brilliant novels and short stories in the history of the SF genre, and is now being widely recognized as one of the major authors of the late twentieth century, in any genre. He won a Hugo Award for his novel The Man in the High Castle, *and his many other novels include* Ubik, Martian Time Slip, The Three Stigmata of Palmer Eldrich, Time Out of Joint, *and* Do Androids Dream of Electric Sheep, *which was somewhat disappointingly filmed as* Bladerunner. *His most recent books, published posthumously, include* The Transmigration of Timothy Archer, Radio Free Albemuth, Puttering About in a Small Land, The Man Whose Teeth Were All Exactly Alike, *and the massive three-volume set* The Collected Stories of Philip K. Dick.

The nightmarish story that follows, "Second Variety," may well be the progenitor of most of the stories about high-tech future war that have followed it over the years. Although dated in some ways—there's no longer a Soviet Union, for instance—in the ways that really count, *it's perhaps even more germane than it used to be, closer by far to becoming a reality, as scientists and military technicians take us ever farther down the road Dick prophesied we'd follow all the way back in 1953. Phil Dick may well be smiling bitterly in Heaven as we ignore the harrowing fictional warning you're about to read and spend millions of dollars to create nearly autonomous killer robots and weapons systems, machines designed to kill enemy machines as well as to kill enemy* humans, *machines that, as military experts confidently tell us, will soon make the human soldier obsolete on the battlefield.*

Let's hope they don't make humans *obsolete as well . . .*

("Second Variety" was filmed, somewhat loosely, as the movie Screamers.)

The Russian soldier made his way nervously up the ragged side of the hill, holding his gun ready. He glanced around him, licking his dry lips, his face set. From time to time he reached up a gloved hand and wiped perspiration from his neck, pushing down his coat collar.

Eric turned to Corporal Leone. "Want him? Or can I have him?" He adjusted the view sight so the Russian's features squarely filled the glass, the lines cutting across his hard, somber features.

Leone considered. The Russian was close, moving rapidly, almost running. "Don't fire. Wait." Leone tensed. "I don't think we're needed."

The Russian increased his pace, kicking ash and piles of debris out of his way. He reached the top of the hill and stopped, panting, staring around him. The sky was overcast, with drifting clouds of gray particles. Bare trunks of trees jutted up occasionally; the ground was level and bare, rubble-strewn, with the ruins of buildings standing out here and there like yellowing skulls.

The Russian was uneasy. He knew something was wrong. He started down the hill. Now he was only a few paces from the bunker. Eric was getting fidgety. He played with his pistol, glancing at Leone.

"Don't worry," Leone said. "He won't get here. They'll take care of him."

"Are you sure? He's got damn far."

"They hang around close to the bunker. He's getting into the bad part. Get set!"

The Russian began to hurry, sliding down the hill, his boots sinking into the heaps of gray ash, trying to keep his gun up. He stopped for a moment, lifting his field glasses to his face.

"He's looking right at us," Eric said.

The Russian came on. They could see his eyes, like two blue stones. His mouth was open a little. He needed a shave; his chin was stubbled. On one bony cheek was a square of tape, showing blue at the edge. A fungoid spot. His coat was muddy and torn. One glove was missing. As he ran, his belt counter bounced up and down against him.

Leone touched Eric's arm. "Here one comes."

Across the ground something small and metallic came, flashing in the dull sunlight of midday. A metal sphere. It raced up the hill after the Russian, its treads flying. It was small, one of the baby ones. Its claws were out, two razor projections spinning in a blur of white steel. The Russian heard it. He turned instantly, firing. The sphere dissolved into particles. But already a second had emerged and was following the first. The Russian fired again.

A third sphere leaped up to the Russian's leg, clicking and whirring. It jumped to the shoulder. The spinning glades disappeared into the Russian's throat.

Eric relaxed. "Well, that's that. God, those damn things give me the creeps. Sometimes I think we were better off before."

"If we hadn't invented them, they would have." Leone lit a cigarette shakily. "I wonder why a Russian would come all this way alone. I didn't see anyone covering him."

Lieutenant Scott came slipping up the tunnel, into the bunker. "What happened? Something entered the screen."

"An Ivan."

"Just one?"

Eric brought the viewscreen around. Scott peered into it. Now there were numerous metal spheres crawling over the prostrate body, dull metal globes clicking and whirring, sawing up the Russian into small parts to be carried away.

"What a lot of claws," Scott murmured.

"They come like flies. Not much game for them any more."

Scott pushed the sight away, disgusted. "Like flies. I wonder why he was out there. They know we have claws all around."

A larger robot had joined the smaller spheres. A long blunt tube with projecting eyepieces, it was directing operations. There was not much left of the soldier. What remained was being brought down the hillside by the host of claws.

"Sir," Leone said, "If it's all right, I'd like to go out there and take a look at him."

"Why?"

"Maybe he came with something."

Scott considered. He shrugged. "All right. But be careful."

"I have my tab." Leone patted the metal band at his wrist. "I'll be out of bounds."

He picked up his rifle and stepped carefully up to the mouth of the bunker, making his way between blocks of concrete and steel prongs, twisted and bent. The air was cold at the top. He crossed over the ground toward the remains of the soldier, striding across the soft ash. A wind blew around him, swirling gray particles up in his face. He squinted and pushed on.

The claws retreated as he came close, some of them stiffening into immobility. He touched his tab. The Ivan would have given something for that! Short hard radiation emitted from the tab neutralized the claws, put them out of commission. Even the big robot with its two waving eyestalks retreated respectfully as he approached.

He bent down over the remains of the soldier. The gloved hand was closed tightly. There was something in it. Leone pried the fingers apart. A sealed container, aluminum. Still shiny.

He put it in his pocket and made his way back to the bunker. Behind him the claws came back to life, moving into operation again. The procession resumed, metal spheres moving through the gray ash with their loads. He could hear their treads scrabbling against the ground. He shuddered.

Scott watched intently as he brought the shiny tube out of his pocket. "He had that?"

"In his hand." Leone unscrewed the top. "Maybe you should look at it, sir."

Scott took it. He emptied the contents out in the palm of his hand. A small piece of silk paper, carefully folded. He sat down by the light and unfolded it.

"What's it say, sir?" Eric said. Several officers came up the tunnel. Major Hendricks appeared.

"Major," Scott said. "Look at this."

Hendricks read the slip. "This just come?"

"A single runner. Just now."

"Where is he?" Hendricks asked sharply.

"The claws got him."

Major Hendricks grunted. "Here." He passed it to his companions. "I think this is what we've been waiting for. They certainly took their time about it."

"So they want to talk terms," Scott said. "Are we going along with them?"

"That's not for us to decide." Hendricks sat down. "Where's the communications officer? I want the Moon Base."

Leone pondered as the communications officer raised the outside antenna cautiously, scanning the sky above the bunker for any sign of a watching Russian ship.

"Sir," Scott said to Hendricks. "It's sure strange they suddenly came around. We've been using the claws for almost a year. Now all of a sudden they start to fold."

"Maybe claws have been getting down in their bunkers."

"One of the big ones, the kind with stalks, got into an Ivan bunker last week," Eric said. "It got a whole platoon of them before they got their lid shut."

"How do you know?"

"A buddy told me. The thing came back with—with remains."

"Moon Base, sir," the communications officer said.

On the screen the face of the lunar monitor appeared. His crisp uniform contrasted to the uniforms in the bunker. And he was cleanshaven. "Moon Base."

"This is forward command L-Whistle. On Terra. Let me have General Thompson."

The monitor faded. Presently General Thompson's heavy features came into focus. "What is it, Major?"

"Our claws got a single Russian runner with a message. We don't know whether to act on it—there have been tricks like this in the past."

"What's the message?"

"The Russians want us to send a single officer on policy level over to their lines. For a conference. They don't state the nature of the conference. They say that matters of—" He consulted the slip: "—matters of grave urgency make it advisable that discussion be opened between a representative of the UN forces and themselves."

He held the message up to the screen for the general to scan. Thompson's eyes moved.

"What should we do?" Hendricks said.

"Send a man out."

"You don't think it's a trap?"

"It might be. But the location they give for their forward command is correct. It's worth a try, at any rate."

"I'll send an officer out. And report the results to you as soon as he returns."

"All right, Major." Thompson broke the connection. The screen died. Up above, the antenna came slowly down.

Hendricks rolled up the paper, deep in thought.

"I'll go," Leone said.

"They want somebody at policy level." Hendricks rubbed his jaw. "Policy level. I haven't been outside in months. Maybe I could use a little air."

"Don't you think it's risky?"

Hendricks lifted the view sight and gazed into it. The remains of the Russian were gone. Only a single claw was in sight. It was folding itself back, disappearing into the ash, like a crab. Like some hideous metal crab . . . "That's the only thing that bothers me." Hendricks rubbed his wrist, "I know I'm safe as long as I have this on me. But there's something about them. I hate the damn things. I wish we'd never invented them. There's something wrong with them. Relentless little—"

"If we hadn't invented them, the Ivans would have."

Hendricks pushed the sight back. "Anyhow, it seems to be winning the war. I guess that's good."

"Sounds like you're getting the same jitters as the Ivans."

Hendricks examined his wristwatch. "I guess I had better get started, if I want to be there before dark."

He took a deep breath and then stepped out onto the gray rubbled ground. After a minute he lit a cigarette and stood gazing around him. The landscape was dead. Nothing stirred. He could see for miles, endless ash and slag, ruins of buildings. A few trees without leaves or branches, only the trunks. Above him the eternal rolling clouds of gray, drifting between Terra and the sun.

Major Hendricks went on. Off to the right something scuttled, something round and metallic. A claw, going lickety-split after something. Probably after a small animal, a rat. They got rats, too. As a sort of sideline.

He came to the top of the little hill and lifted his field glasses.

The Russian lines were a few miles ahead of him. They had a forward command post there. The runner had come from it.

A squat robot with undulating arms passed by him, its arms weaving inquiringly. The robot went on its way, disappearing under some debris. Hendricks watched it go. He had never seen that type before. There were getting to be more and more types he had never seen, new varieties and sizes coming up from the underground factories.

Hendricks put out his cigarette and hurried on. It was interesting, the use of artificial forms in warfare. How had they got started? Necessity. The Soviet Union had gained great initial success, usual with the side that got the war going. Most of North America had been blasted off the map. Retaliation was quick in coming, of course. The sky was full of circling diskbombers long before the war began; they had been up there for years. The disks began sailing down all over Russia within hours after Washington got it.

But that hadn't helped Washington.

The American bloc governments moved to the Moon Base the first year. There was not much else to do. Europe was gone, a slag heap with dark weeds growing from the ashes and bones. Most of North America was useless; nothing could be planted, no one could live. A few million people kept going up in Canada and down in South America. But during the second year Soviet parachutists began to drop, a few at first, then more and more. They wore the first really effective anti-radiation equipment; what was left of American production moved to the Moon along with the governments.

All but the troops. The remaining troops stayed behind as best they could, a few thousand here, a platoon there. No one knew exactly where they were; they stayed where they could, moving around at night, hiding in ruins, in sewers, cellars, with the rats and snakes. It looked as if the Soviet Union had the war almost won. Except for a handful of projectiles fired off from the Moon daily, there was almost no weapon in use against them. They came and went as they pleased. The war, for all practical purposes, was over. Nothing effective opposed them.

And then the first claws appeared. And overnight the complexion of the war changed.

The claws were awkward, at first. Slow. The Ivans knocked them off almost as fast as they crawled out of their underground tunnels. But then they got better, faster and more cunning. Factories, all on Terra, turned them out. Factories a long way underground, behind the Soviet lines, factories that had once made atomic projectiles, now almost forgotten.

The claws got faster, and they got bigger. New types appeared, some with feelers, some that flew. There were a few jumping kinds. The best technicians on the Moon were working on designs, making them more and more intricate, more flexible. They became uncanny; the Ivans were having a lot of trouble with them. Some of the little claws were learning to hide themselves, burrowing down into the ash, lying in wait.

And then they started getting into the Russian bunkers, slipping down when the lids were raised for air and a look around. One claw inside a bunker, a churning sphere of blades and metal—that was enough. And when one got in others followed. With a weapon like that the war couldn't go on much longer.

Maybe it was already over.

Maybe he was going to hear the news. Maybe the Politburo had decided to throw in the sponge. Too bad it had taken so long. Six years. A long time for war like that, the way they had waged it. The automatic retaliation disks, spinning down all over Russia, hundreds of thousands of them. Bacteria crystals. The Soviet guided missiles, whistling through the air. The chain bombs. And now this, the robots, the claws—

The claws weren't like other weapons. They were *alive*, from any practical standpoint, whether the Governments wanted to admit it or not. They were not machines. They were living things, spinning, creeping, shaking themselves up suddenly from the gray ash and darting toward a man, climbing up him, rushing for his throat. And that was what they had been designed to do. Their job.

They did their job well. Especially lately, with the new designs coming up. Now they repaired themselves. They were on their own. Radiation tabs protected the UN troops, but if a man lost his tab he was fair game for the claws, no matter what his uniform. Down below the surface, automatic machinery stamped them out. Human beings stayed a long way off. It was too risky; nobody wanted to be around them. They were left to themselves. And they seemed to be doing all right. The new designs were faster, more complex. More efficient.

Apparently they had won the war.

Major Hendricks lit a second cigarette. The landscape depressed him. Nothing but ash and ruins. He seemed to be alone, the only living thing in the whole world. To the right the ruins of a town rose up, a few walls and heaps of debris. He tossed the dead match away, increasing his pace. Suddenly he stopped, jerking up his gun, his body tense. For a minute it looked like—

From behind the shell of a ruined building a figure came, walking slowly toward him, walking hesitantly.

Hendricks blinked. "Stop!"

The boy stopped. Hendricks lowered his gun. The boy stood silently, looking at him. He was small, not very old. Perhaps eight. But it was hard to tell. Most of the kids who remained were stunted. He wore a faded blue sweater, ragged with dirt, and short pants. His hair was long and matted. Brown hair. It hung over his face and around his ears. He held something in his arms.

"What's that you have?" Hendricks said sharply.

The boy held it out. It was a toy, a bear. A teddy bear. The boy's eyes were large, but without expression.

Hendricks relaxed. "I don't want it. Keep it."

The boy hugged the bear again.

"Where do you live?" Hendricks said.

"In there."

"The ruins?"

"Yes."

"Underground?"

"Yes."

"How many are there?"

"How—how many?"

"How many of you. How big's your settlement?"

The boy did not answer.

Hendricks frowned. "You're not all by yourself, are you?"

The boy nodded.

"How do you stay alive?"

"There's food."

"What kind of food?"

"Different."

Hendricks studied him. "How old are you?"

"Thirteen."

It wasn't possible. Or was it? The boy was thin, stunted. And probably sterile. Radiation exposure, years straight. No wonder he was so small. His arms and legs were like pipe cleaners, knobby and thin. Hendricks touched the boy's arm. His skin was dry and rough; radiation skin. He bent down, looking into the boy's face. There was no expression. Big eyes, big and dark.

"Are you blind?" Hendricks said.

"No. I can see some."

"How do you get away from the claws?"

"The claws?"

"The round things. That run and burrow."

"I don't understand."

Maybe there weren't any claws around. A lot of areas were free. They collected mostly around bunkers, where there were people. The claws had been designed to sense warmth, warmth of living things.

"You're lucky." Hendricks straightened up. "Well? Which way are you going? Back—back there?"

"Can I come with you?"

"With *me*?" Hendricks folded his arms. "I'm going a long way. Miles. I have to hurry." He looked at his watch. "I have to get there by nightfall."

"I want to come."

Hendricks fumbled in his pack. "It isn't worth it. Here." He tossed down the food cans he had with him. "You take these and go back. Okay?"

The boy said nothing.

"I'll be coming back this way. In a day or so. If you're around here when I come back you can come along with me. All right?"

"I want to go with you now."

"It's a long walk."

"I can walk."

Hendricks shifted uneasily. It made too good a target, two people walking along. And the boy would slow him down. But he might not come back this way. And if the boy were really all alone—

"Okay. Come along."

The boy fell in beside him. Hendricks strode along. The boy walked silently, clutching the teddy bear.

"What's your name?" Hendricks said, after a time.

"David Edward Derring."

"David? What—what happened to your mother and father?"

"They died."

"How?"

"In the blast."

"How long ago?"

"Six years?"

Hendricks slowed down. "You've been alone six years?"

"No. There were other people for a while. They went away."

"And you've been alone since?"

"Yes."

Hendricks glanced down. The boy was strange, saying very little. Withdrawn. But that was the way they were, the children who had survived. Quiet. Stoic. A strange kind of fatalism gripped them. Nothing came as a surprise. They accepted anything that came along. There was no longer any *normal*, any natural course of things, moral or physical, for them to expect. Custom, habit, all the determining forces of learning were gone; only brute experience remained.

"Am I walking too fast?" Hendricks said.

"No."

"How did you happen to see me?"

"I was waiting."

"Waiting?" Hendricks was puzzled. "What were you waiting for?"

"To catch things."

"What kind of things?"

"Things to eat."

"Oh." Hendricks set his lips grimly. A thirteen-year-old boy, living on rats and gophers and half-rotten canned food. Down in a hole under the ruins of a town. With radiation pools and claws, and Russian dive-mines up above, coasting around in the sky.

"Where are we going?" David asked.

"To the Russian lines."

"Russian?"

"The enemy. The people who started the war. They dropped the first radiation bombs. They began all this."

The boy nodded. His face showed no expression.

"I'm an American," Hendricks said.

There was no comment. On they went, the two of them, Hendricks walking a little ahead, David trailing behind him, hugging his dirty teddy bear against his chest.

About four in the afternoon they stopped to eat. Hendricks built a fire in a hollow between some slabs of concrete. He cleared the weeds away and heaped up bits of wood. The Russians' lines were not very far ahead. Around him was what had once been a long valley, acres of fruit trees and grapes. Nothing remained now but a few bleak stumps and the mountains that stretched across the horizon at the far end. And the clouds of rolling ash that blew and drifted with the wind, settling over the weeds and remains of buildings, walls here and there, once in a while what had been a road.

Hendricks made coffee and heated up some boiled mutton and bread. "Here." He handed bread and mutton to David. David squatted by the edge of the fire, his knees knobby and white. He examined the food and then passed it back, shaking his head.

"No."

"No? Don't you want any?"

"No."

Hendricks shrugged. Maybe the boy was a mutant, used to special food. It didn't matter. When he was hungry he would find something to eat. The boy was strange. But there were many strange changes coming over the world. Life was not the same anymore. It would never be the same again. The human race was going to have to realize that.

"Suit yourself," Hendricks said. He ate the bread and mutton by himself, washing it down with coffee. He ate slowly, finding the food hard to digest. When he was done he got to his feet and stamped the fire out.

David rose slowly, watching him with his young-old eyes.

"We're going," Hendricks said.

"All right."

Hendricks walked along, his gun in his arms. They were close; he was tense, ready for anything. The Russians should be expecting a runner, an answer to their own runner, but they were tricky. There was always the possibility of a slip-up. He scanned the landscape around him. Nothing but slag and ash, a few hills, charred trees. Concrete walls. But someplace ahead was the first bunker of the Russian lines, the forward command. Underground, buried deep, with only a periscope showing, a few gun muzzles. Maybe an antenna.

"Will we be there soon?" David asked.

"Yes. Getting tired?"

"No."

"Why, then?"

David did not answer. He plodded carefully along behind, picking his way over the ash. His legs and shoes were gray with dust. His pinched face was streaked, lines of gray ash in riverlets down the pale white of his skin. There was no color to his face. Typical of the new children, growing up in cellars and sewers and underground shelters.

Hendricks slowed down. He lifted his field glasses and studied the ground ahead of him. Were they there, someplace, waiting for him? Watching him, the way his men had watched the Russian runner? A chill went up his back. Maybe they were getting their guns ready, preparing to fire, the way his men had prepared, made ready to kill.

Hendricks stopped, wiping perspiration from his face. "Damn." It made him uneasy. But he should be expected. The situation was different.

He strode over the ash, holding his gun tightly with both hands. Behind him came David. Hendricks peered around, tight-lipped. Any second it might happen. A burst of white light, a blast, carefully aimed from inside a deep concrete bunker.

He raised his arm and waved it around in a circle.

Nothing moved. To the right a long ridge ran, topped with dead tree trunks. A few wild vines had grown up around the trees, remains of arbors. And the eternal dark weeds. Hendricks studied the ridge. Was anything up there? Perfect place for a lookout. He approached the ridge warily, David coming silently behind. If it were his command he'd have a sentry up there, watching for troops trying to infiltrate into the command area. Of course, if it were his command there would be the claws around the area for full protection.

He stopped, feet apart, hands on his hips.

"Are we there?" David said.

"Almost."

"Why have we stopped?"

"I don't want to take any chances." Hendricks advanced slowly. Now the ridge lay directly beside him, along his right. Overlooking him. His uneasy feeling increased. If an Ivan were up there he wouldn't have a chance. He waved his arm again. They should be expecting someone in the UN uniform, in response to the note capsule. Unless the whole thing was a trap.

"Keep up with me." He turned toward David. "Don't drop behind."

"With you?"

"Up beside me! We're close. We can't take any chances. Come on."

"I'll be all right." David remained behind him, in the rear, a few paces away, still clutching his teddy bear.

"Have it your way." Hendricks raised his glasses again, suddenly tense. For a moment—had something moved? He scanned the ridge carefully. Everything was silent. Dead. No life up there, only tree trunks and ash. Maybe a few rats. The big black rats that had survived the claws. Mutants—built their own shelters out of saliva and ash. Some kind of plaster. Adaptation. He started forward again.

A tall figure came out on the ridge above him, cloak flapping. Gray-green. A Russian. Behind him a second soldier appeared, another Russian. Both lifted their guns, aiming.

Hendricks froze. He opened his mouth. The soldiers were kneeling, sighting down the side of the slope. A third figure had joined them on the ridge top, a smaller figure in gray-green. A woman. She stood behind the other two.

Hendricks found his voice. "Stop!" He waved up at them frantically. "I'm—"

The two Russians fired. Behind Hendricks there was a faint *pop*. Waves of heat lapped against him, throwing him to the ground. Ash tore at his face, grinding into his eyes and nose.

Choking, he pulled himself to his knees. It was all a trap. He was finished. The soldiers and the woman were coming down the side of the ridge toward him, sliding down through the soft ash. Hendricks was numb. His head throbbed. Awkwardly, he got his rifle up and took aim. It weighed a thousand tons; he could hardly hold it. His nose and cheeks stung. The air was full of the blast smell, a bitter acrid stench.

"Don't fire," the first Russian said, in heavily accented English.

The three of them came up to him, surrounding him. "Put down your rifle, Yank," the other said.

Hendricks was dazed. Everything had happened so fast. He had been caught. And they had blasted the boy. He turned his head. David was gone. What remained of him was strewn across the ground.

The three Russians studied him curiously. Hendricks sat, wiping blood from his nose, picking out bits of ash. He shook his head, trying to clear it. "Why did you do it?" he murmured thickly. "The boy."

"Why?" One of the soldiers helped him roughly to his feet. He turned Hendricks around. "Look."

Hendricks closed his eyes.

"Look!" The two Russians pulled him forward. "See. Hurry up. There isn't much time to spare, Yank!"

Hendricks looked. And gasped.

"See now? Now do you understand?"

From the remains of David a metal wheel rolled. Relays, glinting metal. Parts, wiring. One of the Russians kicked at the heap of remains. Parts popped out, rolling away, wheels and springs and rods. A plastic section fell in, half charred. Hendricks bent shakily down. The front of the head had come off. He could make out the intricate brain, wires and relays, tiny tubes and switches, thousands of minute studs—

"A robot," the soldier holding his arm said. "We watched it tagging you."

"Tagging me?"

"That's their way. They tag along with you. Into the bunker. That's how they get in."

Hendricks blinked, dazed. "But—"

"Come on." They led him toward the ridge. "We can't stay here. It isn't safe. There must be hundreds of them all around here."

The three of them pulled him up the side of the ridge, sliding and slipping on the ash. The woman reached the top and stood waiting for them.

"The forward command," Hendricks muttered. "I came to negotiate with the Soviet—"

"There is no more forward command. *They* got it. We'll explain." They reached the top of the ridge. "We're all that's left. The three of us. The rest were down in the bunker."

"This way. Down this way." The woman unscrewed a lid, a gray manhole cover set in the ground. "Get in."

Hendricks lowered himself. The two soldiers and the woman came behind him, following him down the ladder. The woman closed the lid after them, bolting it tightly into place.

"Good thing we saw you," one of the two soldiers grunted. "It had tagged you about as far as it was going to."

"Give me one of your cigarettes," the woman said. "I haven't had an American cigarette for weeks."

Hendricks pushed the pack to her. She took a cigarette and passed the pack to the two soldiers. In the corner of the small room the lamp gleamed fitfully. The room was low-ceilinged, cramped. The four of them sat around a small wood table. A few dirty dishes were stacked to one side. Behind a ragged curtain a second room was partly visible. Hendricks saw the corner of a coat, some blankets, clothes hung on a hook.

"We were here," the soldier beside him said. He took off his helmet, pushing his blond hair back. "I'm Corporal Rudi Maxer. Polish. Impressed in the Soviet Army two years ago." He held out his hand.

Hendricks hesitated and then shook. "Major Joseph Hendricks."

"Klaus Epstein." The other soldier shook with him, a small dark man with thinning hair. Epstein plucked nervously at his ear. "Austrian. Impressed God knows when. I don't remember. The three of us were here, Rudie and I, with Tasso." He indicated the woman. "That's how we escaped. All the rest were down in the bunker."

"And—and *they* got in?"

Epstein lit a cigarette. "First just one of them. The kind that tagged you. Then it let others in."

Hendricks became alert. "The *kind?* Are there more than one kind?"

"The little boy. David. David holding his teddy bear. That's Variety Three. The most effective."

"What are the other types?"

Epstein reached into his coat. "Here." He tossed a packet of photographs onto the table, tied with a string. "Look for yourself."

Hendricks untied the string.

"You see," Rudi Maxer said, "that was why we wanted to talk terms. The Russians, I mean. We found out about a week ago. Found out that your claws were beginning to make up new designs on their own. New types of their own. Better types. Down in your underground factories behind our lines. You let them stamp themselves, repair themselves. Made them more and more intricate. It's your fault this happened."

Hendricks examined the photos. They had been snapped hurriedly; they were blurred and indistinct. The first few showed—David. David walking along a road, by himself. David and another David. Three Davids. All exactly alike. Each with a ragged teddy bear.

All pathetic.

"Look at the others," Tasso said.

The next pictures, taken at a great distance, showed a towering wounded soldier sitting by the side of a path, his arm in a sling, the stump of one leg extended, a crude crutch on his lap. Then two wounded soldiers, both the same, standing side by side.

"That's Variety One. The Wounded Soldier." Klaus reached out and took the pictures. "You see, the claws were designed to get to human beings. To find them. Each kind was better than the last. They got farther, closer, past most of our defenses, into our lines. But as long as they were merely *machines*, metal spheres with claws and horns, feelers, they could be picked off like any other object. They could be detected as lethal robots as soon as they were seen. Once we caught sight of them—"

"Variety One subverted our whole north wing," Rudi said. "It was a long time before anyone caught on. Then it was too late. They came in, wounded soldiers, knocking and begging to be let in. So we let them in. And as soon as they were in they took over. We were watching out for machines . . ."

"At that time it was thought there was only the one type," Klaus Epstein said. "No one suspected there were other types. The pictures were flashed to us. When the runner was sent to you, we knew of just one type, Variety One. The big Wounded Soldier. We thought that was all."

"Your line fell to—"

"To Variety Three. David and his bear. That worked even better." Klaus smiled bitterly. "Soldiers are suckers for children. We brought them in and tried to feed them. We found out the hard way what they were after. At least, those who were in the bunker."

"The three of us were lucky," Rudi said. "Klaus and I were—were visiting Tasso when it happened. This is her place." He waved a big hand around. "This little cellar. We finished and climbed the ladder to start back. From the ridge we saw that they were all around the bunker. Fighting was still going on. David and his bear. Hundreds of them. Klaus took the pictures."

Klaus tied up the photographs again.

"And it's going on all along your line?" Hendricks said.

"Yes."

"How about *our* lines?" Without thinking, he touched the tab on his arm. "Can they—"

"They're not bothered by your radiation tabs. It makes no difference to them. Russian, American, Pole, German. It's all the same. They're doing what they were designed to do. Carrying out the original idea. They track down life, wherever they find it."

"They go by warmth," Klaus said. "That was the way you constructed them from the very start. Of course, those you designed were kept back by the radiation tabs you wear. Now they've got around that. These new varieties are lead-lined."

"What's the other variety?" Hendricks asked. "The David type, the Wounded Soldier—what's the other?"

"We don't know." Klaus pointed up at the wall. On the wall

were two metal plates, ragged at the edges. Hendricks got up and studied them. They were bent and dented.

"The one on the left came off a Wounded Soldier," Rudi said. "We got one of them. It was going along toward our old bunker. We got it from the ridge, the same way we got the David tagging you."

The plate was stamped: *I-V.* Hendricks touched the other plate. "And this came from the David type?"

"Yes." The plate was stamped: *III-V.*

Klaus took a look at them, leaning over Hendricks's broad shoulder. "You can see what we're up against. There's another type. Maybe it was abandoned. Maybe it didn't work. But there must be a Second Variety. There's One and Three."

"You were lucky," Rudi said. "The David tagged you all the way here and never touched you. Probably thought you'd get it into a bunker, somewhere."

"One gets in and it's all over," Klaus said. "They move fast. One lets all the rest inside. They're inflexible. Machines with one purpose. They were built for only one thing." He rubbed sweat from his lip. "We saw."

They were silent.

"Let me have another cigarette, Yank," Tasso said. "They are good. I almost forgot how they were."

It was night. The sky was black. No stars were visible through the rolling clouds of ash. Klaus lifted the lid cautiously so that Hendricks could look out.

Rudi pointed into the darkness. "Over that way are the bunkers. Where we used to be. Not over half a mile from us. It was just chance Klaus and I were not there when it happened. Weakness. Saved by our lusts."

"All the rest must be dead," Klaus said in a low voice. "It came quickly. This morning the Politburo reached their decision. They notified us—forward command. Our runner was sent out at once. We saw him start toward the direction of your lines. We covered him until he was out of sight."

"Alex Radrivsky. We both knew him. He disappeared about six o'clock. The sun had just come up. About noon Klaus and I had an hour relief. We crept off, away from the bunkers. No one was watching. We came here. There used to be a town here, a few houses, a street. This cellar was part of a big farmhouse. We knew Tasso would be here, hiding down in her little place. We had come here before. Others from the bunkers came here. Today happened to be our turn."

"So we were saved," Klaus said. "Chance. It might have been others. We—we finished, and then we came up to the surface and started back along the ridge. That was when we saw them, the Davids. We understood right away. We had seen the photos of the First Variety, the Wounded Soldier. Our Commissar distributed them to us with an explanation. If we had gone another step they would have seen us. As it was we had to blast two Davids before we got back. There were hundreds of them, all around. Like ants. We took pictures and slipped back here, bolting the lid tight."

"They're not so much when you catch them alone. We moved faster than they did. But they're inexorable. Not like living things. They came right at us. And we blasted them."

Major Hendricks rested against the edge of the lid, adjusting his eyes to the darkness. "Is it safe to have the lid up at all?"

"If we're careful. How else can you operate your transmitter?"

Hendricks lifted the small belt transmitter slowly. He pressed it against his ear. The metal was cold and damp. He blew against the mike, raising up the short antenna. A faint hum sounded in his ear. "That's true, I suppose."

But he still hesitated.

"We'll pull you under if anything happens," Klaus said.

"Thanks." Hendricks waited a moment, resting the transmitter against his shoulder. "Interesting, isn't it?"

"What?"

"This, the new types. The new varieties of claws. We're completely at their mercy, aren't we? By now they've probably gotten into the UN lines, too. It makes me wonder if we're not seeing the beginning of a new species. *The* new species. Evolution. The race to come after man."

Rudi grunted. "There is no race after man."

"No? Why not? Maybe we're seeing it now, the end of human beings, the beginning of the new society."

"They're not a race. They're mechanical killers. You made

them to destroy. That's all they can do. They're machines with a job."

"So it seems now. But how about later on? After the war is over. Maybe, when there aren't any humans to destroy, their real potentialities will begin to show."

"You talk as if they were alive!"

"Aren't they?"

There was silence. "They're machines," Rudi said. "They look like people, but they're machines."

"Use your transmitter, Major," Klaus said. "We can't stay up here forever."

Holding the transmitter tightly, Hendricks called the code of the command bunker. He waited, listening. No response. Only silence. He checked the leads carefully. Everything was in place.

"Scott!" he said into the mike. "Can you hear me?"

Silence. He raised the gain up full and tried again. Only static.

"I don't get anything. They may hear me but they may not want to answer."

"Tell them it's an emergency."

"They'll think I'm being forced to call. Under your direction." He tried again, outlining briefly what he had learned. But still the phone was silent, except for the faint static.

"Radiation pools kill most transmissions," Klaus said, after awhile. "Maybe that's it."

Hendricks shut the transmitter up. "No use. No answer. Radiation pools? Maybe. Or they hear me, but won't answer. Frankly, that's what I would do, if a runner tried to call from the Soviet lines. They have no reason to believe such a story. They may hear everything I say—"

"Or maybe it's too late."

Hendricks nodded.

"We better get the lid down," Rudi said nervously. "We don't want to take unnecessary chances."

They climbed slowly back down the tunnel. Klaus bolted the lid carefully into place. They descended into the kitchen. The air was heavy and close around them.

"Could they work that fast?" Hendricks said. "I left the bunker this noon. Ten hours ago. How could they move so quickly?"

"It doesn't take them long. Not after the first one gets in. It goes wild. You know what the little claws do. Even *one* of these is beyond belief. Razors, each finger. Maniacal."

"All right." Hendricks moved away impatiently. He stood with his back to them.

"What's the matter?" Rudi said.

"The Moon Base. God, if they've gotten there——"

"The Moon Base?"

Hendricks turned around. "They couldn't have got to the Moon Base. How would they get there? It isn't possible. I can't believe it."

"What is this Moon Base? We've heard rumors, but nothing definite. What is the actual situation? You seem concerned."

"We're supplied from the Moon. The governments are there, under the lunar surface. All our people and industries. That's what keeps us going. If they should find some way of getting off Terra, onto the Moon——"

"It only takes one of them. Once the first one gets in it admits the others. Hundreds of them, all alike. You should have seen them. Identical. Like ants."

"Perfect socialism," Tasso said. "The ideal of the communist state. All citizens interchangeable."

Klaus grunted angrily. "That's enough. Well? What next?"

Hendricks paced back and forth, around the small room. The air was full of smells of food and perspiration. The others watched him. Presently Tasso pushed through the curtain, into the other room. "I'm going to take a nap."

The curtain closed behind her. Rudi and Klaus sat down at the table, still watching Hendricks. "It's up to you," Klaus said. "We don't know your situation."

Hendricks nodded.

"It's a problem." Rudi drank some coffee, filling his cup from a rusty pot. "We're safe here for a while, but we can't stay here forever. Not enough food or supplies."

"But if we go outside——"

"If we go outside they'll get us. Or probably they'll get us. We couldn't go very far. How far is your command bunker, Major?"

"Three or four miles."

"We might make it. The four of us. Four of us could watch all sides. They couldn't slip up behind us and start tagging us. We

have three rifles, three blast rifles. Tasso can have my pistol."
Rudi tapped his belt. "In the Soviet army we didn't have shoes
always, but we had guns. With all four of us armed one of us
might get to your command bunker. Preferably you, Major."

"What if they're already there?" Klaus said.

Rudi shrugged. "Well, then we come back here."

Hendricks stopped pacing. "What do you think the chances are
they're already in the American lines?"

"Hard to say. Fairly good. They're organized. They know
exactly what they're doing. Once they start they go like a horde
of locusts. They have to keep moving, and fast. It's secrecy and
speed they depend on. Surprise. They push their way in before
anyone has any idea."

"I see," Hendricks murmured.

From the other room Tasso stirred. "Major?"

Hendricks pushed the curtain back. "What?"

Tasso looked up at him lazily from the cot. "Have you any
more American cigarettes left?"

Hendricks went into the room and sat down across from her,
on a wood stool. He felt in his pockets. "No. All gone."

"Too bad."

"What nationality are you?" Hendricks asked after a while.

"Russian."

"How did you get here?"

"Here?"

"This used to be France. This was part of Normandy. Did you
come with the Soviet army?"

"Why?"

"Just curious." He studied her. She had taken off her coat,
tossing it over the end of the cot. She was young, about twenty.
Slim. Her long hair stretched out over the pillow. She was staring
at him silently, her eyes dark and large.

"What's on your mind?" Tasso said.

"Nothing. How old are you?"

"Eighteen." She continued to watch him, unblinking, her arms
behind her head. She had on Russian army pants and shirt.
Gray-green. Thick leather belt with counter and cartridges.
Medicine kit.

"You're in the Soviet army?"

"No."

"Where did you get the uniform?"

She shrugged. "It was given to me," she told him.

"How—how old were you when you came here?"

"Sixteen."

"That young?"

Her eyes narrowed. "What do you mean?"

Hendricks rubbed his jaw. "Your life would have been a lot different if there had been no war. Sixteen. You came here at sixteen. To live this way."

"I had to survive."

"I'm not moralizing."

"Your life would have been different, too," Tasso murmured. She reached down and unfastened one of her boots. She kicked the boot off, onto the floor. "Major, do you want to go in the other room? I'm sleepy."

"It's going to be a problem, the four of us here. It's going to be hard to live in these quarters. Are there just the two rooms?"

"Yes."

"How big was the cellar originally? Was it larger than this? Are there other rooms filled up with debris? We might be able to open one of them."

"Perhaps. I really don't know." Tasso loosened her belt. She made herself comfortable on the cot, unbuttoning her shirt. "You're sure you have no more cigarettes?"

"I had only the one pack."

"Too bad. Maybe if we get back to your bunker we can find some." The other boot fell. Tasso reached up for the light cord. "Good night."

"You're going to sleep?"

"That's right."

The room plunged into darkness. Hendricks got up and made his way past the curtain, into the kitchen. And stopped, rigid.

Rudi stood against the wall, his face white and gleaming. His mouth opened and closed but no sounds came. Klaus stood in front of him, the muzzle of his pistol in Rudi's stomach. Neither of them moved. Klaus, his hand tight around his gun, his features set. Rudi, pale and silent, spread-eagled against the wall.

"What—" Hendricks muttered, but Klaus cut him off.

"Be quiet, Major. Come over here. Your gun. Get out your gun."

Hendricks drew his pistol. "What is it?"

"Cover him." Klaus motioned him forward. "Beside me. Hurry!"

Rudi moved a little, lowering his arms. He turned to Hendricks, licking his lips. The whites of his eyes shone wildly. Sweat dripped from his forehead, down his cheeks. He fixed his gaze on Hendricks. "Major, he's gone insane. Stop him." Rudi's voice was thin and hoarse, almost inaudible.

"What's going on?" Hendricks demanded.

Without lowering his pistol Klaus answered. "Major, remember our discussion? The Three Varieties? We knew about One and Three. But we didn't know about Two. At least, we didn't know before." Klaus's fingers tightened around the gun butt. "We didn't know before, but we know now."

He pressed the trigger. A burst of white heat rolled out of the gun, licking around Rudi.

"Major, this is the Second Variety."

Tasso swept the curtain aside. "Klaus! What did you do?"

Klaus turned from the charred form, gradually sinking down the wall onto the floor. "The Second Variety, Tasso. Now we know. We have all three types identified. The danger is less. I—"

Tasso stared past him at the remains of Rudi, at the blackened, smoldering fragments and bits of cloth. "You killed him."

"Him? *It,* you mean. I was watching. I had a feeling, but I wasn't sure. At least, I wasn't sure before. But this evening I was certain." Klaus rubbed his pistol butt nervously. "We're lucky. Don't you understand? Another hour and it might—"

"You were *certain?*" Tasso pushed past him and bent down, over the steaming remains on the floor. Her face became hard. "Major, see for yourself. Bones. Flesh."

Hendricks bent down beside her. The remains were human remains. Seared flesh, charred bone fragments, part of a skull. Ligaments, viscera, blood. Blood forming a pool against the wall.

"No wheels," Tasso said calmly. She straightened up. "No wheels, no parts, no relays. Not a claw. Not the Second Variety."

She folded her arms. "You're going to have to be able to explain this."

Klaus sat down at the table, all the color drained suddenly from his face. He put his head in his hands and rocked back and forth.

"Snap out of it." Tasso's fingers closed over his shoulder. "Why did you do it? Why did you kill him?"

"He was frightened," Hendricks said. "All this, the whole thing, building up around us."

"Maybe."

"What, then? What do you think?"

"I think he may have had a reason for killing Rudi. A good reason."

"What reason?"

"Maybe Rudi learned something."

Hendricks studied her bleak face. "About what?" he asked.

"About him. About Klaus."

Klaus looked up quickly. "You can see what she's trying to say. She thinks I'm the Second Variety. Don't you see, Major? Now she wants you to believe I killed him on purpose. That I'm—"

"Why did you kill him, then?" Tasso said.

"I told you." Klaus shook his head wearily. "I thought he was a claw. I thought I knew."

"Why?"

"I had been watching him. I was suspicious."

"Why?"

"I thought I had seen something. Heard something. I thought I—" He stopped.

"Go on."

"We were sitting at the table. Playing cards. You two were in the other room. It was silent. I thought I heard him—*whirr*."

There was silence.

"Do you believe that?" Tasso said to Hendricks.

"Yes. I believe what he says."

"I don't. I think he killed Rudi for a good purpose." Tasso touched the rifle, resting in the corner of the room. "Major—"

"No." Hendricks shook his head. "Let's stop it right now. One is enough. We're afraid, the way he was. If we kill him we'll be doing what he did to Rudi."

Klaus looked gratefully up at him. "Thanks. I was afraid. You understand, don't you? Now she's afraid, the way I was. She wants to kill me."

"No more killing." Hendricks moved toward the end of the ladder. "I'm going above and try the transmitter once more. If I can't get them we're moving back toward my lines tomorrow morning."

Klaus rose quickly. "I'll come up with you and give you a hand."

The night air was cold. The earth was cooling off. Klaus took a deep breath, filling his lungs. He and Hendricks stepped onto the ground, out of the tunnel. Klaus planted his feet wide apart, the rifle up, watching and listening. Hendricks crouched by the tunnel mouth, tuning the small transmitter.

"Any luck?" Klaus asked presently.

"Not yet."

"Keep trying. Tell them what happened."

Hendricks kept trying. Without success. Finally he lowered the antenna. "It's useless. They can't hear me. Or they hear me and won't answer. Or—"

"Or they don't exist."

"I'll try once more." Hendricks raised the antenna. "Scott, can you hear me? Come in!"

He listened. There was only static. Then, still very faintly—

"This is Scott."

His fingers tightened. "Scott! Is it you?"

"This is Scott."

Klaus squatted down. "Is it your command?"

"Scott, listen. Do you understand? About them, the claws. Did you get my message? Did you hear me?"

"Yes." Faintly. Almost inaudible. He could hardly make out the word.

"You got my message? Is everything all right at the bunker? None of them got in?"

"Everything is all right."

"Have they tried to get in?"

The voice was weaker.

"No."

Hendricks turned to Klaus. "They're all right."

"Have they been attacked?"

"No." Hendricks pressed the phone tighter to his ear. "Scott, I can hardly hear you. Have you notified the Moon Base? Do they know? Are they alerted?"

No answer.

"Scott! Can you hear me?"

Silence.

Hendricks relaxed, sagging. "Faded out. Must be radiation pools."

Hendricks and Klaus looked at each other. Neither of them said anything. After a time Klaus said, "Did it sound like any of your men? Could you identify the voice?"

"It was too faint."

"You couldn't be certain?"

"No."

"Then it could have been—"

"I don't know. Now I'm not sure. Let's go back down and get the lid closed."

They climbed back down the ladder slowly, into the warm cellar. Klaus bolted the lid behind them. Tasso waited for them, her face expressionless.

"Any luck?" she asked.

Neither of them answered. "Well?" Klaus said at last. "What do you think, Major? Was it your officer, or was it one of *them?*"

"I don't know."

"Then we're just where we were before."

Hendricks stared down at the floor, his jaw set. "We'll have to go. To be sure."

"Anyhow, we have food here for only a few weeks. We'd have to go up after that, in any case."

"Apparently so."

"What's wrong?" Tasso demanded. "Did you get across to your bunker? What's the matter?"

"It may have been one of my men," Hendricks said slowly. "Or it may have been one of *them*. But we'll never know standing here." He examined his watch. "Let's turn in and get some sleep. We want to be up early tomorrow."

"Early?"

"Our best chance to get through the claws should be early in the morning," Hendricks said.

The morning was crisp and clear. Major Hendricks studied the countryside through his field glasses.

"See anything?" Klaus said.

"No."

"Can you make out our bunkers?"

"Which way?"

"Here." Klaus took the glasses and adjusted them. "I know where to look." He looked a long time, silently.

Tasso came to the top of the tunnel and stepped up onto the ground. "Anything?"

"No." Klaus passed the glasses back to Hendricks. "They're out of sight. Come on. Let's not stay here."

The three of them made their way down the side of the ridge, sliding in the soft ash. Across a flat rock a lizard scuttled. They stopped instantly, rigid.

"What was it?" Klaus muttered.

"A lizard."

The lizard ran on, hurrying through the ash. It was exactly the same color as the ash.

"Perfect adaptation," Klaus said. "Proves we were right, Lysenko, I mean."

They reached the bottom of the ridge and stopped, standing close together, looking around them.

"Let's go." Hendricks started off. "It's a good long trip, on foot."

Klaus fell in beside him. Tasso walked behind, her pistol held alertly. "Major, I've been meaning to ask you something," Klaus said. "How did you run across the David? The one that was tagging you."

"I met it along the way. In some ruins."

"What did it say?"

"Not much. It said it was alone. By itself."

"You couldn't tell it was a machine? It talked like a living person? You never suspected?"

"It didn't say much. I noticed nothing unusual."

"It's strange, machines so much like people that you can be fooled. Almost alive. I wonder where it'll end."

"They're doing what you Yanks designed them to do," Tasso said. "You designed them to hunt out life and destroy. Human life. Wherever they find it."

Hendricks was watching Klaus intently. "Why did you ask me? What's on your mind?"

"Nothing," Klaus answered.

"Klaus thinks you're the Second Variety," Tasso said calmly, from behind them. "Now he's got his eye on you."

Klaus flushed. "Why not? We sent a runner to the Yank lines and *he* comes back. Maybe he thought he'd find some good game here."

Hendricks laughed harshly. "I came from the UN bunkers. There were human beings all around me."

"Maybe you saw an opportunity to get into the Soviet lines. Maybe you saw your chance. Maybe you—"

"The Soviet lines had already been taken over. Your lines had been invaded before I left my command bunker. Don't forget that."

Tasso came up beside him. "That proves nothing at all, Major."

"Why not?"

"There appears to be little communication between the varieties. Each is made in a different factory. They don't seem to work together. You might have started for the Soviet lines without knowing anything about the work of the other varieties. Or even what the other varieties were like."

"How do you know so much about the claws?" Hendricks said.

"I've seen them. I've observed them take over the Soviet bunkers."

"You know quite a lot," Klaus said. "Actually, you saw very little. Strange that you should have been such an acute observer."

Tasso laughed. "Do you suspect me, now?"

"Forget it," Hendricks said. They walked on in silence.

"Are you going the whole way on foot?" Tasso said, after awhile. "I'm not used to walking." She gazed around at the plain of ash, stretching out on all sides of them, as far as they could see. "How dreary."

"It's like this all the way," Klaus said.

"In a way I wish you had been in your bunker when the attack came."

"Somebody else would have been with you, if not me," Klaus muttered.

Tasso laughed, putting her hands in her pockets. "I suppose so."

They walked on, keeping their eyes on the vast plain of silent ash around them.

The sun was setting. Hendricks made his way forward slowly, waving Tasso and Klaus back. Klaus squatted down, resting his gun butt against the ground.

Tasso found a concrete slab and sat down with a sigh. "It's good to rest."

"Be quiet," Klaus said sharply.

Hendricks pushed up to the top of the rise ahead of them. The same rise the Russian runner had come up, the day before. Hendricks dropped down, stretching himself out, peering through his glasses at what lay beyond.

Nothing was visible. Only ash and occasional trees. But there, not more than fifty yards ahead, was the entrance of the forward command bunker. The bunker from which he had come. Hendricks watched silently. No motion. No sign of life. Nothing stirred.

Klaus slithered up beside him. "Where is it?"

"Down there." Hendricks passed him the glasses. Clouds of ash rolled across the evening sky. The world was darkening. They had a couple of hours of light left, at the most. Probably not that much.

"I don't see anything," Klaus said.

"That tree there. The stump. By the pile of bricks. The entrance is to the right of the bricks."

"I'll have to take your word for it."

"You and Tasso cover me from here. You'll be able to sight all the way to the bunker entrance."

"You're going down alone?"

"With my wrist tab I'll be safe. The ground around the bunker is a living field of claws. They collect down in the ash. Like crabs. Without tabs you wouldn't have a chance."

"Maybe you're right."

"I'll walk slowly all the way. As soon as I know for certain—"

"If they're down inside the bunker you won't be able to get back up here. They go fast. You don't realize."

"What do you suggest?"

Klaus considered. "I don't know. Get them to come up to the surface. So you can see."

Hendricks brought his transmitter from his belt, raising the antenna. "Let's get started."

Klaus signaled to Tasso. She crawled expertly up the side of the rise to where they were sitting.

"He's going down alone," Klaus said. "We'll cover him from here. As soon as you see him start back, fire past him at once. They come quick."

"You're not very optimistic," Tasso said.

"No, I'm not."

Hendricks opened the breech of his gun, checking it carefully. "Maybe things are all right."

"You didn't see them. Hundreds of them. All the same. Pouring out like ants."

"I should be able to find out without going down all the way." Hendricks locked his gun, gripping it in one hand, the transmitter in the other. "Well, wish me luck."

Klaus put out his hand. "Don't go down until you're sure. Talk to them from up here. Make them show themselves."

Hendricks stood up. He stepped down the side of the rise.

A moment later he was walking slowly toward the pile of bricks and debris beside the dead tree stump. Toward the entrance of the forward command bunker.

Nothing stirred. He raised the transmitter, clicking it on. "Scott? Can you hear me?"

Silence.

"Scott! This is Hendricks. Can you hear me? I'm standing outside the bunker. You should be able to see me in the view sight."

He listened, the transmitter gripped tightly. No sound. Only static. He walked forward. A claw burrowed out of the ash and raced toward him. It halted a few feet away and then slunk off. A second claw appeared, one of the big ones with feelers. It moved toward him, studied him intently, and then fell in behind him, dogging respectfully after him, a few paces away. A moment later a second big claw joined it. Silently, the claws trailed him as he walked slowly toward the bunker.

Hendricks stopped, and behind him, the claws came to a halt. He was close now. Almost to the bunker steps.

"Scott! Can you hear me? I'm standing right above you. Outside. On the surface. Are you picking me up?"

He waited, holding his gun against his side, the transmitter tightly to his ear. Time passed. He strained to hear, but there was only silence. Silence, and faint static.

Then, distantly, metallically—

"This is Scott."

The voice was neutral. Cold. He could not identify it. But the earphone was minute.

"Scott! Listen. I'm standing right above you. I'm on the surface, looking down into the bunker entrance."

"Yes."

"Can you see me?"

"Yes."

"Through the view sight? You have the sight trained on me?"

"Yes."

Hendricks pondered. A circle of claws waited quietly around him, gray-metal bodies on all sides of him. "Is everything all right in the bunker? Nothing unusual has happened?"

"Everything is all right."

"Will you come up to the surface? I want to see you for a moment." Hendricks took a deep breath. "Come up here with me. I want to talk to you."

"Come down."

"I'm giving you an order."

Silence.

"Are you coming?" Hendricks listened. There was no response. "I order you to come to the surface."

"Come down."

Hendricks set his jaw. "Let me talk to Leone."

There was a long pause. He listened to the static. Then a voice came, hard, thin, metallic. The same as the other. "This is Leone."

"Hendricks. I'm on the surface. At the bunker entrance. I want one of you to come up here."

"Come down."

"Why come down? I'm giving you an order!"

Silence. Hendricks lowered the transmitter. He looked carefully around him. The entrance was just ahead. Almost at his feet. He lowered the antenna and fastened the transmitter to his belt. Carefully, he gripped his gun with both hands. He moved forward, a step at a time. If they could see him they knew he was starting toward the entrance. He closed his eyes a moment.

Then he put his foot on the first step that led downward.

Two Davids came up at him, their faces identical and expressionless. He blasted them into particles. More came rushing silently up, a whole pack of them. All exactly the same.

Hendricks turned and raced back, away from the bunker, back toward the rise.

At the top of the rise Tasso and Klaus were firing down. The small claws were already streaking up toward them, shining metal spheres going fast, racing frantically through the ash. But he had no time to think about that. He knelt down, aiming at the bunker entrance, gun against his cheek. The Davids were coming out in groups, clutching their teddy bears, their thin knobby legs pumping as they ran up the steps to the surface. Hendricks fired into the main body of them. They burst apart, wheels and springs flying in all directions. He fired again, through the mist of particles.

A giant lumbering figure rose up in the bunker entrance, tall and swaying. Hendricks paused, amazed. A man, a soldier. With one leg, supporting himself with a crutch.

"Major!" Tasso's voice came. More firing. The huge figure moved forward, Davids swarming around it. Hendricks broke out of his freeze. The First Variety. The Wounded Soldier. He aimed and fired. The soldier burst into bits, parts and relays flying. Now many Davids were out on the flat ground, away from the bunker. He fired again and again, moving slowly back, half-crouching and aiming.

From the rise, Klaus fired down. The side of the rise was alive with claws making their way up. Hendricks retreated toward the rise, running and crouching. Tasso had left Klaus and was circling slowly to the right, moving away from the rise.

A David slipped up toward him, its small white face expressionless, brown hair hanging down in its eyes. It bent over suddenly, opening its arms. Its teddy bear hurtled down and leaped across the ground, bounding toward him. Hendricks fired. The bear and the David both dissolved. He grinned, blinking. It was like a dream.

"Up here!" Tasso's voice. Hendricks made his way toward her. She was over by some columns of concrete, walls of a runied building. She was firing past him, with the hand pistol Klaus had given her.

"Thanks." He joined her, gasping for breath. She pulled him back, behind the concrete, fumbling at her belt.

"Close your eyes!" She unfastened a globe from her waist. Rapidly, she unscrewed the cap, locking it into place. "Close your eyes and get down."

She threw the bomb. It sailed in an arc, an expert, rolling and bouncing to the entrance of the bunker. Two Wounded Soldiers stood uncertainly by the brick pile. More Davids poured from behind them, out onto the plain. One of the Wounded Soldiers moved toward the bomb, stooping awkwardly down to pick it up.

The bomb went off. The concussion whirled Hendricks around, throwing him on his face. A hot wind rolled over him. Dimly he saw Tasso standing behind the columns, firing slowly and methodically at the Davids coming out of the raging clouds of white fire.

Back along the rise Klaus struggled with a ring of claws circling around him. He retreated, blasting at them and moving back, trying to break through the ring.

Hendricks struggled to his feet. His head ached. He could hardly see. Everything was licking at him, raging and whirling. His right arm would not move.

Tasso pulled back toward him. "Come on. Let's go."

"Klaus—he's still up there."

"Come on!" Tasso dragged Hendricks back, away from the columns. Hendricks shook his head, trying to clear it. Tasso led him rapidly away, her eyes intense and bright, watching for claws that had escaped the blast.

One David came out of the rolling clouds of flame. Tasso blasted it. No more appeared.

"But Klaus. What about him?" Hendricks stopped, standing unsteadily. "He—"

"Come on!"

They retreated, moving farther and farther away from the bunker. A few small claws followed them for a little while and then gave up, turning back and going off.

At last Tasso stopped. "We can stop here and get our breaths."

Hendricks sat down on some heaps of debris. He wiped his neck, gasping. "We left Klaus back there."

Tasso said nothing. She opened her gun, sliding a fresh round of blast cartridges into place.

Hendricks stared at her, dazed. "You left him back there on purpose."

Tasso snapped the gun together. She studied the heaps of rubble around them, her face expressionless. As if she were watching for something.

"What is it?" Hendricks demanded. "What are you looking for? Is something coming?" He shook his head, trying to understand. What was she doing? What was she waiting for? He could see nothing. Ash lay all around them, ash and ruins. Occasionally stark tree trunks, without leaves or branches. "What—"

Tasso cut him off. "Be still." Her eyes narrowed. Suddenly her gun came up. Hendricks turned, following her gaze.

Back the way they had come a figure appeared. The figure walked unsteadily toward them. Its clothes were torn. It limped as it made its way along, going very slowly and carefully. Stopping now and then, resting and getting its strength. Once it almost fell. It stood for a moment, trying to steady itself. Then it came on.

Klaus.

Hendricks stood up. "Klaus!" He started toward him. "How the hell did you—"

Tasso fired. Hendricks swung back. She fired again, the blast passing him, a searing line of heat. The beam caught Klaus in the chest. He exploded, gears and wheels flying. For a moment he continued to walk. Then he swayed back and forth. He crashed to the ground, his arms flung out. A few more wheels rolled away.

Silence.

Tasso turned to Hendricks. "Now you understand why he killed Rudi."

Hendricks sat down again slowly. He shook his head. He was numb. He could not think.

"Do you see?" Tasso said. "Do you understand?"

Hendricks said nothing. Everything was slipping away from him, faster and faster. Darkness, rolling and plucking at him.

He closed his eyes.

Hendricks opened his eyes slowly. His body ached all over. He tried to sit up but needles of pain shot through his arm and shoulder. He gasped.

"Don't try to get up," Tasso said. She bent down, putting her cold hand against his forehead.

It was night. A few stars glinted above, shining through the drifting clouds of ash. Hendricks lay back, his teeth locked. Tasso watched him impassively. She had built a fire with some wood and weeds. The fire licked feebly, hissing at a metal cup suspended over it. Everything was silent. Unmoving darkness, beyond the fire.

"So he was the Second Variety," Hendricks murmured.

"I had always thought so."

"Why didn't you destroy him sooner?" He wanted to know.

"You held me back." Tasso crossed to the fire to look into the metal cup. "Coffee. It'll be ready to drink in a while."

She came back and sat down beside him. Presently she opened her pistol and began to disassemble the firing mechanism, studying it intently.

"This is a beautiful gun," Tasso said, half aloud. "The construction is superb."

"What about them? The claws."

"The concussion from the bomb put most of them out of action. They're delicate. Highly organized, I suppose."

"The Davids, too?"

"Yes,"

"How did you happen to have a bomb like that?"

Tasso shrugged. "We designed it. You shouldn't underestimate our technology, Major. Without such a bomb you and I would no longer exist."

"Very useful."

Tasso stretched out her legs, warming her feet in the heat of the fire. "It surprised me that you did not seem to understand, after he killed Rudi. Why did you think he—"

"I told you, I thought he was afraid."

"Really? You know, Major, for a little while I suspected you. Because you wouldn't let me kill him. I thought you might be protecting him." She laughed.

"Are we safe here?" Hendricks asked presently.

"For a while. Until they get reinforcements from some other area." Tasso began to clean the interior of the gun with a bit of rag. She finished and pushed the mechanism back into place. She closed the gun, running her finger along the barrel.

"We were lucky," Hendricks murmured.

"Yes. Very lucky."

"Thanks for pulling me away."

Tasso did not answer. She glanced up at him, her eyes bright in the firelight. Hendricks examined his arm. He could not move his fingers. His whole side seemed numb. Down inside him was a dull steady ache.

"How do you feel?" Tasso asked.

"My arm is damaged."

"Anything else?"

"Internal injuries."

"You didn't get down when the bomb went off."

Hendricks said nothing. He watched Tasso pour the coffee from the cup into a flat metal pan. She brought it over to him.

"Thanks." He struggled up enough to drink. It was hard to swallow. His insides turned over and he pushed the pan away. "That's all I can drink now."

Tasso drank the rest. Time passed. The clouds of ash moved across the dark sky above them. Hendricks rested, his mind blank. After a while he became aware that Tasso was standing over him, gazing down at him.

"What is it?" he murmured.

"Do you feel any better?"

"Some."

"You know, Major, if I hadn't dragged you away they would have got you. You would be dead. Like Rudi."

"I know."

"Do you want to know why I brought you out? I could have left you. I could have left you there."

"Why did you bring me out?"

"Because we have to get away from here." Tasso stirred the fire with a stick, peering calmly down into it. "No human being can live here. When their reinforcements come we won't have a chance. I've pondered about it while you were unconscious. We have perhaps three hours before they come."

"And you expect me to get us away?"

"That's right. I expect you to get us out of here."

"Why me?"

"Because I don't know any way." Her eyes shone at him in the half light, bright and steady. "If you can't get us out of here they'll kill us within three hours. I see nothing else ahead. Well, Major? What are you going to do? I've been waiting all night. While you were unconscious I sat here, waiting and listening. It's almost dawn. The night is almost over."

Hendricks considered. "It's curious," he said at last.

"Curious?"

"That you should think I can get us out of here. I wonder what you think I can do."

"Can you get us to the Moon Base?"

"The Moon Base? How?"

"There must be some way."

Hendricks shook his head. "No. There's no way that I know of."

Tasso said nothing. For a moment her steady gaze wavered. She ducked her head, turning abruptly away. She scrambled to her feet. "More coffee?"

"No."

"Suit yourself." Tasso drank silently. He could not see her face. He lay back against the ground, deep in thought, trying to concentrate. It was hard to think. His head still hurt. And the numbing daze still hung over him.

"There might be one way," he said suddenly.

"Oh?"

"How soon is dawn?"

"Two hours. The sun will be coming up shortly."

"There's supposed to be a ship near here. I've never seen it. But I know it exists."

"What kind of a ship?" Her voice was sharp.

"A rocket cruiser."

"Will it take us off? To the Moon Base?"

"It's supposed to. In case of emergency." He rubbed his forehead.

"What's wrong?"

"My head. It's hard to think. I can hardly—hardly concentrate. The bomb."

"Is the ship near here?" Tasso slid over beside him, settling down on her haunches. "How far is it? Where is it?"

"I'm trying to think."

Her fingers dug into his arm. "Nearby?" Her voice was like iron. "Where would it be? Would they store it underground? Hidden underground?"

"Yes. In a storage locker."

"How do we find it? Is it marked? Is there a code marker to identify it?"

Hendricks concentrated. "No. No markings. No code symbol."

"What then?"

"A sign."

"What sort of sign?"

Hendricks did not answer. In the flickering light his eyes were glazed, two sightless orbs. Tasso's fingers dug into his arm.

"What sort of sign? What is it?"

"I—I can't think. Let me rest."

"All right." She let go and stood up. Hendricks lay back against the ground, his eyes closed. Tasso walked away from him, her hands in her pockets. She kicked a rock out of her way and stood staring up at the sky. The night blackness was already beginning to fade into gray. Morning was coming.

Tasso gripped her pistol and walked around the fire in a circle, back and forth. On the ground Hendricks lay, his eyes closed, unmoving. The grayness rose in the sky, higher and higher. The landscape became visible, fields of ash stretching out in all directions. Ash and ruins of buildings, a wall here and there, heaps of concrete, the naked trunk of a tree.

The air was cold and sharp. Somewhere a long way off a bird made a few bleak sounds.

Hendricks stirred. He opened his eyes. "Is it dawn? Already?"

"Yes."

Hendricks sat up a little. "You wanted to know something. You were asking me."

"Do you remember now?"

"Yes."

"What is it?" She tensed. "What?" she repeated sharply.

"A well. A ruined well. It's in a storage locker under a well."

"A well." Tasso relaxed. "Then we'll find a well." She looked at her watch. "We have about an hour, Major. Do you think we can find it in an hour?"

"Give me a hand up," Hendricks said.

Tasso put her pistol away and helped him to his feet. "This is going to be difficult."

"Yes it is." Hendricks set his lips tightly. "I don't think we're going to go very far."

They began to walk. The early sun cast a little warmth down on them. The land was flat and barren, stretching out gray and lifeless as far as they could see. A few birds sailed silently, far above them, circling slowly.

"See anything?" Hendricks said. "Any claws?"

"No. Not yet."

They passed through some ruins, upright concrete and bricks. A cement foundation. Rats scuttled away. Tasso jumped back warily.

"This used to be a town," Hendricks said. "A village. Provincial village. This was all grape country, once. Where we are now."

They came onto a ruined street, weeds and cracks criss-crossing it. Over to the right a stone chimney stuck up.

"Be careful," he warned her.

A pit yawned, an open basement. Ragged ends of pipes jutted up, twisted and bent. They passed part of a house, a bathtub turned on its side. A broken chair. A few spoons and bits of china dishes. In the center of the street the ground had sunk away. The depression was filled with weeds and debris and bones.

"Over here," Hendricks murmured.

"This way?"

"To the right."

They passed the remains of a heavy-duty tank. Hendricks's belt counter clicked ominously. The tank had been radiation-blasted. A few feet from the tank a mummified body lay sprawled out, mouth open. Beyond the road was a flat field. Stones and weeds, and bits of broken glass.

"There," Hendricks said.

A stone well jutted up, sagging and broken. A few boards lay across it. Most of the well had sunk into rubble. Hendricks walked unsteadily toward it, Tasso beside him.

"Are you certain about this?" Tasso said. "This doesn't look like anything."

"I'm sure." Hendricks sat down at the edge of the well, his teeth locked. His breath came quickly. He wiped perspiration from his face. "This was arranged so the senior command officer could get away. If anything happened. If the bunker fell."

"That was you?"

"Yes."

"Where is the ship? Is it here?"

"We're standing on it." Hendricks ran his hands over the surface of the well stones. "The eye-lock responds to me, not to anybody else. It's my ship. Or it was supposed to be."

There was a sharp click. Presently they heard a low grating sound from below them.

"Step back," Hendricks said. He and Tasso moved away from the well.

A section of the ground slid back. A metal frame pushed slowly up through the ash, shoving bricks and weeds out of the way. The action ceased as the ship nosed into view.

"There it is," Hendricks said.

The ship was small. It rested quietly, suspended in its mesh frame like a blunt needle. A rain of ash sifted down into the dark cavity from which the ship had been raised. Hendricks made his way over to it. He mounted the mesh and unscrewed the hatch, pulling it back. Inside the ship the control banks and the pressure seat were visible.

Tasso came and stood beside him, gazing into the ship. "I'm not accustomed to rocket piloting," she said after a while.

Hendricks glanced at her. "I'll do the piloting."

"Will you? There's only one seat, Major. I can see it's built to carry only a single person."

Hendricks's breathing changed. He studied the interior of the ship intently. Tasso was right. There was only one seat. The ship was built to carry only one person. "I see," he said slowly. "And the one person is you."

She nodded.

"Of course."

"Why?"

"*You* can't go. You might not live through the trip. You're injured. You probably wouldn't get there."

"An interesting point. But you see, I know where the Moon Base is. And you don't. You might fly around for months and not find it. It's well hidden. Without knowing what to look for—"

"I'll have to take my chances. Maybe I won't find it. Not by myself. But I think you'll give me all the information I need. Your life depends on it."

"How?"

"If I find the Moon Base in time, perhaps I can get them to send a ship back to pick you up. *If* I find the Base in time. If not, then you haven't a chance. I imagine there are supplies on the ship. They will last me long enough—"

Hendricks moved quickly. But his injured arm betrayed him. Tasso ducked, sliding lithely aside. Her hand came up, lightning fast. Hendricks saw the gun butt coming. He tried to ward off the blow, but she was too fast. The metal butt struck against the side of his head, just above his ear. Numbing pain rushed through him. Pain and rolling clouds of blackness. He sank down, sliding to the ground.

Dimly, he was aware that Tasso was standing over him, kicking him with her toe.

"Major! Wake up."

He opened his eyes, groaning.

"Listen to me." She bent down, the gun pointed at his face. "I have to hurry. There isn't much time left. The ship is ready to go, but you must give me the information I need before I leave."

Hendricks shook his head, trying to clear it.

"Hurry up! Where is the Moon Base? How do I find it? What do I look for?"

Hendricks said nothing.

"Answer me!"

"Sorry."

"Major, the ship is loaded with provisions. I can coast for weeks. I'll find the Base eventually. And in a half-hour you'll be dead. Your only chance of survival—" She broke off.

Along the slope, by some crumbling ruins, something moved. Something in the ash. Tasso turned quickly, aiming. She fired. A puff of flame leaped. Something scuttled away, rolling across the ash. She fired again. The claw burst apart, wheels flying.

"See?" Tasso said. "A scout. It won't be long."

"You'll bring them back here to get me?"

"Yes. As soon as possible."

Hendricks looked up at her. He studied her intently. "You're telling the truth?" A strange expression had come over his face, an avid hunger. "You will come back for me? You'll get me to the Moon Base?"

"I'll get you to the Moon Base. But tell me where it is! There's only a little time left."

"All right." Hendricks picked up a piece of rock, pulling himself to a sitting position. "Watch."

Hendricks began to scratch in the ash. Tasso stood by him, watching the motion of the rock. Hendricks was sketching a crude lunar map.

"This is the Appenine range. Here is the Crater of Archimedes. The Moon Base is beyond the end of the Appenine, about two hundred miles. I don't know exactly where. No one on Terra knows. But when you're over the Appenine, signal with one red flare and a green flare, followed by two red flares in quick succession. The Base monitor will record your signal. The Base is under the surface, of course. They'll guide you down with magnetic grapples."

"And the controls? Can I operate them?"

"The controls are virtually automatic. All you have to do is give the right signal at the right time."

"I will."

"The seat absorbs most of the takeoff shock. Air and temperature are automatically controlled. The ship will leave Terra and pass out into free space. It'll line itself up with the Moon, falling into an orbit around it, about a hundred miles above the surface. The orbit will carry you over the Base. When you're in the region of the Appenine, release the signal rockets."

Tasso slid into the ship and lowered herself into the pressure seat. The arm locks folded automatically around her. She fingered the controls. "Too bad you're not going, Major. All this put here for you, and you can't make the trip."

"Leave me the pistol."

Tasso pulled the pistol from her belt. She held it in her hand, weighing it thoughtfully. "Don't go too far from this location. It'll be hard to find you, as it is."

"No. I'll stay here by the well."

Tasso gripped the takeoff switch, running her fingers over the smooth metal. "A beautiful ship, Major. Well built. I admire your workmanship. You people have always done good work. You build fine things. Your work, your creations, are your greatest achievements."

"Give me the pistol," Hendricks said impatiently, holding out his hand. He struggled to his feet.

"Good-bye, Major." Tasso tossed the pistol past Hendricks. The pistol clattered against the ground, bouncing and rolling away. Hendricks hurried after it. He bent down, snatching it up.

The hatch of the ship clanged shut. The bolts fell into place. Hendricks made his way back. The inner door was being sealed. He raised the pistol unsteadily.

There was a shattering roar. The ship burst up from its metal cage, fusing the mesh behind it. Hendricks cringed, pulling back. The ship shot up into the rolling clouds of ash, disappearing into the sky.

Hendricks stood watching a long time, until even the streamer had dissipated. Nothing stirred. The morning air was chill and silent. He began to walk aimlessly back the way they had come. Better to keep moving around. It would be a long time before help came—if it came at all.

He searched his pockets until he found a package of cigarettes. He lit one grimly. They had all wanted cigarettes from him. But cigarettes were scarce.

A lizard slithered by him, through the ash. He halted, rigid. The lizard disappeared. Above, the sun rose higher in the sky. Some flies landed on a flat rock to one side of him. Hendricks kicked at them with his foot.

It was getting hot. Sweat trickled down his face, into his collar. His mouth was dry.

Presently he stopped walking and sat down on some debris. He unfastened his medicine kit and swallowed a few narcotic capsules. He looked around him. Where was he?

Something lay ahead. Stretched out on the ground. Silent and unmoving.

Hendricks drew his gun quickly. It looked like a man. Then he remembered. It was the remains of Klaus. The Second Variety. Where Tasso had blasted him. He could see wheels and relays and metal parts, strewn around on the ash. Glittering and sparkling in the sunlight.

Hendricks got to his feet and walked over. He nudged the inert form with his foot, turning it over a little. He could see the metal hull, the aluminum ribs and struts. More wiring fell out. Like viscera. Heaps of wiring, switches and relays. Endless motors and rods.

He bent down. The brain cage had been smashed by the fall. The artificial brain was visible. He gazed at it. A maze of circuits. Miniature tubes. Wires as fine as hair. He touched the brain cage. It swung aside. The type plate was visible. Hendricks studied the plate.

And blanched.

IV—V.

For a long time he stared at the plate. Fourth Variety. Not the Second. They had been wrong. There were more types. Not just three. Many more, perhaps. At least four. And Klaus wasn't the Second Variety.

But if Klaus wasn't the Second Variety—

Suddenly he tensed. Something was coming, walking through the ash behind the hill. What was it? He strained to see. Figures. Figures coming slowly along, making their way through the ash.

Coming toward him.

Hendricks crouched quickly, raising his gun. Sweat dripped down into his eyes. He fought down rising panic, as the figures neared.

The first was a David. The David saw him and increased its pace. The others hurried behind it. A second David. A third. Three Davids, all alike, coming toward him silently, without expression, their thin legs rising and falling. Clutching their teddy bears.

He aimed and fired. The first two Davids dissolved into particles. The third came on. And the figure behind it. Climbing silently toward him across the gray ash. A Wounded Soldier, towering over the David. And—

And behind the Wounded Soldier came two Tassos, walking side by side. Heavy belt, Russian army pants, shirt, long hair. The familiar figure, as he had seen her only a little while before. Sitting in the pressure seat of the ship. Two slim, silent figures, both identical.

They were very near. The David bent down suddenly, dropping its teddy bear. The bear raced across the ground. Automatically, Hendricks's fingers tightened around the trigger. The bear was gone, dissolved into mist. The two Tasso types moved on, expressionless, walking side by side, through the gray ash.

When they were almost to him, Hendricks raised the pistol waist high and fired.

The two Tassos dissolved. But already a new group was starting up the rise, five or six Tassos, all identical, a line of them coming rapidly toward him.

And he had given her the ship and the signal code. Because of him she was on her way to the moon, to the Moon Base. He had made it possible.

He had been right about the bomb, after all. It had been

designed with knowledge of the other types, the David Type and the Wounded Soldier Type. And the Klaus Type. Not designed by human beings. It had been designed by one of the underground factories, apart from all human contact.

The line of Tassos came up to him. Hendricks braced himself, watching them calmly. The familiar face, the belt, the heavy shirt, the bomb carefully in place.

The bomb—

As the Tassos reached for him, a last ironic thought drifted through Hendricks's mind. He felt a little better, thinking about it. The bomb. Made by the Second Variety to destroy the other varieties. Made for that end alone.

They were already beginning to design weapons to use against each other.

SALVADOR

Lucius Shepard

Lucius Shepard may have been the most popular and influential new writer of the '80s, rivaled only by William Gibson, Connie Willis, and Kim Stanley Robinson. Although his novels have been generally well received, he has had greater impact with his short fiction, an unusual situation these days. Shepard made his first sale to Terry Carr's Universe *in 1983, and the rest of the decade would see a steady stream of bizarre and powerfully compelling stories that would persist through the '90s as well, stories such as the landmark novella "R&R," which won him a Nebula Award in 1987, "The Jaguar Hunter," "Black Coral," "A Spanish Lesson," "The Man Who Painted the Dragon Griaule," "Shades," "Aymara," "A Traveller's Tale," "How the Wind Spoke at Madaket," "On the Border," "The Scalehunter's Beautiful Daughter," and "Barnacle Bill the Spacer," which won him a Hugo Award in 1993. Shepard also won the John W. Campbell Award in 1985 as the year's Best New Writer; in 1988, he picked up a World Fantasy Award for his monumental short-story collection* The Jaguar Hunter, *following it in 1992 with a second World Fantasy Award for his second collection,* The Ends of the Earth.*

Shepard has made something of a specialty in writing vividly and knowingly about future war in stories such as "Shades" and "Delta Sly Honey," as well as melding stories such as "Fire Zone Emerald" and the above mentioned "R&R" into his well-known novel Life During Wartime—*one of the field's most chilling speculations about a possible future "Vietnam." Perhaps his best handling of the theme, though, is in the harrowing story that follows, in which he shows us that we* do *learn from the experience of war—the only question is, learn* what?

Shepard's other books include the novels Green Eyes, Kalimantan, *and* The Golden. *His most recent book is a new collection,* Barnacle Bill the Spacer, *and he's currently at work on a mainstream novel,* Family Values. *Born in Lynchberg, Virginia, he now lives in Seattle, Washington.*

Three weeks before they wasted Tecolutla, Dantzler had his baptism of fire. The platoon was crossing a meadow at the foot of an emerald-green volcano, and being a dreamy sort, he was idling along, swatting tall grasses with his rifle barrel and thinking how it might have been a first-grader with crayons who had devised this elementary landscape of a perfect cone rising into a cloudless sky, when cap-pistol noises sounded on the slope. Someone screamed for the medic, and Dantzler dove into the grass, fumbling for his ampules. He slipped one from the dispenser and popped it under his nose, inhaling frantically; then, to be on the safe side, he popped another—"A double helpin' of martial arts," as DT would say—and lay with his head down until the drugs had worked their magic. There was dirt in his mouth, and he was very afraid.

Gradually his arms and legs lost their heaviness, and his heart rate slowed. His vision sharpened to the point that he could see not only the pinpricks of fir blooming on the slope, but also the figures behind them, half-obscured by brush. A bubble of grim anger welled up in his brain, hardened to a fierce resolve, and he started moving toward the volcano. By the time he reached the base of the cone, he was all rage and reflexes. He spent the next forty minutes spinning acrobatically through the thickets, spraying shadows with bursts of his M-18; yet part of his mind remained distant from the action, marveling at his efficiency, at the comic-strip enthusiasm he felt for the task of killing. He shouted at the men he shot, and he shot them many more times than was necessary, like a child playing soldier.

"Playin' my ass!" DT would say. "You just actin' natural."

DT was a firm believer in the ampules; though the official line was that they contained tailored RNA compounds and pseudoendorphins modified to an inhalant form, he held the opinion that they opened a man up to his inner nature. He was big, black, with heavily muscled arms and crudely stamped features, and he had come to the Special Forces direct from prison, where he had done a stretch for attempted murder; the palms of his hands were covered by jail tattoos—a pentagram and a horned monster. The words DIE HIGH were painted on his helmet. This was his second tour in Salvador, and Moody—who was Dantzler's buddy—said the drugs had addled DT's brains, that he was crazy and gone to hell.

"He collects trophies," Moody had said. "And not just ears like they done in 'Nam."

When Dantzler had finally gotten a glimpse of the trophies, he had been appalled. They were kept in a tin box in DT's pack and were nearly unrecognizable; they looked like withered brown orchids. But despite his revulsion, despite the fact that he was afraid of DT, he admired the man's capacity for survival and had taken to heart his advice to rely on the drugs.

On the way back down the slope they discovered a live casualty, an Indian kid about Dantzler's age, nineteen or twenty, Black hair, adobe skin, and heavy-lidded brown eyes. Dantzler, whose father was an anthropologist and had done fieldwork in Salvador, figured him for a Santa Ana tribesman; before leaving the States, Dantzler had pored over his father's notes, hoping this would give him an edge, and had learned to identify the various regional types. The kid had a minor leg wound and was wearing fatigue pants and a faded COKE ADDS LIFE T-shirt. This T-shirt irritated DT no end.

"What the hell you know 'bout Coke?" he asked the kid as they headed for the chopper that was to carry them deeper into Morazán Province. "You think it's funny or somethin'?" He whacked the kid in the back with his rifle butt, and when they reached the chopper, he slung him inside and had him sit by the door. He sat beside him, tapped out a joint from a pack of Kools, and asked, "Where's Infante?"

"Dead," said the medic.

"Shit!" DT licked the joint so it would burn evenly. "God-damn beaner ain't no use 'cept somebody else know Spanish."

"I know a little," Dantzler volunteered.

Staring at Dantzler, DT's eyes went empty and unfocused. "Naw," he said. "You don't know no Spanish."

Dantzler ducked his head to avoid DT's stare and said nothing;

he thought he understood what DT meant, but he ducked away from the understanding as well. The chopper bore them aloft, and DT lit the joint. He let the smoke out his nostrils and passed the joint to the kid, who accepted gratefully.

"Qué sabor!" he said, exhaling a billow; he smiled and nodded, wanting to be friends.

Dantzler turned his gaze to the open door. They were flying low between the hills, and looking at the deep bays of shadow in their folds acted to drain away the residue of the drugs, leaving him weary and frazzled. Sunlight poured in, dazzling the oil-smeared floor.

"Hey, Dantzler!" DT had to shout over the noise of the rotors. "Ask him whass his name!"

The kid's eyelids were drooping from the joint, but on hearing Spanish he perked up; he shook his head, though, refusing to answer. Dantzler smiled and told him not to be afraid.

"Ricardo Quu," said the kid.

"Kool!" said DT with false heartiness. "Thass my brand!" He offered his pack to the kid.

"Gracias, no." The kid waved the joint and grinned.

"Dude's named for a goddamn cigarette," said DT disparagingly, as if this were the height of insanity.

Dantzler asked the kid if there were more soldiers nearby, and once again received no reply; but, apparently sensing in Dantzler a kindred soul, the kid leaned forward and spoke rapidly, saying that his village was Santander Jiménez, that his father was—he hesitated—a man of power. He asked where they were taking him. Dantzler returned a stormy glare. He found it easy to reject the kid, and he realized later this was because he had already given up on him.

Latching his hands behind his head, DT began to sing—a wordless melody. His voice was discordant, barely audible above the rotors; but the tune had a familiar ring and Dantzler soon placed it. The theme from "Star Trek." It brought back memories of watching TV with his sister, laughing at the low-budget aliens and Scotty's Actors' Equity accent. He gazed out the door again. The sun was behind the hills, and the hillsides were unfeatured blurs of dark green smoke. Oh, God, he wanted to be home, to be anywhere but Salvador! A couple of the guys joined in the singing at DT's urging, and as the volume swelled, Dantzler's emotion peaked. He was on the verge of tears, remembering tastes and sights, the way his girl Jeanine had smelled, so clean and fresh, not reeking of sweat and perfume like the whores around Ilopango—finding all this substance in the banal touch-stone of his culture and the illusions of the hillsides rushing past. Then Moody tensed beside him, and he glanced up to learn the reason why.

In the gloom of the chopper's belly, DT was as unfeatured as the hills—a black presence ruling them, more the leader of a coven than a platoon. The other two guys were singing their lungs out, and even the kid was getting into the spirit of things. *"Músical!"* he said at one point, smiling at everybody, trying to fan the flame of good feeling. He swayed to the rhythm and essayed a "la-la" now and again. But no one else was responding.

The singing stopped, and Dantzler saw that the whole platoon was staring at the kid, their expressions slack and dispirited.

"Space!" shouted DT, giving the kid a little shove. "The final frontier!"

The smile had not yet left the kid's face when he toppled out the door. DT peered after him; a few seconds later he smacked his hand against the floor and sat back, grinning. Dantzler felt like screaming, the stupid horror of the joke was so at odds with the languor of his homesickness. He looked to the others for reaction. They were sitting with their heads down, fiddling with trigger guards and pack straps, studying their bootlaces, and seeing this, he quickly imitated them.

Morazán Province was spook country. Santa Ana spooks. Flights of birds had been reported to attack patrols; animals appeared at the perimeters of campsites and vanished when you shot at them; dreams afflicted everyone who ventured there. Dantzler could not testify to the birds and animals, but he did have a recurring dream. In it the kid DT had killed was pinwheeling down through a golden fog, his T-shirt visible against the roiling backdrop, and sometimes a voice would boom out of the fog, saying, "You are killing my son." No, no, Dantzler would reply,

it wasn't me, and besides, he's already dead. Then he would
wake covered with sweat, groping for his rifle, his heart racing.

But the dream was not an important terror, and he assigned it
no significance. The land was far more terrifying. Pine-forested
ridges that stood out against the sky like fringes of electrified
hair; little trails winding off into thickets and petering out, as if
what they led to had been magicked away; gray rock faces along
which they were forced to walk, hopelessly exposed to ambush.
There were innumerable booby traps set by the guerrillas, and
they lost several men to rockfalls. It was the emptiest place of
Dantzler's experience. No people, no animals, just a few hawks
circling the solitudes between the ridges. Once in a while they
found tunnels, and these they blew with the new gas grenades;
the gas ignited the rich concentrations of hydrocarbons and sent
flame sweeping through the entire system. DT would praise
whoever had discovered the tunnel and would estimate in a loud
voice how many beaners they had "refried." But Dantzler knew
they were traversing pure emptiness and burning empty holes.
Days, under debilitating heat, they humped the mountains,
traveling seven, eight, even ten klicks up trails so steep that
frequently the feet of the guy ahead of you would be on a level
with your face; nights, it was cold, the darkness absolute, the
silence so profound that Dantzler imagined he could hear the
great humming vibration of the earth. They might have been
anywhere or nowhere. Their fear was nourished by the isolation,
and the only remedy was "martial arts."

Dantzler took to popping the pills without the excuse of
combat. Moody cautioned him against abusing the drugs, citing
rumors of bad side effects and DT's madness; but even he was
using them more and more often. During basic training, Dantzler's D.I. had told the boots that the drugs were available only to
the Special Forces, that their use was optional; but there had been
too many instances of lackluster battlefield performance in the
last war, and this was to prevent a reoccurrence.

"The chickenshit infantry should take 'em," the D.I. had said.
"You bastards are brave already. You're born killers, right?"

"Right, sir!" they had shouted.

"What are you?"

"Born killers, sir!"

But Dantzler was not a born killer; he was not even clear as to how he had been drafted, less clear as to how he had been manipulated into the Special Forces, and he had learned that nothing was optional in Salvador, with the possible exception of life itself.

The platoon's mission was reconnaissance and mop-up. Along with other Special Forces platoons, they were to secure Morazán prior to the invasion of Nicaragua; specifically, they were to proceed to the village of Tecolutla, where a Sandinista patrol had recently been spotted, and following that they were to join up with the First Infantry and take part in the offensive against León, a provincial capital just across the Nicaraguan border. As Dantzler and Moody walked together, they frequently talked about the offensive, how it would be good to get down into flat country; occasionally they talked about the possibility of reporting DT, and once, after he had led them on a forced night march, they toyed with the idea of killing him. But most often they discussed the ways of the Indians and the land, since this was what had caused them to become buddies.

Moody was slightly built, freckled, and red-haired; his eyes had the "thousand-yard stare" that came from too much war. Dantzler had seen winos with such vacant, lusterless stares. Moody's father had been in 'Nam, and Moody said it had been worse than Salvador because there had been no real commitment to win; but he thought Nicaragua and Guatemala might be the worst of all, especially if the Cubans sent in troops as they had threatened. He was adept at locating tunnels and detecting booby traps, and it was for this reason Dantzler had cultivated his friendship. Essentially a loner, Moody had resisted all advances until learning of Dantzler's father; thereafter he had buddied up, eager to hear about the field notes, believing they might give him an edge.

"They think the land has animal traits," said Dantzler one day as they climbed along a ridgetop. "Just like some kinds of fish look like plants or sea bottom, parts of the land look like plain ground, jungle . . . whatever. But when you enter them, you find you've entered the spirit world, the world of *Sukias*."

"What's *Sukias*?" asked Moody.

"Magicians." A twig snapped behind Dantzler, and he spun

around, twitching off the safety of his rifle. It was only Hodge—a lanky kid with the beginnings of a beer gut. He stared hollow-eyed at Dantzler and popped an ampule.

Moody made a noise of disbelief. "If they got magicians, why ain't they winnin'? Why ain't they zappin' us off the cliffs?"

"It's not their business," said Dantzler. "They don't believe in messing with worldly affairs unless it concerns them directly. Anyway, these places—the ones that look like normal land but aren't—they're called . . ." He drew a blank on the name. "*Aya*-something. I can't remember. But they have different laws. They're where your spirit goes to die after your body dies."

"Don't they got no Heaven?"

"Nope. It just takes longer between everything and nothing."

"Nothin'," said Moody disconsolately, as if all his hopes for an afterlife had been dashed. "Don't make no sense to have spirits and not have no Heaven."

"Hey," said Dantzler, tensing as wind rustled the pine boughs. "They're just a bunch of damn primitives. You know what their sacred drink is? Hot chocolate! My old man was a guest at one of their funerals, and he said they carried cups of hot chocolate balanced on these little red towers and acted like drinking it was going to wake them to the secrets of the universe." He laughed, and the laughter sounded tinny and psychotic to his own ears. "So you're going to worry about fools who think hot chocolate's holy water?"

"Maybe they just like it," said Moody. "Maybe somebody dyin' just gives 'em an excuse to drink it."

But Dantzler was no longer listening. A moment before, as they emerged from pine cover onto the highest point of the ridge, a stony scarp open to the winds and providing a view of rumpled mountains and valleys extending to the horizon, he had popped an ampule. He felt so strong, so full of righteous purpose and controlled fury, it seemed only the sky was around him, that he was still ascending, preparing to do battle with the gods themselves.

Tecolutla was a village of whitewashed stone tucked into a notch between two hills. From above, the houses—with their shadow-blackened windows and doorways—looked like an unlucky

throw of dice. The streets ran uphill and down, diverging around
boulders. Bougainvilleas and hibiscuses speckled the hillsides,
and there were tilled fields on the gentler slopes. It was a sweet,
peaceful place when they arrived, and after they had gone it was
once again peaceful; but its sweetness had been permanently
banished. The reports of Sandinistas had proved accurate, and
though they were casualties left behind to recuperate, DT had
decided their presence called for extreme measures. Fu gas, frag
grenades, and such. He had fired an M-60 until the barrel melted
down, and then had manned the flamethrower. Afterward, as
they rested atop the next ridge, exhausted and begrimed, having
radioed in a chopper for resupply, he could not get over how one
of the houses he had torched had come to resemble a toasted
marshmallow.

"Ain't that how it was, man?" he asked, striding up and down
the line. He did not care if they agreed about the house; it was a
deeper question he was asking, one concerning the ethics of their
actions.

"Yeah," said Dantzler, forcing a smile. "Sure did."

DT grunted with laughter. "You *know* I'm right, don'tcha
man?"

The sun hung directly behind his head, a golden corona
rimming a black oval, and Dantzler could not turn his eyes away.
He felt weak and weakening, as if threads of himself were being
spun loose and sucked into the blackness. He had popped three
ampules prior to the firefight, and his experience of Tecolutla
had been a kind of mad whirling dance through the streets,
spraying erratic bursts that appeared to be writing weird names
on the walls. The leader of the Sandinistas had worn a mask—a
gray face with a surprised hole of a mouth and pink circles
around the eyes. A ghost face. Dantzler had been afraid of the
mask and had poured round after round into it. Then, leaving
the village, he had seen a small girl standing beside the shell
of the last house, watching them, her colorless rag of a dress
tattering in the breeze. She had been a victim of that malnutrition
disease, the one that paled your skin and whitened your hair and
left you retarded. He could not recall the name of the disease—
things like names were slipping away from him—nor could he

believe anyone had survived, and for a moment he had thought
the spirit of the village had come out to mark their trail.

That was all he could remember of Tecolutla, all he wanted to
remember. But he knew he had been brave.

Four days later, they headed up into a cloud forest. It was the dry
season, but dry season or not, blackish gray clouds always
shrouded these peaks. They were shot through by ugly glimmers
of lightning, making it seem that malfunctioning neon signs were
hidden beneath them, advertisements for evil. Everyone was
jittery, and Jerry LeDoux — a slim dark-haired Cajun kid — flat-
out refused to go.

"It ain't reasonable," he said. "Be easier to go through the
passes."

"We're on recon, man! You think the beaners be waitin' in the
passes, wavin' their white flags?" DT whipped his rifle into
firing position and pointed it at LeDoux. "C'mon, Louisiana
man. Pop a few, and you feel different."

As LeDoux popped the ampules, DT talked to him.

"Look at it this way, man. This is your big adventure. Up there
it be like all them animal shows on the tube. The savage
kingdom, the unknown. Could be like Mars or something'.
Monsters and shit, with big red eyes and tentacles. You wanna
miss that, man? You wanna miss bein' the first grunt on Mars?"

Soon LeDoux was raring to go, giggling at DT's rap.

Moody kept his mouth shut, but he fingered the safety of his
rifle and glared at DT's back. When DT turned to him, however,
he relaxed. Since Tecolutla he had grown taciturn, and there
seemed to be a shifting of lights and darks in his eyes, as if
something were scurrying back and forth behind them. He had
taken to wearing banana leaves on his head, arranging them
under his helmet so the frayed ends stuck out the sides like
strange green hair. He said this was camouflage, but Dantzler
was certain it bespoke some secretive irrational purpose. Of
course DT had noticed Moody's spiritual erosion, and as they
prepared to move out, he called Dantzler aside.

"He done found someplace inside his head that feel good to
him," said DT. "He's tryin' to curl up into it, and once he do that
he ain't gon' be responsible. Keep an eye on him."

Dantzler mumbled his assent, but was not enthused.

"I know he your fren', man, but that don't mean shit. Not the way things are. Now me, I don't give a damn 'bout you personally. But I'm your brother-in-arms, and thass somethin' you can count on . . . y'understand."

To Dantzler's shame, he did understand.

They had planned on negotiating the cloud forest by nightfall, but they had underestimated the difficulty. The vegetarian beneath the clouds was lush—thick, juicy leaves that mashed underfoot, tangles of vines, trees with slick, pale bark and waxy leaves—and the visibility was only about fifteen feet. They were gray wraiths passing through grayness. The vague shapes of the foliage reminded Dantzler of fancifully engraved letters, and for a while he entertained himself with the notion that they were walking among the half-formed phrases of a constitution not yet manifest in the land. They barged off the trail, losing it completely, becoming veiled in spiderwebs and drenched by spills of water; their voices were oddly muffled, the tag ends of words swallowed up. After seven hours of this, DT reluctantly gave the order to pitch camp. They set electric lamps around the perimeter so they could see to string the jungle hammocks; the beam of light illuminated the moisture in the air, piercing the murk with jeweled blades. They talked in hushed tones, alarmed by the eerie atmosphere. When they had done with the hammocks, DT posted four sentries—Moody, LeDoux, Dantzler, and himself. Then they switched off the lamps.

It grew pitch-dark, and the darkness was picked out by plips and plops, the entire spectrum of dripping sounds. To Dantzler's ears they blended into a gabbling speech. He imagined tiny Santa Ana demons talking about him, and to stave off paranoia he popped two ampules. He continued to pop them, trying to limit himself to one every half hour; but he was uneasy, unsure where to train his rifle in the dark, and he exceeded his limit. Soon it began to grow light again, and he assumed that more time had passed than he had thought. That often happened with the ampules—it was easy to lose yourself in being alert, in the wealth of perceptual detail available to your sharpened senses. Yet on checking his watch, he saw it was only a few minutes after two o'clock. His system was too inundated with the drugs to allow panic, but he twitched his head from side to side in tight little arcs to determine the source of the brightness. There did not appear to be a single source; it was simply that filaments of the cloud were gleaming, casting a diffuse golden glow, as if they were elements of a nervous system coming to life. He started to call out, then held back. The others must have seen the light, and they had given no cry; they probably had a good reason for their silence. He scrunched down flat, pointing his rifle out from the campsite.

Bathed in the golden mist, the forest had acquired an alchemic beauty. Beads of water glittered with gemmy brilliance; the leaves and vines and bark were gilded. Every surface shimmered with light . . . everything except a fleck of blackness hovering between two of the trunks, its size gradually increasing. As it swelled in his vision, he saw it had the shape of a bird, its wings beating, flying toward him from an inconceivable distance— inconceivable, because the dense vegetation did not permit you to see very far in a straight line, and yet the bird was growing larger with such slowness that it must have been coming from a long way off. It was not really flying, he realized; rather, it was as if the forest were painted on a piece of paper, as if someone were holding a lit match behind it and burning a hole, a hole that maintained the shape of a bird as it spread. He was transfixed, unable to react. Even when it had blotted out half the light, when he lay before it no bigger than a mote in relation to its huge span, he could not move or squeeze the trigger. And then the blackness swept over him. He had the sensation of being borne along at incredible speed, and he could no longer hear the dripping of the forest.

"Moody!" he shouted. "DT!"

But the voice that answered belonged to neither of them. It was hoarse, issuing from every part of the surrounding blackness, and he recognized it as the voice of his recurring dream.

"You are killing my son," it said. "I have led you here, to this *ayahuamaco*, so he may judge you."

Dantzler knew to his bones the voice was that of the *Sukia* of the village of Santander Jiménez. He wanted to offer a denial, to explain his innocence, but all he could manage was, "No." He said it tearfully, hopefully, his forehead resting on his rifle barrel.

Then his mind gave a savage twist, and his soldiery self regained control. He ejected an ampule from his dispenser and popped it.

The voice laughed—malefic, damning laughter whose vibrations shuddered Dantzler. He opened up with the rifle, spraying fire in all directions. Filigrees of golden holes appeared in the blackness, tendrils of mist coiled through them. He kept on firing until the blackness shattered and fell in jagged sections toward him. Slowly. Like shards of black glass dropping through water. He emptied the rifle and flung himself flat, shielding his head with his arms, expecting to be sliced into bits; but nothing touched him. At last he peeked between his arms; then—amazed, because the forest was now a uniform lustrous yellow—he rose to his knees. He scraped his hand on one of the crushed leaves beneath him, and blood welled from the cut. The broken fibers of the leaf were as stiff as wires. He stood, a giddy trickle of hysteria leaking up from the bottom of his soul. It was no forest, but a building of solid gold worked to resemble a forest—the sort of conceit that might have been fabricated for the child of an emperor. Canopied by golden leaves, columned by slender golden trunks, carpeted by golden grasses. The water beads were diamonds. All the gleam and glitter soothed his apprehension; here was something out of a myth, a habitat for princesses and wizards and dragons. Almost gleeful, he turned to the campsite to see how the others were reacting.

Once, when he was nine years old, he had sneaked into the attic to rummage through the boxes and trunks, and he had run across an old morocco-bound copy of *Gulliver's Travels*. He had been taught to treasure old books, and so he had opened it eagerly to look at the illustrations, only to find that the centers of the pages had been eaten away, and there, right in the heart of the fiction, was a nest of larvae. Pulpy, horrid things. It had been an awful sight, but one unique in his experience, and he might have studied those crawling scraps of life for a very long time if his father had not interrupted. Such a sight was now before him, and he was numb with it.

They were all dead. He should have guessed they would be; he had given no thought to them while firing his rifle. They had been struggling out of their hammocks when the bullets hit, and as a result they were hanging half-in, half-out, their limbs

dangling, blood pooled beneath them. The veils of golden mist made them look dark and mysterious and malformed, like monsters killed as they emerged from their cocoons. Dantzler could not stop staring, but he was shrinking inside himself. It was not his fault. That thought kept swooping in and out of a flock of less acceptable thoughts; he wanted it to stay put, to be true, to alleviate the sick horror he was beginning to feel.

"What's your name?" asked a girl's voice behind him.

She was sitting on a stone about twenty feet away. Her hair was a tawny shade of gold, her skin a half-tone lighter, and her dress was cunningly formed out of the mist. Only her eyes were real. Brown heavy-lidded eyes—they were at variance with the rest of her face, which had the fresh, unaffected beauty of an American teenager.

"Don't be afraid," she said, and patted the ground, inviting him to sit beside her.

He recognized the eyes, but it was no matter. He badly needed the consolation she could offer; he walked over and sat down. She let him lean his head against her thigh.

"What's your name?" she repeated.

"Dantzler," he said. "John Dantzler." And then he added, "I'm from Boston. My father's . . ." It would be too difficult to explain about anthropology. "He's a teacher."

"Are there many soldiers in Boston?" She stroked his cheek with a golden finger.

The caress made Dantzler happy. "Oh, no," he said. "They hardly know there's a war going on."

"This is true?" she said, incredulous.

"Well, they *do* know about it, but it's just news on the TV to them. They've got more pressing problems. Their jobs, families."

"Will you let them know about the war when you return home?" she asked. "Will you do that for me?"

Dantzler had given up hope of returning home, of surviving, and her assumption that he would do both acted to awaken his gratitude. "Yes," he said fervently. "I will."

"You must hurry," she said. "If you stay in the *ayahuamaco* too long, you will never leave. You must find the way out. It is a way not of directions or trails, but of events."

"Where is this place?" he asked, suddenly aware of how much he had taken it for granted.

She shifted her leg away, and if he had not caught himself on the stone, he would have fallen. When he looked up, she had vanished. He was surprised that her disappearance did not alarm him; in reflex he slipped out a couple of ampules, but after a moment's reflection he decided not to use them. It was impossible to slip them back into the dispenser, so he tucked them into the interior webbing of his helmet for later. He doubted he would need them, though. He felt strong, competent, and unafraid.

Dantzler stepped carefully between the hammocks, not wanting to brush against them; it might have been his imagination, but they seemed to be bulged down lower than before, as if death had weighed out heavier than life. That heaviness was in the air, pressuring him. Mist rose like golden steam from the corpses, but the sight no longer affected him—perhaps because the mist gave the illusion of being their souls. He picked up a rifle with a full magazine and headed off into the forest.

The tips of the golden leaves were sharp, and he had to ease past them to avoid being cut; but he was at the top of his form, moving gracefully, and the obstacles barely slowed his pace. He was not even anxious about the girl's warning to hurry; he was certain the way out would soon present itself. After a minute or so he heard voices, and after another few seconds he came to a clearing divided by a stream, one so perfectly reflecting that its banks appeared to enclose a wedge of golden mist. Moody was squatting to the left of the stream, staring at the blade of his survival knife and singing under his breath—a wordless melody that had the erratic rhythm of a trapped fly. Beside him lay Jerry LeDoux, his throat slashed from ear to ear. DT was sitting on the other side of the stream; he had been shot just above the knee, and though he had ripped up his shirt for bandages and tied off the leg with a tourniquet, he was not in good shape. He was sweating, and a gray chalky pallor infused his skin. The entire scene had the weird vitality of something that had materialized in a magic mirror, a bubble of reality enclosed within a gilt frame.

DT heard Dantzler's footfalls and glanced up. "Waste him!" he shouted, pointing at Moody.

Moody did not turn from contemplation of the knife. "No," he said, as if speaking to someone whose image was held in the blade.

"Waste him, man!" screamed DT. "He killed LeDoux!"

"Please," said Moody to the knife. "I don't want to."

There was blood clotted on his face, more blood on the banana leaves sticking out of his helmet.

"Did you kill Jerry?" asked Dantzler; while he addressed the question to Moody, he did not relate to him as an individual, only as part of a design whose message he had to unravel.

"Jésus Christ! Waste him!" DT smashed his fist against the ground in frustration.

"Okay," said Moody. With an apologetic look, he sprang to his feet and charged Dantzler, swinging the knife.

Emotionless, Dantzler stitched a line of fire across Moody's chest; he went sideways into the bushes and down.

"What the hell was you waitin' for!" DT tried to rise, but winced and fell back. "Damn! Don't know if I can walk."

"Pop a few," Dantzler suggested mildly.

"Yeah. Good thinkin', man." DT fumbled for his dispenser.

Dantzler peered into the bushes to see where Moody had fallen. He felt nothing, and this pleased him. He was weary of feeling.

DT popped an ampule with a flourish, as if making a toast, and inhaled. "Ain't you gon' to do some, man?"

"I don't need them," said Dantzler. "I'm fine."

The stream interested him; it did not reflect the mist, as he had supposed, but was itself a seam of the mist.

"How many you think they was?" asked DT.

"How many what?"

"Beaners, man! I wasted three or four after they hit us, but I couldn't tell how many they was."

Dantzler considered this in light of his own interpretation of events and Moody's conversation with the knife. It made sense. A Santa Ana kind of sense.

"Beats me," he said. "But I guess there's less than there used to be."

DT snorted. "You got *that* right!" He heaved to his feet and limped to the edge of the stream. "Gimme a hand across."

Dantzler reached out to him, but instead of taking his hand, he grabbed his wrist and pulled him off-balance. DT teetered on his good leg, then toppled and vanished beneath the mist. Dantzler had expected him to fall, but he surfaced instantly, mist clinging to his skin. Of course, thought Dantzler; his body would have to die before his spirit would fall.

"What you doin', man?" DT was more disbelieving than enraged.

Dantzler planted a foot in the middle of his back and pushed him down until his head was submerged. DT bucked and clawed at the foot and managed to come to his hands and knees. Mist slithered from his eyes, his nose, and he choked out the words ". . . kill you . . ." Dantzler pushed him down again; he got into pushing him down and letting him up, over and over. Not so as to torture him. Not really. It was because he had suddenly understood the nature of the *ayahuamaco*'s laws, that they were approximations of normal laws, and he further understood that his actions had to approximate those of someone jiggling a key in a lock. DT was the key to the way out, and Dantzler was jiggling him, making sure all the tumblers were engaged.

Some of the vessels in DT's eyes had burst, and the whites were occluded by films of blood. When he tried to speak, mist curled from his mouth. Gradually his struggles subsided; he clawed runnels in the gleaming yellow dirt of the bank and shuddered. His shoulders were knobs of black land foundering in a mystic sea.

For a long time after DT sank from view, Dantzler stood beside the stream, uncertain of what was left to do and unable to remember a lesson he had been taught. Finally he shouldered his rifle and walked away from the clearing. Morning had broken, the mist had thinned, and the forest had regained its usual coloration. But he scarcely noticed these changes, still troubled by his faulty memory. Eventually, he let it slide—it would all come clear sooner or later. He was just happy to be alive. After a while he began to kick the stones as he went, and to swing his rifle in a carefree fashion against the weeds.

When the First Infantry poured across the Nicaraguan border and wasted León, Dantzler was having a quiet time at the VA hospital

in Ann Arbor, Michigan; and at the precise moment the bulletin
flashed nationwide, he was sitting in the lounge, watching the
American League playoffs between Detroit and Texas. Some of
the patients ranted at the interruption, while others shouted them
down, wanting to hear the details. Dantzler expressed no reaction
whatsoever. He was solely concerned with being a model patient;
however, noticing that one of the staff was giving him a clinical
stare, he added his weight on the side of the baseball fans. He did
not want to appear too controlled. The doctors were as suspicious
of that sort of behavior as they were of its contrary. But the funny
thing was—at least it was funny to Dantzler—that his feigned
annoyance at the bulletin was an exemplary proof of his control,
his expertise at moving through life the way he had moved
through the golden leaves of the cloud forest. Cautiously,
gracefully, efficiently. Touching nothing, and being touched by
nothing. That was the lesson he had learned—to be as perfect a
counterfeit of a man as the *ayahuamaco* had been of the land; to
adopt the various stances of a man, and yet, by virtue of his
distance from things human, to be all the more prepared for the
onset of crisis or a call to action. He saw nothing aberrant in this;
even the doctors would admit that men were little more than
organized pretense. If he was different from other men, it was
only that he had a deeper awareness of the principles on which
his personality was founded.

When the battle of Managua was joined, Dantzler was living
at home. His parents had urged him to go easy in readjusting to
civilian life, but he had immediately gotten a job as a management trainee in a bank. Each morning he would drive to work
and spend a controlled, quiet eight hours; each night he would
watch TV with his mother, and before going to bed, he would
climb to the attic and inspect the trunk containing his souvenirs
of war—helmet, fatigues, knife, boots. The doctors had insisted
he face his experiences, and this ritual was his way of following
their instructions. All in all, he was quite pleased with his
progress, but he still had problems. He had not been able to force
himself to venture out at night, remembering too well the
darkness in the cloud forest, and he had rejected his friends,
refusing to see them or answer their calls—he was not secure
with the idea of friendship. Further, despite his methodical

approach to life, he was prone to a nagging restlessness, the feeling of a chore left undone.

One night his mother came into his room and told him that an old friend, Phil Curry, was on the phone. "Please talk to him, Johnny," she said. "He's been drafted, and I think he's a little scared."

The word *drafted* struck a responsive chord in Dantzler's soul, and after brief deliberation he went downstairs and picked up the receiver.

"Hey," said Phil. "What's the story, man? Three months, and you don't even give me a call."

"I'm sorry," said Dantzler. "I haven't been feeling so hot."

"Yeah, I understand.." Phil was silent a moment. "Listen, man. I'm leavin', y'know, and we're havin' a big send-off at Sparky's. It's goin' on right now. Why don't you come down?"

"I don't know."

"Jeanine's here, man. Y'know, she's still crazy 'bout you, talks 'bout you alla time. She don't go out with nobody."

Dantzler was unable to think of anything to say.

"Look," said Phil, "I'm pretty weirded out by this soldier shit. I hear it's pretty bad down there. If you got anything you can tell me 'bout what it's like, man, I'd 'preciate it."

Dantzler could relate to Phil's concern, his desire for an edge, and besides, it felt right to go. Very right. He would take some precautions against the darkness.

"I'll be there," he said.

It was a foul night, spitting snow, but Sparky's parking lot was jammed. Dantzler's mind was flurried like the snow, crowded like the lot—thoughts whirling in, jockeying for position, melting away. He hoped his mother would not wait up, he wondered if Jeanine still wore her hair long, he was worried because the palms of his hands were unnaturally warm. Even with the car windows rolled up, he could hear loud music coming from inside the club. Above the door the words SPARKY'S ROCK CITY were being spelled out a letter at a time in red neon, and when the spelling was complete, the letters flashed off and on and a golden neon explosion bloomed around them. After the explosion, the entire sign went dark for a split second, and the big ramshackle building seemed to grow large and merge with

the black sky. He had an idea it was watching him, and he
shuddered—one of those sudden lurches downward of the kind
that take you just before you fall asleep. He knew the people
inside did not intend him any harm, but he also knew that places
have a way of changing people's intent, and he did not want to
be caught off guard. Sparky's might be such a place, might be a
huge black presence camouflaged by neon, its true substance one
with the abyss of the sky, the phosphorescent snowflakes
jittering in his headlights, the wind keening through the side
vent. He would have liked very much to drive home and forget
about his promise to Phil; however, he felt a responsibility to
explain about the war. More than a responsibility, an evangelistic
urge. He would tell them about the kid falling out of the chopper,
the white-haired girl in Tecolutla, the emptiness. God, yes! How
you went down chock-full of ordinary American thoughts and
dreams, memories of smoking weed and chasing tail and hanging
out and freeway flying with a case of something cold, and how
you smuggled back a human-shaped container of pure Salvador-
ian emptiness. Primo grade. Smuggled it back to the land of silk
and money, of minkfuck video games and topless tennis matches
and fast-food solutions to the nutritional problem. Just a taste of
Salvador would banish all those trivial obsessions. Just a taste. It
would be easy to explain.

Of course, some things beggared explanation.

He bent down and adjusted the survival knife in his boot so the
hilt would not rub against his calf. From his coat pocket he
withdrew the two ampules he had secreted in his helmet that
long-ago night in the cloud forest. As the neon explosion flashed
once more, glimmers of gold coursed along their shiny surfaces.
He did not think he would need them; his hand was steady, and
his purpose was clear. But to be on the safe side, he popped them
both.

FLOATING DOGS

Ian McDonald

There's an old saying about politics making strange bedfellows. But, as the bizarre and pyrotechnic story that follows will demonstrate, war can make ever stranger ones . . .

British author Ian McDonald is an ambitious and daring writer with a wide range and an impressive amount of talent. His first story was published in 1982, and since then he has appeared with some frequency in Interzone, Asimov's Science Fiction, New Worlds, Zenith, Other Edens, Amazing, *and elsewhere. He was nominated for the John W. Campbell Award in 1985, and in 1989 he won the* Locus *"Best First Novel" Award for his novel* Desolation Road. *He won the Philip K. Dick Award in 1992 for his novel* King of Morning, Queen of Day. *His other books include the novels* Out On Blue Six *and* Hearts, Hands and Voices, *and the acclaimed* Evolution's Shore, *and two collections of his short fiction,* Empire Dreams *and* Speaking in Tongues. *His most recent books include the new novels* Terminal Cafe *and* Sacrifice of Fools. *Born in Manchester, England, in 1960, McDonald has spent most of his life in Northern Ireland, and now lives and works in Belfast.*

And there in a wood, a Piggy-wig stood . . .
Edward Lear: *The Owl and the Pussy-cat*

On the third day beyond the womb we come to the cool cool river. Peeg and Porcospino and Ceefer and papavator and I. We stand among the trees that come down to the edge and watch the river flow. The sun is high above us; light shines and gleams from the moving water. Peeg is fascinated. He has never seen true water. Only the dream water when he was a seed high in heaven. He goes down over the stones to touch his trunk to the flowing river.

"Alive!" he says. "Alive."

It is only water, I tell him but Peeg cannot accept this. There cannot be enough water in the world for all this flowing: no, it must be some great coiling creature, flowing across the earth, up into heaven and back to earth again. A circle of never-ending movement. For a creature of no hands and very little words, Peeg has much opinion about the hardworld. Opinions should be left to beings like me who have much words, and clever hands. Why, he does not even know his own true name. He calls himself *Peeg* because that is the name he found on his tongue when he woke in the womb of mamavator. I tell him, *You are not a pig, a boar, you are a tapir. A tapir, that is what you are. See, you have a trunk, a snout, pigs do not have trunks or snouts.* He will not be told. *Peeg* is his name, Peeg is what he is. Creatures with few words should not toy with powerful things like names.

Ceefer flexes her claws, cleans between her toes.

"What it is is not important," she says. "How we get across it is." She is a law to herself, Ceefer. She has as many words as I; this I know because she has the smart look in the back of her eyes. You cannot hide that look. But she keeps her words much to herself. If she has a name, one she found on her tongue in mamavator, she keeps that also to herself. So I have my own name for her. Ceefer. Ceefer Cat.

We follow the river to a place where the smooth shining water breaks over rocks and stones into white spray.

"Here we will cross," I say. "Ceefer will go first to make sure there are no traps or snares." She grimaces at the white water; she loves to fish but hates to get her fur wet. In a few bounds she is across, sitting on the far side shaking water from her feet. We follow; Porcospino, then Peeg, then papavator, then me. The Team Leader must be last so he can watch over his team. I can see that Peeg's small feet are far from safe on the slippery rocks.

"Peeg!" I say. "Be careful careful careful." But the glitter and shimmer of the running water have dazzled him. His small feet lose their balance. In he goes. Screaming. Splashing. Feet clawing, kicking, but there is nowhere for them to catch hold.

And the current has hold of him, is sweeping him towards a gap in the rocks to wedge him, drag him down, drown him.

Flash blue silver: papavator steps over me, straddles his long, thin metal legs to form a good steady base, unfolds an arm. *Down* goes the arm, *in* go the fingers locking in the mass of hair and circuitry at the back of Peeg's neck, *up* comes Peeg thrashing and squealing. In three strides papavator is on the far bank. Peeg is a dismal, dripping huddle on the shore.

"Up, up," I say. "Move move. We must go on. We have far to go this day to get to our Destination." But Peeg will not move. He stands shivering, saying over and over and over again these words: *Bit me bit me bad being bad being bit me bit me bad being bad being.* The river being that seemed so wonderful, so friendly to him has turned evil and hostile. I go to talk to him, I stroke the coils of circuitry around his head, stroke the bulge on his side that covers the lance. He will not be consoled by my words and my touching. He is beginning to upset the others. I cannot allow that. We shall have to wait until Peeg is ready before we go on. I signal for papavator to unfold the arm with the needleful of dreams on it. Great dreams there are in the needle. Perhaps the flying dream: that is the one Peeg loves best: that he is back in heaven, flying, laughing and crying and pissing himself with happiness as the angels look down upon him and smile at their Peeg. He lifts his trunk to touch the needle. Dream good, Peeg.

Papavator settles on his metal legs, opens his belly. Time to feed. Porcospino and I suck greedily from the titties. Ceefer flares her nostrils in displeasure. She prefers the taste of gut and bone and blood. Tonight, she will hunt by the light of the moon and the shine of her eyes. She will kill. She will swallow down blood and bones and guts and all. Disgusting creature. Not a being at all.

Ceefer. Peeg. Porcospino. Papavator. Me, Coon-ass. One more in our team to make it the full one-hand's-worth-and-one. Here she comes now, down the beams of light that slant into the shadows among the trees of the river's edge: she does not need dreams to fly in. Only Peeg and I have the gift of colour-seeing, and Peeg is rolling and grunting in his needle-dream. The others cannot see as I do how the colours flow from blue to green across her wings and back, the cap of brilliant red, the beak and feet of brightest yellow. This, I think, is the world called *beautiful*. She settles on papavator's outstretched arm. No pulp, no pap for her. She feeds on pellets from the hand of papavator himself. But for all her colours, she has only one word; that is the trade the angels made: one word, two syllables that she sings over and over and over. Bir-dee. Bir-dee. Bir-dee.

Ceefer Cat looks up from her eternal cleaning, cleaning, cleaning, sudden, sniffing. In the backs of her eyes are the red moving shapes that are her gift from the angels. She stiffens, bares her teeth, just a little. That is enough. One of the things that goes with having hands and colours, and much, much words, is more fear than others: the fear that looks at what might be and shivers. *Anxiety*, that is the name for it.

Danger. Bir-dee leaps up into the air again, darting and many-coloured, brilliant, dashing through the air, and then I can see her no longer through the canopy of tree-tops. But I do not fear that she will fly away out of all seeing and never come back, she is keyed to my scent, she will always come back to me, however far she flies.

Ceefer is waiting in the shadows beneath the trees, Porcospino is ruffling and rattling his quills, papavator has closed himself up and is lurching on to his silly thin legs. But Peeg sleeps on. He grumbles and mumbles and drools in his dream. It must be a very good dream that papavator has in his needle. "Peeg, Peeg, danger coming, danger coming! Awake! Awake! The others have reached the dark of the deep forest, they are looking back; why do we not come?"

I do not have the senses of Ceefer, but I can feel the thing she feels; huge and heavy, moving through the forest on the other side of the river.

There are secrets that mamavator gave only to me, to be shared with none other; secrets whispered to me in the warmth of the womb, in the dream-forest that is so like, and so unlike, this hard-forest. The middle finger of my left hand is one of the secrets told to none but I. It is made from the same almost-living stuff as the emplants that trail almost to the ground from the sockets behind my ears, from the skulls of all my team.

Quick. Quick. Out comes the emplant in the back of Peeg's head.

Quick. Quick. In goes the middle finger of my left hand.

Up, I think. *Up.* Peeg twitches in his sleep, a great heaving twitch. *Up.* He staggers to his feet. *Forward,* I think and the thought pours out of my finger into his head and as he moves forward, still dreaming his needle-dream, I hop up on his back, ride him with my finger. *Move. Move. Run. Run. Fear.* He wails in his dreams, breaks into a trot, a canter. I lash him into a gallop. We fly over the dark, dark earth. Porcospino and Ceefer run at my side, papavator covers the ground with his long, clicking strides. The trees rise up all around us, taller and darker and huger than any dreaming of them. *Run Peeg run.* The dream of the needle is beginning to wear thin, the hardworld is pouring in through the tears and cracks in the dream, but I do not release him from my mind. From far behind comes a tremendous crashing, as if the dark, huge trees are being torn up and thrown into heaven; and the sound of mighty explosions. We run until all running is run out of us. Full of fear, we stop, listening, waiting. Presently, there is the smell of burning. The red shapes in the backs of Ceefer's eyes flicker and shift: she is scanning. She sits to clean herself.

"Whatever it is, is gone now," is all she will say. She licks her crotch.

We sit, we pant, we wait. The rain begins, dripping in fat drops from the forest canopy. Soon the smell of burning is gone. As I sit with the rain running down my fur, Bir-dee comes to me, perches on my hand, singing her glad two-note song. I stroke her neck, ruffle her feathers, smooth down her glossy blue wings. Only when the others are asleep with the rain from high high above falling heavily upon them, do I extract the reconnaissance chip from her head and plug it into the socket beside my right eye.

Flight. Soaring. Trees and clouds and sun, the bright shine and coil of a river, the curved edge of the world: all crazy, all turned on end. Then, something huge as the moon: huger even than mamavator when we saw her for the first time, steaming in the forest clearing where we were born: something earthbound and stamping, stamping out of the forest, into the river, standing with the water flowing around its feet while it fires and fires and fires, explosion after explosion after explosion tearing apart the trees and rocks of the river bank where we rested. Before it stamps away down the river it sets the smashed trees alight with flames from its chest.

I blank the chip with a thought, extrude it, give it back to Bir-dee. To have hands, and colour, and much, much words, to *know;* this is the worst punishment of the angels.

> The bravest animals in the land
> Arc Captain Bcaky and his band.
> *Captain Beaky*

Who made you?

The angels made me from a seed.

The angels planted a seed in the womb of mamavator and nurtured it, and grew it. Flesh of the flesh of mamavator. She suckled and fed us.

What are you?

The servants of the angels, the agents of their work upon this world.

Two natures of service, two natures of servant have the angels; the soft and the hard; those of the inorganic and those of the organic. The service of the inorganic is not greater than the service of the organic, the service of the soft is not greater than the service of the hard; both were created in the likeness of the angels to complement each other in their weakness.

Recite the weaknesses of the organic.

Pain. Hunger. Tiredness. Sleep. Emotion. Defecation. Death.

Recite the weaknesses of the inorganic.

Noise. Expense. Energy. Breakdown. Vulnerability. Stupidity.

Why have the angels, themselves perfect, created such imperfection?

Because the angels alone are perfect.

Because no created thing, no thing of the hands, may assume to the perfection of the angels, that is the great sin. What is the name of the greatest sin?

Pride.

How may we purge ourselves of the sin of pride?

By the faithful service of the angels. By the humble obedience of their will. By the execution of their assignments.

To the letter.

To the letter.

I have always wondered what that final part of the Litany means. *To the letter.* I think that it has something to do with the dark marks on papavator's skin; those regular, orderly marks; and they have something to do with *words,* but the understanding of it is not a gift the angels have chosen to give this Coon-ass. Perhaps they are the prayers of the inorganic: papavator himself takes no part in our nightly recitations; his own hard, inorganic devotions he makes well apart from us; long, thin legs folded up under him, arms and antennae drawn in. It is not sleep, the inorganic do not sleep, not as we sleep. Strange, the lives of the inorganics. How marvellous, the will of the angels, that has made us so different, so weak in ourselves, yet so strong together to their service.

Every night, when Ceefer has sniffed out a place free from traps and poisons for us, we gather in a circle in the forest for the Litany. I lead, they respond as best they can. Bir-dee has only two words, yet no matter how far she is flying, however high, she always returns to sit with the others, shifting from foot to foot because she is not made to stand on the ground, cocking her head from side to side as if the wonder of the words is being communicated to her by some spiritual channel I do not understand. And Peeg loves the Litany, would have me say the words over and over and over because though I know that he does not understand what he is saying—they are just sounds he was born with in his skull—inside the words he can see the angels reaching down to lift him up into heaven and set him flying among the stars.

I have said that papavator does not take part in our worship. There is another, sad to say. Ceefer says that she does not believe. There are no angels, there is no heaven, she says. They are comfortable words we have invented because we know that we all must die and the knowing frightens us. She thinks that is brave. I think it foolish. It is certain that we must die, and that is frightening, but would she say it is wrong to comfort ourselves with dreams, like the dreams papavator keeps in his needle? I

have tried to steer her right but she will not believe. She is a
stubborn animal. Our arguing upsets Peeg; he has a great faith
but the light shines through it, like sun through the leaf canopy,
easily stirred by the wind. I would order Ceefer to believe, but
she would laugh that dreadful cat-laugh at me; so every night
when we recite she sits and cleans herself, licking licking
licking. That licking, it is as bad as any laughter.

At the end, after Porcospino has scraped a hole in the
leaf-litter and one after the other we shit into it, Peeg asks for a
bible story.

"What story would you like to hear?" I ask.

"Angels. War," says Peeg. "Lights. Flying."

Ceefer growls. She stalks away. She thinks it is a stupid story.
She thinks all the bible stories she was taught by mamavator are
stupid. I must admit there is much in them that does not make
sense to me, but Peeg would have them told over and over and
over again, every night if he could. He rolls on to his side, his
safe side, closes his eyes. The tip of the lance slides out of the
fold of skin on his side, like a metal penis. He seems to have
forgotten all about the river. He does not have the circuits for
long memory. Fortunate Peeg.

"In the days of days," I say, "there were only angels and
animals. The animals looked like us, and smelled like us, but
they were only animals, not *beings*. They were called animals by
the angels because all they possessed was an *anima,* a livingness, but no words or spirit. The angels and the animals had
existed together in the world for always so that no one could
remember which had made the other, or whether they had both
been made by something different altogether.

"In those days of days, as in these days of days, animals
served angels, but the angels, being as they were mighty
creatures, with moods and feelings that are not to be judged by
beings, grew tired of the animals and their limitations and
created new servants to be better than the animals. They created
servants stronger than you, Peeg"—he hears my voice in his
near-sleep, the high-pressure lance slides out to almost its full
length—"that could see better and farther than you, Ceefer"—
though she is out, patrolling in the darkness, it is part of the
story—"that could fly higher and carry more than you, Bir-dee,

that were smarter and could remember better and think faster than me, an old raccoon; and that could kill better and more than you, Porcospino.

"So excellent were the new servants that the angels were able to fly up into heaven itself, where they have been flying ever since with their hands held out at their sides.

"Now I have said that the wisdom of the angels is greater than the wisdom of beings, and if the angels turn to war among themselves, as they did, not once, but many times in the days of days, what are we to question them? But there was war, a great and terrible war, fought by the terrible servants they had made for themselves; servants that could knock flat whole forests, that could set fire to the sky and turn the sea to piss. A war so terrible that it was fought not just upon the hard world, but in heaven also. So mighty a war that the angels in the end called upon their old servants, the animals, to aid them, and from those wordless, spiritless creatures created, by the shaping of their hands, *beings* like us.

"Though lowly and lesser and stained by the sin of our failure to serve the angels as they wished to be served, we were permitted to redeem ourselves by aiding the angels in their war. Thus we were given wonderful weapons, mighty enough to destroy the works of angels, both organic and inorganic; mighty enough"—and here I always draw my words into a hushed whisper— *"to destroy the angels themselves."*

As they gaze into my words and in them see the angels smiling and holding out their hands to them, I go to them in turn, as I have every night since we came into the hardworld, and touch the third finger of my left hand to the sockets between their eyes, the finger that sends them down down into holy sleep.

Unseen, unheard, black as the night herself, Ceefer returns from her patrol as I end my story.

"Stupid," she says. "What kind of a god is it that can be killed by beings?"

"I do not know," I say. "That is what faith is for. So we can believe what we cannot know."

"I hope it is a big faith you have," says Ceefer, extending her hard inorganic claws to lick off the forest dirt, carefully,

carefully. "Big enough for another to sit on the back of it. I will have need of your faith tomorrow."

"What do you mean?" I ask.

She blinks her round round eyes at heaven, flares her nostrils. Sensing.

"It will be a hard day, tomorrow," she says, and, refusing any further words with me, stalks away to find a comfortable nest among the root buttresses of the great great trees.

> "Bonedigger, bonedigger, dogs in the
> moonlight . . ."
> Paul Simon: *Call Me Al.*

I have these pictures in my head. I suppose they must be the vision of angels, for I can see the forest spread out below me, from sea to shining sea, all its hills and valleys and rivers and lakes laid out before me. But it is more than just as if seeing from on high; it is as if I can see through the canopy of the trees; see through the trees themselves. I can see with a detail surely not possible from so great a height: I can see the place where mamavator left us before returning to the sky in lights and fire; that is a ball of blueness. I can see us, the Team, five yellow dots with a sixth moving some way ahead of us. And I can see the place where we are to go. Our Destination. The shape of that is a black, pulsing star.

The six yellow points are now closer to the black pulsing star than they are to the blue ball.

Every time Bir-dee returns with her pictures for me, my heavenly sight becomes clearer. I see now the war machine that destroyed the river bank where Peeg dreamed as a red triangle moving off to our left, along the river we crossed. It has lost interest in us. Between us and the black star is an area of open ground. When I look at it in my head, the words "lumpy ground" come to me. It is little more than a morning's walk for us to the lumpy ground.

On the lumpy ground we will decide what we are to do when we reach the Destination. So our orders go.

Between the lumpy ground and the black star the picture looks

as if ten, twenty, many many red stars have fallen out of heaven
on to the earth.

The outer defences.

Ceefer leads us through the dark beneath the great trees
towards the Destination, sensing for any traps and nets and
snares that might await us. Now it is we who must ride on her
back. We must have faith that she can see and hear and smell
what we cannot, we must trust her to see what cannot be known,
for to know, to see, to taste and touch, would be to die. I have
learned a new word today. Ceefer's words of the night before
have made it come bubbling up out of my head like deep deep
water. *Foreboding.* Such a duty, the angels have laid upon us.
But would they have given us a task they knew we could not
perform?

Ceefer's screech sends my angel-pictures whirling away in
many many torn pieces. The wail dies slowly into a growl:
Ceefer crouches, eyes wide, whiskers and ears folded flat, staring
at the thing she has found in the dark under-forest.

It has been dead a long long time. The smell of it has been
dissolved away into the smell of forest: guts and eyes pecked out
by pecking pecking birds and insects, skin pulled away from
teeth bared in the final snap at death. Pelt a dried tatter of fur and
leather. The metal spike of the spring trap is driven out through
the back of its neck. Some kind of possum, or small, biting
marsupial: I cannot tell, it is so old and dead.

There are bright metal sockets beneath its ears, and torn
strands of circuitry. Nestled among its bare ribs are long, thin,
steel somethings.

Cat-cool recovered, Ceefer brushes past, moves on. Porcospino pauses to sniff at the dried corpse, papavator steps past on
his metal legs. He is a machine, he does not have the weakness
of feeling. But Peeg is terrified. Peeg will not go past it. Peeg
cowers away from it; it is a bad sign, he says, *bad sign, bad sign,
bad sign.*

"It cannot harm you," I say. "Its duty is done. Its soul flies in
heaven with the angels. You too have a duty, given you by the
angels, that you must do."

I do not want to have to use the circuits in my finger again.
Wide-eyed with terror, Peeg approaches. Any moment he will

break and run, I think. I have circuits in my hand for that possibility, too. Keeping as far as he can from the dead impaled thing, Peeg edges past. Ceefer waits, head turned, eyes shining red, tail lashing impatiently.

But Peeg is right. It is a bad sign.

We enter a clearing. Ceefer is suspicious, looking to the sky, sniffing all around her. Nothing registers on her sensors but she is not happy. If Ceefer is not happy, I am not happy. Porcospino, too, is uncomfortable; blinking his tiny eyes in the light. He is a creature of the forests, of the darkness of the forests; he is naked in open terrain. Naked sky frightens him. Peeg looks across the clearing to the great great trees.

"Look at the trees, Coon-ass," he says, pointing with his trunk. "Dead dead trees, with leaves on them."

I look where he is pointing. And I am afraid. For the great trees are dead, bare, blasted wood, killed by black air and war, but the branches are hung with black leaves.

"Quick, quick!" I cry. "This is a trap!"

And the leaves rise from the branches of the dead trees and we understand. They are not leaves at all. They are bats, rising up in a cloud of beating, roaring wings so dark they shut out the sun.

Those red dots in my inner vision as many as the stars in heaven . . .

"Quick! Quick!" I try to watch the sky as we run across the clearing beneath the wheeling, chittering mass of bats. They swoop down upon us: I can see the shine of circuitry in their fur. I can see the shine of weapons clutched between their feet.

"Quick! Quick!"

The ground rises up in front of me in a burst of noise and earth: the explosion sends me reeling backwards. I plunge onward, blindly, guided by older, baser, truer instincts. The bats release their bombs and flap away. Explosions to the right of me, explosions to the left of me, explosions before me, explosions behind me. We run on; the sky is gone. There are only bats, wheeling, croaking, screaming. The edge of the forest is close, the cover of the trees. So many bats could not safely fly there. Not day-bats, as these are. I look back, see papavator lurching unsteadily across the clearing. Then the bright bombs fall, there is an explosion, flying metal and machine juices. Arms and legs wave, flail, fall dead.

When I am sure I can no longer hear the beating of wings or the sound of bat-voices, I call a halt. We have lost more with papavator than needle-dreams, I say. Without his picking and purging and preparing digested pap for us to suck from his titties, we must take the time to forage and find our own food. This is a dangerous thing for us to do: we cannot be certain that food we find is not enemy food, or tainted with the black air poisons that papavator's stomach removed, and there are always the traps and snares and nets.

"Hungry now," says Peeg. "Hungry *now.*"

"We all must feed ourselves," I say. "There is no more papavator."

For me to grub and dig for food is a fearful, animal thing; the fat maggots and wild honey I dig with my hands, my fine, clever hands, from the hollow of a dead tree and share with Peeg and Porcospino are crude and disgusting compared to the milk of papavator. For Ceefer to hunt, to bring some small forest thing back dripping in her jaws, is a joy. Her sensor eyes glow red as the tears the small thing she has killed with her steel claws. She offers me a piece of hairy flesh gently grasped in her teeth.

"You are a raccoon," she says, setting it down before me in the way of a wicked joke. "You are an omnivore. You can eat anything." I would sooner eat my own shit. Clever clever Ceefer with your smart, clever words, and your smart eyes that can see things no one else can, and your sharp little claws, and your confident belief in disbelief.

We come to the lumpy ground as the day is growing old. It is a strange terrain indeed; full of hummocks and mounds and hollows and dark pits. As if something huge and unshapely had died long ago and let the forest grow over it. Scattered across the open space are stranger spires and pillars of heaped earth. There is a smell to this place I cannot identify but which stirs the hairs along my spine; a smell, and a sound, a deep, deep humming, everywhere and nowhere.

There is a dark shape moving among the shadows and hollows: a creature. A peccary, rooting. I order Porcospino forward. He raises his quills, growls in his throat.

"Tell him to put his spines down," says Ceefer. "It is not a being. It is just an animal. Come, Peeg, with your lance. That is our evening meal, out there." Off she goes, a black shadow flowing across the lumpy ground. Poor, silly Peeg trots after her. The peccary looks up, bolts for the forest edge. The vague troubling noise has become a definite sound, a buzzing, a droning.

Streams of black vapour pour from the strange earth pillars.

"Ceefer! Peeg! Come back at once!" I say. They need no warning from me, they are already flying back across the lumpy ground. The dark vapour forms a cloud around the peccary. The frantic animals tries to flee but the swarm follows it. The peccary twists, turns, plunges; and falls. And I understand. It is not black air, as I had feared. It is much worse. It is insects. Flying, stinging insects. Millions upon millions of insects. They swarm up from the dead peccary, a dark, droning tower looming above the lumpy ground, leaning over us.

What is this Coon-ass to do if he is to obey the will of the angels? I stare, mesmerised, at the whirlwind of insects, moving slowly across the open ground towards me. We cannot fight. We cannot run. We cannot escape. Then I hear Porcospino's voice.

"In. Now."

Has the fear overloaded his circuitry? What is he talking about? He is scratching at a dark hole at the foot of an oddly shaped green mound.

"Others already in. You. Now."

"Bir-dee," I say. "What about Bir-dee?"

"If she is out there, already too late," says Porcospino. "In. In."

I scuttle into the hole as the storm of insects breaks. Porcospino works with his strong feet, kicking at the dirt to seal up the tunnel. A few insects have crawled inside, I strike at them with my hands and feet, crush them into the earth.

"Come. Come. Fast. Fast," says Porcospino as he leads me down, down, downward. To me, a being of the light, with hands and much much words, this is a foreboding of death; dark, pressing close all around, fear, down down downward into the gnawing earth. To Porcospino this is his place of places, underground, grubbing, sniffing.

When I was a seed in the womb of mamavator, adrift in highest heaven, I had a dream in which I was shown the shape of the world. In this dream the world was a bubble of light and air and life surrounded by earth and soil and stone that went on and on and on beyond all counting, for always. In the dream, a voice told me that somewhere lost in this never-endingness of earth and soil were other worlds like our own, of light and air and life.

Of course, it is the foolish imagining of a raccoon, but when I find myself in light and air and space after so long in the dark I think that we have dug our way through the bottom of the world and emerged in some other earth.

It is a very small world, this bubble of air and light, barely big enough for Ceefer and Peeg and Porcospino and Coon-ass. The air is stale, dead, and tastes of old, used-up poison. The light is strange, dim, blue, coming not from one sun, but from flat squares above us. It is a square world altogether, this world, square-sided, everything sharp-edged. It has the smell of a work of angels.

Peeg is looking as if he is going to cry with confusion.

"I think this must be an old defensive position," I say. I hope that he will trust my words and knowledge. "It must come from the very very early time of the war, so long ago the forest grew over it and forgot it. Look: see?" I point at more flat, square things fixed to the sides of the world. They are covered in tiny red and yellow lights, like the shapes in the pictures in my head. "Machine servants. This is a place made by angels."

"More than machine servants," says Ceefer. "Come. See."

She leads us through an opening, along a tunnel into another blue-lit square-cut chamber. There are more inorganics on the walls with their red and yellow stars. On the floor are the bodies of organics.

The dead possum-thing we encountered on the forest path was frightening because it still retained a memory of life. These things are so long dead that they are not even memories. Beyond fearing, they are merely curious.

"What beings these?" asks Porcospino. I cannot answer, I have never seen creatures like these before. Very tall they are, very thin. Long long legs, very big and fine hands at the ends of their forelegs. Fur only on the tops of their heads. Double-skinned: that is the only way I can describe them. Over the middle of their bodies and their legs they wear a second skin, very soft and fine, though ill-fitting. When I touch it, it falls into dust.

"I will tell you what manner of beings are these," says Ceefer. "They are angels. That is what they are. Dead angels."

Peeg whimpers.

"No," I say. "That cannot be. The angels are all in heaven."

"The stories say that the angels fought upon earth and heaven," says Ceefer. "And this is a very old place. And the stories say that the angels can die. Can be destroyed by *beings.*"

"No," I say, though fears and doubts rise up around me like stinging insects. "No. No. They are monkeys. That is what they are. See the skull, the jaw? Monkeys, created and shaped to the will of the angels, but no more than monkeys."

Ceefer sniffs at the body, delicately bares her teeth and picks up a bone. She coughs, spits it out.

"Piss and dust, that is how angel-meat tastes," she says.

> *Sit Ubu, sit. Good dog.*
> American TV sit-com production
> company sound-byte.

Peeg will destroy.
  How?
  Peeg will know.
  How will Peeg know?
  You will give Peeg the knowledge.
  Knowledge that I do not myself know?
  Strange indeed, and wonderful, are the ways of the angels.

Peeg slept a black sleep last night, down in the square chamber among the strange bodies. There was no papavator with his needleful of dreams to send him flying through the night. I listened to him crying and whimpering, under the blue square lights. The world is too much for him.

Ceefer's eyes, which see in any darkness, lead us through many chambers under the earth full of the strange dead beings before finding a scratchway up into the real world again. It is little more than a scrape; bulging with weapons, Peeg can barely fit through. For one moment we think he has jammed good. He screams and screams and screams in terror as Porcospino digs around him to widen the tunnel. I can understand the fear of the earth closing in all around, I have been learning much about fear.

We emerge into the morning. The sun is high above us. The ground is covered in dead insects, like black dust. They are too dangerous for their angels to allow them to live long. From the lumpy ground we pass into forest again. We scavenge. We scratch. We shit.

From the forest we pass into the smouldering land.

The line between the two is as sharp as the edge of a claw. From the cover of the root buttresses, we survey a land burned clean of life: trees, creepers, ferns, fungi, every living thing, every creature, swept away, stripped down to the sick, shit-coloured earth. A dusting of white ash covers the earth, the smell of burning is strong; here, there the charred stump of a tree has resisted the burning.

There is a shadow on the land. A giant shadow. Before us, above us, on the edge of the burnt land that smoulders further than my eyes can see, stands the hulk of a huge war machine. Some terrible weapon has blown away the upper half of its body, the ground is littered with its torn metal flesh. The wind from across the ashlands moans over the jagged, ripped shell.

"The outer defences," I say, quietly. Porcospino rattles his quills. Peeg whimpers in dread. Ceefer hisses. No one need ask *What could have done this?* There are forces here that can shatter even mamavator: that is why we were set down on earth so far from the Destination, to trek through dread and danger and death. Yet we beings, in all our sinful imperfection, may slip through to work the will of the angels where the mighty machines fail.

We pass between the feet of the destroyed war machine. The wind-blown ash stings my eyes. In the picture in my head, the Destination has grown huge, throbbing like a black heart, filling all my inner vision with its beating, throbbing. The ground is warm beneath my hands and feet. Ceefer quests ahead of us, sniffing a path through the soft white ash.

One scream. One warning. That is all we get. That is all Ceefer is allowed before the dogs, bursting up from under the ground, are upon her. Black hurtling dogs, many many many of them; in an instant she is snatched up, tossed into the air. I see her little steel claws flex, her teeth bare in rage, then the waiting jaws catch her, shake her, tear her in two, shake out her guts and blood and bones and scatter her across the burning earth.

Peeg squeals, lowers her stupid head. The tip of the metal lance slides from its housing on his side.

"No Peeg, no. Let Porcospino!" I say.

The dogs hurl themselves upon us. Porcospino hisses, raises his spines. He flicks loose a flight of quills. The lead dogs go down, kicking their paws and writhing and twisting until their backs snap from the pain of the poisons the angels have put on Porcospino's quills. The second wave of dogs comes bounding on, over the bodies of their brothers. They have red eyes and silver metal jaws. Emplants stud the backs of their necks. Again Porcospino throws his neurotoxic spines and they go down on the right and on the left. A black dog leaps: I see his metal jaws open in my face, smell the stinking steam of his breath. Porcospino raises his tail but Peeg catches the dog in the belly with his high-pressure lance. Intestines bursting from its open mouth, blood spraying from its eyes, it goes spinning away to fall among the bodies of its littermates.

And the third wave is on us. They have ferocity, but no conception of strategy. All they know is to run, and to leap, and to savage. Squealing with excitement, Peeg thrusts with his lance, again, and again, and again: the black evil dogs go down, shattered, smashed, impaled and spasming, stuck full of Porcospino's needles.

Then there are no more for they all lie dead on the soft white ash beneath the war machine. All the dead dogs. And the sun is low on the edge of the world, red and huge behind the thin smoke that rises from the smouldering land.

"Come," I order.

"Ceefer . . ." says Peeg. Soon it will hit him, and I have no dreams to stop him crying.

"She is gone. The angels hold her in their hands. Believe me."

But I am no longer sure I believe what I am telling them they must believe. Where do the faithless go? Is there a lonely place, dark and sad, for those who deny the angels? Or is death death?

Nothing? *Nothing?* As we pick our slow and careful way through the ashlands under the rising moon, I find myself drawn to this thought, over and over and over. *Nothing.* It is a terrible thought. I cannot imagine it. Yet over and over and over, I am drawn to it.

Peeg snuffles out a hollow between the burned roots of a tree stump, digs a small scrape where we lie together.

"Hungry," says Peeg.

"We are all hungry," I say. "There is nothing here for us. We will have to be hungry a little longer."

I lie in the scrape. The moon stands over me. A little lower than the moon, strange lights cross the sky, moving fast, fast, from horizon to horizon in a breath. I cannot sleep. I dare not sleep. If I sleep, I will see Ceefer broken apart and all her words and knowledge and strange unbelief that, in truth, was a kind of belief, spilled out and lost.

In the night, Peeg wakes.

"Coon-ass."

"Yes."

"Give me."

"Give you what?"

"Give me knowledge."

"I do not know how. I do not know what this knowledge is."

"Peeg know. Mamavator give Peeg words. Mamavator say: 'Say Coon-ass: *Load File B13 echelon 7.*'"

And it is as if those words, which Peeg could not possibly know unless he had, indeed, been given them by mamavator, gather all my *beingness* and roll it up like clay in a hand, push it away away to the very back of my head so that I may watch but am helpless to act as I feel my hands reach round to the back of my neck and pull out an emplant. And I see those hands that look like my hands reach out and slide the emplant into an empty socket beneath Peeg's ear. And the ears that hear like my ears hear Peeg sigh, and gasp, and say, in a voice I have never heard Peeg speak in before:

"Reset normal sentience simulation parameters."

I shake my head, try to shake my *Coon-ass* back into every corner of my being. I am frightened: clever, proud, wise Coon-ass, mastered and ridden like a . . . like an *animal.* I lie and watch the lights crossing the sky, feeling small, small, smaller than the smallest thing I can imagine. *Nothing.*

The black, beating star beat-beats all night, so huge and close it has spilled out of the place in my head where the pictures are to fill everything with its beating.

> *All together now, all together now, all together now.*
> *In No Man's Land.*
> The Farm.

In the morning my eyes and hands are raw sore with the white ash that covers the burned lands. We are all very hungry but we know among ourselves it is better not to speak about such things. Peeg offers to let me ride on his back. I am glad to accept. With Porcospino trotting beside us, we enter the inner defences. The borderline is clearly marked. A metal arm jutting from the ash bars our path. Clenched in its steel grip is a rodent-like being, furious even in death. The steel fingers crush the rodent's neck, the rodent's teeth are sunk into the arm's brightly coloured wiring. Both are long, long dead.

It is both warning and welcome.

Much occupied with our own thoughts, whatever kind of thoughts the angels have given us to think, we pass into a landscape of terrible, terrible destruction. As far as we can see, the ash is littered with bodies of beings organic and inorganic, locked together in embraces that seem to this Coon-ass almost tender. Paws clawing for the light; mouths open to snap bright teeth one last time at the sun. Torn and twisted metal; gnaw-bones, jawbones. Hanks of hair and wind-dried hide. Dead birds, pulled out of the sky, sky-wise wings splayed out, feathers rustling in the wind, beaks and eyeless eyesockets silted up with drifting ash. Standing guard over them, half-clogged to the waist in ash and mud, the machines: shattered, crushed, twisted apart by ancient explosions, smashed metal limbs swinging, creaking, red sensor eyes dull dead dark.

A cat hanging from a wire noose.

A bird shot through with a metal spike.

Three bloated dogs floating in a crater full of rainwater.

Porcospino lets out a cry. It is the first sound to break the silence of the ashlands. He has seen the body of a brother porcupine, lying close by in a hollow in the ash, surrounded by the skin-draped skeletons of dogs.

"Leave it, leave it," I say. "You can do nothing here. It is dead, it has been dead for time beyond counting."

But Porcospino will not listen; it is as if this rattle of dead, dry quills and spines is a comrade to him, a comfort in the dreadfulness all around him. A lost littermate he never had. He nuzzles the dead thing, pushes it with his nose, as if he might push life back into it, push it into movement and joy. He pulls at its pelt with his teeth; clumps of emplants come away in his teeth.

"Leave it leave it leave it!" I say. "There is too much danger here!"

The ash hears me. The ash stirs. The ash moves. The ash opens. Like a flower blooming, the machine unfolds from beneath the earth. Its head quests; back, forth, back, forth. Red machine eyes open, staring.

"Run run run!" I say, but the weaving head on the long flexing neck has fascinated Porcospino, like the snake I once saw in my mamavator dreams, which could dazzle you with its dancing, weaving, flexing. The huge red sensor eyes fasten on Porcospino. He gazes up into the huge red eyes.

The machine spews out a sheet of fire. Porcospino goes up in a shriek of burning. He tries to beat at the flames with his tiny useless hands, rolls on to his back to roll them out. The fire roars up and eats him.

The head on its long neck wavers, collapses into the ash. Its red sensor eyes go black. Its work is done. I curl my fingers into the circuitry on Peeg's neck, urge him onward.

"To the Destination," I say. "The Destination."

A thin trail of smoke goes up behind us; the wind changes direction and bends it low over us as we pick our way across the battlefield. As Peeg carries me along, he tells me about what the chip has told him about the Destination he is to destroy. It is a *strategic manufacturing installation,* he says. His words are large and strange, not Peeg words. It builds machines and grows beings, this *strategic manufacturing installation.*

"Like mamavator?" I ask.

"Like mamavator," says Peeg, "but this one does not fly in heaven. This one is buried deep under the ground. Deep deep, way down deep. It is very old. Very very old. The angels have been trying to destroy it for long long years. Attack after attack after attack they have sent, from heaven first, and then by machine, and then by beings. Attack after attack after attack. After so many attacks, it must be tired now, old. It cannot have much energy left. That is how we will be able to reach the Destination."

"How will we know when we reach the Destination?" I ask.

"We will know," says Peeg. "That is what the chip tells me."

"And then you will destroy it?"

"And then Peeg will destroy it."

"How?"

Peeg does not know. But Peeg trusts that the angels, in their great wisdom, having told him much already, will tell him that also when he needs to know.

Angels, in their great wisdom. Peeg would have cried, once. Peeg would have cried for Porcospino. Peeg would have cried for each one of those many many beings, more than many many hands can count, that died so that Peeg and Coon-ass can reach their Destination. What did the angels take away to make room for their great wisdom?

We will know, the angel voices in the chip said. Why must they be so very very true in everything they say? We will know, I will know, I have known, since I stumbled, blinking from the warm wet womb into the forest morning. The Destination is the great black star in the picture in my head taken out and pressed into the earth; real, actual. Huge. The black star is bigger than I can cover with both hands spread out in front of my eyes. Many many hours walk across. Heat shimmers and dances over the star: I cannot see its further edge. Now that the shock is passing, I see that it is not the same as that other star, my inner star. It is not as sharp-edged, as definite; it has many many rays, the shiny black of it is streaked and stained with colours, its surface is crazed and cracked, like something that has fallen from heaven to earth.

Fallen, or cast down? We stand at the edge of the great black star, a raccoon riding on the back of a tapir.

"You must get down now," says Peeg. "I am to go on my own."

"Where?" I touch the blackness with my hand, it is smooth, slippery, warm to the touch.

Peeg points with his trunk out across the black.

"I hear voices," he says in that voice, with those words, which are not his own. "Voices, coming from big bright lights. Wonderful wonderful lights."

"Peeg, you cannot go, I must go too, you need me."

"On my own," Peeg says, looking far into the heat haze. "I will destroy it on my own. Then I will come back to you."

"You will come back to me?"

"Yes."

"Do you promise?"

"I do not understand what that means."

"It means that when you say that you will come back, you will come back, that nothing will stop you coming back."

"Yes."

"Then I will do as you say."

"It is the will of the angels," says Peeg, and walks out on his little, neat feet, out across the black glass star, until the heathaze swallows him and I can see him no more. I sit. I wait. The sun moves across the sky, I watch it reflected in the blackness before me. In the reflection I can see where the wars of the angels have left their marks even there. The face of the sun is scarred with dark pock-marks. Craters. Black starbursts. The heathaze runs over the black, melted land like water. In the shiver and the shimmer I am no longer certain what is true, what is false. For in the silver shining I see a distant dark figure standing. Then the heathaze flows and runs and I see clearly: it is Peeg out there in the black lands.

"Peeg!" I shout, "Peeg!" but he cannot hear me. He is looking into the sky, questing up with his trunk, like one who has been given a vision of angels.

"Peeg!" I call again, and start to run to him, across the black glass star. "You have come back!" I run and run and run; the soles of my feet and hands blister on the burning black glass, but however hard I run, however much I call, I never seem to come

any closer. Peeg remains a tiny, wavering dark figure in the huge
silver shimmer of the heathaze.

"Peeg!" I call one final time.

And Peeg looks round.

And the sky turns white with a light so bright that it burns
through my closed eyelids as if they were not there, burns
through my hands that I clamp over my eyes, a burning burning
light as if the sun has burst and died. Belly, hands, face are seared
by the light, the fur shrivels and crisps away in an instant.

And after the light, is darkness.

And after the darkness is a thunder like the sound of heaven
falling, so loud that it becomes more than sound, it becomes a
voice, a cry of angels.

And after the thunder is a rushing mighty wind; a screaming,
scorching wind that does not seem like a thing of air, but a thing
of earth, a solid, material thing that strikes like a fist, strikes the
breath from me, sends me hurling, tumbling backward in the
tearing whirl of ash and dust and roaring air, away away away
from Peeg's Destination, into the ashlands.

And after the rushing mighty wind is darkness again, beautiful
darkness, and in the beautiful darkness; silence.

> . . . *and dance by the light of the moon.*
>   "Thirtysomething": Production company sound-byte.

Am forgetting. Am losing. Words. Rememberings. Knowings.
Feel with fingers, for darkness still in eyes; feel the chips, feel
the emplants; they feel not right, they feel melted, burned. The
blast must have damaged my circuitry. Words come, words go,
sentences, memories. Words from deep deep in the chips. Words
that I once knew. Words that I have forgotten. Words I was meant
to forget. Words I now remember, stirred up like silt in a river by
the explosion. Words like *implanted nanotok warhead*. Words
like *containment field generator*. Words like *mass/energy con-
version*. I take the words in these clever hands of mine and
understand. Everything. I understand what has been done to me,
to Porcospino and Ceefer and Bir-dee, and every other creature
trapped and impaled and dismembered and burned to nothing out

there in the ashlands. Most of all I understand what has been done to Peeg.

Enough intelligence to carry out the mission, but not to understand. Never to understand, merely to obey.

Blind, burning, I crossed the ashlands. Nothing harmed me, nothing knew of my existence. Dead. All dead now. In my blindness I pushed down down down into my memories, down into the deep deep river of remembering, down beyond our birth from the womb of mamavator into this hardworld, down past the dreamforest in which we ran and played and swam while we were yet seeds in the metal womb. And there I found words. Words like *programmed neural simulation,* and *pre-natal environmental conditioning,* like shadows in a heathaze.

I came to the forest. The trees were tumbled and fallen, brought down by the blast. I felt my way over the trees, picked out fat grubs and beetles with my fingers, crunched them down with my small teeth. *Anima.* The spirit of livingness. When I felt coolness and shade on my pelt, and smelled dampness, and growing, I knew I had passed under the canopy of the living forest.

Grubbing. Sniffing. Feeling. When will seeing be again? When will hearing be again? When this hissing, ringing no more?

There. Do I hear? Look up in darkness, turning turning, under cool cool trees, *again,* do I hear, a whisper, a whistle, a call? Two notes. Two tones. Hi-lo. Hi-lo. Hi-lo. *Hush,* you whistling, chirping, rustling things, in my head or in the world, Coon-ass must listen. Hi-lo. Hi-lo. Hi-lo. Two words.

Blind, I hold up my hand into the warmth of a beam of sunlight. And, light as light, she comes to rest on my fingers, singing her two-word name. Bir-dee. Bir-dee. Bir-dee.

Colours gone. Sweet flashing darting movement, up through leaves, branches, into heaven: gone.

"Bir-dee." Name remains. "Bir-dee." She sings her two-note song. I feel her bobbing, impatient, on my finger. *Chip. Chip. Pull chip. See pictures. See pictures.*

No, Bir-dee, no. Gently gently, I bring her in front of my face, gently gently move close until my lips touch the back of her head. No fear. Trust. I press my lips to her blue blue feathers, then, one by one, pull the chips and emplants from their sockets and drop them, one by one, to the ground. When they are all gone, I lift Bir-dee high, high as my arm will reach, into the warmth of the sun.

"Go, Bir-dee, go. Be animal again. Be full of joy. Fly!" I cast her up into the light. Wings beat, I imagine bright darting colours rising up, rising up, above the forest, into light. I look up into the light: do I see shapes, movings, loomings, like motion of angels? I touch long, trailing coils of circuits and chips, trace them back to the metal sockets in my skull.

Then one by one, I pull them out and let them fall.

THE PRIVATE WAR OF PRIVATE JACOB

Joe Haldeman

Here's a disturbing little story about the call of duty that shows us that maybe you don't have as much choice about answering it as you think you do . . .

Born in Oklahoma City, Oklahoma, Joe Haldeman took a B.S. degree in physics and astronomy from the University of Maryland, and did postgraduate work in mathematics and computer science. But his plans for a career in science were cut short by the U.S. Army, which sent him to Vietnam in 1968 as a combat engineer. Seriously wounded in action, Haldeman returned home in 1969 and began to write. He sold his first story to Galaxy in 1969, and by 1976 had garnered both the Nebula Award and the Hugo Award for his famous novel The Forever War, one of the landmark books of the '70s. He took another Hugo Award in 1977 for his story "Tricentennial," won the Rhysling Award in 1983 for the best science fiction poem of the year (although usually thought of primarily as a "hard-science" writer, Haldeman is, in fact, also an accomplished poet, and has sold poetry to most of the major professional markets in the genre), and won both the Nebula and the Hugo Award in 1991 for the novella version of The Hemingway Hoax. His story "None So Blind" won the Hugo Award in 1995. His other books include two mainstream novels, War Year and 1969, the SF novels Mindbridge, All My Sins Remembered, There Is No Darkness (written with his brother, SF writer Jack C. Haldeman II), Worlds, Worlds Apart, Worlds Enough and Time, Buying Time, and The Hemingway Hoax, the "techno-thriller" Tools of the Trade, the collections Infinite Dreams, Dealing in Futures, Vietnam and Other Alien Worlds, and None So Blind, and, as editor, the anthologies Study War No More, Cosmic Laughter, and Nebula Award Stories Seventeen. His most recent book is the long awaited follow-up to The Forever War, called Forever

Peace, which has just won the John W. Campbell Memorial
Award. Haldeman lives part of the year in Boston, where he
teaches writing at the Massachusetts Institute of Technology,
and the rest of the year in Florida, where he and his wife Gay
make their home.

With each step your boot heel cracks through the sun-dried
crust and your foot hesitates, drops through an inch of red talcum
powder, and then you draw it back up with another crackle. Fifty
men marching in a line through this desert and they sound like a
big bowl of breakfast cereal.

Jacob held the laser projector in his left hand and rubbed his
right in the dirt. Then he switched hands and rubbed his left in
the dirt. The plastic handles got very slippery after you'd
sweated on them all day long, and you didn't want the damn
thing to squirt out of your grip when you were rolling and
stumbling and crawling your way to the enemy, and you couldn't
use the strap, noplace off the parade ground; goddamn slide-rule
jockey figured out where to put it, too high, take the damn thing
off if you could. Take the goddamn helmet off too, if you could.
No matter you were safer with it on. They said. And they were
pretty strict, especially about the helmets.

"Look happy, Jacob." Sergeant Melford was always all smile
and bounce before a battle. During a battle, too. He smiled at the
tanglewire and beamed at his men while they picked their way
through it—if you go too fast you get tripped and if you go too
slow you get burned—and he had a sad smile when one of his
men got zeroed and a shriek a happy shriek when they first saw
the enemy and glee when an enemy got zeroed and nothing but
smiles smiles smiles through the whole sorry mess. "If he *didn't*
smile, just once," young-old Addison told Jacob, a long time ago,
"just once he cried or frowned, there would be fifty people
waiting for the first chance to zero that son of a bitch." And
Jacob asked why and he said, "You just take a good look inside
yourself the next time you follow that crazy son of a bitch into
hell and you come back and tell me how you felt about him."

Jacob wasn't stupid, that day or this one, and he did keep an inside eye on what was going on under his helmet. What old Sergeant Melford did for him was mainly to make him glad that he wasn't crazy too, and no matter how bad things got, at least Jacob wasn't enjoying it like that crazy laughing grinning old Sergeant Melford.

He wanted to tell Addison and ask him why sometimes you were really scared or sick and you would look up and see Melford laughing his crazy ass off, standing over some steaming roasted body, and you'd have to grin, too, was it just so insane horrible or? Addison might have been able to tell Jacob but Addison took a low one and got hurt bad in both legs and the groin and it was a long time before he came back and then he wasn't young-old anymore but just old. And he didn't say much anymore.

With both his hands good and dirty, for a good grip on the plastic handles, Jacob felt more secure and he smiled back at Sergeant Melford.

"Gonna be a good one, Sarge." It didn't do any good to say anything else, like it's been a long march and why don't we rest a while before we hit them, Sarge or, I'm scared and sick and if I'm gonna die I want it at the very first, Sarge: no. Crazy old Melford would be down on his hunkers next to you and give you a couple of friendly punches and josh around and flash those white teeth until you were about to scream or run but instead you wound up saying, "Yeah Sarge, gonna be a good one."

We most of us figured that what made him so crazy was just that he'd been in this crazy war so long, longer than anybody could remember anybody saying he remembered; and he never got hurt while platoon after platoon got zeroed out from under him by ones and twos and whole squads. He never got hurt and maybe that bothered him, not that any of us felt sorry for the crazy son of a bitch.

Wesley tried to explain it like this: "Sergeant Melford is an improbability locus." Then he tried to explain what a locus was and Jacob didn't really catch it, and he tried to explain what an improbability was, and that seemed pretty simple but Jacob couldn't see what it all had to do with math. Wesley was a good talker though, and he might have one day been able to clear it up but he tried to run through the tanglewire, you'd think not even a civilian would try to do that, and he fell down and the little metal bugs ate his face.

It was twenty or maybe twenty-five battles later, who keeps track, when Jacob realized that not only did old Sergeant Melford never get hurt, but he never killed any of the enemy either. He just ran around singing out orders and being happy and every now and then he'd shoot off his projector but he always shot high or low or the beam was too broad. Jacob wondered about it but by this time he was more afraid, in a way, of Sergeant Melford than he was of the enemy, so he kept his mouth shut and he waited for someone else to say something about it.

Finally Cromwell, who had come into the platoon only a couple of weeks after Jacob, noticed that Sergeant Melford never seemed to zero anybody and he had this theory that maybe the crazy old son of a bitch was a spy for the other side. They had fun talking about that for a while, and then Jacob told them about the old improbability locus theory, and one of the new guys said he sure is an imperturbable locust all right, and they all had a good laugh, which was good because Sergeant Melford came by and joined in after Jacob told him what was so funny, not about the improbability locus, but the old joke about how do you make a hormone? You don't pay her. Cromwell laughed like there was no tomorrow and for Cromwell there wasn't even any sunset, because he went across the perimeter to take a crap and got caught in a squeezer matrix.

The next battle was the first time the enemy used the drainer field, and of course the projectors didn't work and the last thing a lot of the men learned was that the light plastic stock made a damn poor weapon against a long knife, of which the enemy had plenty. Jacob lived because he got in a lucky kick, aimed for the groin but got the kneecap, and while the guy was hopping around trying to stay upright he dropped his knife and Jacob picked it up and gave the guy a new orifice, eight inches wide and just below the navel.

The platoon took a lot of zeros and had to fall back, which they did very fast because the tanglewire didn't work in a drainer field, either. They left Addison behind, sitting back against a crate with his hands in his lap and a big drooly red grin not on his face.

With Addison gone, no other private had as much combat time as Jacob. When they rallied back at the neutral zone, Sergeant Melford took Jacob aside and wasn't really smiling at all when he said: "Jacob, you know that now if anything happens to me, you've got to take over the platoon. Keep them spread out and keep them advancing, and most of all, keep them happy."

Jacob said, "Sarge, I can tell them to keep spread out and I think they will, and all of them know enough to keep pushing ahead, but how can I keep them happy when I'm never very happy myself, not when you're not around."

That smile broadened and turned itself into a laugh. You crazy son of a bitch, Jacob thought and because he couldn't help himself, he laughed too. "Don't worry about that," Sergeant Melford said. "That's the kind of thing that takes care of itself when the time comes."

The platoon practiced more and more with knives and clubs and how to use your hands and feet but they still have to carry the projectors into combat because, of course, the enemy could turn off the drainer field whenever he wanted to. Jacob got a couple of scratches and a piece of his nose cut off, but the medic put some cream on it and it grew back. The enemy started using bows and arrows so the platoon had to carry shields, too, but that wasn't too bad after they designed one that fit right over the protector, held sideways. One squad learned how to use bows and arrows back at the enemy and things got as much back to normal as they had ever been.

Jacob never knew exactly how many battles he had fought as a private, but it was exactly forty-one. And actually, he wasn't a private at the end of the forty-first.

Since they got the archer squad, Sergeant Melford had taken to standing back with them, laughing and shouting orders at the platoon and every now and then loosing an arrow that always landed on a bare piece of ground. But this particular battle (Jacob's forty-first) had been going pretty poorly, with the initial advance stopped and then pushed back almost to the archers; and then a new enemy force breaking out on the other side of the archers.

Jacob's squad maneuvered between the archers and the new enemy soldiers and Jacob was fighting right next to Sergeant Melford, fighting pretty seriously while old Melford just laughed his fool head off, crazy son of a bitch. Jacob felt that split-second funny feeling and ducked and a heavy club whistled just over his head and bashed the side of Sergeant Melford's helmet and sheared the top of his helmet off just as neat as you snip the end off a soft-boiled egg. Jacob fell to his knees and watched the helmet full of stuff twirl end over end in back of the archers and he wondered why there were little glass marbles and cubes inside the grey-blue blood-streaked mushy stuff and then everything just went

Inside a mountain of crystal under a mountain of rock, a tiny piezoelectric switch, sixty-four molecules in a cube, flipped over to the OFF *position and the following transaction took place at just less than the speed of light:*

UNIT 10011001011MELFORD ACCIDENTALLY DEACTI-
VATED.
SWITCH UNIT 1101011100JACOB TO CATALYST STATUS.
(SWITCHING COMPLETED).
ACTIVATE AND INSTRUCT UNIT 1101011100JACOB.

and came back again just like that. Jacob stood up and looked around. The same old sun-baked plain, but everybody but him seemed to be dead. Then he checked and the ones that weren't obviously zeroed were still breathing a bit. And, thinking about it, he knew why. He chuckled.

He stepped over the collapsed archers and picked up Melford's bleedy skull-cap. He inserted the blade of a knife between the helmet and the hair, shorting out the induction tractor that held the helmet on the head and served to pick up and transmit signals. Letting the helmet drop to the ground, he carefully bore the grisly balding bowl over to the enemy's crapper. Knowing exactly where to look, he fished out all the bits and pieces of crystal and tossed them down the smelly hole. Then he took the unaugmented brain back to the helmet and put it back the way he had found it. He returned to his position by Melford's body.

The stricken men began to stir and a few of the most hardy wobbled to their hands and knees.

Jacob threw back his head and laughed and laughed.

SPIREY AND THE QUEEN

Alastair Reynolds

New writer Alastair Reynolds is a frequent contributor to
Interzone, *and has also sold to* Asimov's Science Fiction *and
elsewhere. A professional scientist with a PhD in astronomy, he
comes from Wales, but lives in the Netherlands.*

*In the slambang, relentlessly paced adventure that follows,
he throws us headlong into the midst of a bitter and long-term
war being fought in deep space, and shows us that the smallest
of actions can set in motion a chain of circumstances that can
eventually have the largest and most unexpected of conse-
quences—for both good and ill.*

Part One

Space war is godawful *slow.*

Mouser's long-range sensors had sniffed the bogey two days
ago, but it had taken all that time just to creep within kill-range.
I figured it had to be another dud. With ordnance, fuel and
morale all low, we were ready to slink back to Tiger's Eye
anyway; let one of the other thickships pick up the sweep in this
sector.

So—still groggy after frogsleep—I wasn't exactly wetting
myself with excitement; not even when *Mouser* began spiking
the thick with combat-readiness psychogens. Even when we
went to Attack-Con-One, all I did was pause the neurodisney I
was tripping (*Hellcats of Solar War Three,* since you asked),
slough my hammock and swim languidly up to the bridge.

"Junk," I said, looking over Yarrow's shoulder at the readout.
"War debris or another of those piss-poor chondrites. Betcha."

"Sorry, kid. Everything checks out."

"Hostiles?"

"Nope. Positive on the exhaust; dead ringer for the stolen ship." She traced a webbed hand across the swathe of decorations which already curled around her neck. "Want your stripes now or when we get back?"

"You actually think this'll net us a pair of tigers?"

"Damn right it will."

I nodded, and thought: *she isn't necessarily wrong*. No defector, no stolen military secrets reaching the Royalists. Ought to be worth a medal, maybe even a promotion.

So why did I feel something wasn't right?

"All right," I said, hoping to drown qualms in routine. "How soon?"

"Missiles are already away, but she's five light-minutes from us, so the quacks won't reach her for six hours. Longer if she makes a run for cover."

"Run for cover? That's a joke."

"Yeah, hilarious." Yarrow swelled one of the holographic displays until it hovered between us.

It was a map of the Swirl, tinted to show zones controlled by us or the Royalists. An enormous slowly rotating disc of primordial material, 800 AU edge to edge; wide enough that light took more than four days to traverse it.

Most of the action was near the middle, in the light-hour of space around the central star Fomalhaut. Immediately around the sun was a material-free void which we called the Inner Clearing Zone, but beyond that began the Swirl proper; metal-rich lanes of dust condensing slowly into rocky planets. Both sides wanted absolute control of those planet-forming Feeding Zones—prime real estate for the day when one side beat the other and could recommence mining operations—so that was where our vast armies of wasps mainly slugged things out. We humans— Royalist and Standardist both—kept much further out, where the Swirl thinned to metal-depleted icy rubble. Even hunting the defector hadn't taken us within ten light-hours of the Feeding Zones, and we'd become used to having a lot of empty space to ourselves. Apart from the defector, there shouldn't have been anything else out here to offer cover.

But there was. Big too, not much more than a half light-minute from the rat.

"Practically pissing distance," Yarrow observed.

"Too close for coincidence. What is it?"

"Splinter. Icy planetesimal, if you want to get technical."

"Not this early in the day." But I remembered how one of our tutors back at the academy had put it: *Splinters are icy slag, spat out of the Swirl. In a few hundred thousand years there'll be a baby solar system around Fomalhaut, but there'll also be shitloads of junk surrounding it, leftovers on million-year orbits.*

"Worthless to us," Yarrow said, scratching at the ribbon of black hair which ran all the way from her brow to fluke. "But evidently not to ratty."

"What if the Royalists left supplies on the splinter? She could be aiming to refuel before the final hop to their side of the Swirl."

Yarrow gave me her best withering look.

"Yeah, okay," I said. "Not my smartest ever suggestion."

Yarrow nodded sagely. "Ours is not to question, Spirey. Ours is to fire and forget."

Six hours after the quackheads had hared away from *Mouser*, Yarrow floated in the bridge, fluked tail coiled beneath. She resembled an inverted question mark, and if I'd been superstitious I'd have said that wasn't necessarily the best of omens.

"You kill me," she said.

An older pilot called Quillin had been the first to go *siren*—first to swap legs for tail. Yarrow followed a year later. Admittedly it made sense, an adaptation to the fluid-filled environment of a high-gee thickship. And I accepted the cardiovascular modifications that enabled us to breathe thick, as well as the biomodified skin which let us tolerate cold and vacuum far longer than any unmodified human. Not to mention the billions of molecule-sized demons which coursed through our bodies, or the combat-specific psycho-modifications. But swapping your legs for a tail touched off too many queasy resonances in me. Had to admire her nerve, though.

"What?" I said.

"That neurodisney shit. Isn't a real space war good enough for you?"

"Yeah, except I don't think this is it. When was the last time one of us actually looked a Royalist in the eye?"

She shrugged. "Something like 400 years."

"Point made. At least in *Solar War Three* you get some blood. See, it's all set on planetary surfaces—Titan, Europa, all those moons they've got back in Sol system. Trench warfare; hand-to-hand stuff. You know what adrenaline is, Yarrow?"

"Managed without it until now. And there's another thing: Don't know much about Greater Earth history, but there was never a Solar War Three."

"It's conjectural," I said. "And in any case it almost happened; they almost went to the brink."

"Almost?"

"It's set in a different timeline."

She grinned, shaking her head. "I'm telling you, you kill me."

"She made a move yet?" I asked.

"What?"

"The defector."

"Oh, we're back in reality now?" Yarrow laughed. "Sorry, this is going to be slightly less exciting than *Solar War Three*."

"Inconsiderate," I said. "Think the bitch would give us a run for our money." And as I spoke the weapons readout began to pulse faster and faster, like the cardiogram of a fluttering heart. "How long now?"

"One minute, give or take a few seconds."

"Want a little bet?"

Yarrow grinned, sallow is the red alert lighting. "As if I'd say no, Spirey."

So we hammered out a wager; Yarrow betting 50 tiger-tokens the rat would attempt some last-minute evasion. "Won't do her a blind bit of good," she said. "But that won't stop her. It's human nature."

Me, I suspected our target was either dead or asleep.

"Bit of an empty ritual, isn't it?"

"What?"

"I mean, the attack happened the best part of five minutes ago, realtime. The rat's already dead, and nothing we can do can influence that outcome."

Yarrow bit on a nicotine stick. "Don't get all philosophical on me, Spirey."

"Wouldn't dream of it. How long?"

"Five seconds. Four . . ."

She was somewhere between three and four when it happened. I remember thinking that there was something of disdainful about the rat's actions: that she'd deliberately waited until the last possible moment, and that she'd dispensed with our threat with the least effort possible.

That was how it felt, anyway.

Nine of the quackheads detonated prematurely, way beyond kill-range. For a moment the tenth remained, zeroing in on the defector—but instead it failed to detonate, until it was just beyond range.

For long moments there was silence, while we absorbed what had happened. Yarrow broke it, eventually.

"Guess I just made myself some money," she said.

Colonel Wendigo's hologram delegated appeared, momentarily frozen before shivering to life. With her too-clear, too-young eyes she fixed first Yarrow and then me.

"Intelligence was mistaken," she said. "Seems the defector doctored records to conceal the theft of those countermeasures. But you harmed her anyway?"

"Just," said Yarrow. "Her quackdrive's spewing out exotics like Spirey after a bad binge. No hull damage, but . . ."

"Assessment?"

"Making a run for the splinter."

Wendigo nodded. "And then?"

"She'll set down and make repairs." Yarrow paused, added: "Radar says there's metal on the surface. Must've been a wasp battle there, before the splinter got lobbed out of the Swirl."

The delegate nodded in my direction. "Concur, Spirey?"

"Yes sir," I said, trying to suppress the nervousness I always felt around Wendigo, even though almost all my dealings with her had been via simulations like this. Yarrow was happy to edit the conversation afterwards, inserting the correct honorifics before transmitting the result back to Tiger's Eye—but I could never free myself of the suspicion that Wendigo would somehow unravel the unedited version, with all its implicit insubordination. Not that any of us didn't inwardly accord Wendigo all the respect she was due. She'd nearly died in the Royalist strike against Tiger's Eye 15 years ago—the one in which my mother was killed. Actual attacks against our two mutually opposed comet bases were rare, not happening much more than every other generation—more gestures of spite than anything else. But this had been an especially bloody one, killing an eighth of our number and opening city-sized portions of our base to vacuum. Wendigo was caught in the thick of the kinetic attack. Now she was chimeric, lashed together by cybernetics. Not much of this showed externally—except that the healed parts of her were too flawless, more porcelain than flesh. Wendigo had not allowed the surgeons to regrow her arms. Story was she lost them trying to pull one of the injured through an open airlock, back into the pressurised zone. She's almost made it, fighting against the gale of escaping air. Then some no-brainer hit the emergency door control, and when the lock shut it took Wendigo's arms off at the shoulder, along with the head of the person she was saving. She wore prosthetics now; gauntleted in chrome.

"She'll get there a day ahead of us," I said. "Even if we pull 20 gees."

"And probably gone to ground by the time you get there."

"Should we try a live capture?"

Yarrow backed me up with a nod. "It's not exactly been possible before."

The delegate bided her time before answering. "Admire your dedication," she said, after a suitably convincing pause. "But you'd only be postponing a death sentence. Kinder to kill her now, don't you think?"

Mouser entered kill-range 19 hours later, a wide pseudo-orbit 3,000 klicks out. The splinter—17 by 12 klicks across—was far too small to be seen as anything other than a twinkling speck, like a grain of sugar at arm's length. But everything we wanted to know was clear: topology, gravimetrics, and the site of the downed ship. That wasn't hard. Quite apart from the fact that it hadn't buried itself completely, it was hot as hell.

"Doesn't look like the kind of touchdown you walk away from," Yarrow said.

"Think they ejected?"

"No way." Yarrow sketched a finger through a holographic enlargement of the ship, roughly cone-shaped, vaguely stream-lined just like our own thickship, to punch through the Swirl's thickest gas belts. "Clock those dorsal hatches. Evac pods still in place."

She was right. The pods could have flung them clear before the crash, but evidently they hadn't had time to bail out. The ensuing impact—even cushioned by the ship's manifold of thick—probably hadn't been survivable.

But there was no point taking chances.

Quackheads would have finished the job, but we'd used up our stock. *Mouser* carried a particle beam battery, but we'd have to move uncomfortably close to the splinter before using it. What remained were the molemines, and they should have been perfectly adequate. We dropped 15 of them, embedded in a cloud of 200 identical decoys. Three of the 15 were designated to dust the wreck, while the remaining 12 would bury deeper into the splinter and attempt to shatter it completely.

That at least was the idea.

It all happened very quickly, not in the dreamy slow-motion of a neurodisney. One instant the molemines were descending toward the splinter, and then the next instant they weren't there. Spacing the two instants had been an almost subliminally brief flash.

"Starting to get sick of this," Yarrow said.

Mouser digested what had happened. Nothing had emanated from the wreck. Instead, there'd been a single pulse of energy seemingly from the entire volume of space around the splinter. Particle weapons, *Mouser* diagnosed. Probably single-use drones, each tinier than a pebble but numbering hundreds or even thousands. The defector must have sewn them on her approach.

But she hadn't touched us.

"It was a warning," I said. "Telling us to back off."

"I don't think so."

"What?"

"I think the warning's on its way."

I stared at her blankly for a moment, before registering what she had already seen: arcing from the splinter was something too fast to stop, something against which our minimally-armoured thickship had no defense, not even the option of flight.

Yarrow started to mouth some exotic profanity she'd reserved for precisely this moment. There was an eardrum-punishing bang and *Mouser* shuddered—but we weren't suddenly chewing vacuum.

And that was very bad news indeed.

Antiship missiles come in two main flavours: quackheads and sporeheads. You know which immediately after the weapon has hit. If you're still thinking—if you still exist—chances are it's a sporehead. And at that point your problems are just beginning.

Invasive demon attack, *Mouser* shrieked. Breather manifold compromised . . . which meant something uninvited was in the thick. That was the point of a sporehead: to deliver hostile demons into an enemy ship.

"Mm," Yarrow said. "I think it might be time to suit up."

Except our suits were a good minute's swim away back into the bowels of *Mouser*, through twisty ducts which might skirt the infection site. Having no choice, we swam anyway, Yarrow insisting I take the lead even though she was a quicker swimmer. And somewhere—it's impossible to know exactly where—demons reached us, seeping invisibly into our bodies via the thick. I couldn't pinpoint the moment; it wasn't as if there was a jagged transition between lucidity and demon-manipulated irrationality. Yarrow and I were terrified enough as it was. All I know is it began with a mild agoraphilia; an urge to escape *Mouser*'s flooded confines. Gradually it phased into claustrophobia, and then became fully-fledged panic, making *Mouser* seem as malevolent as a haunted house.

Yarrow ignored her suit, clawing the hull until her fingers spooled blood.

"Fight it," I said. "It's just demons triggering our fear centres, trying to drive us out!"

Of course, knowing so didn't help.

Somehow I stayed still long enough for my suit to slither on. Once sealed, I purged the tainted thick with the suit's own supply—but I knew it wasn't going to help much. The phobia already showed that hostile demons had reached my brain, and now it was even draping itself in a flimsy logic. Beyond the ship we'd be able to think rationally. It would only take a few minutes for the thick's own demons to neutralize the invader—and then we'd be able to reboard. Complete delusion, of course.

But that was the point.

Part Two

When something like coherent thought returned I was outside.

Nothing but me and the splinter.

The urge to escape was only a background anxiety, a flock of stomach-butterflies urging me against returning. Was that demon-manipulated fear or pure common sense? I couldn't tell—but what I knew was that the splinter seemed to be beckoning me forward, and I didn't feel like resisting. Sensible, surely: we'd exhausted all conventional channels of attack against the defector, and now all that remained was to confront her on the territory she'd staked as her own.

But where was Yarrow?

Suit's alarm chimed. Maybe demons were still subjugating my emotions, because I didn't react with my normal speed. I just blinked, licked my lips and stifled a yawn.

"Yeah, what?"

Suit informed me: something massing slightly less than me, two klicks closer to the splinter, on a slightly different orbit. I knew it was Yarrow; also that something was wrong. She was drifting. In my blackout I'd undoubtedly programmed suit to take me down, but Yarrow appeared not to have done anything except bail out.

I jetted closer. And then saw why she hadn't programmed her suit. Would have been tricky. She wasn't wearing one.

I hit ice an hour later.

Cradling Yarrow—she wasn't much of a burden, in the splinter's weak gravity—I took stock. I wasn't ready to mourn her, not just yet. If I could quickly get her to the medical suite aboard the defector's ship there was a good chance of revival. But where the hell was the wreck?

Squandering its last reserves of fuel, suit had deposited us in a clearing among the graveyard of ruined wasps. Half submerged in ice, they looked like scorched scrap-iron sculptures; phantoms from an entomologist's worst nightmare. So there'd been a battle here, back when the splinter was just another drifting lump of ice. Even if the thing was seamed with silicates or organics, it would not have had any commercial potential to either side. But it might still have had strategic value, and that was why the wasps had gone to war on its surface. Trouble was—as we'd known before the attack—the corpses covered the entire surface, so there was no guessing where we'd come down. The wrecked ship might be just over the nearest hillock—or another ten kilometres in any direction.

I felt the ground rumble under me. Hunting for the source of the vibration, I saw a quill of vapour reach into the sky, no more than a klick away. It was a geyser of superheated ice.

I dropped Yarrow and hit dirt, suit limiting motion so I didn't bounce. Look back, I expected to see a dimple in the permafrost, where some rogue had impacted.

Instead, the geyser was still present. Worse, it was coming steadily closer, etching a neat trench. A beam weapon was making that plume, I realized—like one of the party batteries aboard ship. Then I wised up. That was *Mouser*. The demons had worked their way into its command infrastructure, reprogramming it to turn against us. Now *Mouser* worked for the defector.

I slung Yarrow over one shoulder and loped away from the boiling impact point. Fast as the geyser moved, its path was predictable. If I made enough lateral distance the death-line would sear past—

Except the damn thing turned to follow me.

Now a second flanked it, shepherding me through the thickest zone of wasp corpses. Did they have some significance for the defector? Maybe so, but I couldn't see it. The corpses were a rough mix of machines from both sides: Royalist wasps marked with yellow shell symbols, ours with grinning tiger-heads. Generation 35 units, if I remembered Mil-Hist, when both sides toyed with pulse-hardened optical thinkware. In the 70-odd

subsequent generations there'd been numerous further jumps:
ur-quantum logics, full-spectrum reflective wasp armour, cha-
meleoflage, quackdrive powerplants and every weapon system
the human mind could devise. We'd tried to encourage the wasps
to make these innovations for themselves, but they never
managed to evolve beyond strictly linear extrapolation. Which
was good, or else we human observers would have been out of
a job.

Not that it really mattered now.

A third geyser had erupted behind mc, and a fourth ahead,
boxing me in. Slowly, the four points of fire began to con-
verge. I stopped, but kept holding Yarrow. I listened to my own
breathing, harsh above the basso tremor of the drumming
ground.

Then steel gripped my shoulder.

She said we'd be safer underground. Also that she had friends
below who might be able to do something for Yarrow.

"If you weren't defecting," I began, as we entered a roughly-
hewn tunnel into the splinter's crust, "what the hell was it?"

"Trying to get home. Least that was the idea, until we realized
Tiger's Eye didn't want us back." Wendigo knuckled the ice with
one of her steel fists, her suit cut away to expose her prosthetics.
"Which is when we decided to head here."

"You almost made it," I said. Then added: "Where were you
trying to get home from?"

"Isn't it obvious?"

"Then you did defect."

"We were trying to make contact with the Royalists. Trying to
make peace." In the increasingly dim light I saw her shrug. "It
was a long shot, conducted in secrecy. When the mission went
wrong, it was easy for Tiger's Eye to say we'd been defecting."

"Bullshit."

"I wish."

"But you sent us."

"Not in person."

"But your delegate—"

"Is just software. It could be made to say anything my enemies
chose. Even to order my own execution as a traitor."

We paused to switch on our suit lamps. "Maybe you'd better tell me everything."

"Gladly," Wendigo said. "But if this hasn't been a good day so far, I'm afraid it's about to go downhill."

There had been a clique of high-ranking officers who believed that the Swirl war was intrinsically unwinnable. Privy to information not released to the populace, and able to see through Tiger's Eye's own carefully filtered internal propaganda, they realized that negotiation—contact—was the only way out.

"Of course, not everyone agreed. Some of my adversaries wanted us dead before we even reached the enemy." Wendigo sighed. "Too much in love with the war's stability—and who can blame them? Life for the average citizen in Tiger's Eye isn't that bad. We're given a clear goal to fight for, and the likelihood of any one of us dying in a Royalist attack is small enough to ignore. The idea that all of that might be about to end after 400 years; that we all might have to rethink our roles . . . well, it didn't go down too well."

"About as welcome as a fart in a vac-suit, right?"

Wendigo nodded. "I think you understand."

"Go on."

Her expedition—Wendigo and two pilots—had crossed the Swirl unchallenged. Approaching the Royalist cometary base, they'd expected to be questioned—perhaps even fired upon—but nothing had happened. When they entered the stronghold, they understood why.

"Deserted," Wendigo said. "Or we thought so, until we found the *Royalists*." She expectorated the word. "Feral, practically. Naked, grubby subhumans. Their wasps feed them and treat their illnesses, but that's as far as it goes. They grunt, and they've been toilet-trained, but they're not quite the military geniuses we've been led to believe."

"Then . . ."

"The war is . . . nothing we thought." Wendigo laughed, but the confines of her helmet rendered it more like the squawking of a jack-in-the-box. "And now you wonder why home didn't want us coming back?"

•   •   •

Before Wendigo could explain further, we reached a wider
bisecting tunnel, glowing with its own insipid chlorine-coloured
light. Rather than the meandering bore of the tunnel in which we
walked, it was as cleanly cut as a rifle barrel. In one direction the
tunnel was blocked by a bullet-nosed cylinder, closely modelled
on the trains in Tiger's Eye. Seemingly of its own volition, the
train lit up and edged forward, a door puckering open.

"Get in," Wendigo said. "And lose the helmet. You won't need
it where we're going."

Inside I coughed phlegmy ropes of thick from my lungs.
Transitioning between breathing modes isn't pleasant—more so
since I'd breathed nothing but thick for six weeks. But after a
few lungfuls of the train's antiseptic air, the dark blotches around
my vision began to recede.

Wendigo did likewise, only with more dignity.

Yarrow lay on one of the couches, stiff as a statue carved in
soap. Her skin was cyanotic, a single all-enveloping bruise. Pilot
skin is a better vacuum barrier than the usual stuff, and vacuum
itself is a far better insulator against heat loss than air. But where
I'd lifted her my gloves had embossed fingerprints into her flesh.
Worse was the broad stripe of ruined skin down her back and the
left side of her tail, where she had lain against the splinter's
surface.

But her head looked better. When she hit vac, biomodified
seals would have shut within her skull, barricading every
possible avenue for pressure, moisture or blood loss. Even her
eyelids would have fused tight. Implanted glands in her carotid
artery would have released droves of friendly demons, quickly
replicating via nonessential tissue in order to weave a protective
scaffold through her brain.

Good for an hour or so—maybe longer. But only if the hostile
demons hadn't screwed with Yarrow's native ones.

"You were about to tell me about the wasps," I said, as curious
to hear the rest of Wendigo's story as I was to blank my doubts
about Yarrow.

"Well, it's rather simple. They got smart."

"The wasps?"

She clicked the steel fingers of her hand. "Overnight. Just over a hundred years ago."

I tried not to look too overwhelmed. Intriguing as all this was, I wasn't treating it as anything other than an outlandish attempt to distract me from the main reason for my being here, which remained killing the defector. Wendigo's story explained some of the anomalies we'd so far encountered—but that didn't rule out a dozen more plausible explanations. Meanwhile, it was amusing to try and catch her out. "So they got smart," I said. "You mean our wasps, or theirs?"

"Doesn't mean a damn any more. Maybe it just happened to one machine in the Swirl, and then spread like wildfire to all the trillions of other wasps. Or maybe it happened simultaneously, in response to some stimulus we can't even guess at."

"Want to hazard a guess?"

"I don't think it's important, Spirey." She sounded as though she wanted to put a lot of distance between herself and this topic. "Point is it happened. Afterwards, distinctions between us and the enemy—at least from the point of view of the wasps—completely vanished."

"Workers of the Swirl unite."

"Something like that. And you understand why they kept it to themselves, don't you?"

I nodded, more to keep her talking.

"They needed us, of course. They still lacked something. Creativity, I guess you'd call it. They could evolve themselves incrementally, but they couldn't make the kind of sweeping evolutionary jumps we'd been feeding them."

"So we had to keep thinking there was a war on."

Wendigo looked pleased. "Right. We'd keep supplying them with innovations, and they'd keep pretending to do each other in." She halted, scratching at the unwrinkled skin around one eye with the alloy finger of one hand. "Clever little bastards."

Part Three

We'd arrived somewhere.

It was a chamber, large as any enclosed space I'd ever seen. I felt gravity; too much of the stuff. The whole chamber must have been gimballed and spun within the splinter, like one of the gee-load simulators back in Tiger's Eye. The vaulted ceiling, hundreds of meters "above," now seemed vertiginously higher.

Apart from its apex, it was covered in intricate frescos—dozens of pictorial facets, each a cycling hologram. They told the history of the Swirl, beginning with its condensation from intersteller gas, the ignition of its star, the onset of planetary formation. Then the action cut to the arrival of the first Standardist wasp, programmed to dive into the Swirl and breed like a rabbit, so that one day there'd be a sufficiently huge population to begin mining the thing; winnowing out metals, silicates and precious organics for the folks back home. Of course, it never happened like that. The Royalists wanted in on the action, so they sent their own wasps, programmed to attack ours. The rest is history. The frescos showed the war's beginning, and then a little while later the arrival of the first human observers, beamed across space as pure genetic data, destined to be born in artificial wombs in hollowed out comet-cores, raised and educated by wasps, imprinted with the best tactical and strategic knowledge available. Thereafter they taught the wasps. From then on things hotted up, because the observers weren't limited by years of timelag. They were able to intervene in wasp evolution in realtime.

That ought to have been it, because by then we were pretty up-to-date, give or take 400 years of the same.

But the frescos carried on.

There was one representing some future state of the Swirl, neatly ordered into a ticking orrery of variously sized and patterned worlds, some with beautiful rings or moon systems. And finally—like medieval conceptions of Eden—there was a triptych of lush planetary landscapes, with weird animals in the foreground, mountains and soaring cloudbanks behind.

"Seen enough to convince you?" Wendigo asked.

"No," I said, not entirely sure whether I believed myself. Craning my neck, I looked up toward the apex.

Something hung from it.

It was a pair of wasps, fused together. One was complete, the other was only fully-formed, seemingly in the process of

splitting from the complete wasp. The fused pair looked to have
been smothered in molten bronze, left to dry in waxy nodules.

"You know what this is?" Wendigo asked.

"I'm waiting."

"Wasp art."

I looked at her.

"This wasp was destroyed mid-replication," Wendigo continued. "While it was giving birth. Evidently the image has some
poignancy for them. How I'd put it in human terms I don't
know . . ."

"Don't even think about it."

I followed her across the marbled terrazzo which floored the
chamber. Arched porticos surrounded it, each of which held a
single dead wasp, their body designs covering a hundred
generations of evolution. If Wendigo was right, I supposed these
dead wasps were the equivalent of venerated old ancestors
peering from oil paintings. But I wasn't convinced just yet.

"You knew this place existed?"

She nodded. "Or else we'd be dead. The wasps back in the
Royalist stronghold told us we could seek sanctuary here, if
home turned against us."

"And the wasps—what? Own this place?"

"And hundreds like it, although the others are already far
beyond the Swirl, on their way out to the halo. Since the wasps
came to consciousness, most of the splinters flung out of the
Swirl have been infiltrated. Shrewd of them—all along, we've
never suspected that the splinters are anything other than cosmic
trash."

"Nice decor, anyway."

"Florentine," Wendigo said, nodding. "The frescos are in the
style of a painter called Masaccio; one of Brunelleschi's dis-
ciples. Remember, the wasps had access to all the cultural data
we brought with us from GE—every byte of it. That's how they
work, I think—by constructing things according to arbitrary
existing templates."

"And there's a point to all this?"

"I've been here precisely one day longer than you, Spirey."

"But you said you had friends here; people who could help
Yarrow."

"They're here all right," Wendigo said, shaking her head. "Just hope you're ready for them."

On some unspoken cue they emerged, spilling from a door which until then I'd mistaken for one of the surrounding porticos. I flinched, acting on years of training. Although wasps have never intentionally harmed a human being—even the enemy's wasps—they're nonetheless powerful, dangerous machines. There were 12 of them; divided equally between Standardist and Royalist units. Six-legged, their two-metre-long segmented alloy bodies sprouted weapons, sensors and specialized manipulators. So far so familiar, except that the way the wasps moved was subtly wrong. It was as if the machines choreographed themselves, their bodies defining the extremities of a much larger form which I sensed more than saw.

The 12 whisked across the floor.

"They are—or rather *it* is—a queen," Wendigo said. "From what I've gathered, there's one queen for every splinter. Splinterqueens, I call them."

The swarm partially surrounded us now—but retained the brooding sense of oneness.

"She told you all this?"

"Her demons did, yes." Wendigo tapped the side of her head. "I got a dose after our ship crashed. You got one after we hit your ship. It was a standard sporehead from our arsenal, but the Splinterqueen loaded it with her own demons. For the moment that's how she speaks to us—via symbols woven by demons."

"Take your word for it."

Wendigo shrugged. "No need to."

And suddenly I knew. It was like eavesdropping a topologist's fever dream—only much stranger. The burst of Queen's speech couldn't have lasted more than a tenth of a second, but its after-images seemed to persist much longer, and I had the start of a migraine before it had ended. But like Wendigo had implied before, I sensed planning—that every thought was merely a step toward some distant goal, the way each statement in a mathematical proof implies some final *QED*.

Something big indeed.

"You deal with that shit?"

"My chimeric parts must filter a lot."

"And she understands you?"

"We get by."

"Good," I said. "Then ask her about Yarrow."

Wendigo nodded and closed both eyes, entering intense rapport with the Queen. What followed happened quickly: six of her components detached from the extended form and swarmed into the train we had just exited. A moment later they emerged with Yarrow, elevated on a loom formed from dozens of wasp manipulators.

"What happens now?"

"They'll establish a physical connection to her neural demons," Wendigo said. "So that they can map the damage."

One of the six reared up and gently positioned its blunt, anvil-shaped "head" directly above Yarrow's frost-mottled scalp. Then the wasp made eight nodding movements, so quickly that the motion was only a series of punctuated blurs. Looking down, I saw eight bloodless puncture marks on Yarrow's head. Another wasp replaced the driller and repeated the procedure, executing its own blurlike nods. This time, glistening fibres trailed from Yarrow's eight puncture points into the wasp, which looked as if it was sucking spaghetti from my compatriot's skull.

Long minutes of silence followed, while I waited for some kind of report.

"It isn't good," Wendigo said eventually.

"Show me."

And I got a jolt of Queen's speech, feeling myself *inside* Yarrow's hermetically sealed head, feeling the chill that had gasped against her brain core, despite her pilot augs. I sensed the two intermingled looms of native and foreign demons, webbing the shattered matrix of her consciousness.

I also sensed—what? Doubt?

"She's pretty far gone, Spirey."

"Tell the Queen to do what she can."

"Oh, she will. Now she's glimpsed Yarrow's mind, she'll do all she can not to lose it. Minds mean a lot to her—particularly in view of what the Splinterqueens have in mind for the future. But don't expect miracles."

"Why not? We seem to be standing in one."

"Then you're prepared to believe some of what I've said?"

"What it means," I started to say—

But I didn't finish the sentence. As I was speaking the whole chamber shook violently, almost dashing us off our feet.

"What was that?"

Wendigo's eyes glazed again, briefly.

"Your ship," she said. "It just self-destructed."

"What?"

A picture of what remained of *Mouser* formed in my head: a dulling nebula, embedding the splinter. "The order to self-destruct came from Tiger's Eye," Wendigo said. "It cut straight to the ship's quackdrive subsystems, at a level the demons couldn't rescind. I imagine they were rather hoping you'd have landed by the time the order arrived. The blast would have destroyed the splinter."

"You're saying home just tried to kill us?"

"Put it like this," Wendigo said. "Now might not be a bad time to rethink your loyalties."

Tiger's Eye had failed this time—but they wouldn't stop there. In three hours they'd learn of their mistake, and three or more hours after that we would learn of their countermove, whatever it happened to be.

"She'll do something, won't she? I mean, the wasps wouldn't go to the trouble of building this place only to have Tiger's Eye wipe it out."

"Not much she can do," Wendigo said, after communing with the Queen. "If home chooses to use kinetics against us—and they're the only weapon which could hit us from so far—then there really is no possible defence. And remember there are a hundred other worlds like this, in or on their way to the halo. Losing one would make very little difference."

Something in me snapped. "Do you have to sound so damned indifferent to it all? Here we are talking about how we're likely to be dead in a few hours and you're acting as if it's only a minor inconvenience." I fought to keep the edge of hysteria out of my voice. "How do you know so much anyway? You're mighty well informed for someone who's only been here a day, Wendigo."

She regarded me for a moment, almost blanching under the slap of insubordination. Then Wendigo nodded, without anger.

"Yes, you're right to ask how I know so much. You can't have failed to notice how hard we crashed. My pilots took the worst."

"They died?"

Hesitation. "One at least—Sorrel. But the other, Quillin, wasn't in the ship when the wasps pulled me out of the wreckage. At the time I assumed they'd already retrieved her."

"Doesn't look that way."

"No, it doesn't, and . . ." She paused, then shook her head. "Quillin was why we crashed. She tried to gain control, to stop us landing . . ." Again Wendigo trailed off, as if unsure how far to commit herself. "I think Quillin was a plant, put aboard by those who disagreed with the peace initiative. She'd been primed—altered psychologically to reject any Royalist peace overtures."

"She was born like that—with a stick up her ass."

"She's dead, I'm sure of it."

Wendigo almost sounded glad.

"Still, you made it."

"Just, Spirey. I'm the humpty who fell off the wall twice. This time they couldn't find all the pieces. The Splinterqueen pumped me full of demons; gallons of them. They're all that's holding me together, but I don't think they can keep it up forever. When I speak to you, at least some of what you hear is the Splinterqueen herself. I'm not really sure where you draw the line."

I let that sink in, then said: "About your ship. Repair systems would have booted when you hit. Any idea when she'll fly again?"

"Another day, day and a half."

"Too damn long."

"Just being realistic. If there's a way to get off the splinter within the next six hours, ship isn't it."

I wasn't giving up so easily. "What if wasps help? They could supply materials. Should speed things."

Again that glazed look. "All right," she said. "It's done. But I'm afraid wasp assistance won't make enough difference. We're still looking at 12 hours."

"So I won't start any long disneys." I shrugged. "And maybe we can hold out until then." She looked unconvinced, so I said:

"Tell me the rest. Everything you know about this place. *Why*, for starters."

"Why?"

"Wendigo, I don't have the faintest damn idea what any of us are doing here. All I do know is that in six hours I could be suffering from acute existence failure. When that happens, I'd be happier knowing what was so important I had to die for it."

Wendigo looked toward Yarrow, still nursed by the detached elements of the Queen. "I don't think our being here will help her," she said. "In which case, maybe I should show you something." A near-grin appeared on Wendigo's face. "After all, it isn't as if we don't have time to kill."

Part Four

So we rode the train again, this time burrowing deeper into the splinter.

"This place," Wendigo said, "and the hundred others already beyond the Swirl—and the hundreds, thousands more which will follow—are *arks*. They're carrying life into the halo; the cloud of left-over material around the Swirl."

"Colonization, right?"

"Not quite. When the time's right the splinters will return to the Swirl. Only there won't be one any more. There'll be a solar system, fully formed. When the colonization does begin, it will be of new worlds around Fomalhaut, seeded from the life-templates held in the splinters."

I raised a hand. "I was following you there . . . until you mentioned life-templates."

"Patience, Spirey."

Wendigo's timing couldn't have been better, because at that moment light flooded the train's brushed-steel interior.

The tunnel had become a glass tube, anchored to one wall of a vast cavern suffused in emerald light. The far wall was tiered, draping rafts of foliage. Our wall was steep and forested, oddly-curved waterfalls draining into stepped pools. The waterfalls were bent away from true "vertical" by coriolis force, evidence that—just like the first chamber—this entire space was independently spinning within the splinter. The stepped pools were surrounded by patches of grass, peppered with moving forms which might have been naked people. There were wasps as well—tending the people.

As the people grew clearer I had that flinch you get when your gaze strays onto someone with a shocking disfigurement. Roughly half of them were *males*.

"Imported Royalists," Wendigo said. "Remember I said they'd turned feral? Seems there was an accident, not long after the wasps made the jump to sentience. A rogue demon, or something. Decimated them."

"They have both sexes."

"You'll get used to it, Spirey—conceptually anyway. Tiger's Eye wasn't always exclusively female, you know that? It was just something we evolved into. Began with you pilots, matter of fact. Fem physiology made sense for pilots—women were smaller, had better gee-load tolerance, better stress psychodynamics and required fewer consumables than males. We were products of bio-engineering from the outset, so it wasn't hard to make the jump to an all-fem culture."

"Makes me want to . . . I don't know." I forced my gaze away from the Royalists. "Puke or something. It's like going back to having hair all over your body."

"That's because you grew up with something different."

"Did they always have both sexes?"

"Probably not. What I do know is that the wasps bred from the survivors, but something wasn't right. Apart from the reversion to dimorphism, the children didn't grow up normally. Some part of their brains hadn't developed right."

"Meaning what?"

"They're morons. The wasps keep trying to fix things of course. That's why the Splinterqueen will do everything to help Yarrow—and us, of course. If she can study or even capture our thought patterns—and the demons make that possible—maybe she can use them to imprint consciousness back onto the Royalists. Like the Florentine architecture I said they copied, right? That was one template, and Yarrow's mind will be another."

"That's supposed to cheer me up?"

"Look on the bright side. A while from now, there might be a whole generation of people who think along lines laid down by Yarrow."

"Scary thought." Then wondered why I was able to crack a joke, with destruction looming so close in the future. "Listen, I still don't get it. What makes them want to bring life to the Swirl?"

"It seems to boil down to two . . . *imperatives,* I suppose you'd call them. The first's simple enough. When wasps were first opening up Greater Earth's solar system back in the mid-21st century, we sought the best way for them to function in large numbers without supervision. We studied insect colonies and imprinted the most useful rules straight into the wasps' programming. More than 600 years later, those rules have percolated to the top. Now the wasps aren't content merely to organize themselves along patterns derived from living proto-types. Now they want to become—or at least give rise to—living forms of their own."

"Life envy."

"Or something very like it."

I thought about what Wendigo had told me, then said: "What about the second imperative?"

"Trickier. Much trickier." She looked at me hard, as if debating whether to broach whatever subject was on her mind. "Spirey, what do you know about Solar War Three?"

The wasps had given up on Yarrow while we travelled. They'd left her on a corniced plinth in the middle of the terrazzo; poised on her back, arms folded across her chest, tail and fluke draping asymmetrically over one side.

"She didn't necessarily fail, Spirey," Wendigo said, taking my arm in her own unyielding grip. "That's only Yarrow's body, after all."

"The Queen managed to read her mind?"

There was no opportunity to answer. The chamber shook, more harshly than when *Mouser* had gone up. The vibration keeled us to the floor, Wendigo's metal arms cracking against the tessellated marble. As if turning in her sleep, Yarrow slipped from the plinth.

"Home," Wendigo said, raising herself from the floor.

"Impossible. Can't have been more than two hours since *Mouser* was hit. There shouldn't be any response for another four!"

"They probably decided to attack us regardless of the outcome of their last attempt. Kinetics."

"You sure there's no defence?"

"Only good luck." The ground lashed at us again, but Wendigo stayed standing. The roar which followed the first impact was subsiding, fading into a constant but bearable complaint of tortured ice. "The first probably only chipped us—maybe gouged a big crater, but I doubt that it ruptured any of the pressurized areas. Next time could be worse."

And there *would* be a next time, no doubt about it. Kinetics were the only weapon capable of hitting us at such long range, and they did so by sheer force of numbers. Each kinetic was a speck of iron, accelerated to a hair's breadth below the speed of light. Relativity bequeathed the speck a disproportionate amount of kinetic energy—enough that only a few impacts would rip the splinter to shreds. Of course, only one in a thousand of the kinetics they fired at us would hit—but that didn't matter. They'd just fire 10,000.

"Wendigo," I said. "Can we get to your ship?"

"No," she said, after a moment's hesitation. "We can reach it, but it isn't fixed yet."

"Doesn't matter. We'll lift on auxiliaries. Once we're clear of the splinter we'll be safe."

"No good, either. Hull's breached—it'll be at least an hour before even part of it can be pressurized."

"And it'll take us an hour or so just to get there, won't it? So why are we waiting?"

"Sorry, Spirey, but—"

Her words were drowned by the arrival of the second kinetic. This one seemed to hit harder, the impact trailing away into aftergroans. The holographic frescos were all dark now. Then— ever so slowly—the ceiling ruptured, a huge mandible of ice probing into the chamber. We'd lost the false gravity; now all that remained was the splinter's feeble pull, dragging us obliquely toward one wall.

"*But* what?" I shouted in Wendigo's direction.

For a moment she had that absent look which said she was more Queen than Wendigo. Then she nodded in reluctant acceptance. "All right, Spirey. We play it your way. Not because I think our chances are great. Just that I'd rather be doing something."

"Amen to that."

It was uncomfortably dim now, much of the illumination having come from the endlessly cycling frescos. But it wasn't silent. Though the groan of the chamber's off-kilter spin was gone now, what remained was almost as bad: the agonized shearing of the ice which lay beyond us. Helped by wasps, we made it to the train. I carried Yarrow's corpse, but at the door Wendigo said: "Leave her."

"No way."

"She's dead, Spirey. Everything of her that mattered, the Splinterqueen already saved. You have to accept that. It was enough that you brought her here, don't you understand? Carrying her now would only lessen your chances—and that would really have pissed her off."

Some alien part of me allowed the wasps to take the corpse. Then we were inside, helmeted up and breathing thick.

As the train picked up speed, I glanced out the window, intent on seeing the Queen one last time. It should have been too dark, but the chamber looked bright. For a moment I presumed the frescos had come to life again, but then something about the scene's unreal intensity told me the Queen was weaving this image in my head. She hovered above the debris-strewn terrazzo—except that this was more than the Queen I had seen before. This was—what?

How she saw herself?

Ten of her 12 wasp composites were now back together, arranged in constantly shifting formation. They now seemed more living than machine, with diaphanous sunwings, chitin-black bodies, fur-sheened limbs and sensors, and eyes which were faceted crystalline globes, sparkling in the chamber's false light. That wasn't all. Before, I'd sensed the Queen as something implied by her composites. Now I didn't need to imagine her.

Like a ghost in which the composites hung, she loomed vast in the chamber, multi-winged and brooding—

And then we were gone.

We sped towards the surface for the next few minutes, waiting for the impact of the next kinetic. When it hit, the train's cushioned ride smothered the concussion. For a moment I thought we'd made it, then the machine began to decelerate slowly to a dead halt. Wendigo convened with the Queen and told me the line was blocked. We disembarked into vacuum.

Ahead, the tunnel ended in a wall of jumbled ice.

After a few minutes we found a way through the obstruction, Wendigo wrenching aside boulders larger than either of us. "We're only half a klick from the surface," she said, as we emerged into the unblocked tunnel beyond. She pointed ahead, to what might have been a scotoma of absolute blackness against the milky darkness of the tunnel. "After that, a klick overland to the wreck." She paused. "Realize we can't go home, Spirey. Now more than ever."

"Not exactly spoilt for choice, are we?"

"No. It has to be the halo, of course. It's where the splinter's headed anyway; just means we'll get there ahead of schedule. There are other Splinterqueens out there, and at the very least they'll want to keep us alive. Possibly other humans as well— others who made the same discovery as us, and knew there was no going home."

"Not to mention Royalists."

"That troubles you, doesn't it?"

"I'll deal with it," I said, pushing forward.

The tunnel was nearly horizontal, and with the splinter's weak gravity it was easy to make the distance to the surface. Emerging, Fomalhaut glared down at us, a white-cored blood-shot eye surrounded by the wrinkle-like dust lanes of the inner Swirl. Limned in red, wasp corpses marred the landscape.

"I don't see the ship."

Wendigo pointed to a piece of blank caramel-coloured horizon. "Curvature's too great. We won't see it until we're almost on top of it."

"Hope you're right."

"Trust me. I know this place like, well . . ." Wendigo regarded one of her limbs. "Like the back of my hand."

"Encourage me, why don't you."

Three or four hundred metres later we crested a scallop-shaped rise of ice and halted. We could see the ship now. It didn't look in much better shape than when Yarrow and I had scoped it from *Mouser*.

"I don't see any wasps."

"Too dangerous for them to stay on the surface," Wendigo said.

"That's cheering. I hope the remaining damage is cosmetic," I said. "Because if it isn't—"

Suddenly I wasn't talking to anyone.

Wendigo was gone. After a moment I saw her, lying in a crumpled heap at the foot of the hillock. Her guts stretched away like a rusty comet-tail, half way to the next promontory.

Quillin was 50 metres ahead, risen from the concealment of a chondrite boulder.

When Wendigo had mentioned her, I'd put her out of mind as any kind of threat. How could she pose any danger beyond the inside of a thickship, when she'd traded her legs for a tail and fluke, just like Yarrow? On dry land, she'd be no more mobile than a seal pup. Well, that was how I'd figured things.

But I'd reckoned without Quillin's suit.

Unlike Yarrow's—unlike any siren suit I'd ever seen—it sprouted legs. Mechanized, they emerged from the hip, making no concessions to human anatomy. The legs were long enough to lift Quillin's tail completely free of the ice. My gaze tracked up her body, registering the crossbow which she held in a double-handed grip.

"I'm sorry," Quillin's deep voice boomed in my skull. "Check-in's closed."

"Wendigo said you might be a problem."

"Wise up. It was staged from the moment we reached the Royalist stronghold." Still keeping the bow on me, she began to lurch across the ice. "The ferals were actors, playing dumb. The wasps were programmed to feed us bullshit."

"It isn't a Royalist trick, Quillin."

"Shit. See I'm gonna have to kill*you* as well."

The ground jarred, more violently than before. A nimbus of white light puffed above the horizon, evidence of an impact on the splinter's far side. Quillin stumbled, but her legs corrected the accident before it tripped her forward.

"I don't know if you're keeping up with current events," I said. "But that's our own side."

"Maybe you didn't think hard enough. Why did wasps in the Swirl get smart before the trillions of wasps back in Sol System? Should have been the other way round."

"Yeah?"

"Of course, Spirey. GE's wasps had a massive head start." She shrugged, but the bow stayed rigidly pointed. "Okay, war sped up wasp evolution here. But that shouldn't have made so much difference. That's where the story breaks down."

"Not quite."

"What?"

"Something Wendigo told me. About what she called the second imperative. I guess it wasn't something she found out until she went underground."

"Yeah? Astonish me."

Well, something astonished Quillin at that point—but I was only marginally less surprised by it myself. An explosion of ice, and a mass of swiftly-moving metal erupting from the ground around her. The wasp corpses were partially dismembered, blasted and half-melted—but they still managed to drag Quillin to the ground. For a moment she thrashed, kicking up plumes of frost. Then the whole mass lay deathly still, and it was just me, the ice and a lot of metal and blood.

The Queen must have coaxed activity out of a few of the wasp corpses, ordering them to use their last reserves of power to take out Quillin.

Thanks, Queen.

But no cigar. Quillin hadn't necessarily meant to shoot me at that point, but—bless her—she had anyway. The bolt had transected me with the precision of one of the Queen's theorems, somewhere below my sternum. Gut-shot. The blood on the ice was my own.

Part Five

I tried moving. A couple of light-years away I saw my body undergo a frail little shiver. It didn't hurt, but there was nothing in the way of proprioceptive feedback to indicate I'd actually managed to twitch any part of my body.

Quillin was moving too. Wriggling, that is, since her suit's legs had been cleanly ripped away by the wasps. Other than that she didn't look seriously injured. Ten or so metres from me, she flopped around like a maggot and groped for her bow. What remained of it anyway.

Chalk one to the good guys.

By which time I was moving, executing a marginally quicker version of Quillin's slug crawl. I couldn't stand up—there are limits to what pilot physiology can cope with—but my legs gave me leverage she lacked.

"Give up, Spirey. You have a head start on me, and right now you're a little faster—but that ship's still a long way off." Quillin took a moment to catch her breath. "Think you can sustain that pace? Gonna need to, if you don't want me catching up."

"Plan on rolling over me until I suffocate?"

"That's an option. If this doesn't kill you first."

Enough of her remained in my field-of-view to see what she meant. Something sharp and bladelike had sprung from her wrist, a bayonet projecting half a metre ahead of her hand. It looked like a nasty little toy—but I did my best to push it out of mind and get on with the job of crawling towards the ship. It was no more than 200 metres away now—what little of it protruded above the ice. The external airlock was already open, ready to clamp shut as soon as I wriggled inside—

"You never finished telling me, Spirey."

"Telling you what?"

"About this—what did you call it? The second imperative?"

"Oh, that." I halted and snatched breath. "Before I go on, I want you to know I'm only telling you this to piss you off."

"Whatever bakes your cake."

"All right," I said. "Then I'll begin by saying you were right.

Greater Earth's wasps should have made the jump to sentience long before those in the Swirl, simply because they'd had longer to evolve. *And that's what happened.*"

Quillin coughed, like gravel in a bucket. "Pardon?"

"They beat us to it. About a century and a half ago. Across Sol system, within just a few hours, every single wasp woke up and announced its intelligence to the nearest human being it could find. Like babies reaching for the first thing they see." I stopped, sucking in deep lungfuls. The wreck had to be closer now—but it hardly looked it.

Quillin, by contrast, looked awfully close now—and that blade awfully sharp.

"So the wasps woke," I said, damned if she wasn't going to hear the whole story. "And that got some people scared. So much, some of them got to attacking the wasps. Some of their shots went wide, because within a day the whole system was one big shooting match. Not just humans against wasps—but humans against humans." Less than 50 metres now, across much smoother ground than we'd so far traversed. "Things just escalated. Ten days after Solar War Three began, only a few ships and habitats were still transmitting. They didn't last long."

"Crap," Quillin said—but she sounded less cocksure than she had a few moments before. "There was a war back then, but it never escalated into a full-blown Solar War."

"No. It went the whole hog. From then on every signal we ever got from GE was concocted by wasps. They daren't break the news to us—at least not immediately. We've only been allowed to find out because we're never going home. Guilt, Wendigo called it. They couldn't let it happen again."

"What about our wasps?"

"Isn't it obvious? A while later the wasps here made the same jump to sentience—presumably because they'd been shown the right moves by the others. Difference was, ours kept it quiet. Can't exactly blame them, can you?"

There was nothing from Quillin for a while, both of us concentrating on the last patch of ice before Wendigo's ship.

"I suppose you have an explanation for this too," she said eventually, swiping her tail against the ground. "C'mon, blow my mind."

So I told her what I knew. "They're bringing life to the Swirl. Sooner than you think, too. Once this charade of a war is done, the wasps breed in earnest. Trillions out there now, but in a few decades it'll be *billions* of trillions. They'll outweigh a good-sized planet. In a way the Swirl will have become sentient. It'll be directing its own evolution."

I spared Quillin the details—how the wasps would arrest the existing processes of planetary formation so that they could begin anew, only this time according to a plan. Left to its own devices, the Swirl would contract down to a solar system comprised solely of small, rocky planets—but such a system could never support life over billions of years. Instead, the wasps would exploit the system's innate chaos to tip it toward a state where it would give rise to at least two much larger worlds— planets as massive as Jupiter or Saturn, capable of shepherding left-over rubble into tidy, world-avoiding orbits. Mass extinctions had no place in the Splinterqueens' vision of future life.

But I guessed Quillin probably didn't care.

"Why are you hurrying, Spirey?" she asked, between harsh grunts as she propelled herself forward. "The ship isn't going anywhere."

The edge of the open airlock was a metre above the ice. My fingers probed over the rim, followed by the crest of my battered helmet. Just lifting myself into the lock's lit interior seemed to require all the energy I'd already expended in the crawl. Somehow I managed to get half my body length into the lock.

Which is when Quillin reached me.

There wasn't much pain when she dug the bayonet into my ankle; just a form of cold I hadn't imagined before, even lying on the ice. Quillin jerked the embedded blade to and forth, and the knot of cold seemed to reach out little feelers, into my foot and lower leg. I sensed she wanted to retract the blade for another stab, but my suit armour was gripping it tight.

The bayonet taking her weight, Quillin pulled herself up to the rim of the lock. I tried kicking her away, but the skewered leg no longer felt a part of me.

"You're dead," she whispered.

"News to me."

Her eyes rolled wide, then locked on me with renewed venom.

She gave the bayonet a violent twist. "So tell me one thing. That story—bullshit, or what?"

"I'll tell you," I said. "But first consider this." Before she could react I reached out and palmed a glowing panel set in the lock wall. The panel whisked aside, revealing a mushroom-shaped red button. "You know that story they told about Wendigo, how she lost her arms?"

"You weren't meant to swallow that hero guff, Spirey."

"No? Well get a load of this. My hand's on the emergency pressurization control, Quillin. When I hit it, the outer door's going to slide down quicker than you can blink."

She looked at my hand, then down at her wrist, still attached to my ankle via the jammed bayonet. Slowly the situation sank in. "Close the door, Spirey, and you'll be a leg short."

"And you an arm, Quillin."

"Stalemate, then."

"Not quite. See, which of us is more likely to survive? Me inside, with all the medical systems aboard this ship, or you all on your lonesome outside? Frankly, I don't think it's any contest."

Her eyes opened wider. Quillin gave a shriek of anger and entered one final furious wrestling match with the bayonet.

I managed to laugh. "As for your question, it's true, every word of it." Then, with all the calm I could muster, I thumbed the control. "Pisser, isn't it?"

I made it, of course.

Several minutes after the closing of the door, demons had lathered a protective cocoon around the stump and stomach wound. They allowed me no pain—only a muggy sense of detachment. Enough of my mind remained sharp to think about my escape—problematic given that the ship still wasn't fixed.

Eventually I remembered the evac pods.

They were made to kick away from the ship fast, if some quackdrive system went on the fritz. They had thrusters for that; nothing fancy, but here they'd serve another purpose. They'd boost me from the splinter, punch me out of its grav well.

So I did it.

Snuggled into a pod and blew out of the wreck, feeling the

gee-load even within the thick. It didn't last long. On the evac pod's cam I watched the splinter drop away until it was pebble-sized. The main body of the kinetic attack was hitting it by then, impacts every ten or so seconds. After a minute of that the splinter just came apart. Afterwards, there was only a sooty veil where it had been, and then only the Swirl.

I hoped the Queen had made it. I guess it was within her power to transmit what counted of herself out to sisters in the halo. If so, there was a chance for Yarrow as well. I'd find out eventually. Afterwards, I used the pod's remaining fuel to inject into a slow elliptical orbit, one that would graze the halo in a mere 50 or 60 years.

That didn't bother me. I wanted to close my eyes and let the thick nurse me whole again—and sleep an awful long time.

A DRY, QUIET WAR

Tony Daniel

One of the fastest-rising new stars of the '90s, Tony Daniel grew up in Alabama, lived for a while on Vashon Island in Washington State, and in recent years, in the best tradition of the young Bohemian artist, has been restlessly on the move— from Vashon Island to Europe, from Europe to New York City, from New York City to Alabama, and, most recently, back to New York City again. He attended the Clarion West Writers Workshop in 1989, and since then has become a frequent contributor to Asimov's Science Fiction, *as well as to markets such as* The Magazine of Fantasy and Science Fiction, Amazing, SF Age, Universe, Full Spectrum, *and elsewhere.*

Like many writers of his generation, Tony Daniel first made an impression on the field with his short fiction. He made his first sale, to Asimov's, *in 1990, "The Passage of Night Trains," and followed it up with a long string of well-received stories both there and elsewhere throughout the first few years of the '90s, stories such as "The Careful Man Goes West," "Sun So Hot I Froze To Death," "Prism Tree," "Death of Reason," "Candle," "No Love in All of Dwingeloo," "The Joy of the Sidereal Long-Distance Runner," "The Robot's Twilight Companion," and many others. His story "Life on the Moon" was a finalist for the Hugo Award in 1996, and won the* Asimov's Science Fiction *Readers Award poll. His first novel,* Warpath, *was released simultaneously in America and England in 1993, and he subsequently won $2000 and the T. Morris Hackney Award for his as-yet-unpublished mountain-climbing novel* Ascension. *In 1997, he published a major new novel,* Earthling, *which has gotten enthusiastic reviews everywhere from* Interzone *to* The New York Times.

In "A Dry, Quiet War," he spins a colorful and exotic story of a battle-weary veteran who returns from a bewilderingly strange high-tech future war only to face his greatest and most sinister challenge right at home . . .

I *cannot tell* you what it meant to me to see the two suns of Ferro set behind the dry mountain east of my home. I had been away twelve billion years. I passed my cabin to the pump well, and taking a metal cup from where it hung from a set-pin, I worked the handle three times. At first it creaked, and I believed it was rusted tight, but then it loosened, and within fifteen pulls, I had a cup of water.

Someone had kept the pump up. Someone had seen to the house and the land while I was away at the war. For me, it had been fifteen years; I wasn't sure how long it had been for Ferro. The water was tinged red and tasted of iron. Good. I drank it down in a long draft, then put the cup back onto its hanger. When the big sun, Hemingway, set, a slight breeze kicked up. Then Fitzgerald went down and a cold, cloudless night spanked down onto the plateau. I shivered a little, adjusted my internals, and stood motionless, waiting for the last of twilight to pass, and the stars—my stars—to come out. Steiner, the planet that is Ferro's evening star, was the first to emerge, low in the west, methane blue. Then the constellations. Ngal. Gilgamesh. The Big Snake, half-coiled over the southwestern horizon. There was no moon tonight. There was never a moon on Ferro, and that was right.

After a time, I walked to the house, climbed up the porch, and the house recognized me and turned on the lights. The place was dusty, the furniture covered with sheets, but there were no signs of rats or jinjas, and all seemed in repair. I sighed, blinked, tried to feel something. Too early, probably. I started to take a covering from a chair, then let it be. I went to the kitchen and checked the cupboard. An old malt-whiskey bottle, some dry cereal, some spices. The spices had been my mother's, and I seldom used them before I left for the end of time. I considered that the whiskey might be perfectly aged by now. But, as the saying goes on Ferro, we like a bit of food with our drink, so I left the house and took the road to town, to Heidel.

It was a five-mile walk, and though I could have enhanced and covered the ground in ten minutes or so, I walked at a regular pace under my homeworld stars. The road was dirt, of course, and my pant legs were dusted red when I stopped under the outside light of Thredmartin's Pub. I took a last breath of cold air, then went inside to the warm.

It was a good night at Thredmartin's. There were men and women gathered around the fire hearth, usas and splices in the cold corners. The regulars were at the bar, a couple of whom I recognized—so old now, wizened like stored apples in a barrel. I looked around for a particular face, but she was not there. A jukebox sputtered some core-cloud deak, and the air was thick with smoke and conversation. Or was, until I walked in. Nobody turned to face me. Most of them couldn't have seen me. But a signal passed and conversation fell to a quiet murmur. Somebody quickly killed the jukebox.

I blinked up an internals menu into my peripheral vision and adjusted to the room's temperature. Then I went to the edge of the bar. The room got even quieter. . . .

The bartender, old Thredmartin himself, reluctantly came over to me.

"What can I do for you, sir?" he asked me.

I looked over him, to the selection of bottles, tubes, and cans on display behind him. "I don't see it," I said.

"Eh?" He glanced back over his shoulder, then quickly returned to peering at me.

"Bone's Barley," I said.

"We don't have any more of that," Thredmartin said, with a suspicious tone.

"Why not?"

"The man who made it died."

"How long ago?"

"Twenty years, more or less. I don't see what business of—"

"What about his son?"

Thredmartin backed up a step. Then another. "Henry," he whispered. "Henry Bone."

"Just give me the best that you do have, Peter Thredmartin," I said. "In fact, I'd like to buy everybody a round on me."

"Henry Bone! Why, you looked to me like a bad 'un indeed when you walked in here. I took you for one of them glims, I did," Thredmartin said. I did not know what he was talking about. Then he smiled an old devil's crooked smile. "Your money's no good here, Henry Bone. I do happen to have a couple of bottles of your old dad's whiskey stowed away in back. Drinks are on the house."

And so I returned to my world, and for most of those I'd left behind it seemed as if I'd never really gone. My neighbors hadn't changed much in the twenty years local that had passed, and of course, they had no conception of what had happened to me. They knew only that I'd been to the war—the Big War at the End of Time—and evidently everything turned out okay, for here I was, back in my own time and my own place. I planted Ferro's desert barley, brought in peat from the mountain bogs, bred the biomass that would extract the minerals from my hard ground water, and got ready for making whiskey once again. Most of the inhabitants of Ferro were divided between whiskey families and beer families. Bones were distillers, never brewers, since the Settlement, ten generations before.

It wasn't until she called upon me that I heard the first hints of the troubles that had come. Her name was Alinda Bexter, but since we played together under the floorplanks of her father's hotel, I had always called her Bex. When I left for the war, she was twenty, and I twenty-one. I still recognized her at forty, five years older than I was now, as she came walking down the road to my house, a week after I'd returned. She was taller than most women on Ferro, and she might be mistaken for a usa-human splice anywhere else. She was rangy, and she wore a khaki dress that whipped in the dry wind as she came toward me. I stood on the porch, waiting for her, wondering what she would say.

"Well, this is a load off of me," she said. She was wearing a brimmed hat. It had ribbon to tie under her chin, but Bex had not done that. She held her hand on it to keep it from blowing from her head. "This damn ranch has been one big thankless task."

"So it was you who kept it up," I said.

"Just kept it from falling apart as fast as it would have otherwise," she replied. We stood and looked at one another for a moment. Her eyes were green. Now that I had seen an ocean, I could understand the kind of green they were.

"Well then," I finally said. "Come on in."

I offered her some sweetcake I'd fried up, and some beer that my neighbor, Shin, had brought by, both of which she declined. We

sat in the living room, on furniture covered with the white sheets
I had yet to remove. Bex and I took it slow, getting to know each
other again. She ran her father's place now. For years, the only
way to get to Heidel was by freighter, but we had finally gotten
a node on the Flash, and even though Ferro was still a backwater
planet, there were more strangers passing through than there ever
had been—usually en route to other places. But they sometimes
stayed a night or two in the Bexter Hotel. Its reputation was
spreading, Bex claimed, and I believed her. Even when she was
young, she had been shrewd but honest, a combination you don't
often find in an innkeeper. She was a quiet woman—that is, until
she got to know you well—and some most likely thought her
conceited. I got the feeling that she hadn't let down her reserve
for a long time. When I knew her before, Bex did not have many
close friends, but for the ones she had, such as me, she poured
out her thoughts, and her heart. I found that she hadn't changed
much in that way.

"Did you marry?" I asked her, after hearing about the hotel
and her father's bad health.

"No," she said. "No, I very nearly did, but then I did not. Did
you?"

"No. Who was it?"

"Rall Kenton."

"Rall Kenton? Rall Kenton whose parents run the hops
market?" He was a quarter-splice, a tall man on a world of tall
men. Yet, when I knew him, his long shadow had been deceptive.
There was no spark or force in him. "I can't see that, Bex."

"Tom Kenton died ten years ago," she said. "Marjorie retired,
and Rall owned the business until just last year. Rall did all right;
you'd be surprised. Something about his father's passing gave
him a backbone. Too much of one, maybe."

"What happened?"

"He died," she said. "He died too, just as I thought you had."
Now she told me she would like a beer after all, and I went to get
her a bottle of Shin's ale. When I returned, I could tell that she'd
been crying a little.

"The glims killed Rall," said Bex, before I could ask her about
him. "That's their name for themselves, anyway. Humans,
repons, kaliwaks, and I don't know what else. They passed

through last year and stayed for a week in Heidel. Very bad. They made my father give over the whole hotel to them, and then they had a . . . trial, they called it. Every house was called and made to pay a tithe. The glims decided how much. Rall refused to pay. He brought along a pistol—Lord knows where he got it—and tried to shoot one of them. They just laughed and took it from him." Now the tears started again.

"And then they hauled him out into the street in front of the hotel." Bex took a moment and got control of herself. "They burnt him up with a p-gun. Burned his legs off first, then his arms, then the rest of him after they'd let him lie there a while. There wasn't a trace of him after that; we couldn't even bury him."

I couldn't take her to me, hold her, not after she'd told me about Rall. Needing something to do, I took some tangled banwood from the tinder box and struggled to get a fire going from the burnt-down coals in my hearth. I blew into the fireplace and only got a nose full of ashes for my trouble. "Didn't anybody fight?" I asked.

"Not after that. We just waited them out. Or they got bored. I don't know. It was bad for everybody, not just Rall." Bex shook her head, sighed, then saw the trouble I was having and bent down to help me. She was much better at it than I, and the fire was soon ablaze. We sat down and watched it flicker.

"Sounds like war-ghosts," I said.

"The glims?"

"Soldiers who don't go home after the war. The fighting gets into them and they don't want to give it up, or can't. Sometimes they have . . . modifications that won't let them give it up. They wander the timeways—and since they don't belong to the time they show up in, they're hard to kill. In the early times, where people don't know about the war, or have only heard rumors of it, they had lots of names. Vampires. Hagamonsters. Zombies."

"What can you do?"

I put my arm around her. It had been so long. She tensed up, then breathed deeply, serenely.

"Hope they don't come back," I said. "They are bad ones. Not the worst, but bad."

We were quiet for a while, and the wind, blowing over the chimney's top, made the flue moan as if it were a big stone flute.

"Did you love him, Bex?" I asked. "Rall?"

She didn't even hesitate in her answer this time. "Of course not, Henry Bone. How could you ever think such a thing? I was waiting to catch up with you. Now tell me about the future."

And so I drew away from her for a while, and told her—part of it at least. About how there is not enough dark matter to pull the cosmos back together again, not enough mass to undulate in an eternal cycle. Instead, there *is* an end, and all the stars are either dead or dying, and all that there is is nothing but dim night. I told her about the twilight armies gathered there, culled from all times, all places. Creatures, presences, machines, weapons fighting galaxy-to-galaxy, system-to-system, fighting until the critical point is reached, when entropy flows no more, but pools, pools in endless, stagnant pools of nothing. No light. No heat. No effect. And the universe is dead, and so those who remain . . . inherit the dark field. They win.

"And did you win?" she asked me. "If that's the word for it."

The suns were going down. Instead of answering, I went outside to the woodpile and brought in enough banwood to fuel the fire for the night. I thought maybe she would forget what she'd asked me—but not Bex.

"How does the war end, Henry?"

"You must never ask me that." I spoke the words carefully, making sure I was giving away nothing in my reply. "Every time a returning soldier tells that answer, he changes everything. Then he has two choices. He can either go away, leave his own time, and go back to fight again. Or he can stay, and it will all mean nothing, what he did. Not just who won and who lost, but all the things he did in the war spin off into nothing."

Bex thought about this for a while. "What could it matter? What in God's name could be worth fighting *for*?" she finally asked. "Time ends. Nothing matters after that. What could it possibly matter who won . . . who wins?"

"It means you can go back home," I said. "After it's over."

"I don't understand."

I shook my head and was silent. I had said enough. There was no way to tell her more, in any case—not without changing things. And no way to *say* what it was that had brought those forces together at the end of everything. And what the hell do *I* know, even now? All I know is what I was told, and what I was trained to do. If we don't fight at the end, there won't be a beginning. For there to be people, there must be a war to fight at the end of things. We live in that kind of universe, and not another, they told me. They told me, and then I told myself. And I did what I had to do so that it would be over and I could go home, come back.

"Bex, I never forgot you," I said. She came to sit with me by the fire. We didn't touch at first, but I felt her next to me, breathed the flush of her skin as the fire warmed her. Then she ran her hand along my arm, felt the bumps from the operational enhancements.

"What have they done to you?" she whispered.

Unbidden the old words of the skyfallers' scream, the words that were yet to be, surfaced in my mind.

> *They sucked down my heart*
> *to a little black hole.*
> *You cannot stab me.*

> *They wrote down my brain*
> *on a hard knot of space.*
> *You cannot turn me.*

> *Icicle spike*
> *from the eye of a star.*
> *I've come to kill you.*

I almost spoke them, from sheer habit. But I did not. The war was over. Bex was here, and I knew it was over. I was going to *feel* something, once again, something besides guilt, hate, and rage. I didn't yet, that was true, but I *could* feel the possibility.

"I don't really breathe anymore, Bex; I pretend to so I won't put people off," I told her. "It's been so long, I can't even remember what it was like to *have* to."

Bex kissed me then. At first, I didn't remember how to do that either. And then I did. I added wood to the fire, then ran my hand along Bex's neck and shoulders. Her skin had the health of youth still, but years in the sun and wind had made a supple leather of it, tanned and grained fine. We took the sheet from the couch and pulled it near to the warmth, and she drew me down to her on it, to her neck and breasts.

"Did they leave enough of you for me?" she whispered.

I had not known until now. "Yes," I answered. "there's enough." I found my way inside her, and we made love slowly, in a way that might seem sad to any others but us, for there were memories and years of longing that flowed from us, around us, like amber just at the melting point, and we were inside and there was nothing but this present with all of what was, and what would be, already passed. No time. Finally, only Bex and no time between us.

We fell asleep on the old couch, and it was dim half-morning when we awoke, with Fitzgerald yet to rise in the west and the fire a bed of coals as red as the sky.

Two months later, I was in Thredmartin's when Bex came in with an evil look on her face. We had taken getting back together slow and easy up till then, but the more time we spent around each other, the more we understood that nothing basic had changed. Bex kept coming to the ranch and I took to spending a couple of nights a week in a room her father made up for me at the hotel. Furly Bexter was an old-style McKinnonite. Men and women were to live separately and only meet for business and copulation. But he liked me well enough, and when I insisted on paying for my room, he found a loophole somewhere in the Tracts of McKinnon about cohabitation being all right in hotels and hostels.

"The glims are back," Bex said, sitting down at my table. I was in a dark corner of the pub. I left the fire for those who could not adjust their own internals to keep them warm. "They've taken over the top floor of the hotel. What should we do?"

I took a draw of beer—Thredmartin's own thick porter—and looked at her. She was visibly shivering, probably more from agitation than fright.

"How many of them are there?" I asked.

"Six. And something else, some splice I've never seen, how-ever many that makes."

I took another sip of beer. "Let it be," I said. "They'll get tired, and they'll move on."

"What?" Bex's voice was full of astonishment. "What are you saying?"

"You don't want a war here, Bex," I replied. "You have no idea how bad it can get."

"They killed Rall. They took our *money*."

"Money." My voice sounded many years away, even to me.

"It's muscle and worry and care. You know how hard people work on Ferro. And for those . . . *things* . . . to come in and take it! We cannot let them—"

"—Bex," I said. "I am not going to do anything."

She said nothing; she put a hand on her forehead as if she had a sickening fever, stared at me for a moment, then looked away.

One of the glims chose that moment to come into Thredmar-tin's. It was a halandana, a splice—human and jan—from up-time and a couple of possible universes over. It was nearly seven feet tall, with a two-foot-long neck, and it stooped to enter Thredmartin's. Without stopping, it went to the bar and de-manded morphine.

Thredmartin was at the bar. He pulled out a dusty rubber, little used, and before he could get out an injector, the halandana reached over, took the entire rubber and put it in the pocket of the long gray coat it wore. Thredmartin started to speak, then shook his head, and found a spray shooter. He slapped it on the bar, and started to walk away. The halandana's hand shot out and pushed the old man. Thredmartin stumbled to his knees.

I felt the fingers of my hands clawing, clenching. Let them loosen; let them go.

Thredmartin rose slowly to one knee. Bex was up, around the bar, and over to him, steadying his shoulder. The glim watched this for a moment, then took its drug and shooter to a table, where it got itself ready for an injection.

I looked at it closely now. It was female, but that did not mean much in halandana splices. I could see it phase around the edges with dead, gray flames. I clicked in wideband overspace, and I could see through the halandana to the chair it was sitting in and the unpainted wood of the wall behind it. And I saw more, in the spaces between spaces. The halandana was keyed in to a websquad; it wasn't really an individual anymore. Its fate was tied to that of its unit commander. So the war-ghosts—the glims—were a renegade squad, most likely, with a single leader calling the shots. For a moment, the halandana glanced in my direction, maybe feeling my gaze somewhere outside of local time, and I banded down to human normal. It quickly went back to what it was doing. Bex made sure Thredmartin was all right, then came back over to my table.

"We're not even in its timeline," I said. "It doesn't think of us as really being alive."

"Oh God," Bex said. "This is just like before."

I got up and walked out. It was the only solution. I could not say anything to Bex. She would not understand. I understood— not acting was the rational, the *only*, way, but not *my* way. Not until now.

I enhanced my legs and loped along the road to my house. But when I got there, I kept running, running off into the red sands of Ferro's outback. The night came down, and as the planet turned, I ran along the length of the Big Snake, bright and hard to the southwest, and then under the blue glow of Steiner, when she rose in the moonless, trackless night. I ran for miles and miles, as fast as a jaguar, but never tiring. How could I tire when parts of me stretched off into dimensions of utter stillness, utter rest? Could Bex see me for what I *was,* she would not see a man, but a kind of colonial creature, a mass of life pressed into the niches and fault lines of existence like so much grit and lichen. A human is anchored with only his heart and his mind; sever those, and he floats away. Floats away. What was I? A medusa fish in an ocean of time? A tight clump of nothing, disguised as a man? Something else?

Something damned hard to kill, that was certain. And so were the glims. When I returned to my house in the star-bright night, I half expected to find Bex, but she was not there. And so I rattled about for a while, powered down for an hour at down and rested on a living-room chair, dreaming in one part of my mind, completely alert in another. The next day, Bex still did not come, and I began to fear something had happened to her. I walked partway into Heidel, then cut off the road and stole around the outskirts, to a mound of shattered, volcanic rocks—the tailings of some early prospector's pit—not far from the town's edge. There I stepped up my vision and hearing, and made a long sweep of Main Street. Nothing. Far, far too quiet, even for Heidel.

I worked out the parabolic to the Bexter Hotel, and after a small adjustment, heard Bex's voice, then her father's. I was too far away to make out the words, but my quantitatives gave it a positive ID. So Bex was all right, at least for the moment. I made my way back home, and put in a good day's work making whiskey.

The next morning—it was the quarteryear's double dawn, with both suns rising in the east nearly together—Bex came to me. I brought her inside, and the moted sunlight of my family's living room, where I now took my rest, when I rested, Bex told me that the glims had taken her father.

"He held back some old Midnight Livet down in the cellar, and didn't deliver it when they called for room service." Bex rubbed her left fist with her right fingers, expertly, almost mechanically, as she'd kneaded a thousand balls of bread dough. "How do they know these things? How do they know, Henry?"

"They can see *around* things," I said. "Some of them can, anyway."

"So they read our thoughts? What do we have left?"

"No, no. They can't see in *there*, at least I'm sure they can't see in your old man's McKinnonite nut lump of a brain. But they probably saw the whiskey down in the cellar, all right. A door isn't a very solid thing for a war-ghost out of its own time and place."

Bex gave her hand a final squeeze, spread it out upon her lap. She stared down at the lines of her palm, then looked up at me. "If you won't fight, then you have to tell *me* how to fight them," she said. "I won't let them kill my father."

"Maybe they won't."

"I can't take that chance."

Her eyes were blazing green, as the suns came full through the window. Her face was bright-lit and shadowed, as if by the steady coals of a fire. You have loved this woman a long time, I thought. You have to tell her something that will be of use. But what could possibly be of use against a creature that had survived—*will* survive—that great and final war—and so must survive *now*? You can't kill the future. That's how the old sergeants would explain battle fate to the recruits. If you are meant to be there, they'd say, then nothing can hurt you. And if you're not, then you'll just fade, so you might as well go out fighting.

"You can only irritate them," I finally said to Bex. "There's a way to do it with the Flash. Talk to that technician, what's his name—"

"Jurven Dvorak."

"Tell Dvorak to strobe the local interrupt, fifty, sixty tetra-cycles. It'll cut off all traffic, but it will be like a wasp nest to them; and they won't want to get close enough to turn it off. Dvorak better stay near the node after that too."

"All right," Bex said. "Is that all?"

"Yes," I said. I rubbed my temples, felt the vague pain of a headache, which quickly receded as my internals rushed more blood to my scalp. "Yes, that's it."

Later that day, I heard the crackle of random quantum-tunnel spray, as split, unsieved particles decided their spin, charm, and color without guidance from the world of gravity and cause. It was an angry buzz, like the hum of an insect caught between screen and windowpane, tremendously irritating to listen to for hours on end, if you were unlucky enough to be sensitive to the effect. I put up with it, hoping against hope that it would be enough to drive off the glims.

Bex arrived in the early evening, leading her father, who was ragged and half-crazed from two days without light or water. The glims had locked him in a cleaning closet, in the hotel, where he'd sat cramped and doubled over. After the buzz started, Bex opened the lock and dragged the old man out. It was as if the glims had forgotten the whole affair.

"Maybe," I said. "We can hope."

She wanted me to put the old man up at my house, in case the glims suddenly remembered. Old Furly Bexter didn't like the idea. He rattled on about something in McKinnon's "Letter to the Canadians," but I said yes, he could stay. Bex left me with her father in the shrouds of my living room.

Some time that night, the quantum buzz stopped. And in the early morning, I saw them—five of them—stalking along the road, kicking before them the cowering, stumbling form of Jurven Dvorak. I waited for them on the porch. Furly Bexter was asleep in my parents' bedroom. He was exhausted from his ordeal, and I expected him to stay that way for a while.

When they came into the yard, Dvorak ran to the pump and held to the handle, as if it were a branch suspending him over a bottomless chasm. And for him it was. They'd broken his mind and given him a dream of dying. Soon to be replaced by reality, I suspected, and no pump-handle hope of salvation.

Their leader—or the one who did the talking—was human-looking. I'd have to band out to make a full ID, and I didn't want to give anything away for the moment. He saved me the trouble by telling me himself.

"My name's Marek," he said. "Come from a D-line, not far down-time from here."

I nodded, squinting into the red brightness reflected off my hardpan yard.

"We're just here for a good time," the human continued. "What you want to spoil that for?"

I didn't say anything for a moment. One of Marek's gang spat into the dryness of my dirt.

"Go ahead and have it," I said.

"All right," Marek said. He turned to Dvorak, then pulled out a weapon—not really a weapon though, for it is the tool of behind-the-lines enforcers, prison interrogators, confession extractors. It's called an algorithmic truncheon, a *trunch*, in the parlance. A trunch, used at full load, will strip the myelin sheath from axons and dendrites; it will burn up a man's nerves as if they were fuses. It is a way to kill with horrible pain. Marek walked over and touched the trunch to the leg of Dvorak, as if he were lighting a bonfire.

The Flash technician began to shiver, and then to seethe, like a teapot coming to boil. The motion traveled up his legs, into his chest, out his arms. His neck began to writhe, as if the corded muscles were so many snakes. Then Dvorak's brain burned, as a teapot will when all the water has run out and there is nothing but flame against hot metal. And then Dvorak screamed. He screamed for a long, long time. And then he died, crumpled and spent, on the ground in front of my house.

"I don't know you," Marek said, standing over Dvorak's body and looking up at me. "I know *what* you are, but I can't get a read on *who* you are, and that worries me," he said. He kicked at one of the Flash tech's twisted arms. "But now you know *me*."

"Get off my land," I said. I looked at him without heat. Maybe I felt nothing inside, either. That uncertainty had been my companion for a long time, my grim companion. Marek studied me for a moment. If I kept his attention, he might not look around me, look inside the house, to find his other fun, Furly Bexter, half-dead from Marek's amusements. Marek turned to the others.

"We're going," he said to them. "We've done what we came for." They turned around and left by the road on which they'd come, the only road there was. After a while, I took Dvorak's body to a low hill and dug him a grave there. I set up a sandstone marker, and since I knew Dvorak came from Catholic people, I scratched into the stone the sign of the cross. Jesus, from the Milky Way. Another glim. Hard to kill.

It took old-man Bexter only a week or so to fully recover; I should have known by knowing Bex that he was made of a tougher grit. He began to putter around the house, helping me out where he could, although I ran a tidy one-man operation, and he was more in the way than anything. Bex risked a trip out once that week. Her father again insisted he was going back into town, but Bex told him the glims were looking for him. So far, she'd managed to convince them that she had no idea where he'd gotten to.

I was running low on food and supplies, and had to go into town the following Firstday. I picked up a good backpack load at the mercantile and some chemicals for treating the peat at the druggist, then risked a quick look-in on Bex. A sign on the desk told all that they could find her at Thredmartin's, taking her lunch, should they want her. I walked across the street, set my load down just inside Thredmartin's door, in the cloakroom, then passed through the entrance into the afternoon dank of the pub.

I immediately sensed glims all around, and hunched myself in, both mentally and physically. I saw Bex in her usual corner, and walked toward her across the room. As I stepped beside a table in the pub's middle, a glim—it was the halandana—stuck out a long, hairy leg. Almost, I tripped—and in that instant, I almost did the natural thing and cast about for some hold that was not present in the three-dimensional world—but I did not. I caught myself, came to a dead stop, then carefully walked around the glim's outstretched leg.

"Mind if I sit down?" I said as I reached Bex's table. She nodded toward a free chair. She was finishing a beer, and an empty glass stood beside it. Thredmartin usually had the tables clear as soon as the last drop left a mug. Bex was drinking fast. Why? Working up her courage, perhaps.

I lowered myself into the chair, and for a long time, neither of us said anything to the other. Bex finished her beer. Thredmartin appeared, looked curiously at the two empty mugs. Bex signaled for another, and I ordered my own whiskey.

"How's the ranch," she finally asked me. Her face was flush and her lips trembled slightly. She was angry, I decided. At me, at the situation. It was understandable. Completely understandable.

"Fine," I said. "The ranch is fine."

"Good."

Again a long silence. Thredmartin returned with our drinks. Bex sighed, and for a moment, I thought she would speak, but she did not. Instead, she reached under the table and touched my hand. I opened my palm, and she put her hand into mine. I felt the tension in her, the bonework of her hand as she squeezed tightly. I felt her fear and worry. I felt her love.

And then Marek came into the pub looking for her. He stalked across the room and stood in front of our table. He looked hard at me, then at Bex, and then he swept an arm across the table and sent Bex's beer and my whiskey flying toward the wall. The beer mug broke, but I quickly reached out and caught my tumbler of scotch in midair without spilling a drop. Of course, no ordinary human could have done it.

Bex noticed Marek looking at me strangely and spoke with a

loud voice that got his attention. "What do you want? You were looking for me at the hotel?"

"Your sign says you're open," Marek said in a reasonable, ugly voice. "I rang for room service. Repeatedly."

"Sorry," Bex said. "Just let me settle up and I'll be right there."

"Be right there *now*," Marek said, pushing the table from in front of her. Again, I caught my drink, held it on a knee while I remained sitting. Bex started up from her chair and stood facing Marek. She looked him in the eyes. "I'll *be* there directly," she said.

Without warning, Marek reached out and grabbed her by the chin. He didn't seem to be pressing hard, but I knew he must have her in a painful grip. He pulled Bex toward him. Still, she stared him in the eyes. Slowly, I rose from my chair, setting my tumbler of whiskey down on the warm seat where I had been.

Marek glanced over at me. Our eyes met, and at that close distance, he could plainly see the enhancements under my corneas. I could see his.

"Let go of her," I said.

He did not let go of Bex.

"Who the hell are you?" he asked. "That you tell *me* what to do?"

"I'm just a grunt, same as you," I said. "Let go of her."

The halandana had risen from its chair and was soon standing behind Marek. It-she growled mean and low. A combat schematic of how to handle the situation iconed up into the corner of my vision. The halandana was a green figure, Marek was red, Bex was a faded rose. I blinked once to enlarge it. Studied it in a fractional second. Blinked again to close it down. Marek let go of Bex.

She stumbled back, hurt and mad, rubbing her chin.

"I don't think we've got a grunt here," Marek said, perhaps to the halandana, or to himself, but looking at me. "I think we've got us a genuine skyfalling space marine."

The halandana's growl grew deeper and louder, filling ultra and subsonic frequencies.

"How many systems'd you take out, skyfaller?" Marek asked. "A couple of galaxies worth?" The halandana made no advance on me, but Marek put out his hand to stop it. "Where do you get off? This ain't nothing but small potatoes next to what *you've* done."

In that moment, I spread out, stretched a bit in ways that Bex could not see, but that Marek could—to some extent at last. I encompassed him, all of him, and did a thorough ID on both him and the halandana. I ran the data through some trans-d personnel files tucked into a swirl in n-space. I'd never expected to access again. Marek Lambrois. Corporal of a back-line military-police platoon assigned to the local cluster in a couple of possible worlds, deserters all in a couple of others. He was aggression enhanced by trans-weblink anti-alg coding. The squad's fighting profile was notched to the top level at all times. They were bastards who were now *preprogrammed* bastards. Marek was right about them being small potatoes. He and his gang were nothing but mean-ass grunts, small-time goons for some of the nonaligned contingency troops.

"What the hell?" Marek said. He noticed my analytics, although it was too fast for him to get a good glimpse of me. But he did understand something in that moment, something it didn't take enhancement to figure out. And in that moment, everything was changed, had I but seen. Had I but seen.

"You're some bigwig, ain't you, skyfaller? Somebody that *matters* to the outcome," Marek said. "This is your actual, and you don't want to fuck yourself up-time, so you won't fight." He smiled crookedly. A diagonal of teeth, straight and narrow, showed whitely.

"Don't count on it," I said.

"You won't," he said, this time with more confidence. "I don't know what I was worrying about! I can do anything I want here."

"Well," I said. "Well." And then I said nothing.

"Get on over there and round up some grub," Marek said to Bex. "I'll be waiting for it in room fifty-five, little lady."

"I'd rather—"

"Do it," I said. The words were harsh and did not sound like my voice. But they were my words, and after a moment, I remembered the voice. It was mine. From far, far in the future. Bex gasped at their hardness, but took a step forward, moved to obey.

"Bex," I said, more softly. "Just get the man some food." I turned to Marek. "If you hurt her, I don't care about anything. Do you understand? Nothing will matter to me."

Marek's smile widened into a grin. He reached over, slowly, so that I could think about it, and patted my cheek. Then he deliberately slapped me, hard. Hard enough to turn my head. Hard enough to draw a trickle of blood from my lip. It didn't hurt very much, of course. Of course it didn't hurt.

"Don't you worry, skyfaller," he said. "I know exactly where I stand now." He turned and left, and the halandana, its drugs unfinished on the table where it had sat, trailed out after him.

Bex looked at me. I tried to meet her gaze, but did not. I did not look down, but stared off into Thredmartin's darkness. She reached over and wiped the blood from my chin with her little finger.

"I guess I'd better go," she said.

I did not reply. She shook her head sadly, and walked in front of me. I kept my eyes fixed, far away from this place, this time, and her passing was a swirl of air, a red-brown swish of hair, and Bex was gone. Gone.

> *They sucked down my heart*
> *to a little black hole.*
> *You cannot stab me.*

"Colonel Bone, we've done the prelims on sector eleven sixty-eight, and there are fifty-six class-one civilizations along with two-hundred seventy rationals in stage-one or -two development."

"Fifty-six. Two hundred seventy. Ah. Me."

"Colonel, sir, we can evac over half of them within thirty-six hours local."

"And have to defend them in the transcendent. Chaos neutral. Guaranteed forty percent casualties for us."

"Yes, sir. But what about the civs at least. We can save a few."

> *They wrote down my brain*
> *on a hard knot of space.*
> *You cannot turn me.*

"Unacceptable, soldier."

"Sir?"

"Unacceptable."

"Yes, sir."

All dead. All those millions of dead people. But it was the end of time, and they had to die, so that they—so that we *all*, all in time—could live. But they didn't know, those civilizations. Those people. It was the end of time, but you loved life all the same, and you died the same hard way as always. For nothing. It would be for nothing. Outside, the wind had kicked up. The sky was red with Ferro's dust, and a storm was brewing for the evening. I coated my sclera with a hard and glassy membrane, and unblinking, I stalked home with my supplies through a fierce and growing wind.

That night, on the curtains of dust and thin rain, on the heave of the storm, Bex came to my house. Her clothes were torn and her face was bruised. She said nothing, as I closed the door behind her, led her into the kitchen, and began to treat her wounds. She said nothing as her worried father sat at my kitchen table and watched, and wrung his hands, and watched because there wasn't anything he could do.

"Did that man . . ." her father said. The old man's voice broke. "Did he?"

"I tried to take the thing, the trunch, from him. He'd left it lying on the table by the door." Bex spoke in a hollow voice. "I thought that nobody was going to do anything, not even Henry, so I had to. I had to." Her facial bruises were superficial. But she held her legs stiffly together, and clasped her hands to her stomach. There was vomit on her dress. "The trunch had some kind of alarm set on it," Bex said. "So he caught me."

"Bex, are you hurting?" I said to her. She looked down, then carefully spread her legs. "He caught me and then he used the trunch on me. Not full strength. Said he didn't want to do permanent damage. Said he wanted to save me for later." Her voice sounded far away. She covered her face with her hands. "He put it in me," she said.

Then she breathed deeply, raggedly, and made herself look at me. "Well," she said. "So."

I put her into my bed, and he sat in the chair beside it, standing watch for who knew what? He could not defend his daughter, but he must try, as surely as the suns rose, now growing farther apart, over the hard pack of my homeworld desert.

Everything was changed.

"Bex," I said to her, and touched her forehead. Touched her fine, brown skin. "Bex, in the future, we won, I won, my command won it. Really, really big. That's why we're here. That's why we're all here."

Bex's eyes were closed. I could not tell if she'd already fallen asleep. I hoped she had.

"I have to take care of some business, and then I'll do it again," I said in a whisper. "I'll just have to go back up-time and do it again."

Between the first and second rising, I'd reached Heidel, and as Hemingway burned red through the storm's dusty leavings, I stood in the shadows of the entrance of the Bexter Hotel. There I waited.

The halandana was the first up—like me, they never really slept—and it came down from its room looking, no doubt, to go out and get another rubber of its drug. Instead, it found me. I didn't waste time with the creature. With a quick twist in n-space, I pulled it down to the present, down to a local concentration of hate and lust and stupidity that I could kill with a quick thrust into its throat. But I let it live; I showed it myself, all of me spread out and huge, and I let it fear.

"Go and get Marek Lambrois," I told it. "Tell him Colonel Bone wants to see him. Colonel Henry Bone of the Eighth Sky and Light."

"Bone," said the halandana. "I thought—"

I reached out and grabbed the creature's long neck. This was the halandana weak point, and this halandana had a ceramic implant as protection. I clicked up the power in my forearm a level and crushed the collar as I might a tea cup. The halandana's neck carapace shattered to platelets and shards, outlined in fine cracks under its skin.

"Don't think," I said. "Tell Marek Lambrois to come into the street and I will let him live."

This was untrue, of course, but hope never dies, I'd discov-

ered, even in the hardest of soldiers. But perhaps I'd underestimated Marek. Sometimes I still wonder.

He stumbled out, still partly asleep, onto the street. Last night
had evidently been a hard and long one. His eyes were a red no
detox nano could fully clean up. His skin was the color of paste.

"You have something on me," I said. "I cannot abide that."

"Colonel Bone," he began. "If I'd knowed it was *you*—"

"Too late for that."

"It's never too late, that's what you taught us all when you
turned that offensive around out on the Husk and gave the Chaos
the what-for. I'll just be going. I'll take the gang with me. It's to
no purpose, our staying now."

"You knew enough *yesterday*—enough to leave." I felt the
rage, the old rage that was to be, once again. "Why did you do
that to her?" I asked. "Why did you—"

And then I looked into his eyes and saw it there. The quiet
desire—beaten down by synthesized emotions, but now triumphant, sadly triumphant. The desire to finally, finally *die*. Marek
was not the unthinking brute I'd taken him for after all. Too bad
for him.

I took a step toward Marek. His instincts made him reach
down, go for the trunch. But it was a useless weapon on me. I
don't have myelin sheaths on my nerves. I don't have nerves
anymore; I have *wiring*. Marek realized this was so almost
instantly. He dropped the trunch, then turned and ran. I caught
him. He tried to fight, but there was never any question of him
beating me. That would be absurd. I'm Colonel Bone of the
Skyfalling 8th. I kill so that there might be life. *Nobody* beats me.
It is my fate, and yours too.

I caught him by the shoulder, and I looped my other arm
around his neck and reined him to me—not enough to snap
anything. Just enough to calm him down. He was strong, but had
no finesse.

Like I said, glims are hard to kill. They're the same as snails
in shells in a way, and the trick is to draw them out—way out.
Which is what I did with Marek. As I held him physically, I
caught hold of him, all of him, *over there*, in the place I can't tell
you about, can't describe. The way you do this is by holding a
glim still and causing him great suffering, so that they can't

withdraw into the deep places. That's what vampire stakes and Roman crosses are all about.

And, like I told Bex, glims are bad ones, all right. But, but not the worst. *I* am the worst.

> *Icicle spike*
> *from the eye of a star.*
> *I've come to kill you.*

I sharpened my nails. Then I plunged them into Marek's stomach, through the skin, into the twist of his guts. I reached around there and caught hold of something, a piece of intestine. I pulled it out. This I tied to the porch of the Bexter Hotel.

Marek tried to untie himself and pull away. He was staring at his insides, rolled out, raw and exposed, and thinking—I don't know what. I haven't died. I don't know what it is like to die. He moaned sickly. His hands fumbled uselessly in the grease and phlegm that coated his very own self. There was no undoing the knots I'd tied, no pushing himself back in.

I picked him up, and as he whimpered, I walked down the street with him. His guts trailed out behind us, like a pink ribbon. After I'd gotten about twenty feet, I figured this was all he had in him. I dropped him into the street.

Hemingway was in the northeast and Fitzgerald directly east. They both shone at different angles on Marek's crumple, and cast crazy, mazy shadows down the length of the street.

"Colonel Bone," he said. I was tired of his talking. "Colonel—"

I reached into his mouth, past his gnashing teeth, and pulled out his tongue. He reached for it as I extracted it, so I handed it to him. Blood and drool flowed from his mouth and colored the red ground even redder about him. Then, one by one, I broke his arms and legs, then I broke each of the vertebrae in his backbone, moving up his spinal column with quick pinches. It didn't take long.

This is what I did in the world that people can see. In the twists of other times and spaces, I did similar things, horrible, irrevocable things, to the man. I killed him. I killed him in such a way that he would never come to life again, not in any possible place, not in any possible time. I wiped Marek Lambrois from existence. Thoroughly. And with his death the other glims died, like lights going out, lights ceasing to exist, bulb, filament and all. Or like the quick loss of all sensation after a brain is snuffed out.

Irrevocably gone from this timeline, and that was what mattered. Keeping this possible future uncertain, balanced on the fulcrum of chaos and necessity. Keeping it *free*, so that I could go back and do my work.

I left Marek lying there, in the main street of Heidel. Others could do the mopping up; that wasn't my job. As I left town, on the way back to my house and my life there, I saw that I wasn't alone in the dawn-lit town. Some had business out at this hour, and they had watched. Others had heard the commotion and come to windows and porches to see what it was. Now they knew. They knew what I was, what I was to be. I walked alone down the road, and found Bex and her father both sound asleep in my room.

I stroked her fine hair. She groaned, turned in her sleep. I pulled my covers up to her chin. Forty years old, and as beautiful as a child. Safe in my bed. Bex. Bex. I will miss you. Always, always, Bex.

I went to the living room, to the shroud-covered furniture. I sat down in what had been my father's chair. I sipped a cup of my father's best barley-malt whiskey. I sat, and as the suns of Ferro rose in the hard-iron sky, I faded into the distant, dying future.

RORVIK'S WAR

Geoffrey A. Landis

A physicist who works for NASA, and who has recently been working on the Martian Lander program, Geoffrey A. Landis is a frequent contributor to Analog *and to* Asimov's Science Fiction, *and has also sold stories to markets such as* Interzone, Amazing *and* Pulphouse. *Landis is not a prolific writer, by the high-production standards of the genre, but he is popular. His story, "A Walk in the Sun," won him a Nebula and a Hugo Award in 1992; his story, "Ripples in the Dirac Sea," won him a Nebula Award in 1990; and his story, "Elemental," was on the Final Hugo Ballot a few years back. His first book was the collection,* Myths, Legends, and True History. *He lives in Brook Park, Ohio.*

In the vivid and feverdream-intense story that follows, he shows us that sometimes the toughest war a soldier can fight is the battle to stay human—*and in the ultra–high-tech world of future warfare, that may turn out to be almost impossible . . .*

1.

A spaz launcher lies beside Private Rorvik, broken in the lee of a crushed building. The air is crisp with the tang of smokeless powder.

He is dying. The hole in his belly leaks blood around his clenched fingers, around the spike of crimson pain that shoots through the core of his being, turning dry Boston dirt into red-brown mud. There is a lot of mud; hours' worth. Try to ignore the pain, try to forget you're dying.

He is tired, so tired, but he can't sleep. The pain won't let him move. Each breath stabs like a bayonet into his stomach. His fear is gone, along with hope, and he is left with only pain.

The sky is blue, impossibly blue for a day so gray, brilliant burnished blue, the blue of boredom, babbling burning broken blue, bright baking burning bleeding . . . Stop it. Stop it stop it stop it. Think of something else. There is a taste of copper in his mouth. Maybe he would be rescued. The sounds of battle as the Russians are driven back, the rumble of microtanks. The purple glint of sunlight off a video lens, peeking around the corner, the shout of discovery: "Hey! There's somebody alive here!" Soldiers—Americans, thank God! Scurrying people all around, a ripping sound as someone pulls the tab of a smoke grenade and tosses it into the clear area behind him, boiling red smoke twisted like an insubstantial genie to guide the helicopter into the hot zone. "You all right there? Hang on, we've called for medics. Help is coming. You'll be okay, just hang on." *Whop whop whop* as the chopper comes in, and a stab of pain as the medevac team lifts him up, the pain is there but it's distant because it's going to be all right. He grins stoically and the men cheer at his bravery. The chopper takes off, Russian stingers swarming after it but the decoys and the door-gunner get them all. It's going to be all right, it's going to be all right, it's going to be . . . Stop it.

You're dying. There will be no rescue. The American forces are in retreat. The best you can hope for is the Russian advance.

Think of something else. Think of your family. Think about Lissy. He tries to recall his daughter's face, but can't. Brown hair, freckles, pixie nose. It means nothing to him. How she used to beg him for rides on his knee, pretending it was a pony, no, a *horse*, Daddy, ponies are for *children* and suddenly he sees her there, right in front of him, she is really there and he tries to smile for her and tell her it is all right and that he loves her more than anything but his smile turns into a grimace and all he can do is croak. When he tries to reach out to her the pain hits him in his belly like fifty millimeter cannon fire. He clenches his jaw to keep from screaming, then spits the blood out of his mouth. She isn't there, she has never been there at all and he will never see her again.

And then he can hear them, a low rumbling throbbing of the dirt beneath him, treads and six-legged walkers rumbling across the broken pavement of the city. But this isn't a hallucination; this is real. God! Could it be?

He tries to move, to look, but the pain is too much. Something winks in the corner of his vision, and he slowly turns his head. Indicators on the broken spaz launcher suddenly glow to life. The IFF light flickers, on and off, red. Foe. And another light insistently green: targets acquired and locked, warheads armed and ready.

The spaz launcher is still working! Somehow the advancing Russians have missed it; the broken building must have shielded it from their surveillance drones. Guessing from the rumbling in the distance, the advancing mechs must be a whole division. He could put a big hole in their advance, if he gives the launch command.

And then their drones will home in on him and blow him away.

Or he could wait, he could disable the launcher, he could wait for them to find him. Surely they take prisoners of war? They would bring him to a hospital, fix him up, and maybe someday in a POW exchange he'll be sent home, disabled but still alive. A hero. Nobody would have to know about the launcher. Nobody would ever know . . .

He looks at the launcher. Go away, he thinks. I don't want you. I didn't ask for you. I never asked to be a soldier.

He could go home a hero, but inside he would know. And the Russians would advance, they would take Boston, and Worcester, and Springfield. Lissy would grow up speaking Russian, she would go to Russian schools, and after a while she would learn to hate him.

He can hear scrabbling, something coming up the hill. A lens pokes around the corner, just as he'd imagined it, but it is a Russian lens, attached to a camera on six spidery metal legs, an unarmed battlefield surveillance unit. It looks at him, humming softly to itself.

They've found him. It is now or never.

He pulls his hand away from the wound in his belly and tries to sit up. The hole opens up afresh, and a new flow of blood wells into his lap. He tries not to look at it. He tries to ignore the pain. The drone—unarmed, thank God!—continues to watch him.

He reaches out to the panel and hits *actuate*. The launcher shudders and vibrates like an epileptic having a seizure, as armor-piercing hunter-seekers chuff from the aperture. The hum of the drone watching him changes pitch and he knows that the Russians are zeroed in, but it is too late; too late for them, too late for him. He leans back and gasps. For a moment, the world goes purple-black. Far away, he can hear the *chumpf* of explosions as his missiles find their targets, and closer, much closer, the rising whistle of incoming shells.

The first shell explodes a few meters away, and the ground swells up like a wave and tosses him casually against the broken building. He opens his eyes, and after a moment, they focus. In a frozen moment of perfect clarity, he sees the shell that will kill him swell in an instant from a speck into an absolutely perfect circle, deadly black against the blue, blue sky.

And then there is nothing at all.

2.

Rorvik remembered the day his draft notice had come as clearly as if it had happened yesterday. It had been seven-thirty in the morning, and Angela was about ready to head for work. As she kissed him, promising to hurry home, there was a knock on the door.

Angela pulled away from him and turned. "Who could that be, at this hour?"

"Probably a salesman." The knock came again, three measured raps. He was annoyed. The few minutes in the morning while Lissy was still asleep and before Angela went off to work was about the only time he had Angela to himself. "I'll get it." He jerked open the door, ready to give somebody an earful. "Yes?"

It was a balding man in a plain blue suit. Standing just behind him, flanking him on either side, were two larger men. The man looked at a piece of paper. "Mr. Davis C. Rorvik?"

"What do you want?"

"Excuse me. You *are* Mr. Rorvik?"

"Yes, but—"

The man glanced toward Angela, and then back. "May we speak to you alone for a moment, Mr. Rorvik?"

"You may not," Angela said sharply, coming up behind him. "If you have something to tell him, you can say it right here." She made a show of looking at her watch. "And quickly."

The man shrugged, and addressed Mr. Rorvik. "Mr. Rorvik, as a duly authorized agent of the United States Selective Service, it is my duty to inform you that as of this moment, you are a member of the United States Armed Forces."

"Wait one moment—"

The man opened a folder and removed a stack of photocopied papers. He ran his finger down the top page to the signatures, and then showed it to Rorvik. An ancient student loan application. "This is your signature?"

He didn't remember the particular document, but the signature was clearly his. It had seemed a good bargain at the time: tuition money for college in return for a promise to serve if needed, and they probably wouldn't even need him anyway. With the collapse of communism across the globe, there was no prospect of war in sight. "Yes, but . . ."

The man nodded at one of the goons, who pulled something out from under his jacket.

"I'm too . . ." There was a hiss, and Rorvik felt a cool sting at the back of his neck. ". . . too . . ." His knees suddenly buckled, and he slid slowly to the ground. Inside the house, Angela screamed.

He couldn't move. His muscles felt like warm pudding; his head felt as if somebody had swathed it in lint. The man continued to speak; presumably to Angela. "Under the provisions of Emergency order 09-13A, you are forbidden under the penalty of law to discuss this draft notice or to divulge any information concerning the whereabouts of Mr. Rorvik." One of the men wrapped his arms under Rorvik's armpits. The other picked up his legs. "This includes discussing the matter with any agents of the press." Angela had stopped screaming, and was, as far as he could tell, listening in silence. "The provisions of the Emergency order allow for full compensation for any inconvenience occasioned by Mr. Rorvik's service." The two men picked him up and started to take him away to the gray station wagon

idling at the curb. As the two men swung him around, he could
see his next-door neighbor Jack on his way to the subway stop,
briefcase in hand. He was taking an intense interest in the weeds
poking out through the cracks in the sidewalk. He didn't once
look in Rorvik's direction.

As they bundled him into the car, Rorvik managed to complete
the phrase he had started, hours ago ". . . too old to be drafted.
I'm thirty-eight years old. . . ."

3.

"It's the Eff-En-Gee. What's your name, FNG?"

"Rorvik."

"That Swedish?"

"Close enough. It's Norwegian."

"Wrong answer, FNG." The big corporal tapped him on the
chest. "Start counting. I'll tell you when you can stop."

Rorvik dropped down and began doing push-ups. "One! Two!
Three!"

"Either you're an American or you're meat. Got it?"

"Heard and understood."

The corporal—Driscott, his name-tag had said—watched
him for a few moments. "You may think your name's Rorvik, but
I think your name is FNG. You mind that, FNG?"

"No, sir."

"Good. You learn fast, FNG. You know what FNG stands
for?"

"No, sir."

"Stands for Fuckin' New Guy. Means you're dangerous, FNG.
You're going to get us all killed. Forget yourself, go outside. Feel
good to get outside for a few minutes, wouldn't it, FNG?"

"No, sir."

"Good answer. Get yourself specced by a flying Bear eyeball,
and you realize you made a fuck-up when you get pounded to
dust by arty. One tremendous ker-powie is the last thing you're
going to hear. Now, that wouldn't bother me a bit—nobody
much cares if the Army's got one FNG more or less—but that

same arty fire is gonna spread *me* across a few acres of landscape too, and I wouldn't like that very much, no.

"—Count real quiet there, Private FNG, I want you to hear me and hear me good.

"Reason we call you FNG is so that we don't forget, even for a moment, that you're not to be trusted. One FNG is as dangerous as a dozen Bear-eyes. Live 'til the next new guy comes in, maybe you deserve a name of your own, and *he's* the FNG."

Driscott put his foot on Rorvik's back and pressed him against the ground. "'Til then, you don't do nothing outside of rules, and maybe we all live a little longer. Got it?"

"Heard and understood."

"Good. I think I'm gonna get along with you, FNG. I think we're gonna get along fine."

There had been no air travel, of course—Russian microsats could spot an airplane and their SAMs would blow it out of the sky from a thousand miles away. Rorvik, along with half a dozen other draftees, dazed and scared, had been taken across the interdiction zone in an armored convoy that dashed from hardpoint to hardpoint, screened with chaff, decoys, jammers. At first he wondered why it was necessary to get to the battle zone at all; later he was taught that radio relays were weak links in a battle, and that a critical half of their communications was by line-of-sight microwave and laser links that required proximity. No communications link was entirely secure, but the shorter the link, the more reliable it was.

Later yet he realized that it didn't matter where the soldiers were actually located. The fire zone could move a hundred miles in the blink of an eye when the Russian computers made a new guess at the American command location. The front lines were everywhere.

Driscott took his foot away and reached down a hand. It took a moment before Rorvik realized that Driscott was offering him a hand up. "You're gonna learn about this war fast, FNG. First thing you gonna learn, we don't get the information here. They don't tell us nothing."

"Yes, sir."

"You married, FNG? Got a family?"

"Yes."

"Too bad. Forget 'em. War first started, the soldiers stayed back from the lines and let the metal take the fire. Sometimes even got to go home on weekends. That got stopped real quick. Fuckin' Russkies didn't know the rules; too many civvies killed when the Russkies targeted the ops. You're here for the duration, got it?"

"Understood." The funny thing was, he could barely even remember the war starting. He was old enough to remember watching CNN with his parents by the hour during the breakup of the Soviet Union, remembered the sense of relief as the world stood down from the brink of nuclear annihilation. But the rise of the Russian junta and the new cold war had seemed to occur in the blink of an eye when he hadn't been paying attention. In hindsight, it was inevitable—though nobody had predicted it at the time—that a strongman would take over control from the ruins of the Soviet system. It was funny how something so important could seem so distant. He had been too busy marrying, trying to start a family, trying to keep a job in an economy going sour year by year. He knew it intellectually, could quote the headline statistics, but the threat of war had never seemed real to him, even as the cold war turned into a war of hot steel.

And the new threat of war wasn't like the old. It was to be a war of computers, not missiles. "I don't even understand why we're here," Rorvik said to Driscott. "They'd told us that the computers made war obsolete. That battlefield simulations can predict the outcome of every battle, so nobody would actually fight anymore."

"Yeah?" Driscott seemed amused. "Tell me about it, new guy."

"If our battlefield simulations say the same thing the Russian ones do, and they know the outcome of a battle before the first shot is fired, why are we fighting? They said that whoever was going to lose would know, and back down. What happened?"

"You got sold a bill of goods, FNG. Lissen to too many of those TV commentators." Driscott shook his head. "Just goes to show. Nah, them computers don't know everything. Ya can't predict the psy-fucking-cology of the guys in the field. You can put in the numbers, but can you put in morale? Can you put in fuckups?" He tapped Rorvik's chest. "It's you and me, buddy, you and me make the difference. We aren't just fighting a war. No, what we're doing is showing them Russian computers that they don't got a clue about just how tough the American soldier really is. No matter what they throw at us, no matter how tough things get, even if all we have left is rocks, we just keep coming. We never give up. Never. Got it?"

"Got it."

4.

For a moment after he wakes, his dream of being a civilian seems like it had been only yesterday, the memories of civilian life stronger and more alive than those of the war. The feeling fades. It was just that the war had started so *fast*, and his life had changed so quickly and completely, it sometimes feels like he had been a civilian just hours before.

Rorvik is a tactical operator on the fly-eyes, one of the best. A fly-eye is a tiny infrared-visible camera with an encrypted radio transmitter, hung under a plastic flex-wing with a miniature propeller and motor, the whole thing folding up to a streamlined package about the size of a pencil that fits into a rifle. It is up to him to find targets for the artillery, located somewhere in a secured hiding place fifty miles or more distant.

The war is a huge game of hide and seek. When the enemy is found, the smart shells pound cracks through his armor to incinerate the meat within.

Somewhere in the city below, a grunt hiding in the deserted city fires him into the sky. Rorvik knows nothing about the soldier who launches him, nor cares, but waits with a rising sense of anticipation until he hits apogee and spreads his wings. Deployed, silent, nearly radar invisible, he soars over darkened buildings looking for movement, flying in slow zigzags to present a less predictable target. His motor gives him about five minutes of power, but it is a point of pride with the fliers not to use it, but to soar the tiny flexwing on thermals and on the ridge lift from rooftops, prolonging his flights for hours before he has to return to the drab world of concrete and first sergeants and smelly underwear and MRE packages eaten cold to avoid unnecessary IR signature. He hates cold water shaves and the endless pinochle game the E-5 sergeants play in their den; he hates the smell of stale piss that washes over the room whenever one of the men opens up the latrine canister to take a leak, and the rotten-fruit smell of unwashed bodies the rest of the time. (There is a perennial rumor that the enemy is developing an odor-sensitive homing bomb, and that when it is developed the field troops will be subject to a smell discipline as strong as the IR discipline is now. God, he wishes they'd hurry.)

But, flying his eye, he is far from all that. He flies above the city, the flier's electronic eyes becoming his own, heedless of his body controlling the flier far below.

He soars over the darkening city. It is spring, but the few trees left in the city provide scant obstruction to his cameras. A flutter of movement attracts his attention, and he wheels around. Nothing. No, there! He zooms in. A piece of paper blowing in the wind. He circles for a minute, hoping to catch something else, but nothing moves. MI will examine his snapshot of the paper, he knows, trying to determine where it came from, if it is ours or theirs.

"Little Eagle? Word from Uncle Henry that they've seen Bear footprints north in sector Tiger three-niner. They want you to eyeball it for them. Do you need a new bird?"

Tiger 39. He flashes up a map. About a kilometer north of him, in the areas that once used to be north Cambridge. "Negative, unless they're in some real rush about it. I can get there in five minutes."

"Roger. We're standing by."

He can see the pink warmth of a thermal off to his left, and banks around. He increases speed until his wings begin to ripple and lose lift, then backs off a hair.

Four minutes later he is circling the area.

The sky is muddy brown in the falsecolor of his IR display. "It's an evac zone," the voice in his earphones says. "Anything you see will be Bears."

He hears the slight riffle of air behind him. He snap-rolls instantly, and the diving hawk misses him by inches. He pushes into a dive to gain airspeed, with one eye watching the Russian hawk pull up to come around at him again, with the other flashing to his map to find if he is near a sector where he has fire support from the ground. Negative. He flips his mike on.

"Load up another birdy, Wintergreen. I've drawn a hawk."

"No can do, Little Eagle. A couple of Bear eyes moved in too close to our guys on the ground. Advise you run for the green in sector X-ray niner."

The Russian hawk, abandoning stealth, has lit its tiny pulsejet and is coming at him from below. "Negative, negative. It's too far. Blow the eyes away."

"Sorry, Sport. Too many eyes. We don't want to risk the Bears getting a fix on our artillery. You're on your own."

"Fuck you very much, Wintergreen." He starts an evasion pattern. No way he can outrun a hawk; he pushes the stick forward to the edge of flutter and heads in zigzags toward the turbulence of a fragged building.

He'd been hoping he could ride the turbulence, but the gusty wind is too much for him. The wind-rotor grabs him, flips him upside down. He rolls out inches away from smashing against the concrete, pulls out hard, and stalls. Hanging dead in the air for the instant before falling, he feels more than sees the hawk coming at him. He is dead meat.

And in the next instant the hawk flies apart, ripped to shreds by gunfire. He pushes forward, regains flying speed, and hightails down-wind, at the same time keying his mike. "What the hell was that? Fletchette?"

"Birdshot. I found a grunt dumb enough to step outside to take a shot. You owe me one, Sport. Can you make it now?"

"Affirmative."

"Keep your eyes peeled. Local support arty is pinned down, but we have some long-range shoot'n'scoot that can wipe the Bear HQ if you happen to find it in your travels."

"Rog." He finds some lift, gains altitude, and heads for Tiger.

He flies over territory that is familiar to him. He had worked near here once, before he was married. For a moment he wonders why the Russians had invaded. Arming for war had shored up a failed economy, but did it make any sense for the Bears to actually hold territory? They must have had a reason, or at least a pretext for one, but for the moment Rorvik can't remember what it was. But then, who could ever psych out the Russians?

Leave that to the professionals, with their super-computers and tactical models. Not to the soldiers.

Tiger three-niner. Circling the area, he finds a cluster of relatively undamaged buildings, apparently the remains of an old housing project. A bit exposed for a fire base, but still . . . He circles lower, looking for signs of habitation. Nothing. There! Traces of body heat lingering in the still air, a yellowish fog in the IR. He zooms out and follows the heat trace across the city as it brightens into lime green and then the pale blue of recent passage. There, under an overhang, the scarlet flash of a warm body. He checks his map. This is an evac area; a free-fire zone. A flash of movement. "Think I got something here. Hold fire." He banks around.

"Standing by to fire."

He comes in low, stalls, fights the building's turbulence. Another flash of movement; a foot. "Got it! Bogeys, could be a Bear fire-control post." He flashes his IR range finder. "My coords plus five at twenty-two surface, mark. I'm coming around to guide your fire." He rides out and into some slope lift from the breeze flowing up over the facade.

A different voice, the slight echo of multiple radio relays. "Roger. Outgoing, one, two, three." His vision flickers static for a moment from the EM pulse used to dazzle any Bear radars from tracing back the rising shells. It takes a moment for the shells to clear far enough to aero-maneuver, a moment in which he is suddenly aware of sitting in a concrete bunker with a flickering television helmet on his head, and then his vision sharpens back to normal and he is flying again.

The fire support base is miles away; it will be a minute before the shells come in and need his terminal guidance. Something about what he's seen bothers him. He flicks back to his last photo. A foot shows in the shadow of an overhang. He zooms in, enhances contrast. Barefoot. The Russians are that far out of discipline? He circles back, penetrating upwind slowly, searching for a good view. There. He hovers for a moment into the wind, panning his eye around behind him. Shapes move, but the shadow is too deep to distinguish them in visual. He turns up contrast and sharpens his gain. There.

The instant before he stalls out, he gets a good shot.

Three children circle around a suspended object. The oldest is perhaps fourteen, the youngest perhaps nine. One, blindfolded, holds a broken mop handle like a club. In a corner a scruffy yellow dog watches him. He looks closer at the suspended object. He recognizes it as the throw-away cardboard transport tube for an 80-mm Russian antiaircraft missile. It has been decorated, painted bright colors, given old buttons to serve as eyes, four painted cardboard legs and long floppy ears. A crude caricature of a donkey. A piñata.

The voice in his earphones says, "Twenty seconds to incoming. Ready for terminal guidance."

"Abort your rounds! Abort!"

"Say again, Eagle?"

"Abort your rounds! Civilians!"

"Roger." Three sharp cracks in the air above him as the lifting bodies detonate. "Rounds aborted." There is a pause, and then, "Do you have a vector on the target that can avoid the civilians?"

He feels like ash, like he had been burned and there is nothing left. Shooting at shadows is common enough, but it won't endear him to his superiors. "Negative. False alarm. Sorry, guys."

There is a long pause, and then, "Operations wants to talk to you, Rorvik."

Using his name instead of his code is a bad sign. "Acknowledged."

"That means now, Private."

"Roger." He scrambles and finds some lift, prolonging the flight, knowing it might be his last. "I'll be there as soon as I'm down."

Another pause. "Negative, Rorvik. Ops wants to talk to you pronto. Advise you blow the bird and get your butt down here before you get marks for insubordination."

"Heard and understood." No help for it. The critical chips on his bird are set to melt when they lose the carrier wave for more than a few seconds, or if he gives the coded signal. The rest of the bird is just sticks and plastic; no more than a toy. He flicks the cover off the toggle, caresses it for a second, and then presses it with his thumb. His eye-screens flash black for an instant, and then there is nothing left of the world but the whisper and swirl of static.

He pops his helmet, and is in a grimy concrete bunker crammed with equipment and stinking of sweat and hot electronics. Next to his contoured seat, two other fliers sit, faceless in the white plastic of surround helmets, oblivious to him and the rest of the world, except for their birds. His muscles ache from the body English he gave his bird while flying, but the bunker is too cramped for him to stretch. He unpins the throat mike, and goes to explain.

5.

They are kept in the dark about the overall course of the war, but from the consistent, slow retreat, and the way that replacements—men and materiel both—are getting scarcer and scarcer, by the end of the summer Rorvik knows that the war is not going well.

Some of the men from Rorvik's unit keep a Russian lieutenant tied up in a remote bunker, nominally an auxiliary command post but actually just an abandoned garage that hasn't been shelled, with a roof thick enough to mask IR signature. They call her Olga—nobody knows her real name; it had been written on her uniform way back when she'd had one, but none of the gang could read Cyrillic, and she either can't or won't speak English.

Rorvik's unit is all male. Equality be damned, the Army is still segregated by sex. Only Headquarters units and reserves mix genders; every operational unit Rorvik has served in has been all male. There are all-female units too, the subject of a good deal of unlikely stories and rude speculation, but Rorvik's unit rarely meets them, except on the field, where the drones are sexless and the operators invisible, hidden behind labyrinths of encrypted radio relays. The Russian lieutenant is the only female any of them has seen for weeks—some of them, months.

And they know that there is little chance that they will survive the war anyway.

As Rorvik passes by, one of the boys yells out an invitation for him to join them. Rorvik walks faster, and they snicker. "Ol' Davey's too good for us." "No, it's just that he's waiting until we capture a *boy*." "Maybe he's got his own nookie stashed away somewhere, some pretty Russky major."

Their lieutenant pretends not to notice, but he knows. No way he could miss it. They are supposed to turn prisoners over to the authorities—they desperately need Russians for their simulations—but, for the moment, that is impossible. No doubt as soon as they rejoined their battalion the prisoner would be "found," and rescued from the civilian "partisans" who had so cruelly mistreated her.

Could he do anything? Informing headquarters about the prisoner would result in her disappearance, and possibly his own, long before any inspection might get to them. Still, the thought that there could be something he might do chews at Rorvik's conscience and worries him at the odd moments when battle duty or his eight-hour watch leaves him free to think.

As the battle eddies and stalls, with movement by lightning air deployment and half the battle fought by remotes, it is almost pointless to mark battle lines. Most of the Boston area is controlled by neither the Russians nor the American forces, but watched by both. To the extent that anybody can say, though, Rorvik's unit is temporarily behind enemy lines. Or at least, they are cut off from support.

Their control bunker is buried under Dorchester. When the battle moved closer, his unit had to stay inside; but now, with the battle line off in Roxbury, some outside mobility is possible. At work, of course, he is right in the thick of battle, wherever it is.

Rorvik was taken off of tac surveillance to become a drone runner. He alternates with Drejivic, six hours on, six off, controlling four robot warriors. The warriors are intelligent; if the coded remote signal is jammed, they will keep fighting until the interference clears, and their IFF (identify, friend or foe) signals—changed hourly—keep them from shooting each other. But remotes work best if an actual human watches over them to make decisions. In a hard fire-fight, it is best to let them on their own; human reaction time only slows them down. He'll interfere only when indecision about a questionable IFF threatens a gridlock. Occasionally he'll have to call in Rick, who runs another four, to take one of his drones; or Rick will call him in. It is a point of pride not to do this too often.

Angie, Lissy, Gumby, and Pokey, he calls them. Drejivic has other names.

He hooks into the computer. When he runs drones, his body stays in the bunker, but *he*—the important part of him—is the drone. He flits back and forth from one viewpoint to another. When he wears one body, the views from the other three cameras are always visible in the edge of his vision.

When he concentrates on one drone, the others fight on their own initiative.

Angie and Lissy, the fliers, he likes best. These aren't the disposable surveillance flexies he flew when the war was young; these are armed fighting drones. The fliers are pigs for energy use, though, and have to conserve their time aloft. On the ground they are clumsy. More than once he's had to use his rocket-assisted take-off to haul ass out of fire too hot for them to handle. The rasstos are one-shot units; use one up and you have to bring the drone home and wait for a replacement. Like everything else, they are running low. He's been chewed out several times, the sarge drilling in that we are *not* to get into situations where we have to rassto out.

Unfortunately, Angie is waiting for a replacement rassto, and Lissy is out of action. She's taken a couple of rounds of small-caliber fire. The maintenance tech has her now, trying to scrounge parts to put her back together.

Gumby and Pokey are his two bipedal walkers. Running them feels almost like wearing a robot suit. Gumby is the most flexible of his drones. His problem is that they also ran out of ammo for the 3-mm skittergun that is Gumby's utility weapon. He still has the 10-mm armor piercers and rockets, but on his own, Gumby's first move in a firefight is still to bring up the skittergun. The slight hesitation it takes for Gumby's tiny processor to remember it didn't work could be fatal. The unit is supposed to be adaptable enough to remember, but Rorvik guesses that that part of his programming has been shot out.

Pokey is operational, but weaponless until parts become available, after the unit rejoins the main army. Mostly Rorvik stays out of Gumby's viewpoint and lets the drone move around on auto while he scouts from Pokey.

What the drones fight, mostly, are other drones. There are

human infantry in the field, on both sides, but they tend to be dug into stealth emplacements, mobile and heavily protected, only popping out for missions too delicate to be run by drones.

In the distance, the heavy overcast glows orange with reflected light as the ruins of Boston burn.

The status bulletin has given them a clear for an hour. It is rare that their computers can predict a clear for that long; somewhere far away one side or the other must have ferreted a major command center, and a battle must be drawing all of the resources available. For now, Rorvik's area is clear of Russian eyes, and they can move around outside. Drone runners have to take rest shifts of a minimum of three hours to stay at peak effectiveness; the regulations demand it, and so he knows he won't be called back except for a serious emergency.

A block from their bunker is a square that still has a few trees in it; the closest thing to a park within the defense perimeter. He decides to go there for as long as the clear lasts.

Someone else has gotten there before him.

The woman in the park has a SISI gun grafted right to her shoulder, and the eye-shaped barrel turns to aim at him at the same time she raises her head. He takes an involuntary step back; the gun unnerves him. See it, shoot it: he could be dead with a single thought. She must have volunteered to have the gun grafted into her nervous system; the regulations don't allow them to modify you without consent. It means that she is from a live-combat unit, and that is unusual as well, especially for a woman. Women have to volunteer for front-line duty.

He was in a live-combat unit once, during the first battle for Boston. He remembers—but that was early in the war; there is no point in dredging up those memories.

Her insignia shows her to be a Spec-4. He has heard that a female infantry company had temporarily moved in to an area south of them, but hadn't realized that their clear areas would overlap. The gun moves like something alive on her shoulder, pivoting minutely as she shifts her eyes, jerking from target to target with the unblinking attention of a snake.

She watches him eyeing her gun. "It's no safer behind the lines, soldier. I'd rather have it be up front, where I can fight back, than where you are, buried in some concrete bunker and never hear it coming, you know?"

"Doesn't the gun make you a target?"

"Makes me dangerous." She smiles. "I like to be dangerous."

She is too tall, too many muscles and too few curves, and wears a wrinkled jumpsuit made of fireproof fabric that masks what feminine lines she has. She is desirable as all hell.

She can tell he is thinking about that, too, and she laughs. "Soldiers think any woman out here is sex-crazed, you know it? I'm not like that. I've got a husband, and two kids. They're what I'm fighting for."

"I know."

"You married, soldier?"

He nods.

"Happily? Got any kids?"

"A girl."

She nods. "Then you do know." As she unzips the jumpsuit, she says, "They're back at home, and we're here." She runs the tip of one finger along the gun barrel for a second, then does something to it with the other hand, and it stops tracking her gaze. "This didn't happen, you know? It's the war. No commitments, no promises, no looking each other up, after."

"No." He doesn't believe there will be an after, not anymore. He has seen the craters where houses once were, the lines of refugees, miles long, trudging endlessly out of the cities toward areas they believed might be safe. He has seen the ruins of the area where his house had been, where his wife and girl once lived.

But he still believes in now.

Her name is Westermaker, she whispers. She kneels to unzip his pants. He strokes her hair—short, dark and very slightly curled—as she runs her lips along the underside of his cock.

A confused jumble of thoughts crowds through his head all at the same time. He feels himself already beginning to dribble, and wonders if he will be able to hold back, or if he will come the instant she takes him in her mouth. Wonders if he will ever be able to tell Angela about this, and whether she could possibly understand. Wonders if the Army issues female grunts birth control. Wonders if she will stay long enough for him to take her twice.

He reaches down to slide his pants off. She cups his buttocks in a palm as she delicately touches the end of her tongue to the tip of his cock, and the burst of machine-gun fire takes her low in the chest. Her mouth opens to scream as her lungs splatter out the side of her shredded uniform and across the jagged ends of her splintered ribs. An instant later, without a sound, she dies.

He staggers back, his ears ringing with the report, tries to turn around, and trips on the pants tangled around his knees. He rolls over and looks right into the lens of a Russian walker. With the soft whirr of servos, the machine gun tracks to his face.

He squeezes his eyes shut. The smell of blood is very strong. Nothing happens.

After a long moment he opens his eyes. The machine is still there, unblinking; the gun still aimed right for him. It is heavier and clumsier than the American units Rorvik is familiar with, all angles and graceless ceramic armor-plate, and very deadly. Surreptitiously, he reaches behind him and gropes for a rock. The machine does nothing. It takes an eternity to find a rock loose enough to pull out of the ground. When he finally pries one loose he waits for an instant, gauging the distance, and then, with a quick, smooth motion, hurls it at the machine.

It dodges easily, still watching him, still tracking him with the gun, still holding back its fire. The gun must have jammed, he thinks, and then, an instant later, God, it's already called in artillery on me.

But the gun killed Westermaker easily enough, and the remote is making no effort to get clear of incoming artillery.

He should have never gone out, not even to a clear zone, without his sidearm. But he is a drone runner; he isn't supposed to fight face to face. Holding his pants up with one hand, he scrambles to his feet, preparing to make a run for it, and hears the hydraulics start up behind him. He freezes. Suddenly he realizes what the remote is up to.

Where can he go?

It had shot Westermaker. Westermaker had been armed, though her SISI gun had been useless against a threat she never saw. He is no threat. The operator—somewhere miles away—

can shoot him anytime he wanted. But his very presence means that there must be a command post somewhere nearby. Why not let him go, and watch where he went?

The tell-tale on his wrist has started to blink urgently red: return to secure area immediately. A warning that does him no good at all.

A block of ice forms in his lungs. It is suddenly impossible for him to breathe. He doesn't dare go back, it would lead the bears right into his post.

There is no way he can warn his unit, but if he doesn't return they will know, and take measures. Either way, it is too late for him.

The smell of blood has vanished, but the acid smell of spent powder etches his nostrils, fills the entire world. Slowly, slowly, he turns and starts to walk, then run. Crosswise and down hill; in a whole loop away from his bunker, away from safety, away from hope.

6.

In the ruins of Worcester, the triumphant Russian troops are coming up Belmont Street from Boston. The resistance waits for them. Rorvik's unit has managed to find a gas station that was shelled to rubble early in the war, its buried storage tanks are almost untouched. They have filled a Dumpster with gasoline, poured in five dozen bags of nitrate liberated from an old greenhouse supply, and then melted in styrofoam to make it gel. At the bottom of the Dumpster is a pound of black powder, with a detonator made from a lightbulb filament.

The Dumpster is hidden inside the bricked-up front of an abandoned apartment block, just another forgotten piece of debris in a city full of rubble.

Russian air cover is too complete and the computer triangulation and jamming too swift for Rorvik's unit to trust a radio link, even with encrypted relays. They lost two men learning that lesson. Rorvik was odd man out on the coin toss. He has found a concealed niche, across the street from the bomb, and waits, nervous, sweat dripping down his back. Through a tiny hole drilled in the wall, he watches the enemy as it walks, crawls, rolls up the street on jointed steel legs and armor-plated wheels.

Wondering if he will be able to get away, after.

Now.

The explosion is huge, an orgasm in orange and black and glorious rolling thunder. The blast picks up one of the ceramic-armored high-mobility one-man tanks and flips it against the wall. It struggles to right itself, but the move is pointless. As planned, the blast has undermined the stone facade of the building, and a slow-motion avalanche of Fitchburg granite rumbles down over the column. Five tanks and about a dozen mechanicals are swept up in the river of boiling stone, then tossed aside and buried by rubble.

The Russian commander is sharp, and in control. Before the dust has started to settle, Rorvik hears the amplified voice booming out in clipped Russian. "They left a man behind to detonate it! Find him! Squadron A, left side of the street! B, right!"

He should have scrambled the instant he pressed the button, not stayed to see what he accomplished. He could hide forever from ordinary eyes, but to infrared sensors the plume of his breath must glow like a beacon. He has only moments. He dashes through the streets, and can hear the clatter of armored soldiers entering the street behind him.

He dodges down an alley, hoping to stay out of sight of the sky for a few more moments, and only after he enters it sees that the shelling has completely blocked it with rubble. It is too late to run back the way he came; troops are too close behind him. He spots a window into the basement of a dime store, and miraculously the iron grille over the window has been shaken loose, but the glass is still intact. He smashes the glass with a piece of asphalt and drops into the darkness.

He lands awkwardly, bruising his leg. In a few minutes his eyes adjust to the dimnss. The basement is empty save for rubbish; the cement floor damp and glistening. Across from the window a stairway once rose to the main level. It is now just a pile of splintered wood. The door hangs above empty space, and through bullet holes he can see sky.

This, then, will be his last stand. There is nowhere left to run.

Turning, he sees the shadow of an articulated leg fall across the empty window. He limps away from the window, crouches against the wall and pulls out his automatic. The remote stops, hesitates by the window while the operator queries for directions, and then a lens pokes in through the window.

It swivels left, the wrong way. Rorvik aims, but holds his fire, waiting for a better shot. The body of the remote starts to press in through the window at the same time the camera pans right, and an instant before it fixes on him, Rorvik fires.

His shot is aimed at one of the vulnerable hydraulic lines, and the spray of hot fluid tells him he damaged it. Before he can shoot again, two more shatter the door above. He hears the shot an instant after he feels it hit him in the chest. The second shot, an instant later, he never hears: the one that blows apart his skull.

7.

Then he awoke. The memory of being drafted was fresh in his mind, as it always was when he awoke from a long sleep. All that had been long ago. He'd been captured; the US had fallen. He was, like many others, in a reeducation camp. Since he'd been drafted, not volunteered, the camp bureaucracy had considered him a victim of the imperialist aggressors, rather than a war criminal. That fact had earned him a chance at reeducation, instead of the bullet in the back of the head that had awaited most of his fellow soldiers.

As he stood in the line for the "voluntary" evening reeducation lecture, a man behind him put a hand on his shoulder and whispered.

"Resistance meeting tonight. Strike a blow for freedom!"

How crazy were they? Didn't they know that the Bears had stoolies and paid informants everywhere? Hey, he could even earn brownie points—maybe even a chance to see Angela and Lissy—by passing along what he'd heard.

The lecture was about economics and simulation war. Very little of the war, he discovered, had actually been fought; most of it had been simulation. Both sides' tactical computers could model the outcome of every battle, and the side that would have lost would always withdraw without actually fighting.

In theory.

"What the capitalist computers failed to take into account," said the lecturer, a tall Hispanic man with a Stalin moustache and a habit of nervously looking over his shoulder, "was that the loyal soldiers of the Hegemony have the force of history with them. Citizens of a democracy are by nature unable to act in harmony. Knowing that history is invincible, the soldiers of the Hegemony are unswerving. Purity of ideology gives them strength. How could the computers of an obsolete political system calculate this? Only with the data from actual battles, showing the staggering battlefield superiority of Hegemony troops. Victory of the Hegemony was inevitable. Even now, with algorithms bolstered with actual battle data, the computers of the aggressor capitalist governments have correctly calculated their inevitable defeat. The capitalist government has surrendered unconditionally to the provisional government, and asked all its soldiers to lay down arms. Resistance of any sort is treason, and will be dealt with as such."

Rorvik listened to it sleeping with his eyes open, automatically noting phrases to parrot back in the group-reeducation sessions the next morning. Attending the lecture would earn him points, maybe a second piece of toast at breakfast the next time supplies came to the camp.

Later, after the official lecture, the lecturer—who had been a high-school history teacher before the war—casually gathered interested parties for the second talk, this one quite unofficial. The Americans had a clandestine school system of their own in the camps, and whenever the Russkies' lecturers gave any information from the disputed territories or talked on how the resistance was going, they tried to sort out the kernel of truth from the shell of propaganda. The resistance was still alive, they said, and the Russians were having a tough time trying to govern the territory they had captured. If they could hold out, frustrate their captors at every turn, soon the alleycats would . . .

"Resistance" was a forbidden word, and anyone caught using it could be shot without hesitation. The slang for the day was to call the remnants of the armed forces who had escaped capture "alleycats."

But nothing changed, and if there really were alleycats, he'd heard plenty of talk but seen no real signs of them in the camp. Until now.

As the man spoke, barely loud enough to hear, Rorvik's attention drifted. The talk was about the necessity for computer models to be grounded in data, something Rorvik had no need to be taught again. His mind was running on another track. He couldn't actually remember being captured, and suddenly that had struck him as odd. Surely that was an important moment in his life; he ought to have vivid memories, or at least some recollection of how it had happened. He must have blacked out, that was it. The time he had been wounded, bleeding to death in the rubble . . . but no, he hadn't been captured then, he remembered it vividly, remembered the artillery, remembered dying.

No, that was impossible, he had survived, joined the resistance, set off the bomb and been chased into . . . no, that couldn't be. He had died then, too. There was something wrong with his memory. Had he hallucinated it? But it had been real, he was sure of it, as real as the barbed wire and concrete surrounding him.

One of the other men in the camp, Povelli, brushed past him on the way to the latrine. Rorvik looked up, and Povelli, without looking at him, bent over, untied his shoe, and then carefully retied it. "Wait a few minutes, then get up and make like you gotta go to the crapper," Povelli said softly. Rorvik glanced around. No one was paying attention to them. "Past the crapper, you know the tool shed? Ten minutes. Whistle once when you approach."

Rorvik nodded slightly, as if agreeing with something the professor said, and Povelli finished tying his shoe and got up.

The lecture was breaking up anyway; it was dangerous to gather in groups of more than two or three for very long. Rorvik stretched and looked around. Nobody was paying particular attention to him. He strolled toward the latrine.

Before he got halfway to the meeting, just outside the prefab, Khokhlov stopped him. They had two reeducation counselors to assist them in learning correct political thought. Khokhlov was the nicer of the two, and spoke British-accented English with a bare trace of gutteral Slavic vowels.

He offered Rorvik a cigarette. The Russians all smoked heavily. Rorvik accepted it, but only puffed on it enough to show that he appreciated the courtesy.

"You have come very far in your thinking, Mr. Rorvik," Khokhlov said. "I believe you are one of my best students."

Rorvik nodded and gave him a wide smile. "Thank you. I have been doing my best."

"Are you dissatisfied at all?" Khokhlov waved his hand. "Of course, I know that food here is not as plentiful as it could be. I assure you that we all are under the same conditions, even guards."

Rorvik wondered what Khokhlov could be after. Did he know about the meeting? "No, no—everything is fine," he said. He knew quite as well as Khokhlov that complaining was a sure sign of regressive-thinking. "Really."

"Perhaps we could chat a bit?" said Khokhlov. He took Rorvik by the arm. "I have been very disturbed by something I heard, my friend. One of the people I have been chatting with—you won't object if I don't mention his name?—said that he believed you were sympathetic to the resistance. I, of course, told him this could not be correct, but he quite insisted on the point."

"No, no," Rorvik said hastily. "Absolutely not. I steer clear of them, let me assure you."

Khokhlov looked interested. "Really? Then you know who they are?"

He wanted to kick himself for speaking without thinking, but tried to keep his expression innocent and candid. "Well, no— that is, not really. I've heard rumors, of course—"

"I am quite interested in rumors."

"It wouldn't be fair—"

Khokhlov cut him off. "I am judge of fairness in this camp, Mr. Rorvik. Please, we are not barbarians here. Let me give you my assurance that I am here to help people adjust to scientific society, not to punish them for retrograde thinking. If you are hearing rumors, I should be aware of them. If people are spreading tales—gossips, this is correct word?—spreading the gossips without foundation, I should know this, in order to better guide people to correct thinking. Please, do not hesitate to speak completely candidly with me."

Rorvik smiled ingratiatingly, trying to assume the puppy-dog expression of a convert to correct-thinking. "I don't know any specific names."

"I am afraid that you are not being completely open with me, Mr. Rorvik," Khokhlov said, his face expressing deep sorrow mixed with sternness, the expression of a teacher with a willfully disobedient pupil. "Perhaps I have been overly hasty in evaluating your progress toward objective political thought. You are aware, I am sure, that this camp is quite the luxury dacha. You are guests here, not prisoners. In other places food is not quite so plentiful, and discipline is a bit more . . . severe. Please, I beg of you, tell me some names." He smiled. "I do believe that we could . . . work together."

"I'm afraid not, sir."

Khokhlov frowned. "I am not stupid, Mr. Rorvik. Let me point something out to you. I know that there are resistance sympathizers in this camp, and I know something is going on. I can feel it in the air, and I also have my . . . sources. I suspect that you know what is going on. Now, consider. We have been talking for quite the while. Ten minutes? Don't think we haven't been noticed. Now, what are these resistance sympathizers to think, as they watch us talk? Even if you assure them you told me nothing, how can they trust you? Talk to me, and I will see to your safety—I have my means in this camp, I assure you—or else . . ." He shook his head. "It is not me you should be afraid of. You are tagged for being a pigeon whether you talk or not."

Khokhlov was right, he realized. Even though he hadn't joined the resistance, he knew too much. Had there been any way he could have avoided talking to Khokhlov? No; the reeducation counselors were all-powerful within the boundary of the camps. Even the guards feared them, and a prisoner who deliberately refused to talk when asked politely could expect to be denounced, or even shot. But it was the wrong night to be talking to him. He wouldn't survive the night without Khokhlov's protection.

His muscles were knotted up, and he had to force himself to breathe normally. He knew the feeling intimately; it was the feeling of having hostile, invisible eyes watching from the sky, the feeling of being a target for inevitable death.

But just what, really, did he have to live for? If he talked, other people would die. It wasn't fair—he'd never even joined the camp resistance!—but he understood war very well by now. He shook his head slowly. "I'm sorry. I really am."

The muscles in his neck didn't loosen, but he realized that he could breathe again.

"I am, too, Mr. Rorvik." Khokhlov waited for one more moment, then shook his head and strode briskly away, as if he wanted to have nothing more to do with Rorvik, abandoning him to his fate. "I am, too."

Rorvik knew that his one chance was to find Povelli—or somebody, anybody with a line to the resistance—and try to explain. There was a bare possibility that they might take a chance on him, if he went to them immediately, showing he had nothing to hide.

He didn't move.

There was something wrong. He desperately needed to find somewhere to think. There was nowhere; standing here by the barbed wire was as good as anywhere.

He squeezed his eyes tightly shut. Where the hell was he?

In a camp.

Was he?

The memory of the draft was still fresh in his mind. His biceps still ached from the pushups that Driscott had made him do, back when he was still a FNG, what, two years ago?

That was impossible.

He had died. Unambiguously, totally. Shot in the chest, shot in the head, blown to pieces by artillery.

That was impossible, too.

Simulations. That was the key. He remembered that from his civilian days, as the superpowers of Europe and Japan and America jockeyed and maneuvered for position, watching their simulations of what would happen in every possible attack scenario, each waiting until they found one where they'd have the advantage. Much of battle was mathematical, a matter of strategy and tactics, faceless forces fighting other faceless forces.

But in some situations, the people mattered. They would need to know how real troops react in battle before they could believe the computer models. God, Driscott had told him that, right out; Driscott had told him everything, and he had been too dumb to understand.

He opened his eyes, and tried to disbelieve what he saw. There was no camp; no war. When he'd been drafted, there had been no war. How long ago was that? A few days? A month? It was ridiculous to think that the Russians would invade the United States; what would they get out of it? The whole war made no sense, not unless it was a scenario, an elaborate set-up to probe how soldiers would act in wartime.

He even knew the technology; it wasn't that much more sophisticated than what he had used to run his drones, except that the resolution would be higher. *Was* higher.

It looked real. There would be micro-lasers somewhere, rastering the image directly onto his retina. If the resolution was high enough, there would be no possible way to tell the difference between real and simulated. He would be drugged, strapped into a contour-couch somewhere, maybe in Washington? Paralytic drugs certainly, to keep his motions from causing problems, while SQUID pickups read the nerve impulses to his muscles. Maybe hypnotics to make him suggestible, make it easier for him to mistake the simulation for reality.

He pinched himself, then punched his arm as hard as he could. It hurt, but that proved nothing. That could be simulated.

There must be other real people in the simulation, too. Who? Westermaker? Driscott? Who was real, and who simulated? Westermaker, he thought. She had to be real. Somewhere she was still alive. Someday she would go back to her husband, back to her kids. In a few days she would be wondering if he had been real or a simulation. And an incident that had been innocent and decent would turn into a pornographic sideshow for some Washington desk-jockeys.

It took him a moment to realize that if this was true, then somewhere—maybe not even far away—Angela and Lissy were alive too, waiting patiently for him at home, oblivious of the nonexistent war. Not starving to death in a relocation camp, not buried in unmarked graves hidden under mountains of rubble. Alive.

God, now he knew what he had been drafted for. Not to be a real soldier, but to play out simulations, perfect computer simulations of possible battle scenarios. The people he'd fought, the ones he'd fought with, weren't real. They needed to know how he'd hold up under stress, how any average American would hold up. They needed the data to make their computer simulations work. He was fighting this war so that, in real life, no one would ever have to fight a war.

He was a pawn.

But was he a pawn of the Americans? Or the Russians? What if the Russians needed to know the reactions of American soldiers, too? What if they really were planning an invasion?

That was ridiculous.

He started to shake his head, first left, then right, watching for a timelag in the video response. It started making him dizzy, but he refused to stop. "Let me out!" He shook his head harder, faster. The other prisoners stared at him. "Stop the simulation! I quit, I tell you! I'm quitting!"

His head hurt, and the world was no less real. He clenched his teeth and slapped himself on the side of the head, ignoring the pain. Blood started to flow down his cheek on the third or fourth punch, but now he thought he could see something, a blur of black-anodized aluminum, out of focus in front of his eyes, the raster-head of a retinal laser-scanner. He shook his head more violently, left and right, up and down, and he could see it more clearly, with the lenses and sensors that kept it focused on his eyes. It had slipped slightly off to the side, and the reeducation camp was the part out of focus now, two-dimensional, the view from each eye skewed. He tried to pull it off his head, but his hands felt nothing. He shook his head harder. The moment before he passed out, the head-mounted display slipped entirely away, and he could see the room, and the computers, and the figures of three doctors bending over him with expressions of alarmed concern.

8.

The man from the Selective Service thanked Rorvik, reminded him of the penalties for talking to any person at any time about his service experiences, and then shook his hand. Rorvik could see Angela waiting for him at the door. The house looked different; smaller, the paint dingier than he remembered. He'd only been gone a week.

Stop that. If it were a simulation, they would have used photographs of the house; it would be perfect in every detail.

He scanned the bushes aromatically, looking for the glint of sun from drone lenses, wishing he had his IR augmented vision. Then he caught himself, forced his muscles to relax. There was no war, no hiding drones.

The government car drove off, and Lissy darted from behind Angela and scampered out to greet him. He spread his arms to receive her, and she almost knocked him over with her enthusiasm. "Daddy! You're home! I missed you!"

He picked her up and swung her around. She was bigger than he remembered. Could she have grown so much in a week? Her hair was darker, her face thinner and more ordinary than in his memories.

"I missed you too, Tiger-cub," he said.

She looked up at him, growling like a tiger but with a wide smile, and he hugged her. Then he nuzzled his face up under her ponytail, and purred at her as loud as he could. She giggled and purred back.

They couldn't possibly simulate that. He opened his arms. Angela joined them, and he hugged them both at the same time. "I missed you, too, Daddy-cat," Angela whispered.

It was real this time.

He was home.

Real.

SECOND SKIN

Paul J. McAuley

Born in Oxford, England, in 1955, Paul J. McAuley now makes his home in London. He is considered to be one of the best of the new breed of British writers (although a few Australian writers could be fit in under this heading as well) who are producing that sort of revamped, updated, widescreen Space Opera sometimes referred to as "radical hard science fiction," and is a frequent contributor to Interzone, *as well as to markets such as* Amazing, The Magazine of Fantasy and Science Fiction, Asimov's Science Fiction, When the Music's Over, *and elsewhere. His first novel,* Four Hundred Billion Stars, *won the Philip K. Dick Award. His other books include* Of the Fall, Eternal Light *and* Pasquale's Angel, *two collections of his short work,* The King of the Hill and Other Stories *and* The Invisible Country, *and an original anthology co-edited with Kim Newman,* In Dreams. *His acclaimed novel,* Fairyland *won both the Arthur C. Clarke Award and the John W. Campbell Award in 1996. His most recent book is* Child of the River, *the first volume of a major new trilogy of ambitious scope and scale,* Confluence, *set ten million years in the future.*

In the suspenseful and richly inventive story that follows, he takes us on a journey across space to the farthest reaches of the solar system, beneath the frozen surface of the moon Proteus, for a tale that demonstrates that sometimes the most effective warfare is not waged with armies or high-tech weapons, and that sometimes the most dangerous battlefield of all may be the human heart.

The transport, once owned by an outer system cartel and appropriated by Earth's Pacific Community after the Quiet War, ran in a continuous, ever-changing orbit between Saturn, Uranus, and Neptune. It never docked. It mined the solar wind for hydrogen to mix with the nanogram of antimatter that could power it for a century, and once or twice a year, during its intricate gravity-assisted loops between Saturn's moons, maintenance drones attached remoralike to its hull, and fixed whatever its self-repairing systems couldn't handle.

Ben Lo and the six other members of the first trade delegation to Proteus since the war were transferred onto the transport as it looped around Titan, still sleeping in the hibernation pods they'd climbed into in Earth orbit. Sixty days later, they were released from the transport in individual drop capsules of structural diamond, like so many seeds scattered by a pod.

Ben Lo, swaddled in the crash web that took up most of the volume of the drop capsule's little bubble, watched with growing vertigo as the battered face of Proteus drew closer. He had been awakened only a day ago, and was as weak and unsteady as a new-born kitten. The sun was behind the bubble's braking chute. Ahead, Neptune's disc was tipped in star-sprinkled black above the little moon. Neptune was subtly banded with blue and violet, its poles capped with white cloud, its equator streaked with cirrus. Slowly, slowly, Proteus began to eclipse it. The transport had already dwindled to a bright point amongst the bright points of the stars, on its way to spin up around Neptune, loop past Triton, and head on out for the next leg of its continuous voyage, halfway across the solar system to Uranus.

Like many of the moons of the outer planets, Proteus was a ball of ice and rock. Over billions of years, most of the rock had sunk to the core, and the moon's icy, dirty white surface was splotched with a scattering of large impact craters with black interiors, like well-used ash trays, and dissected by large stress fractures, some running halfway round the little globe.

The spy fell toward Proteus in a thin transparent bubble of carbon, wearing a paper suit and a diaper, and trussed up in a cradle of smart cabling like an early Christian martyr. He could barely move a muscle. Invisible laser light poured all around him—the capsule was opaque to the frequency used—gently pushing against the braking sail which had unfolded and spun into a twenty kilometer diameter mirror after the capsule had been released by the transport. Everything was fine.

The capsule said, "Only another twelve hours, Mr. Lo. I

suggest that you sleep. Elfhame's time zone is ten hours behind
Greenwich Mean Time."

Had he been asleep for a moment? Ben Lo blinked and said,
"Jet lag," and laughed.

"I don't understand," the capsule said politely. It didn't need to
be very intelligent. All it had to do was control the altitude of the
braking sail, and keep its passenger amused and reassured until
landing. Then it would be recycled.

Ben Lo didn't bother to try to explain. He was feeling the
same kind of yawning apprehension that must have gripped
ninety-year-old airline passengers at the end of the twentieth
century. A sense of deep dislocation and estrangement. How
strange that I'm here, he thought. And, how did it happen? When
he'd been born, spaceships had been crude, disposable chemical
rockets. The first men on the moon. President Kennedy's
assassination. No, that happened before I was born. For a
moment, his yawning sense of dislocation threatened to swallow
him whole, but then he had it under control and it dwindled to
mere strangeness. It was the treatment, he thought. The treatment
and the hibernation.

Somewhere down there in the white moonscape, in one of the
smaller canyons, was Ben Lo's first wife. But he mustn't think of
that. Not yet. Because if he did . . . no, he couldn't remember.
Something bad, though.

"I can offer a variety of virtualities," the capsule said. Its voice
was a husky contralto. It added, "Certain sexual services are also
available."

"What I'd like is a chateaubriand steak butterfried and
well-grilled over hickory wood, a Caesar salad, and a 1998
Walnut Creek Cabernet Sauvignon."

"I can offer a range of nutritive pastes, and eight flavors of
water, including a balanced electrolyte," the capsule said. A
prissy note seemed to have edged into its voice. It added, "I
would recommend that you restrict intake of solids and fluids
until after landing."

Ben Lo sighed. He had already had his skin scrubbed and
repopulated with strains of bacteria and yeast native to the
Protean ecosystem, and his GI tract had been reamed out and

packed with a neutral gel containing a benign strain of *E. coli*. He said, "Give me an inflight movie."

"I would recommend virtualities," the capsule said. "I have a wide selection."

Despite the capsule's minuscule intelligence, it had a greater memory capacity than all the personal computers on Earth at the end of the millennium. Ben Lo had downloaded his own archives into it.

"*Wings of Desire,*" he said.

"But it's in black and white! And flat. And only two senses—"

"There's color later on. It has a particular relevance to me, I think. Once upon a time, capsule, there was a man who was very old, and became young again, and found that he'd lost himself. Run the movie, and you'll understand a little bit about me."

The moon, Neptune, the stars, fell into a single point of light. The light went out. The film began.

Falling through a cone of laser light, the man and the capsule watched how an angel became a human being, out of love.

The capsule skimmed the moon's dirty-white surface and shed the last of its relative velocity in the inertia buffers of the target zone, leaving its braking sail to collapse across kilometers of moonscape. It was picked up by a striding tripod that looked like a prop from *The War of the Worlds*, and carried down a steeply sloping tunnel through triple airlocks into something like the ER room of a hospital. With the other members of the trade delegation, Ben Lo, numbed by neural blocks, was decanted, stripped, washed, and dressed in fresh paper clothes.

Somewhere in the press of nurses and technicians he thought he glimpsed someone he knew, or thought he knew. A woman, her familiar face grown old, eyes faded blue in a face wrinkled as a turtle's. . . . But then he was lifted onto a gurney and wheeled away.

Waking, he had problems with remembering who he was. He knew he was nowhere on Earth. A universally impersonal hotel room, but he was virtually in free fall. Some moon, then. But what role was he playing?

He got up, moving carefully in the fractional gravity, and pulled aside the floor-to-ceiling drapes. It was night, and across a kilometer of black air was a steep dark mountainside or perhaps a vast building, with lights wound at its base, shimmering on a river down there. . . .

Proteus. Neptune. The trade delegation. And the thing he couldn't think about, which was fractionally nearer the surface now, like a word at the back of his tongue. He could feel it, but he couldn't shape it. Not yet.

He stripped in the small, brightly lit sphere of the bathroom and turned the walls to mirrors and looked at himself. He was too young to be who he thought he was. No, that was the treatment, of course. His third. Then why was his skin this color? He hadn't bothered to tint it for . . . how long?

That sci-fi version of *Othello*, a century and a half ago, when he'd been a movie star. He remembered the movie vividly, although not the making of it. But that was the color he was now, his skin a rich dark mahogany, gleaming as if oiled in the lights, his hair a cap of tight black curls.

He slept again, and dreamed of his childhood home. San Francisco. Sailboats scattered across the blue bay. He'd had a little boat, a Laser. The cold salt smell of the sea. The pinnacles of the rust-red bridge looming out of banks of fog, and the fog horn booming mournfully. Cabbage leaves in the gutters of Spring Street. The crowds swirling under the crimson and gold neon lights of the trinket shops of Grant Avenue, and the intersection of Grant and California tingling with trolley car bells.

He remembered everything as if he had just seen it in a movie. Nonassociational aphasia. It was a side effect of the treatment he'd just had. He'd been warned about it, but it was still unsettling. The woman he was here to . . . Avernus. Her name now. But when they had been married, a hundred and sixty-odd years ago, she had been called Barbara Reiner. He tried to remember the taste of her mouth, the texture of her skin, and could not.

The next transport would not swing by Proteus for a hundred and seventy days, so there was no hurry to begin the formal business of the trade delegation. For a while, its members were treated as favored tourists, in a place that had no tourist industry at all.

The sinuous rill canyon which housed Elfhame had been burned to an even depth of a kilometer, sealed under a construction diamond roof, and pressurized to 750 millibars with a nitrox mix enriched with 1 percent carbon dioxide to stimulate plant growth. The canyon ran for fifty kilometers through a basaltic surface extrusion, possibly the remnant of the giant impact that had resurfaced the farside hemisphere of the moon a billion years ago, or the result of vulcanism caused by thermal drag when the satellite had been captured by Neptune.

The sides of the canyon were raked to form a deep vee in profile, with a long narrow lake lying at the bottom like a black ribbon, dusted with a scattering of pink and white coral keys. The Elfhamers called it the Skagerrak. The sides of the canyon were steeply terraced, with narrow vegetable gardens, rice paddies, and farms on the higher levels, close to the lamps that, strung from the diamond roof, gave an insolation equivalent to that of the Martian surface. Farther down, amongst pocket parks and linear strips of designer wilderness, houses clung to the steep slopes like soap bubbles, or stood on platforms or bluffs, all with panoramic views of the lake at the bottom and screened from their neighbors by soaring ginkgoes, cypress, palmettos, bamboo (which grew to fifty meters in the microgravity), and dragon's blood trees. All the houses were large and individually designed; Elfhamers went in for extended families. At the lowest levels were the government buildings, commercial malls and parks, the university and hospital, and the single hotel, which bore all the marks of having been recently constructed for the trade delegation. And then there was the lake, the Skagerrak, with its freshwater corals and teeming fish, and slow, ten-meter-high waves. The single, crescent-shaped beach of black sand at what Elfhamers called the North End was very steeply raked, and constantly renewed; the surfing was fabulous.

There was no real transportation system except for a single tube train line that shuttled along the west side, and moving lines with T-bar seats, like ski lifts, that made silver lines along the steep terrace slopes. Mostly, people bounded around in huge kangaroo leaps, or flew using startlingly small wings of diamond foil or little hand-held airscrews—the gravity was so low, 0.007g, that human flight was ridiculously easy. Children rode airboards or simply dived from terrace to terrace, which strictly speaking was illegal, but even adults did it sometimes, and it seemed to be one of those laws to which no one paid much attention unless someone got hurt. It *was* possible to break a bone if you jumped from the top of a canyon and managed to land on one of the lakeside terraces, but you'd have to work at it. Some of the kids did—the latest craze was terrace bouncing, in which half a dozen screaming youngsters tried to find out how quickly they could get from top to bottom with the fewest touchdown points.

The entire place, with its controlled, indoor weather, its bland affluent sheen, and its universal cleanliness, was ridiculously vulnerable. It reminded Ben Lo of nothing so much as an old-fashioned shopping mall, the one at Santa Monica, for instance. He'd had a bit part in a movie made in that mall, somewhere near the start of his career. He was still having trouble with his memory. He could remember every movie he'd made, but couldn't remember *making* any one of them.

He asked his guide if it was possible to get to the real surface. She was taken aback by the request, then suggested that he could access a mobot using the point-of-presence facility of his hotel room.

"Several hundred were released fifty years ago, and some of them are still running, I suppose. Really, there is nothing up there but some industrial units."

"I guess Avernus has her labs on the surface."

Instantly, the spy was on the alert, suppressing a thrill of panic.

His guide was a very tall, thin, pale girl called Marla. Most Elfhamers were descended from Nordic stock, and Marla had the high cheekbones, blue eyes, blond hair, and open and candid manner of her counterparts on Earth. Like most Elfhamers, she was tanned and athletically lithe, and wore a distractingly small amount of fabric: tight shorts, a band of material across her small breasts, plastic sandals, a communications bracelet.

At the mention of Avernus, Marla's eyebrows dented over her slim, straight nose. She said, "I would suppose so, yah, but there's nothing interesting to see. The program, it is reaching the end of its natural life, you see. The surface is not interesting, and it is dangerous. The cold and the vacuum, and still the risk of micrometeorites. Better to live inside."

Like worms in an apple, the spy thought. The girl was soft and foolish, very young and very naïve. It was only natural that a member of the trade delegation would be interested in Elfhame's most famous citizen. She wouldn't think anything of this.

Ben Lo blinked and said, "Well, yes, but I've never been there. It would be something, for someone of my age to set foot on the surface of a moon of Neptune. I was born two years before the first landing on Earth's moon, you know. Have you ever been up there?"

Marla's teeth were even and pearly white, and when she smiled, as she did now, she seemed to have altogether too many. "By point-of-presence, of course. It is part of our education. It is fine enough in its own way, but the surface is not our home, you understand."

They were sitting on the terrace of a café that angled out over the lake. Resin tables and chairs painted white, clipped bay trees in big white pots, terra-cotta tiles, slightly sticky underfoot, like all the floor coverings in Elfhame. Bulbs of schnapps cooled in an ice bucket.

Ben Lo tipped his chair back and looked up at the narrow strip of black sky and its strings of brilliant lamps that hung high above the steep terraces on the far side of the lake. He said, "You can't see the stars. You can't even see Neptune."

"Well, we *are* on the farside," Marla said, reasonably. "But by point-of-presence mobot I have seen it, several times. I have been on Earth the same way, and Mars, but those were fixed, because of the single lag."

"Yes, but you might as well look at a picture!"

Marla laughed. "Oh, yah. Of course. I forget that you were once a capitalist—" the way she said it, he might have been a dodo, or a dolphin—"from the United States of the Americas, as it was called then. That is why you put such trust in what you call *real*. But really, it is not such a big difference. You put on a mask, or you put on a pressure suit. It is all barriers to experience. And what is to see? Dusty ice, and the same black sky as home, but with more and weaker lamps. We do not need the surface."

Ben Lo didn't press the point. His guide was perfectly

charming, if earnest and humorless, and brightly but brainlessly enthusiastic for the party line, like a cadre from one of the supernats. She was transparently a government spy, and was recording everything—she had shown him the little button camera and asked his permission.

"Such a historical event this is, Mr. Lo, that we wish to make a permanent record of it. You will I hope not mind?"

So now Ben Lo changed the subject, and asked why there were no sailboats on the lake, and then had to explain to Marla what a sailboat was.

Her smile was brilliant when she finally understood. "Oh yah, there are some I think who use such boards on the water, like surfing boards with sails."

"Sailboards, sure."

"The waves are very high, so it is not easy a sport. Not many are allowed, besides, because of the film."

It turned out that there was a monomolecular film across the whole lake, to stop great gobs of it floating off into the lakeside terraces.

A gong beat softly in the air. Marla looked at her watch. It was tattooed on her slim, tanned wrist. "Now it will rain soon. We should go inside, I think. I can show you the library this afternoon. There are several real books in it that one of our first citizens brought all the way from Earth."

When he was not sight-seeing or attending coordination meetings with the others in the trade delegation (he knew none of them well, and they were all so much younger than him, and as bright and enthusiastic as Marla), he spent a lot of time in the library. He told Marla that he was gathering background information that would help finesse the target packages of economic exchange, and she said that it was good, this was an open society, they had nothing to hide. Of course, he couldn't use his own archive, which was under bonded quarantine, but he was happy enough typing away at one of the library terminals for hours on end, and after a while, Marla left him to it. He also made use of various point-of-presence mobots to explore the surface, especially around Elfhame's roof.

And then there were the diplomatic functions to attend: a party in the prime minister's house, a monstrous construction of pine logs and steeply pitched roofs of wooden shingles cantilevered above the lake; a reception in the assembly room of the parliament, the Riksdag; others at the university and the Supreme Court. Ben Lo started to get a permanent crick in his neck from looking up at the faces of his etiolated hosts while making conversation.

At one, held in the humid, rarefied atmosphere of the research greenhouses near the top of the East Wall of Elfhame, Ben Lo glimpsed Avernus again. His heart lifted strangely, and the spy broke off from the one sided conversation with an earnest hydroponicist and pushed through the throng toward his target, the floor sucking at his sandals with each step.

The old woman was surrounded by a gaggle of young giants, set apart from the rest of the party. The spy was aware of people watching when he took Avernus's hand, something that caused a murmur of unrest amongst her companions.

"An old custom, dears," Avernus told them. "We predate most of the plagues that made such gestures taboo, even after the plagues were defeated. Ben, dear, what a surprise. I had hoped never to see you again. Your employers have a strange sense of humor."

A young man with big, red-framed data glasses said, "You know each other?"

"We lived in the same city," Avernus said, "many years ago." She had brushed her vigorous grey hair back from her forehead. The wine-dark velvet wrap did not flatter her skinny old woman's body. She said to Ben, "You look so young."

"My third treatment," he confessed.

Avernus said, "It was once said that in American lives there was no second act—but biotech has given almost everyone who can afford it a second act, and for some a third one, too. But what to *do* in them? One simply can't pretend to be young again—one is too aware of death, and has too much at stake, too much invested in *self*, to risk being young."

"There's no longer any America," Ben Lo said. "Perhaps that helps."

"To be without loyalty," the old woman said, "except to one's own continuity."

The spy winced, but did not show it.

The old woman took his elbow. Her grip was surprisingly strong. "Pretend to be interested, dear," she said. "We are having a delightful conversation in this delightful party. Smile. That's better!"

Her companions laughed uneasily at this. Avernus said quietly to Ben, "You must visit me."

"I have an escort."

"Of course you do. I'm sure someone as resourceful as you will think of something. Ah, this must be your guide. What a tall girl!"

Avernus turned away, and her companions closed around her, turning their long bare backs on the Earthman.

Ben Lo asked Marla what Avernus was doing there. He was dizzy with the contrast between what his wife had been, and what she had become. He could hardly remember what they had talked about. Meet. They had to meet. They would meet.

It was beginning.

Marla said, "It is a politeness to her. Really, she should not have come, and we are glad she is leaving early. You do not worry about her, Mr. L. She is a sideline. We look inward, we reject the insane plans of the previous administration. Would you like to see the new oil-rich strains of *Chlorella* we use?"

Ben Lo smiled diplomatically. "It would be very interesting."

There had been a change of government, after the war. It had been less violent and more serious than a revolution, more like a change of climate, or of religion. Before the Quiet War (that was what it was called on Earth. for although tens of thousands had died in the war, none had died on *Earth*), Proteus had been loosely allied with, but not committed to, an amorphous group which wanted to exploit the outer reaches of the solar system, beyond Plato's orbit; after the war, Proteus dropped its expansionist plans and sought to reestablish links with the trading communities of Earth.

Avernus had been on the losing side of the change in political climate. Brought in by the previous regime because of her skills in gengeneering vacuum organisms, she found herself sidelined and ostracized, her research group disbanded and replaced by government cadres, funds for her research suddenly diverted to new projects. But her contract bound her to Proteus for the next ten years, and the new government refused to release her. She had developed several important new dendrimers, light-harvesting molecules used in artificial photosynthesis, and established several potentially valuable genelines, including a novel form of photosynthesis based on a sulphur-spring *Chloroflexus* bacterium. The government wanted to license them, but to do that it had to keep Avernus under contract, even if it would not allow her to work.

Avernus wanted to escape, and Ben Lo was there to help her. The Pacific Community had plenty of uses for vacuum organisms—there was the whole of the Moon to use as a garden, to begin with—and was prepared to overlook Avernus's political stance in exchange for her expertise and her knowledge.

He was beginning to remember more and more, but there was still so much he didn't know. He supposed that the knowledge had been buried, and would flower in due course. He tried not to worry about it.

Meanwhile, the meetings of the trade delegation and Elfhame's industrial executive finally began. Ben Lo spent most of the next ten days in a closed room dickering with Parliamentary speakers on the Trade Committee over marginal rates for exotic organics. When the meetings were finally over, he slept for three hours and then, still logy from lack of sleep but filled with excess energy, went body surfing at the black beach at the North End. It was the first time he had managed to evade Marla. She had been as exhausted as he had been by the rounds of negotiations, and he had promised that he would sleep all day so that she could get some rest.

The surf was tremendous, huge smooth slow glassy swells falling from thirty meters to batter the soft, sugary black sand with giant's paws. The air was full of spinning globs of water, and so hazed with spray, like a rain of foamy flowers, that it was necessary to wear a filtermask. It was what the whole lake would be like, without its monomolecular membrane.

Ben Lo had thought he would still have an aptitude for body surfing, because he'd done so much of it when he had been living in Los Angeles, before his movie career really took off. But he

was as helpless as a kitten in the swells, his boogie board turning
turtle as often as not and twice he was caught in the undertow.
The second time, a pale naked giantess got an arm around his
chest and hauled him up onto dry sand.

After he hawked up a couple of lungs-full of fresh water, he
managed to gasp his thanks. The woman smiled. She had black
hair in a bristle cut, and startlingly green eyes. She was very tall
and very thin, and completely naked. She said, "At last you are
away from that revisionist bitch."

Ben Lo sat up, abruptly conscious, in the presence of this
young naked giantess, of his own nakedness. "Ah. You are one
of Avernus's—"

The woman walked away with her boogie board under her
arm, pale buttocks flexing. The spy unclipped the ankle line that
tethered him to his rented board, bounded up the beach in two
leaps, pulled on his shorts, and followed.

Sometime later, he was standing in the middle of a vast red-lit
room at blood heat and what felt like a hundred percent
humidity. Racks of large-leaved plants receded into infinity;
those nearest him towered high above, forming a living green
wall. His arm stung, and the tall young woman, naked under a
green gown open down the front, but masked and wearing
disposable gloves, deftly caught the glob of expressed blood—
his blood—in a capillary straw, took a disc of skin from his
forearm with a spring-loaded punch, sprayed the wound with
sealant and went off with her samples.

A necessary precaution, the old woman said, Avernus. He
remembered now. Or at least could picture it. Taking a ski lift all
the way to the top. Through a tunnel lined with tall plastic bags
in which green *Chlorella* cultures bubbled under lights strobing
in fifty millisecond pulses. Another attack of memory loss—
they seemed to be increasing in frequency! Stress, he told
himself.

"Of all the people I could identify," Avernus said, "they had to
send *you.*"

"Ask me anything," Ben Lo said, although he wasn't sure that
he recalled very much of their brief marriage.

"I mean identify genetically. We exchanged strands of hair in amber, do you remember? I kept mine. It was mounted in a ring."

"I didn't think that you were sentimental."

"It was my idea, and I did it with all my husbands. It reminded me of what I once was."

"My wife."

"An idiot."

"I must get back to the hotel soon. If they find out I've been wandering around without my escort, they'll start to suspect."

"Good. Let them worry. What can they do? Arrest me? Arrest you?"

"I have diplomatic immunity."

Avernus laughed. "Ben, Ben, you always were so status-conscious. That's why I left. I was just another thing you'd collected. A trophy, like your Porsche, or your Picasso."

He didn't remember.

"It wasn't a very good Picasso. One of his fakes—do you know that story?"

"I suppose I sold it."

The young woman in the green gown came back. "A positive match," she said. "Probability of a negative identity point oh oh one or less. But he is doped up with immunosuppressants and testosterone.

"The treatment," the spy said glibly. "Is this where you do your research?"

"Of course not. They certainly would notice if you turned up there. This is one of the pharm farms. They grow tobacco here, with human genes inserted to make various immunoglobulins. They took away my people, Ben, and replaced them with spies. Ludmilla is one of my original team. They put her to drilling new agricultural tunnels."

"We are alone here," Ludmilla said.

"Or you would have made your own arrangements."

"I hate being dependent on people. Especially from Earth, if you'll forgive me. And especially you. Are the others in your trade delegation . . . ?"

"Just a cover," the spy said. "They know nothing. They are looking forward to your arrival in Tycho. The laboratory is ready to be fitted out to your specifications."

"I swore I'd never go back, but they are fools here. They stand on the edge of greatness, the next big push, and they turn their backs on it and burrow into the ice like maggots."

The spy took her hands in his. Her skin was loose on her bones, and dry and cold despite the humid heat of the hydroponic greenhouse. He said, "Are you ready? Truly ready?"

She did not pull away. "I have said so. I will submit to any test, if it makes your masters happy. Ben, you are exactly as I remember you. It is very strange."

"The treatments are very good now. You must use one."

"Don't think I haven't, although not as radical as yours. I like to show my age. You could shrivel up like a Struldbrugg, and I don't have to worry about *that*, at least. That skin color, though. Is it a fashion?"

"I was Othello, once. Don't you like it?" Under the red lights his skin gleamed with an ebony luster.

"I always thought you'd make a good Iago, if only you had been clever enough. I asked for someone I knew, and they sent you. It almost makes me want to distrust them."

"We were young, then." He was trying to remember, searching her face. Well, it was two hundred years ago. Still, he felt as if he trembled at a great brink, and a tremendous feeling of nostalgia for what he could not remember swept through him. Tears grew like big lenses over his eyes and he brushed them into the air and apologized.

"I am here to do a job," he said, and said it as much for his benefit as hers.

Avernus said, "Be honest, Ben. You hardly remember anything."

"Well, it *was* a long time ago." But he did not feel relieved at this admission. The past was gone. No more than pictures, no longer a part of him.

Avernus said, "When we got married, I was in love, and a fool. It was in the Wayfarer's Chapel, do you remember? Hot and dry, with a Santa Ana blowing, and Channel Five's news helicopter hovering overhead. You were already famous, and two years later you were so famous I no longer recognized you."

They talked a little while about his career. The acting, the successful terms as state senator, the unsuccessful term as

congressman, the fortune he had made in land deals after the
partition of the USA, his semi-retirement in the upper house of
the Pacific Community parliament. It was a little like an
interrogation, but he didn't mind it. At least he knew *this* story
well.

The tall young woman, Ludmilla, took him back to the hotel.
It seemed natural that she should stay for a drink, and then that
they should make love, with a languor and then an urgency that
surprised him, although he had been told that restoration of his
testosterone levels would sometimes cause emotional or physical
cruxes that would require resolution. Ben Lo had made love in
microgravity many times, but never before with someone who
had been born to it. Afterward, Ludmilla rose up from the bed
and moved gracefully about the room, dipping and turning as she
pulled on her scanty clothes.

"I will see you again," she said, and then she was gone.

The negotiations resumed, a punishing schedule taking up at
least twelve hours a day. And there were the briefings and
summary sessions with the other delegates, as well as the other
work the spy had to attend to when Marla thought he was asleep.
Fortunately, he had a kink that allowed him to build up sleep
debt and get by on an hour a night. He'd sleep long when this
was done, all the way back to Earth with his prize. Then at last
it was all in place, and he only had to wait.

Another reception, this time in the little zoo halfway up the
West Side. The Elfhamers were running out of novel places to
entertain the delegates. Most of the animals looked vaguely
unhappy in the microgravity and none were very large. Bush-
babies, armadillos, and mice; a pair of hippopotami no larger
than domestic cats; a knee-high pink elephant with some kind of
skin problem behind its disproportionately large ears.

Ludmilla brushed past Ben Lo as he came out of the rest room
and said, "When can she go?"

"Tonight," the spy said.

Everything had been ready for fourteen days now. He went to
find something to do now that he was committed to action.

Marla was feeding peanuts to the dwarf elephant. Ben Lo

said, "Aren't you worried that the animals might escape? You wouldn't want mice running around Shangri-la."

"They all have a kink in their metabolism. An artificial amino acid they need. That girl you talked with was one of Avernus's assistants. She should not be here."

"She propositioned me." Marla said nothing. He said, "There are no side deals. If someone wants anything, they have to bring it to the table through the proper channels."

"You are an oddity here, it is true. Too much muscles. Many women would sleep with you, out of curiosity."

"But *you* have never asked, Marla. I'm ashamed." He said it playfully, but he saw that Marla suspected something. It didn't matter. Everything was in place.

They came for him that night, but he was awake and dressed, counting off the minutes until his little bundle of surprises started to unpack itself. There were two of them, armed with tasers and sticky foam canisters. The spy blinded them with homemade capsicum spray (he'd stolen chilli pods from one of the hydroponic farms and suspended a water extract in a perfume spray) and killed them as they blundered about, screaming and pawing at their eyes. One of them was Marla, another a well-muscled policeman who must have spent a good portion of each day in a centrifuge gym. The spy disabled the sprinkler system, set fire to his room, kicked out the window, and ran.

There were more police waiting outside the main entrance of the hotel. The spy ran right over the edge of the terrace and landed two hundred meters down amongst blue pines grown into bubbles of soft needles in the microgravity. Above, the fire touched off the homemade plastic explosive, and a fan of burning debris shot out above the spy's head, seeming to hover in the black air for a long time before beginning to flutter down toward the Skagerrak. Briefly, he wondered if any of the delegation had survived. It didn't matter. The young, enthusiastic, and naive delegates had always been expendable.

Half the lights were out in Elfhame, and all of the transportation systems, the phone system was crashing and resetting every five minutes, and the braking lasers were sending twenty-millisecond pulses to a narrow wedge of the sky. It was a dumb bug, only a thousand lines long. The spy had laboriously typed it from memory into the library system, which connected with everything else. It wouldn't take long to trace, but by then, other things would start happening.

The spy waited in the cover of the bushy pine trees. One of his teeth was capped and he pulled it out and unraveled the length of monomolecular diamond wire coiled inside.

In the distance, people called to each other over a backdrop of ringing bells and sirens and klaxons. Flashlights flickered in the darkness on the far side of the Skagerrak's black gulf; on the terrace above the spy's hiding place, the police seemed to have brought the fire in the hotel under control. Then the branches of the pines started to doff as a wind came up; the bug had reached the air conditioning. In the darkness below, waves grew higher on the Skagerrak, sloshing and crashing together, as the wind drove waves toward the beach at the North End and reflected waves clashed with those coming onshore. The monomolecular film over the lake's surface was not infinitely strong. The wind began to tear spray from the tops of the towering waves, and filled the lower level of the canyon with flying foam flowers. Soon the waves would grow so tall that they'd spill over the lower levels.

The spy counted out ten minutes, and then started to bound up the terraces, putting all his strength into his thigh and back muscles. Most of the setbacks between each terrace were no more than thirty meters high; for someone with muscles accustomed to one gee, it was easy enough to scale them with a single jump in the microgravity, even from a standing start.

He was halfway there when the zoo's elephant charged past him in the windy semidarkness. Its trunk was raised above its head and it trumpeted a single despairing cry as it ran over the edge of the narrow terrace. Its momentum carried it a long way out into the air before it began to fall, outsized ears flapping as if trying to lift it. Higher up, the plastic explosive charges the spy had made from sugar, gelatin, and lubricating grease blew out hectares of plastic sheeting and structural frames from the long greenhouses.

The spy's legs were like wood when he reached the high agricultural regions; his heart was pounding and his lungs were burning as he tried to strain oxygen from the thin air. He grabbed a fire extinguisher and mingled with panicked staff, ricocheting down long corridors and bounding across windblown fields of crops edged by shattered glass walls and lit by stuttering red emergency lighting. He was only challenged once, and he struck the woman with the butt end of the fire extinguisher and ran on without bothering to check if she was dead or not.

Marla had shown him the place where they stored genetic material on one of her endless tours. Everything was kept in liquid nitrogen, and there was a wide selection of dewar flasks. He chose one about the size of a human head, filled it, and clamped on the lid.

Then through a set of double pressure doors, banging the switch that closed them behind him, setting down the flask and dropping the coil of diamond wire beside it, stepping into a dressing frame, and finally pausing, breathing hard, dry-mouthed and suddenly trembling, as the vacuum suit was assembled around him. As the gold-filmed bubble was lowered over his head and clamped to the neck seal, Ben Lo started, as if waking. Something was terribly wrong. What was he doing here?

Dry air hissed around his face; headup displays stuttered and scrolled down. The spy walked out of the frame, stowed the diamond wire in one of the suit's utility pockets, picked up the flask of liquid nitrogen, and started the airlock cycle, ignoring the computer's contralto as it recited a series of safety precautions while the room revolved, and opened on a flood of sunlight.

The spy came out at the top of the South End of Elfhame. The canyon stretched away to the north, its construction-diamond roof like black sheet-ice: a long, narrow lake of ice curving away downhill, it seemed, between odd, rounded hills like half-buried snowballs, their sides spattered with perfect round craters. He bounded around the tangle of pipes and fins of some kind of distillery or cracking plant, and saw the line of the railway arrowing away across a glaring white plain toward an horizon as close as the top of a hill.

The railway was a single rail hung from smart A-frames whose carbon fiber legs compensated for movements in the icy surface. Thirteen hundred kilometers long, it described a complete circle around the little moon from pole to pole, part of the infrastructure left over from Elfhame's expansionist phase, when it was planned to string sibling settlements all the way around the moon.

The spy kangaroo-hopped along the sunward side of the railway, heading south toward the rendezvous point they had agreed upon. In five minutes, the canyon and its associated domes and industrial plant had disappeared beneath the horizon behind him. The ice was rippled and cracked and blistered, and crunched under the cleats of his boots at each touchdown.

"That was some diversion," a voice said over the open channel. "I hope no one was killed."

"Just an elephant, I think. Although if it landed in the lake, it might have survived." He wasn't about to tell Avernus about Marla and the policeman.

The spy stopped in the shadow of a carbon-fiber pillar, and scanned the icy terrain ahead of him. The point-of-presence mobots hadn't been allowed into this area. The ice curved away to the east and south like a warped checkerboard. There was a criss-cross pattern of ridges that marked out regular squares about two hundred meters on each side, and each square was a different color. Vacuum organisms. He'd reached the experimental plots.

Avernus said over the open channel, "I can't see the pickup."

He started along the line again. At the top of his leap, he said, "I've already signaled to the transport using the braking lasers. It'll be here in less than an hour. We're a little ahead of schedule."

The transport was a small gig with a brute of a motor taking up most of its hull, leaving room for only a single hibernation pod and a small storage compartment. If everything went according to plan, that was all he would need.

He came down and leaped again, and then he saw her on the far side of the curved checkerboard of the experimental plots, a tiny figure in a transparent vacuum suit sitting on a slope of black ice at what looked like the edge of the world. He bounded across the fields toward her.

The ridges were only a meter high and a couple of meters across, dirty water and methane ice fused smooth as glass. It was

easy to leap over each of them—the gravity was so light that the
spy could probably get into orbit if he wasn't careful. Each field
held a different growth. A corrugated grey mold that gave like
rubber under his boots. Flexible spikes the color of dried blood,
all different heights and thicknesses, but none higher than his
knees. More grey stuff, this time mounded in discrete blisters
each several meters from its nearest neighbors, with fat grey
ropes running beneath the ice. Irregular stacks of what looked
like black plates that gave way, halfway across the field, to a
blanket of black stuff like cracked tar.

The figure had turned to watch him, its helmet a gold bubble
that refracted the rays of the tiny, intensely bright star of the sun.
As the spy made the final bound across the last of the experimental plots—more of the black stuff, like a huge wrinkled
vinyl blanket dissected by deep wandering cracks—Avernus
said in his ear, "You should have kept to the boundary walls."

"It doesn't matter now."

"Ah, but I think you'll find it does."

Avernus was sitting in her pressure suit on top of a ridge of
upturned strata at the rim of a huge crater. Her suit was
transparent, after the fashion of the losing side of the Quiet War.
It was intended to minimize the barrier between the human and
the vacuum environments. She might as well have flown a flag
declaring her allegiance to the outer alliance. Behind her, the
crater stretched away south and west, and the railway ran right
out above its dark floor on pillars that doubled and tripled in
height as they stepped away down the inner slope. The crater was
so large that its far side was hidden beyond the little moon's
curvature. The black stuff had overgrown the ridge, and flowed
down into the crater. Avernus was sitting in the only clear spot.

She said, "This is my most successful strain. You can see how
vigorous it is. You didn't get that suit from my lab, did you? I
suggest you keep moving around. This stuff is thixotropic in the
presence of foreign bodies, like smart paint. It spreads out,
flowing under pressure, over the neighboring organisms, but
doesn't overgrow itself."

The spy looked down, and saw that the big cleated boots of his
pressure suit had already sunken to the ankles in the black stuff.
He lifted one, then the other; it was like walking in tar. He took

a step toward her, and the ground collapsed beneath his boots and he was suddenly up to his knees in black stuff.

"My suit," Avernus said, "is coated with the protein by which the strain recognizes its own self. You could say I'm like a virus, fooling the immune system. I dug a trench, and that's what you stepped into. Where is the transport?"

"On its way, but you don't have to worry about it," the spy said, as he struggled to free himself. "This silly little trap won't hold me for long."

Avernus stepped back. She was four meters away, and the black stuff was thigh deep around the spy now, sluggishly flowing upward. The spy flipped the catches on the flask and tipped liquid nitrogen over the stuff. The nitrogen boiled up in a cloud of dense vapor and evaporated. It had made no difference at all to the stuff's integrity.

A point of light began to grow brighter above the close horizon of the moon, moving swiftly aslant the field of stars.

"It gets brittle at close to absolute zero," Avernus said, " but only after several dozen hours." She turned, and added, "There's the transport."

The spy snarled at her. He was up to his waist, and had to fold his arms across his chest, or else they would be caught fast.

Avernus said, "You never were Ben Lo, were you? Or at any rate no more than a poor copy. The original is back on Earth, alive or dead. If he's alive, no doubt he'll claim that this is all a trick of the outer alliance against the Elfhamers and their new allies, the Pacific Community."

He said, "There's still time, Barbara. We can do this together."

The woman in the transparent pressure suit turned back to look at him. Sun flared on her bubble helmet. "Ben, poor Ben. I'll call you that for the sake of convenience. Do you know what happened to you? Someone used you. That body isn't even yours. It isn't anyone's. Oh, it looks like you, and I suppose the altered skin color disguises the rougher edges of the plastic surgery. The skin matches your genotype, and so does the blood, but the skin was cloned from your original, and the blood must come from marrow implants. No wonder there's so much immunosuppressant in your system. If we had just trusted your skin and blood, we would not have known. But your sperm—it was all female. Not a single Y chromosome. I think you're probably haploid, a construct from an unfertilized blastula. You're not even male, except somatically—you're swamped with testosterone, probably have been since gastrulation. You're a *weapon*, Ben. They used things like you as assassins in the Quiet War."

He was in a pressure suit, with dry air blowing around his head and headup displays blinking at the bottom of the clear helmet. A black landscape, and stars high above, with something bright pulsing, growing closer. A spaceship! That was important, but he couldn't remember why. He tried to move, and discovered that he was trapped in something like tar that came to his waist. He could feel it clamping around his legs, a terrible pressure that was compromising the heat exchange system of his suit. His legs were freezing cold, but his body was hot, and sweat prickled across his skin, collecting in the folds of the suit's undergarment.

"Don't move," a woman's voice said. "It's like quicksand. It flows under pressure. You'll last a little longer if you keep still. Struggling only makes it more liquid."

Barbara. No, she called herself Avernus now. He had the strangest feeling that someone else was there, too, just out of sight. He tried to look around, but it was terribly hard in the half-buried suit. He had been kidnapped. It was the only expla-nation. He remembered running from the burning hotel. . . . He was suddenly certain that the other members of the trade delegation were dead, and cried out, "Help me!"

Avernus squatted in front of him, moving carefully and slowly in her transparent pressure suit. He could just see the outline of her face through the gold film of her helmet's visor. "There are two personalities in there, I think. The dominant one let you back, Ben, so that you would plead with me. But don't plead, Ben. I don't want my last memory of you to be so undignified, and anyway, I won't listen. I won't deny you've been a great help. Elfhame always was a soft target, and you punched just the right buttons, and then you kindly provided the means of getting where I want to go. They'll think I was kidnapped." Avernus turned and pointed up at the sky. "Can you see? That's your transport. Ludmilla is going to reprogram it."

"Take me with you, Barbara."

"Oh, Ben, Ben. But I'm not going to Earth. I considered it, but when they sent you, I knew that there was something wrong. I'm going *out*, Ben. Further out. Beyond Pluto, in the Kuiper Disk, where there are more than fifty thousand objects with a diameter of more than a hundred kilometers, and a billion comet nuclei ten kilometers or so across. And then there's the Oort Cloud, and its billions of comets. The fringes of *that* mingle with the fringes of Alpha Centauri's cometary cloud. Life spreads. That's its one rule. In ten thousand years, my children will reach Alpha Centauri, not by starship, but simply through expansion of their territory."

"That's the way you used to talk when we were married. All that sci-fi you used to read!"

"You don't remember it, Ben. Not really. It was fed to you. All my old interviews, my books and articles, all your old movies. They did a quick construction job, and just when you started to find out about it, the other one took over."

"I don't think I'm quite myself. I don't understand what's happening, but perhaps it is something to do with the treatment I had. I told you about that."

"Hush, dear. There was no treatment. That was when they fixed you in the brain of this empty vessel."

She was too close, and she had half-turned to watch the moving point of light grow brighter. He wanted to warn her, but something clamped his lips and he almost swallowed his tongue. He watched as his left hand stealthily unfastened a utility pocket and pulled out a length of glittering wire fine as a spider-thread. Monomolecular diamond. Serrated along its length, except for five centimeters at each end, it could easily cut through pressure suit material and flesh and bone.

He knew then. He knew what he was.

The woman looked at him and said sharply, "What are you doing, Ben?"

And for that moment, he was called back, and he made a fist around the thread and plunged it into the black stuff. The spy screamed and reached behind his helmet and dumped all oxygen from his main pack. It hissed for a long time, but the stuff gripping his legs and waist held firm.

"It isn't an anaerobe," Avernus said. She hadn't moved. "It is a vacuum organism. A little oxygen won't hurt it."

Ben Lo found that he could speak. He said, "He wanted to cut off your head."

"I wondered why you were carrying that flask of liquid nitrogen. You were going to take my head back with you—and what? Use a bush robot to strip my brain neuron by neuron and read my memories into a computer? How convenient to have a genius captive in a bottle!"

"It's me, Barbara. I couldn't let him do that to you." His left arm was buried up the elbow.

"Then thank you, Ben. I'm in your debt."

"I'd ask you to take me with you, but I think there's only one hibernation pod in the transport. You won't be able to take your friend, either."

"Well, Ludmilla has her family here. She doesn't want to leave. Or not yet."

"I can't remember that story about Picasso. Maybe you heard it after we—after the divorce."

"You told it to me, Ben. When things were good between us, you used to tell stories like that."

"Then I've forgotten."

"It's about an art dealer who buys a canvas in a private deal, that is signed 'Picasso.' This is in France, when Picasso was working in Cannes, and the dealer travels there to find if it is genuine. Picasso is working in his studio. He spares the painting a brief glance and dismisses it as a fake."

"I had a Picasso, once. A bull's head. I remember that, Barbara."

"You thought it was a necessary sign of your wealth. You were photographed beside it several times. I always preferred Georges Braque myself. Do you want to hear the rest of the story?"

"I'm still here."

"Of course you are, as long as I stay out of reach. Well, a few months later, the dealer buys another canvas signed by Picasso. Again he travels to the studio; again Picasso spares it no more than a glance, and announces that it is a fake. The dealer protests that this is the very painting he found Picasso working on the first time he visited but Picasso just shrugs and says, 'I often paint fakes.'"

His breathing was becoming labored. Was there something wrong with the air system? The black stuff was climbing his chest. He could almost see it move a creeping wave of black devouring him centimeter by centimeter.

The star was very close to the horizon, now.

He said, "I know a story."

"There's no more time for stories, dear. I can release you, if you want. You only have your reserve air in any case."

"No. I want to see you go."

"I'll remember you. I'll tell your story far and wide."

Ben Lo heard the echo of another voice across their link, and the woman in the transparent suit stood and lifted a hand in salute and bounded away.

The spy came back, then, but Ben Lo fought him down. There was nothing he could do, after all. The woman was gone. He said, as if to himself, "I know a story. About a man who lost himself, and found himself again, just in time. Listen. *Once upon a time . . .*"

Something bright rose above the horizon and dwindled away into the outer darkness.

THE WAR MEMORIAL

Allen Steele

Here's a visit to a curious memorial on a historic battlefield on a battle-torn moon, and the poignant and surprising story of how it came to be there . . .

Allen Steele made his first sale to Asimov's Science Fiction *magazine in 1988, soon following it up with a long string of other sales to* Asimov's, *as well as to markets such as* The Magazine of Fantasy and Science Fiction *and* Science Fiction Age. *In 1990, he published his critically acclaimed first novel,* Orbital Decay, *which subsequently won the Locus Poll as Best First Novel of the year, and soon Steele was being compared to Golden Age Heinlein by no less an authority than Gregory Benford. His other books include the novels* Clarke County, Space, Lunar Descent, Labyrinth of Night, The Weight, *and* The Tranquillity Alternative, *and a collection,* Rude Astronauts. *His most recent book is the novel* A King of Infinite Space. *He won a Hugo Award in 1996 for his novella "The Death of Captain Future," and his novella ". . . Where Angels Fear to Tread" is on the Hugo Ballot as I type these words. Born in Nashville, Tennessee, he has worked for a variety of newspapers and magazines, covering science and business assignments, and is now a full-time writer living in Massachusetts with his wife Linda.*

The *first-wave* assault is jinxed from the very beginning. Even before the dropship touches down, its pilot shouts over the comlink that a Pax missile battery seven klicks away has locked in on their position, despite the ECM buffer set up by the lunarsats. So it's going to be a dustoff; the pilot has done his job by getting the men down to the surface, and he doesn't want to be splattered across Mare Tranquillitatis.

It doesn't matter anyway. Baker Company has been deployed for less than two minutes before the Pax heatseekers pummel the ground around them and take out the dropship even as it begins its ascent.

Giordano hears the pilot scream one last obscenity before his ugly spaceship is reduced to metal rain, then something slams against his back and everything within the suit goes black. For an instant he believes he's dead, that he's been nailed by one of the heatseekers, but it's just debris from the dropship. The half-ton ceramic-polymer shell of the Mark III Valkyrie Combat Armor Suit has absorbed the brunt of the impact.

When the lights flicker back on within his soft cocoon and the flatscreen directly in front of his face stops fuzzing, he sees that not everyone has been so lucky. A few dozen meters away at three o'clock, there's a new crater that used to be Robinson. The only thing left of Baker Company's resident card cheat is the severed rifle arm of his CAS.

He doesn't have time to contemplate Robinson's fate. He's in the midst of battle. Sgt. Boyle's voice comes through the com-link, shouting orders. Traveling overwatch, due west, head for Marker One-Eight-Five. Kemp, take Robinson's position. Cortez, you're point. Stop staring, Giordano (yes sir). Move, move, move. . . .

So they move, seven soldiers in semi-robotic heavy armor, bounding across the flat silver-gray landscape. Tin men trying to outrun the missiles plummeting down around them, the sound-less explosions the missiles make when they hit. For several kilometers around them, everywhere they look, there are scores of other tin men doing the same, each trying to survive a silent hell called the Sea of Tranquillity.

Giordano is sweating hard, his breath coming in ragged gasps. He tells himself that if he can just make Marker One-Eight-Five—crater Arago, or so the map overlay tells him—then everything will be okay. The crater walls will protect them. Once Baker Company sets up its guns and erects a new ECM buffer, they can dig in nice and tight and wait it out; the beachhead will have been established by then and the hard part of Operation Monkey Wrench will be over.

But the crater is five-and-a-half klicks away, across plains as flat and wide-open as Missouri pasture, and between here and there a lot of shitfire is coming down. The Pax Astra guns in the foothills of the lunar highlands due west of their position can see them coming; the enemy has the high ground, and they're throwing everything they can at the invading force.

Sgt. Boyle knows his platoon is in trouble. He orders everyone to use their jumpjets. Screw formation; it's time to run like hell.

Giordano couldn't agree more whole-heartedly. He tells the Valkyrie to engage the twin miniature rockets mounted on the back of his carapace.

Nothing happens.

Once again, he tells the voice-activated computer mounted against the back of his neck to fire the jumpjets. When there's still no response, he goes to manual, using the tiny controls nestled within the palm of his right hand inside the suit's artificial arm.

At that instant, everything goes dark again, just like it did when the shrapnel from the dropship hit the back of his suit.

This time, though, it stays dark.

A red LCD lights above his forehead, telling him that there's been a total system crash.

Cursing, he finds the manual override button and stabs it with his little finger. As anticipated, it causes the computer to completely reboot itself; he hears servomotors grind within the carapace as its limbs move into neutral position, until his boots are planted firmly on the ground and his arms are next to his sides, his rifle pointed uselessly at the ground.

There is a dull click from somewhere deep within the armor, then silence.

Except for the red LCD, everything remains dark.

He stabs frantically at the palm buttons, but there's no power to any of the suit's major subsystems. He tries to move his arms and legs, but finds them frozen in place.

Limbs, jumpjets, weapons, ECM, comlink . . . nothing works.

Now he's sweating more than ever. The impact of that little bit of debris from the dropship must have been worse than he thought. Something must have shorted out, badly, within the Valkyrie's onboard computer.

He twists his head to the left so he can gaze through the

eyepiece of the optical periscope, the only instrument within the
suit that isn't dependent upon computer control. What he sees
terrifies him: the rest of his platoon jumpjetting for the security
of the distant crater, while missiles continue to explode all
around him.

Abandoning him. Leaving him behind.

He screams at the top of his lungs, yelling for Boyle and Kemp
and Cortez and the rest, calling them foul names, demanding that
they wait or come back for him, knowing that it's futile. They
can't hear him. For whatever reason, they've already determined
that he's out of action; they cannot afford to risk their lives by
coming back to lug an inert CAS across a battlefield.

He tries again to move his legs, but it's pointless. Without
direct interface from the main computer, the limbs of his suit are
immobile. He might as well be wearing a concrete block.

The suit contains three hours of oxygen, fed through pumps
controlled by another computer tucked against his belly, along
with the rest of its life-support systems. So at least he won't
suffocate or fry. . . .

For the next three hours, at any rate.

Probably less. The digital chronometer and life-support gauges
are dead, so there's no way of knowing for sure.

As he watches, even the red coal of the LCD warning lamp
grows dim until it finally goes cold, leaving him in the dark.

He has become a living statue. Fully erect, boots firmly placed
upon the dusty regolith, arms held rigid at his sides, he is in
absolute stasis.

For three hours. Certainly less.

For all intents and purposes, he is dead.

In the smothering darkness of his suit, Giordano prays to a god
in which he has never really believed. Then, for lack of anything
else to do, he raises his eyes to the periscope eyepiece and
watches as the battle rages on around him.

He fully expects—and, after at time, even hopes—for a Pax
missile to relieve him of his ordeal, but this small mercy never
occurs. Without an active infrared or electromagnetic target to
lock in upon, the heatseekers miss the small spot of ground he
occupies, instead decimating everything around him.

Giordano becomes a mute witness to the horror of the worst

conflict of the Moon War, what historians will later call the Battle of Mare Tranquillitatis. Loyalty, duty, honor, patriotism . . . all the things in which he once believed are soon rendered null and void as he watches countless lives being lost.

Dropships touch down near and distant, depositing soldiers in suits similar to his own. Some don't even make it to the ground before they become miniature supernovas.

Men and women like himself are torn apart even as they charge across the wasteland for the deceptive security of distant craters and rills.

An assault rover bearing three lightsuited soldiers rushes past him, only to be hit by fire from the hills. It is thrown upside down, crushing two of the soldiers beneath it. The third man, his legs broken and his suit punctured, manages to crawl from the wreckage. He dies at Giordano's feet, his arms reach out to him.

He has no idea whether Baker Company has survived, but he suspects it hasn't, since he soon sees a bright flash from the general direction of the crater it was supposed to occupy and hold.

In the confines of his suit, he weeps and screams and howls against the madness erupting around him. In the end, he goes mad himself, cursing the same god to whom he'd prayed earlier for the role to which he has been damned.

If God cares, it doesn't matter. By then, the last of Giordano's oxygen reserves have been exhausted; he asphyxiates long before his three hours are up, his body still held upright by the Mark III Valkyrie Combat Armor Suit.

When he is finally found, sixty-eight hours later, by a patrol from the victorious Pax Astra Free Militia, they are astonished that anything was left standing on the killing ground. This sole combat suit, damaged only by a small steel pipe wedged into its CPU housing, with a dead man inexplicably sealed inside, is the only thing left intact. All else has been reduced to scorched dust and shredded metal.

So they leave him standing.

They do not remove the CAS from its place, nor do they attempt to prise the man from his armor. Instead, they erect a circle of stones around the Valkyrie. Later, when peace has been negotiated and lunar independence has been achieved, a small plaque is placed at his feet.

The marker bears no name. Because so many lives were lost during the battle, nobody can be precisely certain of who was wearing this particular CAS on that particular day.

An eternal flame might have been placed at his feet, but it can't, because nothing burns on the Moon.

A SPECIAL
KIND OF MORNING

Gardner Dozois

*Gardner Dozois has won two Nebula Awards for his own short
fiction, as well as ten Hugo Awards as the year's Best Editor.
He is the editor of* Asimov's Science Fiction *magazine, and
also the editor of the annual anthology series* The Year's Best
Science Fiction, *now up to its Fifteenth Annual Collection. He
is the author or editor of over seventy books, including a long
string of Ace anthologies co-edited with Jack Dann. His own
short fiction was most recently collected in* Geodesic Dreams:
The Best Short Fiction of Gardner Dozois.*

*Here, in one of the earliest stories to deal with the impli-
cations of the then-oncoming Biological Revolution, he takes
us to a distant future world that has forgotten about War—but
which, alas, has not outgrown its capacity to learn . . .*

> *The Doomsday Machine is the human race.*
> —Graffito in New York subway,
> Seventy-ninth Street Station

Did y'ever hear the one about the old man and the sea?

Halt a minute, lordling; stop and listen. It's a fine story, full of
balance and point and social pith; short and direct. It's not mine.
Mine are long and rambling and parenthetical and they corrode
the moral fiber right out of a man. Come to think, I won't tell you
that one after all. A man of my age has a right to prefer his own
material, and let the critics be damned. I've a prejudice now for
webs of my own weaving.

Sit down, sit down: butt against pavement, yes; it's been done before. Everything has, near about. Now that's not an expression of your black pessimism, or your futility, or what have you. Pessimism's just the commonsense knowledge that there's more ways for something to go wrong than for it to go right, from our point of view anyway—which is not necessarily that of the management, or of the mechanism, if you prefer your cosmos depersonalized. As for futility, everybody dies the true death eventually; even though executives may dodge it for a few hundred years, the hole gets them all in the end, and I imagine that's futility enough for a start. The philosophical man accepts both as constants and then doesn't let them bother him any. Sit down, damn it; don't pretend you've important business to be about. Young devil, you are in the enviable position of having absolutely nothing to do because it's going to take you a while to recover from what you've just done.

There. That's better. Comfortable? You don't look it; you look like you've just sat in a puddle of piss and're wondering what the socially appropriate reaction is. Hypocrisy's an art, boy; you'll improve with age. Now you're bemused, lordling, that you let an old soak chivy you around, and now he's making fun of you. Well, the expression on your face is worth a chuckle; if you could see it you'd laugh yourself. You will see it years from now too, on some other young man's face—that's the only kind of mirror that ever shows it clear. And *you'll* be an old soak by that time, and you'll laugh and insult the young buck's dignity, but you'll be laughing more at the reflection of the man you used to be than at that particular stud himself. And you'll probably have to tell the buck just what I've told you to cool him down, and there's a laugh in that too; listen for the echo of a million and one laughs behind you. I hear a million now.

How do I get away with such insolence? What've I got to lose, for one thing. That gives you a certain perspective. And I'm socially instructive in spite of myself—I'm valuable as an object lesson. For that matter, why is an arrogant young aristo like you sitting there and putting up with my guff? Don't even bother to answer; I knew the minute you came whistling down the street, full of steam and strut. Nobody gets up this early in the morning anymore, unless they're old as I am and begrudge sleep's dry-run of death—or unless they've never been to bed in the first place.

The world's your friend this morning, a toy for you to play with and examine and stuff in your mouth to taste, and you're letting your benevolence slop over onto the old degenerate you've met on the street. You're even happy enough to listen, though you're being quizzical about it, and you're sitting over there feeling benignly superior. And I'm sitting over *here* feeling benignly superior. A nice arrangement, and everyone content. Well, then, mornings make you feel that way. Especially if you're fresh from a night at the Towers, the musk of Lady Nil still warm on your flesh.

A blush—my buck, you *are* new-hatched. How did I know? Boy, you'd be surprised what I know; I'm occasionally startled myself, and I've been working longer to get it catalogued. Besides, hindsight is a comfortable substitute for omnipotence. And I'm not blind yet. You have the unmistakable look of a cub who's just found out he can do something else with it besides piss. An incredible revelation, as I recall. The blazing significance of it will wear a little with the years, though not all that much, I suppose; until you get down to the brink of the Ultimate Cold, when you stop worrying about the identity of warmth, or demanding that it pay toll in pleasure. Any hand of clay, long's the blood still runs the tiny degree that's just enough for difference. Warmth's the only definition between you and graveyard dirt. But morning's not for graveyards, though it works the other way. Did y'know they also used to use that to make babies? 'S'fact; though few know it now. It's a versatile beast. Oh *come*—buck, cub, young cocksman—stop being so damn surprised. People ate, slept, and fornicated before you were born, some of them anyway, and a few will probably even find the courage to keep on at it after you die. You don't have to keep it secret; the thing's been circulated in this region once or twice before. You weren't the first to learn how to make the beast do its trick, though I *know* you don't believe that. *I* don't believe it concerning myself, and I've had a long time to learn.

You make me think, sitting there innocent as an egg and twice as vulnerable; yes, you are definitely about to make me think, and I believe I'll have to think of some things I always regret having thought about, just to keep me from growing maudlin.

Damn it, boy, you *do* make me think. Life's strange—wet-eared
as you are, you've probably had that thought a dozen times
already, probably had it this morning as you tumbled out of your
fragrant bed to meet the rim of the sun; well, I've four times
your age, and a ream more experience, and I still can't think of
anything better to sum up the world: life's strange. 'S been said,
yes. But *think*, boy, how strange: the two of us talking, you
coming, me going; me knowing where you've got to go, you
suspecting where I've been, and the same destination for both. O
strange, very strange! Damn it, you're a deader already if you
can't see the strangeness of that, if you can't sniff the poetry; it
reeks of it, as of blood. And I've smelt blood, buck. It has a very
distinct odor; you know it when you smell it. You're bound for
blood; for blood and passion and high deeds and all the rest of
the business, and maybe for a little understanding if you're lucky
and have eyes to see. Me, I'm bound for nothing, literally. I've
come to rest here in Kos, and while the Red Lady spins her web
of colors across the sky I sit and weave my own webs of words
and dreams and other spider stuff—

What? Yes, I do talk too much; old men like to babble, and
philosophy's a cushion for old bones. But it's my profession now,
isn't it, and I've promised you a story. What happened to my leg?
That's a bloody story, but I said you're bound for blood; I know
the mark. I'll tell it to you then: perhaps it'll help you to
understand when you reach the narrow place, perhaps it'll even
help you to think, although that's a horrible weight to wish on
any man. It's customary to notarize my care before I start, keep
you from running off at the end without paying. Thank you,
young sir. Beware of some of these beggars, buck; they have a
credit tally at Central greater than either of us will ever run up.
They turn a tidy profit out of poverty. I'm an honest pauper,
more's the pity, exist mostly on the subsidy, if you call that
existing—Yes, I know. The leg

We'll have to go back to the Realignment for that, more than
half a century ago, and half a sector away, at World. This was
before World was a member of the Commonwealth. In fact,
that's what the Realignment was about, the old Combine
overthrown by the Quaestors, who then opted for amalgamation

and forced World into the Commonwealth. That's where and when the story starts.

Start it with waiting.

A lot of things start like that, waiting. And when the thing you're waiting for is probable death, and you're lying there loving life and suddenly noticing how pretty everything is and listening to the flint hooves of darkness click closer, feeling the iron-shod boots strike relentless sparks from the surface of your mind, knowing that death is about to fall out of the sky and that there's no way to twist out from under—then, waiting can take time. Minutes become hours, hours become unthinkable horrors. Add enough horrors together, total the scaly snouts, and you've got a day and a half I once spent laying up in a mountain valley in the Blackfriars on World, almost the last day I spent anywhere.

This was just a few hours after D'kotta. Everything was a mess, nobody really knew what was happening, everybody's communication lines cut. I was just a buck myself then, working with the Quaestors in the field, a hunted criminal. Nobody knew what the Combine would do next, we didn't know what *we'd* do next, groups surging wildly from one place to another at random, panic and riots all over the planet, even in the Controlled Environments.

And D'kotta-on-the-Blackfriars was a seventy-mile swath of smoking insanity, capped by boiling umbrellas of smoke that eddied ashes from the ground to the stratosphere and back. At night it pulsed with molten scum, ugly as a lanced blister; lighting up the cloud cover across the entire horizon, visible for hundreds of miles. It was this ugly glow that finally panicked even the zombies in the Environments, probably the first strong emotion in their lives.

It'd been hard to sum up the effects of the battle. We thought that we had the edge, that the Combine was close to breaking, but nobody knew for sure. If they weren't as close to folding as we thought, then we were probably finished. The Quaestors had exhausted most of their hoarded resources at D'Kotta, and we certainly couldn't hit the Combine any harder. If they could shrug off the blow, then they could wear us down.

Personally, I didn't see how anything could shrug *that* off. I'd watched it all and it'd shaken me considerably. There's an old-time expression, "put the fear of God into him." That's what D'kotta had done for me. There wasn't any God anymore, but I'd seen fire vomit from the heavens and the earth ripped wide for rape, and it'd been an impressive enough surrogate. Few people ever realized how close the Combine and the Quaestors had come to destroying World between them, there at D'kotta.

We'd crouched that night—the team and I—on the high stone ramparts of the tallest of the Blackfriars, hopefully far away from anything that could fall on us. There were twenty miles of low, gnarly foothills between us and the rolling savannahland where the city of D'kotta had been minutes before, but the ground under our bellies heaved and quivered like a sick animal, and the rock was hot to the touch: feverish.

We could've gotten farther away, should have gotten farther away, but we had to watch. That'd been decided without anyone saying a word, without any question about it. It was impossible *not* to watch. It never even occurred to any of us to take another safer course of action. When reality is being turned inside out like a dirty sock, you watch, or you are less than human. So we watched it all from beginning to end: two hours that became a single second lasting for eons. Like a still photograph of time twisted into a scream—the scream reverberating on forever and yet taking no duration at all to experience.

We didn't talk. We *couldn't* talk—the molecules of the air itself shrieked too loudly, and the deep roar of explosions was a continual drumroll—but we wouldn't have talked even if we'd been able. You don't speak in the presence of an angry God. Sometimes we'd look briefly at each other. Our faces were all nearly identical: ashen, waxy, eyes of glass, blank, and lost as pale driftwood stranded on a beach by the tide. We'd been driven through the gamut of expressions into *extremis*—rictus: faces so contorted and strained they ached—and beyond to the quietus of shock: muscles too slack and flaccid to respond anymore. We'd only look at each other for a second, hardly focusing, almost not aware of what we were seeing, and then our eyes would be dragged back as if it by magnetism to the Fire.

At the beginning we'd clutched each other, but as the battle progressed we slowly drew apart, huddling into individual agony; the thing so big that human warmth meant nothing, so frightening that the instinct to gather together for protection was reversed, and the presence of others only intensified the realization of how ultimately naked you were. Earlier we'd set up a scattershield to filter the worst of the hard radiation—the gamma and intense infrared and ultraviolet—blunt some of the heat and shock and noise. We thought we had a fair chance of surviving, then, but we couldn't have run anyway. We were fixed by the beauty of horror/horror of beauty, surely as if by a spike driven through our backbones into the rock.

And away over the foothills, God danced in anger, and his feet struck the ground to ash.

What was it like?

Kos still has oceans and storms. Did y'ever watch the sea lashed by high winds? The storm boils the water into froth, whips it white, until it becomes an ocean of ragged lace to the horizon, whirlpools of milk, not a fleck of blue left alive. The land looked like this at D'kotta. The hills *moved*. The Quaestors had a discontinuity projector there, and under its lash the ground stirred like sluggish batter under a baker's spoon; stirred, shuddered, groaned, cracked, broke: acres heaved themselves into new mountains, other acres collapsed into canyons.

Imagine a giant asleep just under the surface of the earth, overgrown by fields, dreaming dreams of rock and crystal. Imagine him moving restlessly, the long rhythm of his dreams touched by nightmare, tossing, moaning, tremors signaling unease in waves up and down his miles-long frame. Imagine him catapulted into waking terror, lurching suddenly to his knees with the bawling roar of ten million burning calves: a steaming claw of rock and black earth raking for the sky. Now, in a wink, imagine the adjacent land hurtling downward, sinking like a rock in a pond, opening a womb a thousand feet wide, swallowing everything and grinding it to powder. Then, almost too quick to see, imagine the mountain and the crater switching, the mountain collapsing all at once and washing the feet of the older Blackfrairs with a tidal wave of earth, then tumbling down to make a pit; at the same time the sinking earth at the bottom of the other crater reversing itself and erupting upward into a quaking fist of rubble. Then they switch again, and keep switching. Like watching the same film clip continuously run forward and backward. Now multiply that by a million and spread it out so that all you can see to the horizon is a stew of humping rock. D'y'visualize it? Not a tenth of it.

Dervishes of fire stalked the chaos, melting into each other, whirlpooling. Occasionally a tactical nuclear explosion would pinch a hole in the night, a brief intense flare that would be swallowed like a candle in a murky snowstorm. Once a tacnuke detonation coincided with the upthrusting of a rubble mountain, with an effect like that of a firecracker exploding inside a swinging sack of grain.

The city itself was gone; we could no longer see a trace of anything man-made, only the stone maelstrom. The river Delva had also vanished, flash-boiled to steam; for a while we could see the gorge of its dry bed stitching across the plain, but then the ground heaved up and obliterated it.

It was unbelievable that anything could be left alive down there. Very little was. Only the remainder of the heavy weapons sections on both sides continued to survive, invisible to us in the confusion. Still protected by powerful phasewalls and scatter-shields, they pounded blindly at each other—the Combine some-what ineffectively with biodeths and tacnukes, the Quaestors responding by stepping up the discontinuity projector. There was only one, in the command module—the Quaestor techni-cians were praying it wouldn't be wiped out by a random strike—and it was a terraforming device and not actually a "weapon" at all, but the Combine had been completely unpre-pared for it, and were suffering horribly as a result.

Everything began to flicker, random swatches of savannahland shimmering and blurring, phasing in and out of focus in a jerky, mismatched manner: that filmstrip run through a spastic projec-tor. At first we thought it must be heat eddies caused by the fires, but then the flickering increased drastically in frequency and tempo, speeding up until it was impossible to keep anything in focus even for a second, turning the wide veldt into a mad kaleidoscope of writhing, interchanging shapes and color-patterns from one horizon to the other. It was impossible to watch it for long. It hurt the eyes and filled us with an oily, inexplicable panic that we were never able to verbalize. We looked away, filled with the musty surgings of vague fear.

We didn't know then that we were watching the first practical application of a process that'd long been suppressed by both the Combine and the Commonwealth, a process based on the starship dimensional "drive" (which isn't a "drive" at all, but the word's passed into the common press) that enabled a high-cycling discontinuity projector to throw time out of phase within a limited area, so that a post *here* would be a couple of minutes ahead or behind a spot a few inches away, in continuity sequence. That explanation would give a psychophysicist fits, since "time" is really nothing at all like the way we "experience" it, so the process "really" doesn't do what I've said it does — doing something *really* abstruse instead — but that's close enough to what it does on a practical level, 'cause even if the time distortion is an "illusionary effect" — like the sun seeming to rise and set — they still used it to kill people. So it threw time out of phase, and kept doing it, switching the dislocation at random: so that in any given square foot of land there might be four or five discrepancies in time sequence that kept interchanging. Like, *here* might be one minute "ahead" of the base "now," and then a second later (language breaks down hopelessly under this stuff, you need the math) *here* would be two minutes behind the now, then five minutes behind, then three ahead, and so on. And all the adjacent zones in that square foot are going through the same switching process at the same time (goddamn this language!). The Combine's machinery tore itself to pieces. So did the people: some died of suffocation because of a five-minute discrepancy between an inhaled breath and oxygen received by the lungs, some drowned in their own blood.

It took about ten minutes, at least as far as we were concerned as unaffected observers. I had a psychophysicist tell me once that "it" had both continued to "happen" forever and had never "happened" at all, and that neither statement canceled out the validity of the other, that *each* statement in fact was both "applicable" and "nonapplicable" to the same situation consecutively — and I did not understand. It took ten minutes.

At the end of that time, the world got very still.

We looked up. The land had stopped churning. A tiny star appeared amongst the rubble in the middle distance, small as a pinhead but incredibly bright and clear. It seemed to suck the

night into it like a vortex, as if it were a pinprick through the
worldstuff into a more intense reality, as if it were gathering a
great breath for a shout.

We buried our heads in our arms as one, instinctively.

There was a very bright light, a light that we could feel
through the tops of our heads, a light that left dazzling after-
images even through closed and shrouded lids. The mountain
leaped under us, bounced us into the air again and again, battered
us into near unconsciousness. We never even heard the roar.

After a while, things got quiet again, except for a continuous
low rumbling. When we looked up, there were thick, sluggish
tongues of molten magma oozing up in vast flows across the
veldt, punctuated here and there by spectacular shower-fountains
of vomited sparks.

Our scattershield had taken the brunt of the blast, borne it just
long enough to save our lives, and then overloaded and burnt
itself to scrap; one of the first times *that's* ever happened.

Nobody said anything. We didn't look at each other. We just
lay there.

The chrono said an hour went by, but nobody was aware of it.

Finally, a couple of us got up, in silence, and started to
stumble aimlessly back and forth. One by one, the rest crawled
to their feet. Still in silence, still trying not to look at each other,
we automatically cleaned ourselves up. You hear someone say
"It made me shit my pants," and you think it's an expression; not
under the right stimuli. Automatically, we treated our bruises and
lacerations, automatically we tidied the camp up, buried the
ruined scatterfield generator. Automatically, we sat down again
and stared numbly at the light show on the savannah.

Each of us knew the war was over—we knew it with the gut
rather than the head. It was an emotional reaction, but very calm,
very resigned, very passive. It was a thing too big for question-
ing; it became a self-evident fact. After D'kotta, there could be
nothing else. Period. The war was over.

We were almost right. But not quite.

In another hour or so, a man from field HQ came up over the
mountain shoulder in a stolen vacform and landed in camp. The
man switched off the vac, jumped down, took two steps toward
the parapet overlooking hell, stopped. We saw his stomach

muscles jump, tighten. He took a stumbling half-step back, then stopped again. His hand went up to shield his throat, dropped, hesitated, went back up. We said nothing. The HQ directing the D'kotta campaign had been sensibly located behind the Black-friars: they had been shielded by the mountain chain and had seen nothing but glare against the cloud cover. This was his first look at the city; at where the city had been. I watched the muscles play in his back, saw his shoulders hunch as if under an unraised fist. A good many of the Quaestor men involved in planning the D'kotta operation committed suicide immediately after the Realignment; a good many didn't. I don't know what category this one belonged in.

The liaison man finally turned his head, dragged himself away. His movements were jerky, and his face was an odd color, but he was under control. He pulled Heynith, our team leader, aside. They talked for a half hour. The liaison man showed Heynith a map, scribbled on a pad for Heynith to see, gave Heynith some papers. Heynith nodded occasionally. The liaison man said good-bye, half-ran to his vacform. The vac lifted with an erratic surge, steadied, then disappeared in a long arc over the gnarled backs of the Blackfriars. Heynith stood in the dirtswirl kicked up by the backwash and watched impassively.

It got quiet again, but it was a little more apprehensive.

Heynith came over, studied us for a while, then told us to get ready to move out. We stared at him. He repeated it in a quiet, firm voice; unendurably patient. Hush for a second, then somebody groaned, somebody else cursed, and the spell of D'kotta was partially broken, for a moment. We awoke enough to ready our gear; there was even a little talking, though not much.

Heynith appeared at our head and led us out in a loose travel formation, diagonally across the face of the slope, then up toward the shoulder. We reached the notch we'd found earlier and started down the other side.

Everyone wanted to look back at D'kotta. No one did.

Somehow, it was still night.

We never talked much on the march, of course, but tonight the silence was spooky: you could hear boots crunch on stone, the slight rasp of breath, the muted jangle of knives occasionally bumping against thighs. You could hear our fear; you could smell it, could see it.

We could touch it, we could taste it.

I was a member of something so old that they even had to dig up the name for it when they were rooting through the rubble of ancient history, looking for concepts to use against the Combine: a "commando team." Don't ask me what it means, but that's what it's called. Come to think, I know what it means in terms of flesh: it means ugly. Long ugly days and nights that come back in your sleep even uglier, so that you don't want to think about it at all because it squeezes your eyeballs like a vise. Cold and dark and wet, with sudden death looming up out of nothing at any time and jarring you with mortality like a rubber glove full of ice water slapped across your face. Living jittery high all the time, so that everything gets so real that it looks fake. You live in an anticipation that's pain, like straddling a fence with a knifeblade for a top rung, waiting for something to come along in the dark and push you off. You get so you like it. The pain's so consistent that you forget it's there, you forget there ever was a time when you didn't have it, and you live on the adrenaline.

We liked it. We were dedicated. We *hated*. It gave us something to do with our hate, something tangible we could see. And nobody'd done it but us for hundreds of years; there was an exultation to that. The Scholars and Antiquarians who'd shared the Quaestor movement—left fullsentient and relatively unwatched so they could better piece together the muddle of prehistory from generations of inherited archives—they'd been smart. They knew their only hope of baffling the Combine was to hit them with radical concepts and tactics, things they didn't have instructions for handling, things out of the Combine's experience. So they scooped concepts out of prehistory, as far back as the archives go, even finding *written* records somewhere and having to figure out how to use them.

Out of one of these things, they got the idea of "guerrilla" war. No, I don't know what that means either, but what it *means* is playing the game by your own rules instead of the enemy's. Oh, you let the enemy keep playing by *his* rules, see, but you play by your own. Gives you a wider range of moves. You *do* things. I mean, *ridiculous* things, but so ancient they don't have any defense against them because they never thought they'd have to defend against *that*. Most of the time they never even knew *that* existed.

Like, we used to run around with those projectile weapons the Quaestors had copied from old plans and mass-produced in the autfacs on the sly by stealing computer time. The things worked by a chemical reaction inside the mechanism that would spit these tiny missiles out at a high velocity. The missile would hit you so hard it would actually lodge itself in your body, puncture internal organs, *kill* you. I know it sounds like an absurd concept, but there were advantages.

Don't forget how tightly controlled a society the Combine's was; even worse than the Commonwealth in its own way. We couldn't just steal energy weapons or biodeths and use them, because all those things operated on broadcast power from the Combine, and as soon as one was reported missing, the Combine would just cut the relay for that particular code. We couldn't make them ourselves, because unless you used the Combine's broadcast power you'd need a ton of generator equipment with each weapon to provide enough energy to operate it, and we didn't have the technology to miniaturize that much machinery. (Later some genius figured out a way to make, say, a functioning biodeth with everything but the energy source and then cut into and tap Combine broadcast power without showing up on the coding board, but that was toward the end anyway, and most of them were stockpiled for the shock troops at D'kotta.) At least the "guns" worked. And there were even unexpected advantages. We found that tanglefields, scattershields, phasewalls, personal warders, all the usual defenses, were unable to stop the "bullets" (the little missiles fired by the "guns")—they were just too sophisticated to stop anything as crude as a lump of metal moving at relatively sluggish ballistic speeds. Same with "bombs" and "grenades"—devices designed to have a chemical reaction violent enough to kill in an enclosed place. And the list went on and on. The Combine thought we couldn't move around, because all vehicles were coded and worked on broadcast power. Did you ever hear of "bicycles"? They're devices for translating mechanical energy into motion, they ride on wheels that you actually make revolve with physical labor. And the bicycles didn't have enough metal or mass to trigger sentryfields or show up on sweep probes, so we could go undetected to places they thought nobody could reach. Communicate? We used mirrors to flash messages, used puffs of smoke as code, had people actually *carry* messages from one place to another.

More important, we *personalized* war. That was the most radical thing, that was the thing that turned us from kids running around and having fun breaking things into men with bitter faces, that was the thing that took the heart out of the Combine more than anything else. That's why people still talk about the Realignment with horror today, even after all these years, especially in the Commonwealth.

We killed people. *We* did it, ourselves. We walked up and stabbed them. I mentioned a knife before, boy, and I knew you didn't know what it was; you bluff well for a kid—that's the way to a reputation for wisdom: look sage and always keep your mouth shut about your ignorance. Well, a knife is a tapering piece of metal with a handle, sharpened on the sides and very sharp at the tapered end, sharp enough so that when you strike someone with it the metal goes right into their flesh, cuts them, rips them open, *kills* them, and there is blood on your hands which feels wet and sticky and is hard to wash off because it dries and sticks to the little hairs on the backs of your wrists. We learned how to hit people hard enough to kill them, snap the bones inside the skin like dry sticks inside oiled cloth. We did. We strangled them with lengths of wire. You're shocked. So was the Combine. They had grown used to killing at a great distance, the push of a button, the flick of a switch, using vast, clean, impersonal forces to do their annihilation. *We* killed people. We killed *people*—not statistics and abstractions. We heard their screams, we saw their faces, we smelled their blood, and their vomit and shit and urine when their systems let go after death. You have to be crazy to do things like that. We *were* crazy. We were a good team.

There were twelve of us in the group, although we mostly worked in sections of four. I was in the team leader's section, and it had been my family for more than two years.

Heynith, stocky, balding, leather-faced; a hard, fair man; brilliant organizer.

Ren, impassive, withdrawn, taciturn, frighteningly competent, of a strange humor.

Goth, young, tireless, bullheaded, given to sudden enthusiasms and depressions; he'd only been with us for about four months, a replacement for Mason, who had been killed while trying to escape from a raid on Cape Itica.

And me.

We were all warped men, emotional cripples one way or the other.

We were all crazy

The Combine could never understand that kind of craziness, in spite of the millions of people they'd killed or shriveled impersonally over the years. They were afraid of that craziness, they were baffled by it, never could plan to counter it or take it into account. They couldn't really believe it.

That's how we'd taken the Blackfriars Transmitter, hours before D'kotta. It had been impregnable—wrapped in layer after layer of defense fields against missile attack, attack by chemical or biological agents, transmitted energy, almost anything. We'd walked in. They'd never imagined anyone would do that, that it was even possible to attack that way, so there was no defense against it. The guardsystems were designed to meet more esoteric threats. And even after ten years of slowly escalating guerrilla action, they still didn't *really* believe anyone would use his body to wage war. So we walked in. And killed everybody there. The staff was a sentient techclone of ten and an executive foreman. No nulls or zombies. The ten identical technicians milled in panic, the foreman stared at us in disbelief, and what I think was distaste that we'd gone so far outside the bounds of procedure. We killed them like you kill insects, not really thinking about it much, except for that part of you that always thinks about it, that records it and replays it while you sleep. Then we blew up the transmitter with chemical explosives. Then, as the flames leaped up and ate holes in the night, we'd gotten on our bicycles and rode like hell toward the Blackfriars, the mountains hunching and looming ahead, as jagged as black snaggleteeth against the industrial glare of the sky. A tanglefield had snatched at us for a second, but then we were gone.

That's all that I personally had to do with the "historic" Battle of D'kotta. It was enough. We'd paved the way for the whole encounter. Without the transmitter's energy, the Combine's weapons and transportation systems—including liftshafts, slide-walks, irisdoors, and windows, heating, lighting, waste dis-posal—were inoperable; D'kotta was immobilized. Without the station's broadcast matter, thousands of buildings, industrial complexes, roadways, and homes collapsed into chaos, literally collapsed. More important, without broadcast nourishment, D'kotta's four major Cerebrums—handling an incredible com-plexity of military/industrial/administrative tasks—were knocked out of operation, along with a number of smaller Cerebrums: the synapses need constant nourishment to function, and so do the sophont ganglion units, along with the constant flow of the psychocybernetic current to keep them from going mad from sensory deprivation, and even the nulls would soon grow intractable as hunger stung them almost to self-awareness, finally to die after a few days. Any number of the lowest-ranking sentient clones—all those without stomachs or digestive sys-tems, mostly in the military and industrial castes—would find themselves in the same position as the nulls; without broadcast nourishment, they would die within days. And without catarcs in operation to duplicate the function of atrophied intestines, the buildup of body wastes would poison them anyway, even if they could somehow get nourishment. The independent food dispens-ers for the smaller percentage of fullsentients and higher clones simply could not increase their output enough to feed that many people, even if converted to intravenous systems. To say nothing of the zombies in the Environments scattered throughout the city.

There were backup fail-safe systems, of course, but they hadn't been used in centuries, the majority of them had fallen into disrepair and didn't work, and other Quaestor teams made sure the rest of them wouldn't work either.

Before a shot had been fired, D'kotta was already a major disaster.

The Combine had reacted as we'd hoped, as they'd been additionally prompted to react by intelligence reports of Quaestor massings in strength around D'kotta that it'd taken weeks to leak to the Combine from unimpeachable sources. The Combine was pouring forces into D'kotta within hours, nearly the full strength of the traditional military caste and a large percentage of the militia they'd cobbled together out of industrial clones when the Quaestors had begun to get seriously troublesome, plus a major portion of their heavy armament. They had hoped to surprise the Quaestors, catch them between the city and the inaccessible portion of the Blackfriars, quarter the area with so much strength it'd be impossible to dodge them, run the Quaestors down, annihilate them, break the back of the movement.

It had worked the other way around.

For years, the Quaestors had strung and run, always retreating when the Combine advanced, never meeting them in conventional battle, never hitting them with anything really heavy. Then, when the Combine had risked practically all of its military resources on one gigantic effort calculated to be effective against the usual Quaestor behavior, we had suddenly switched tactics. The Quaestors had waited to meet the Combine's advance and had hit the Combine forces with everything they'd been able to save, steal, hoard, and buy clandestinely from sympathizers in the Commonwealth in over fifteen years of conspiracy and campaigns aimed at this moment.

Within an hour of the first tacnuke exchange, the city had ceased to exist, everything leveled except two of the Cerebrums and the Escridel Creche. Then the Quaestors activated their terraforming devices—which I believe they bought from a firm here on Kos, as a matter of fact. This was completely insane—terraforming systems used indiscriminately can destroy entire planets—but it was the insanity of desperation, and they did it anyway. Within a half hour, the remaining Combine heavy armaments battalions and the two Cerebrums ceased to exist. A few minutes later, the supposedly invulnerable Escridel Creche ceased to exist, the first time in history a creche had ever been destroyed. Then, as the cycling energies got out of hand and filterfeedback built to a climax, everything on the veldt ceased to exist.

The carnage had been inconceivable.

Take the vast population of D'kotta as a base, the second largest city on World, one of the biggest even in this sector of the Commonwealth. The subfleets had been in, bringing the betja harvest and other goods up the Delva; river traffic was always heaviest at that time of year. The mines and factories had been in full swing, and the giant sprawl of the Westernese Shipyards and Engine Works. Add the swarming inhabitants of the six major Controlled Environments that circled the city. Add the city-within-a-city of Admin South, in charge of that hemisphere. Add the twenty generations of D'kotta Combine fullsentients whose discorporate ego-patterns had been preserved in the mountain of "indestructible" micromolecular circuitry called the Escridel Creche. (Those executives had died the irreversible true death, without hope of resurrection this time, even as disembodied intellects housed within artificial mind-environments: the records of their brain's unique pattern of electrical/psychocybernetic rhythms and balances had been destroyed, and you can't rebuild consciousness from a fused puddle of slag. This hit the Combine where they lived, literally, and had more impact than anything else.) Add the entire strength of both opposing forces; all of our men—who suspected what would happen—had been suicide volunteers. Add all of the elements together.

The total goes up into the multiples of billions.

The number was too big to grasp. Our minds fumbled at it while we marched, and gave up. It was too big.

I stared at Ren's back as we walked, a nearly invisible mannequin silhouette, and tried to multiply that out to the necessary figure. I staggered blindly along, lost and inundated beneath thousands of individual arms, legs, faces; a row of faces blurring off into infinity, all screaming—and the imagining nowhere near the actuality.

Billions.

How many restless ghosts out of that many deaders? Who do they haunt?

Billions.

Dawn caught us about two hours out. It came with no warning, as usual. We were groping through World's ink-dark, moonless night, watched only by the million icy eyes of evening, shreds of witchfire crystal, incredibly cold and distant. I'd watched them night after night for years, scrawling their indecipherable hieroglyphics across the sky, indifferent to man's incomprehension. I stopped for a second on a rise, pushing back the infrared lenses, staring at the sky. What program was printed there, suns for ciphers, worlds for decimal points? An absurd question—I was nearly as foolish as you once, buck—but it was the first fully verbalized thought I'd had since I'd realized the nakedness of flesh, back there on the parapet as my life tore itself apart. I asked it again, half-expecting an answer, watching my breath turn to plumes and tatters, steaming in the silver chill of the stars.

The sun came up like a meteor. It scuttled up from the horizon with that unsettling, deceptive speed that even natives of World never quite get used to. New light washed around us, blue and raw at first, deepening the shadows and honing their edges. The sun continued to hitch itself up the sky, swallowing stars, a watery pink flush wiping the horizon clear of night. The light deepened, mellowed into gold. We floated through silver mist that swirled up around the mountain's knobby knees. I found myself crying silently as I walked the high ridge between mist and sky, absorbing the morning with a new hunger, grappling with a thought that was still too big for my mind and kept slipping elusively away just out of reach. There was a low hum as our warmsuits adjusted to the growing warmth, polarizing from black to white, bleeding heat back into the air. Down the flanks of the Blackfriars and away across the valley below— visible now as the mists pirouetted past us to the summits—the night plants were dying, shriveling visibly in mile-long swaths of decay. In seconds the Blackfriars were gaunt and barren, turned to hills of ash and bone. The sun was now a bloated yellow disk surrounded by haloes of red and deepening scarlet, shading into the frosty blue of rarefied air. Stripped of softening vegetation, the mountains looked rough and abrasive as pumice, gouged by lunar shadows. The first of the day plants began to appear at our feet, the green spiderwebbing, poking up through cracks in the dry earth.

We came across a new stream, tumbling from melting ice, sluicing a dusty gorge.

An hour later we found the valley.

Heynith led us down onto the marshy plain that rolled away from mountains to horizon. We circled wide, cautiously approaching the valley from the lowlands. Heynith held up his hand, pointed to me, Ren, Goth. The others fanned out across the

mouth of the valley, hid, settled down to wait. We went in alone.
The speargrass had grown rapidly; it was chest-high. We crawled
in, timing our movements to coincide with the long soughing of
the morning breeze, so that any rippling of the grass would be
taken for natural movement. It took us about a half hour of dusty,
sweaty work. When I judged that I'd wormed my way in close
enough, I stooped, slowly parted the speargrass enough to peer
out without raising my head.

It was a large vacvan, a five-hundred-footer, equipped with
waldoes for self-loading.

It was parked near the hill flank on the side of the wide valley.
There were three men with it.

I ducked back into the grass, paused to make sure my "gun"
was ready for operation, then crawled laboriously nearer to the
van.

It was very near when I looked up again, about twenty-five
feet away in the center of a cleared space. I could make out the
hologram pictograph that pulsed identification on the side: the
symbol for Urheim, World's largest city and Combine Seat of
Board, half a world away in the Northern Hemisphere. They'd
come a long way; still thought of as long, though ships
whispered between the stars—it was still long for feet and eyes.
And another longer way: from fetuses in glass wombs to men
stamping and jiggling with cold inside the fold of a mountain's
thigh, watching the spreading morning. That made me feel funny
to think about. I wondered if they suspected that it'd be the last
morning they'd ever see. That made me feel funnier. The thought
tickled my mind again, danced away. I checked my gun a second
time, needlessly.

I waited, feeling troubled, pushing it down. Two of them were
standing together several feet in front of the van, sharing a mild
narcotic atomizer, sucking deeply, shuffling with restlessness
and cold, staring out across the speargrass to where the plain
opened up. They had the stiff, rumpled, puff-eyed look of people
who had just spent an uncomfortable night in a cramped place.
They were dressed as fullsentients uncloned, junior officers of
the military caste, probably hereditary positions inherited from
their families, as the case with most of the uncloned cadet
executives. Except for the cadre at Urheim and other major

cities, they must have been some of the few surviving clansmen; hundreds of thousands of military cadets and officers had died at D'kotta (along with uncounted clones and semisentients of all ranks), and the caste had never been extremely large in the first place. The by-laws had demanded that the Combine maintain a security force, but it had become mostly traditional, with minimum function, at least among the uncloned higher ranks almost the last stronghold of old-fashioned nepotism. That was one of the things that had favored the Quaestor uprising, and had forced the Combine to take the unpopular step of impressing large numbers of industrial clones into a militia. The most junior of these two cadets was very young, even younger than me. The third man remained inside the van's cab. I could see his face blurrily through the windfield, kept on against the cold though the van was no longer in motion.

I waited. I knew the others were maneuvering into position around me. I also knew what Heynith was waiting for.

The third man jumped down from the high cab. He was older, wore an officer's hologram: a full executive. He said something to the cadets, moved a few feet toward the back of the van, started to take a piss. The column of golden liquid steamed in the cold air.

Heynith whistled.

I rolled to my knees, parted the speargrass at the edge of the cleared space, swung my gun up. The two cadets started, face muscles tensing into uncertain fear. The older cadet took an involuntary step forward, still clutching the atomizer. Ren and Goth chopped him down, firing a stream of "bullets" into him. The guns made a very loud metallic rattling sound that jarred the teeth, and fire flashed from the ejector ends. Birds screamed upward all along the mountain flank. The impact of the bullets knocked the cadet off his feet, rolled him so that he came to rest belly-down. The atomizer flew through the air, hit, bounced. The younger cadet leaped toward the cab, right into my line of fire. I pulled the trigger; bullets exploded out of the gun. The cadet was kicked backwards, arms swinging wide, slammed against the side of the cab, jerked upright as I continued to fire, spun along the van wall and rammed heavily into the ground. He tottered on one shoulder for a second, then flopped over onto his back. At the sound of the first shot, the executive had whirled—penis still dangling from pantaloons, surplus piss spraying wildly—and dodged for the back of the van, so that Heynith's volley missed and screamed from the van wall, leaving a long scar. The executive dodged again, crouched, came up with a biodeth in one hand, and swung right into a single bullet from Ren just as he began to fire. The impact twirled him in a staggering circle, his finger still pressing the trigger; the carrier beam splashed harmlessly from the van wall, traversed as the executive spun, cut a long swath through the speargrass, the plants shriveling and blackening as the beam swept over them. Heynith opened up again before the beam could reach his clump of grass, sending the executive—somehow still on his feet—lurching past the end of the van. The biodeth dropped, went out. Heynith kept firing, the executive dancing bonelessly backwards on his heels, held up by the stream of bullets. Heynith released the trigger. The executive collapsed: a heap of arms and legs at impossible angles.

When we came up to the van, the young cadet was still dying. His body shivered and arched, his heels drummed against the earth, his fingers plucked at nothing, and then he was still. There was a lot of blood.

The others moved up from the valley mouth. Heynith sent them circling around the rim, where the valley walls dipped down on three sides.

We dragged the bodies away and concealed them in some large rocks.

I was feeling numb again, like I had after D'kotta.

I continued to feel numb as we spent the rest of that morning in frantic preparation. My mind was somehow detached as my body sweated and dug and hauled. There was a lot for it to do. We had four heavy industrial lasers, rock-cutters; they were clumsy, bulky, inefficient things to use as weapons, but they'd have to do. This mission had not been planned so much as thrown together, only two hours before the liaison man had contacted us on the parapet. Anything that could possibly work at all would have to be made to work somehow; no time to do it right, just do it. We'd been the closest team in contact with the field HQ who'd received the report, so we'd been snatched; the lasers were the only things on hand that could even approach potential as a heavy weapon, so we'd use the lasers.

Now that we'd taken the van without someone alerting the combine by radio from the cab, Heynith flashed a signal mirror back toward the shoulder of the mountain we'd quitted a few hours before. The liaison man swooped down ten minutes later, carrying one of the lasers strapped awkwardly to his platvac. He made three more trips, depositing the massive cylinders as carefully as eggs, then gunned his platvac and screamed back toward the Blackfriars in a maniac arc just this side of suicidal. His face was still gray, tight-pressed lips a bloodless white against ash, and he hadn't said a word during the whole unloading procedure. I think he was probably one of the Quaestors who followed the Way of Atonement. I never saw him again. I've sometimes wished I'd had the courage to follow his example, but I rationalize by telling myself that I have atoned with my life rather than my death, and who knows, it might even be somewhat true. It's nice to think so anyway.

It took us a couple of hours to get the lasers into position. We spotted them in four places around the valley walls, dug slanting pits into the slopes to conceal them and tilt the barrels up at the right angle. We finally got them all zeroed on a spot about a hundred feet above the center of the valley floor, the muzzle arrangement giving each a few degrees of leeway on either side. That's where she'd have to come down anyway if she was a standard orbot, the valley being just wide enough to contain the boat and the vacvab, with a safety margin between them. Of course, if they brought her down on the plain outside the valley mouth, things were going to get very hairy; in that case we might be able to lever one or two of the lasers around to bear, or, failing that, we could try to take the orbot on foot once it'd landed, with about one chance in eight of making it. But we thought that they'd land her in the valley; that's where the vacvan had been parked, and they'd want the shelter of the high mountain walls to conceal the orbot from any Quaestor eyes that might be around. If so, that gave us a much better chance. About one out of three.

When the lasers had been positioned, we scattered, four men to an emplacement, hiding in the camouflaged trenches alongside the big barrels. Heynith led Goth and me toward the laser we'd placed about fifty feet up the mountain flank, directly behind and above the vacvan. Ren stayed behind. He stood next to the van—shoulders characteristically slouched, thumbs hooked in his belt, face carefully void of expression—and watched us out of sight. Then he looked out over the valley mouth, hitched up his gun, spat in the direction of Urheim and climbed up into the van cab.

The valley was empty again. From our position the vacvan looked like a shiny toy, sun dogs winking across its surface as it baked in the afternoon heat. An abandoned toy, lost in high weeds, waiting in loneliness to be reclaimed by owners who would never come.

Time passed.

The birds we'd frightened away began to settle back onto the hillsides.

I shifted position uneasily, trying half-heartedly to get comfortable. Heynith glared me into immobility. We were crouched in a trench about eight feet long and five feet deep, covered by a camouflage tarpaulin propped open on the valley side by pegs, a couple of inches of vegetation and topsoil on top of the tarpaulin. Heynith was in the middle, straddling the operator's saddle of the laser. Goth was on his left, I was on his right. Heynith was going to man the laser when the time came; it only took one person. There was nothing for Goth and me to do, would be nothing to do even during the ambush, except take over the firing in the unlikely event that Heynith was killed without the shot wiping out all of us, or stand by to lever the laser around in case that became necessary. Neither was very likely to happen. No, it was Heynith's show, and we were superfluous and unoccupied.

That was bad.

We had a lot of time to think.

That was worse.

I was feeling increasingly numb, like a wall of clear glass had been slipped between me and the world and was slowly thickening, layer by layer. With the thickening came an incredible isolation (isolation though I was cramped and suffocating, though I was jammed up against Heynith's bunched thigh—I couldn't touch him, he was miles away) and with the isolation came a sick, smothering panic. It was the inverse of claustro-phobia. My flesh turned to clear plastic, my bones to glass, and I was naked, ultimately naked, and there was nothing I could wrap me in. Surrounded by an army, I would still be alone; shrouded in iron thirty feet underground, I would still be naked. One portion of my mind wondered dispassionately if I was slipping into shock; the rest of it fought to keep down the scream that gathered along tightening muscles. The isolation increased. I was unaware of my surroundings, except for the heat and the pressure of enclosure.

I was seeing the molten spider of D'kotta, lying on its back and showing its obscene blotched belly, kicking legs of flame against the sky, each leg raising a poison blister where it touched the clouds.

I was seeing the boy, face runneled by blood, beating heels against the ground.

I was beginning to doubt big, simple ideas.

Nothing moved in the valley except wind through grass, spirits circling in the form of birds.

Spider legs.

Crab dance.

The blocky shadow of the vacvan crept across the valley.

Suddenly, with the intensity of vision, I was picturing Ren sitting in the van cab, shoulders resting against the door, legs stretched out along the seat, feet propped up on the instrument board, one ankle crossed over the other, gun resting across his lap, eyes watching the valley mouth through the windfield. He would be smoking a cigarette, and he would take it from his lips occasionally, flick the ashes onto the shiny dials with a finger-nail, smile his strange smile, and carefully burn holes in the plush fabric of the upholstery. The fabric (real fabric; not plastic) would smolder, send out a wisp of bad-smelling smoke, and there would be another charred black hole in the seat. Ren would smile again, put the cigarette back in his mouth, lean back, and puff slowly. Ren was waiting to answer the radio signal from the orbot, to assure its pilot and crew that all was well, to talk them down to death. If they suspected anything was wrong, he would be the first to die. Even if everything went perfectly, he stood a high chance of dying anyway; he was the most exposed.

It was almost certainly a suicide job. Ren said that he didn't give a shit; maybe he actually didn't. Or at least had convinced himself that he didn't. He was an odd man. Older than any of us, even Heynith, he had worked most of his life as a cadet executive in Admin at Urheim, devoted his existence to his job, subjugated all of his energies to it. He had been passed over three times for promotion to executive status, years of redoubled effort and mounting anxiety between each rejection. With the third failure he had been quietly retired to live on the credit subsidy he had earned with forty years of service. The next morning, precisely at the start of his accustomed work period, he stole a biodeth from a security guard in the Admin Complex, walked into his flowsector, killed everyone there, and disappeared from Urheim. After a year on the run, he had managed to contact the Quaestors. After another year of training, he was serving with a commando team in spite of his age. That had been five years ago; I had known him for two. During all that time, he had said little. He did his job very well with a minimum of waste motion, never made mistakes, never complained, never showed emotion. But occasionally he would smile and burn a hole in something. Or someone.

The sun dived at the horizon, seeming to crash into the plain in an explosion of flame. Night swallowed us in one gulp. Black as a beast's belly.

It jerked me momentarily back into reality. I had a bad moment when I thought I'd gone blind, but then reason returned and I slipped the infrared lenses down over my eyes, activated them. The world came back in shades of red. Heynith was working cramped legs against the body of the lasers. He spoke briefly, and we gulped some stimulus pills to keep us awake; they were bitter, and hard to swallow dry as usual, but they kicked up a familiar acid churning in my stomach, and my blood began to flow faster. I glanced at Heynith. He'd been quiet, even for Heynith. I wondered what he was thinking. He looked at me, perhaps reading the thought, and ordered us out of the trench.

Goth and I crawled slowly out, feeling stiff and brittle, slapped our thighs and arms, stamped to restore circulation. Stars were sprinkling across the sky, salt spilled on black porcelain. I still couldn't read them, I found. The day plants had vanished, the day animals had retreated into catalepsy. The night plants were erupting from the ground, fed by the debris of the day plants. They grew rapidly, doubling, then tripling in height as we watched. They were predominantly thick, ropy shrubs with wide, spearhead leaves of dull purple and black, about four feet high. Goth and I dug a number of them up, root systems intact, and placed them on top of the tarpaulin to replace the day plants that had shriveled with the first touch of bitter evening frost. We had to handle them with padded gloves; the leaf surfaces greedily absorbed the slightest amount of heat and burned like dry ice.

Then we were back in the trench, and it was worse than ever. Motion had helped for a while, but I could feel the numbing panic creeping back, and the momentary relief made it even harder to bear. I tried to start a conversation, but it died in monosyllabic grunts; and silence sopped up the echoes. Heynith was methodically checking the laser controls for the nth time. He was tense; I could see it bunch his shoulder muscles, bulge his calves into rock as they pushed against the footplates of the saddle. Goth looked worse than I did; he was somewhat younger, and usually energetic and cheerful. Not tonight.

We should have talked, spread the pain around; I think all of us realized it. But we couldn't; we were made awkward by our own special intimacy. At one time or another, every one of us had reached a point where he *had* to talk or die, even Heynith, even Ren. So we all had talked and all had listened, each of us switching roles sooner or later. We had poured our fears and dreams and secret memories upon each other, until now we knew each other too well. It made us afraid. Each of us was afraid that he had exposed too much, let down too many barriers. We were afraid of vulnerability, of the knife that jabs for the softest fold of the belly. We were all scarred men already, and twice-shy. And the resentment grew that others had seen us that helpless, that vulnerable. So the walls went back up, intensified. And so when we needed to talk again, we could not. We were already too close to risk further intimacy.

Visions returned, ebbing and flowing, overlaying the darkness.

The magma churning, belching a hot breath that stinks of rotten eggs.

The cadet, his face inhuman in the death rictus, blood running down in a wash from his smashed forehead, plastering one eye closed, bubbling at his nostril, frothing around his lips, the lips tautening as his head jerks forward and then backwards, slamming the ground, the lips then growing slack, the body slumping, the mouth sagging open, the rush of blood and phlegm past the tombstone teeth, down the chin and neck, soaking into the fabric of the tunic. The feet drumming at the ground a final time, digging up clots of earth.

I groped for understanding. I had killed people before, and it had not bothered me except in sleep. I had done it mechanically, routine backed by hate, hate cushioned by routine. I wondered if the night would ever end. I remembered the morning I'd watched from the mountain. I didn't think the night would end. A big idea tickled my mind again.

The city swallowed by stone.

The cadet falling, swinging his arms wide.

Why always the cadet and the city in conjunction? Had one sensitized me to the other, and if so, which? I hesitated.

Could both of them be equally important?

One of the other section leaders whistled.

We all started, somehow grew even more tense. The whistle came again, warbling, sound floating on silence like oil on water. Someone was coming. After a while we heard a rustling and snapping of underbrush approaching downslope from the mountain. Whoever it was, he was making no effort to move quietly. In fact he seemed to be blundering along, bulling through the tangles, making a tremendous thrashing noise. Goth and I turned in the direction of the sound, brought our guns up to bear, primed them. That was instinct. I wondered who could be coming *down* the mountain toward us. That was reason. Heynith twisted to cover the opposite direction, away from the noise, resting his gun on the saddle rim. That was caution. The thrasher passed our position about six feet away, screened by the shrubs. There was an open space ten feet farther down, at the head of a talus bluff that slanted to the valley. We watched it. The shrubs at the end of the clearing shook, were torn aside. A figure stumbled out into starlight.

It was a null.

Goth sucked in a long breath, let it hiss out between his teeth.

Heynith remained impassive, but I could imagine his eyes narrowing behind the thick lenses. My mind was totally blank for about three heartbeats, then, surprised: a null! and I brought the gun barrel up, then, uncomprehending: a null? and I lowered the muzzle. Blank for a second, then: how? and trickling in again: how? Thoughts snarled into confusion, the gun muzzle wavered hesitantly.

The null staggered across the clearing, weaving in slow figure-eights. It almost fell down the talus bluff, one foot suspended uncertainly over the drop, then lurched away, goaded by tropism. The null shambled backward a few paces, stopped, swayed, then slowly sank to its knees.

It kneeled: head bowed, arms limp along the ground, palms up.

Heynith put his gun back in his lap, shook his head. He told us he'd be damned if he could figure out where it came from, but we'd have to get rid of it. It could spoil the ambush if it was spotted. Automatically, I raised my gun, trained it. Heynith stopped me. No noise, he said, not now. He told Goth to go out and kill it silently.

Goth refused. Heynith stared at him speechlessly, then began to flush. Goth and Heynith had had trouble before. Goth was a good man, brave as a bull, but he was stubborn, tended to follow his own lead too much, had too many streaks of sentimentality and touchiness, *thought* too much to be a really efficient cog.

They had disagreed from the beginning, something that wouldn't have been tolerated this long if the Quaestors hadn't been desperate for men. Goth was a devil in a fight when aroused, one of the best, and that had excused him a lot of obstinacy. But he had a curious squeamishness, he hadn't developed the layers of numbing scar-tissue necessary for guerrilla work, and that was almost inevitably fatal. I'd wondered before, dispassionately, how long he would last.

Goth was a hereditary fullsentient, one of the few connected with the Quaestors. He'd been a cadet executive in Admin, gained access to old archives that had slowly soured him on the Combine, been hit at the psychologically right moment by increasing Quaestor agitprop, and had defected; after a two-year proving period, he'd been allowed to participate actively. Goth was one of the only field people who was working out of idealism rather than hate, and that made us distrust him. Heynith also nurtured a traditional dislike for hereditary full-sentients. Heynith had been part of an industrial sixclone for over twenty years before joining the Quaestors. His Six had been wiped out in a production accident, caused by standard Combine negligence. Heynith had been the only survivor. The Combine had expressed mild sympathy, and told him that they planned to cut another clone from him to replace the destroyed Six; he of course would be placed in charge of the new Six, by reason of his seniority. They smiled at him, not seeing any reason why he wouldn't want to work another twenty years with biological replicas of his dead brothers and sisters, the men, additionally, reminders of what he'd been as a youth, unravaged by years of pain. Heynith had thanked them politely, walked out, and kept walking, crossing the Gray Waste on foot to join the Quaestors.

I could see all this working in Heynith's face as he raged at Goth. Goth could feel the hate too, but he stood firm. The null was incapable of doing anybody any harm; he wasn't going to kill it. There'd been enough slaughter. Goth's face was bloodless, and I could see D'kotta reflected in his eyes, but I felt no sympathy for him, in spite of my own recent agonies. He was disobeying orders. I thought about Mason, the man Goth had replaced, the man who had died in my arms at Itica, and I hated Goth for being alive instead of Mason. I had loved Mason. He'd been an Antiquarian in the Urheim archives, and he'd worked for the Quaestors almost from the beginning, years of vital service before his activities were discovered by the Combine. He'd escaped the raid, but his family hadn't. He'd been offered an admin job in Quaestor HQ, but had turned it down and insisted on fieldwork in spite of warnings that it was suicidal for a man of his age. Mason had been a tall, gentle, scholarly man who pretended to be gruff and hard-nosed, and cried alone at night when he thought nobody could see. I'd often thought that he could have escaped from Itica if he'd tried harder, but he'd been worn down, sick and guilt-ridden and tired, and his heart hadn't really been in it; that thought had returned to puzzle me often afterward. Mason had been the only person I'd ever cared about, the one who'd been more responsible than anybody for bringing

me out of the shadows and into humanity, and I could have shot
Goth at that moment because I thought he was betraying Mason's
memory.

Heynith finally ran out of steam, spat at Goth, started to call
him something, then stopped and merely glared at him, lips
white. I'd caught Heynith's quick glance at me, a nearly invisible
head-turn, just before he'd fallen silent. He'd almost forgotten
and called Goth a zombie, a widespread expletive on World that
had carefully *not* been used by the team since I'd joined. So
Heynith had never really forgotten, though he'd treated me with
scrupulous fairness. My fury turned to a cold anger, widened out
from Goth to become a sick distaste for the entire world.

Heynith told Goth he would take care of him later, take care
of him good, and ordered me to go kill the null, take him upslope
and out of sight first, then conceal the body.

Mechanically, I pulled myself out of the trench, started
downslope toward the clearing. Anger fueled me for the first few
feet, and I slashed the shrubs aside with padded gloves, but it
ebbed quickly, leaving me hollow and numb. I'd known how the
rest of the team must actually think of me, but somehow I'd
never allowed myself to admit it. Now I'd had my face jammed
in it, and, coming on top of all the other anguish I'd gone through
the last two days, it was too much.

I pushed into the clearing.

My footsteps triggered some response in the null. It surged
drunkenly to its feet, arms swinging limply, and turned to face
me.

The null was slightly taller than me, build very slender, and
couldn't have weighed too much more than a hundred pounds. It
was bald, completely hairless. The fingers were shriveled, limp
flesh dangling from the club of the hand; they had never been
used. The toes had been developed to enable technicians to walk
nulls from one section of the Cerebrum to another, but the feet
had never had a chance to toughen or grow callused: they were
a mass of blood and lacerations. The nose was a rough blob of
pink meat around the nostrils, the ears similarly atrophied. The
eyes were enormous, huge milky corneas and small pupils, like
those of a nocturnal bird; adapted to the gloom of the Cerebrum,
and allowed to function to forestall sensory deprivation; they

aren't cut into the psychocybernetic current like the synapses or the ganglions. There were small messy wounds on the temples, wrists, and spine-base where electrodes had been torn loose. It had been shrouded in a pajamalike suit of nonconductive material, but that had been torn almost completely away, only a few hanging tatters remaining. There were no sex organs. The flesh under the rib cage was curiously collapsed; no stomach or digestive tract. The body was covered with bruises, cuts, gashes, extensive swatches sun-baked to second-degree burns, other sections seriously frostbitten or marred by bad coldburns from the night shrubs.

My awe grew, deepened into archetypical dread.

It was from D'kotta, there could be no doubt about it. Somehow it had survived the destruction of its Cerebrum, somehow it had walked through the boiling hell to the foothills, somehow it had staggered up to and over the mountain shoulder. I doubted if there'd been any predilection in its actions; probably it had just walked blindly away from the ruined Cerebrum in a straight line and kept walking. Its actions with the talus bluff demonstrated that; maybe earlier some dim instinct had helped it fumble its way around obstacles in its path, but now it was exhausted, baffled, stymied. It was miraculous that it had made it this far. And the agony it must have suffered on its way was inconceivable. I shivered, spooked. The short hairs bristled on the back of my neck.

The null lurched toward me.

I whimpered and sprang backwards, nearly falling, swinging up the gun.

The null stopped, its head lolling, describing a slow semicircle. Its eyes were tracking curiously, and I doubted if it could focus on me at all. To it, I must have been a blur of darker gray.

I tried to steady my ragged breathing. It didn't hurt me; it was harmless, nearly dead anyway. Slowly, I lowered the gun, pried my fingers from the stock, slung the gun over my shoulder.

I edged cautiously toward it. The null swayed, but remained motionless. Below, I could see the vacvan at the bottom of the bluff, a patch of dull gunmetal sheen. I stretched my hand out slowly. The null didn't move. This close, I could see its gaunt ribs rising and falling with the effort of its ragged breathing. It was trembling, an occasional convulsive spasm shuddering along its frame. I was surprised that it didn't stink; nulls were rumored to have a strong personal odor, at least according to the talk in field camps—bullshit, like so much of my knowledge at that time. I watched it for a minute, fascinated, but my training told me I couldn't stand out here for long; we were too exposed. I took another step, reached out for it, hesitated. I didn't want to touch it. Swallowing my distaste, I selected a spot on its upper arm free of burns or wounds, grabbed it firmly with one hand.

The null jerked at the touch but made no attempt to strike out or get away. I waited warily for a second, ready to turn my grip into a wrestling hold if it should try to attack. It remained still, but its flesh crawled under my fingers, and I shivered myself in reflex. Satisfied that the null would give me no trouble, I turned and began to force it upslope, pushing it ahead of me.

It followed my shove without resistance, until we hit the first of the night shrubs, then it staggered and made a mewing, inarticulate sound. The plants were burning it, sucking warmth out of its flesh, raising fresh welts, ugly where bits of skin had adhered to the shrubs. I shrugged, pushed it forward. It mewed and lurched again. I stopped. The null's eyes tracked in my direction, and it whimpered to itself in pain. I swore at myself for wasting time, but moved ahead to break a path for the null, dragging it along behind me. The branches slapped harmlessly at my warmsuit as I bent them aside; occasionally one would slip past and lash the null, making it flinch and whimper, but it was spared the brunt of it. I wondered vaguely at my motives for doing it. Why bother to spare someone (some*thing*, I corrected nervously) pain when you're going to have to kill him (*it*) in a minute? What difference could it make? I shelved that and concentrated on the movements of my body; the null wasn't heavy, but it wasn't easy to drag it uphill either, especially as it'd stumble and go down every few yards and I'd have to pull it back to its feet again. I was soon sweating, but I didn't care, as the action helped to occupy my mind, and I didn't want to have to face the numbness I could feel taking over again.

We moved upslope until we were about thirty feet above the trench occupied by Heynith and Goth. This looked like a good place. The shrubs were almost chest-high here, tall enough to

hide the null's body from an aerial search. I stopped. The null
bumped blindly into me, leaned against me, its breath coming in
rasps next to my ear. I shivered in horror at the contact.
Gooseflesh blossomed on my arms and legs, swept across my
body. Some connection sent a memory whispering at my mind,
but I ignored it under the threat of rising panic. I twisted my
shoulder under the null's weight, threw it off. The null slid back
downslope a few feet, almost fell, recovered.

I watched it, panting. The memory returned, gnawing inces-
santly. This time it got through:

Mason scrambling through the sea-washed rocks of Cape Itica
toward the waiting ramsub, while the fire sky-whipping behind
picked us out against the shadows; Mason, too slow in vaulting
over a stone ridge, balancing too long on the razor-edge in
perfect silhouette against the night; Mason jerked upright as a
fusor fired from the high cliff puddled his spine, melted his flesh
like wax; Mason tumbling down into my arms, almost driving
me to my knees; Mason, already dead, heavy in my arms, *heavy
in my arms*; Mason torn away from me as a wave broke over us
and deluged me in spume; Mason sinking from sight as Heynith
screamed for me to come on and I fought my way through the
chest-high surf to the ramsub—

That's what supporting the null had reminded me of: Mason,
heavy in my arms.

Confusion and fear and nausea.

How could the null make me think of Mason?

Sick self-anger that my mind could compare Mason, gentle as
the dream-father I'd never had, to something as disgusting as the
null.

Anger novaed, trying to scrub out shame and guilt.

I couldn't take it. I let it spill out onto the null.

Growling, I sprang forward, shook it furiously until its head
rattled and wobbled on its limp neck, grabbed it by the shoulders,
and hammered it to its knees.

I yanked my knife out. The blade flamed suddenly in starlight.

I wrapped my hand around its throat to tilt its head back.

Its flesh was warm. A pulse throbbed under my palm.

All at once, my anger was gone, leaving only nausea.

I suddenly realized how cold the night was. Wind bit to the bone.

It was *looking* at me.

I suppose I'd been lucky. Orphans aren't as common as they once were—not in a society where reproduction has been relegated to the laboratory—but they still occur with fair regularity. I had been the son of an uncloned junior executive who'd run up an enormous credit debit, gone bankrupt, and been forced into insolvency. The Combine had cut a clone from him so that their man-hours would make up the back discrepancy, burned out the higher levels of his brain, and put him in one of the nonsentier penal Controlled Environments. His wife was also cloned, but avoided brainscrub and went back to work in a lower capacity in Admin. I, as a baby, then became a ward of the State, and was sent to one of the institutional Environments. Imagine an endless series of low noises, repeating over and over again forever, no high or low spots, everything level: MMMMMMMMM MMMMMMMMMMMMMMMMMMMMMMMMMMMMMMMMM MMMMMMMMM. Like that. That's the only way to describe the years in the Environments. We were fed, we were kept warm, we worked on conveyor belts piercing together miniaturized equipment, we were put to sleep electronically, we woke with our fingers already busy in the monotonous, rhythmical motions that we couldn't remember learning, motions we had repeated a million times a day since infancy. Once a day we were fed a bar of food-concentrates and vitamins. Occasionally, at carefully calculated intervals, we would be exercised to keep up muscle tone. After reaching puberty, we were occasionally masturbated by electric stimulation, the seed saved for sperm banks. The administrators of the Environment were not cruel; we almost never saw them. Punishment was by machine shocks; never severe, very rarely needed. The executives had no need to be cruel. All they needed was MMMMMMMMMMMMMMMMMMM MMMMMMMMM. We had been taught at some early stage, probably by shock and stimulation, to put the proper part in the proper slot as the blocks of equipment passed in front of us. We had never been taught to talk, although an extremely limited language of several mood-sounds had independently developed among us; the executives never spoke on the rare intervals when

they came to check the machinery that regulated us. We had
never been told who we were, where we were; we had never
been told anything. We didn't care about any of these things, the
concepts had never formed in our minds, we were only semi-
conscious at best anyway. There was nothing but MMMMMM
MMMMMMMMMMMMMMMMM. The executives weren't concerned with our spiritual development; there was no graduation
from the Environment, there was no place else for us to go in a
rigidly stratified society. The Combine had discharged its obli-
gation by keeping us alive, in a place where we could even be
minimally useful. Though our jobs were sinecures and could
have been more efficiently performed by computer, they gave the
expense of our survival a socially justifiable excuse, they put us
comfortably in a pigeonhole. We were there for life. We would
grow up from infancy, grow old, and die, bathed in MMMM
MMMMMMMMMMMMMMMMM. The first real, separate, and
distinct memory of my life is when the Quaestors raided the
Environment, when the wall of the assembly chamber suddenly
glowed red, buckled, collapsed inward, when Mason pushed out
of the smoke and the debris cloud, gun at the ready, and walked
slowly toward me. That's hindsight. At the time, it was only a
sudden invasion of incomprehensible sounds and lights and
shapes and colors, too much to possibly comprehend, incredibly
alien. It was the first discordant note ever struck in our lives:
MMMMMMMMMMMMM!!!! shattering our world in an instant,
plunging us into another dimension of existence. The Quaestors
kidnapped all of us, loaded us onto vacvans, took us into the
hills, tried to undo some of the harm. That'd been six years ago.
Even with the facilities available at the Quaestor underground
complex—hypnotrainers and analysis computers to plunge me
back to childhood and patiently lead me out again step by step
for ten thousand years of subjective time, while my body
slumbered in stasis—even with all of that, I'd been lucky to
emerge somewhat sane. The majority had died, or been driven
into catalepsy. I'd been lucky even to be a Ward of the State, the
way things had turned out. Lucky to be a zombie. I could have
been a low-ranked clone, without a digestive system, tied forever
to the Combine by unbreakable strings. Or I could have been one
of the thousands of tank-grown creatures whose brains are used

as organic-computer storage banks in the Cerebrum gestalts, completely unsenteient: I could have been a null.

Enormous eyes staring at me, unblinking.

Warmth under my fingers.

I wondered if I was going to throw up.

Wind moaned steadily through the valley with a sound like MMMMMMMMMMMMMMMM.

Heynith hissed for me to hurry up, sound riding the wind, barely audible. I shifted my grip on the knife. I was telling myself: it's never been really sentient anyway. Its brain has only been used as a computer unit for a biological gestalt, there's no individual intelligence in there. It wouldn't make any difference. I was telling myself: it's dying anyway from a dozen causes. It's in pain. It would be kinder to kill it.

I brought up the knife, placing it against the null's throat. I pressed the point in slowly, until it was pricking flesh.

The null's eyes tracked, focused on the knifeblade.

My stomach turned over. I looked away, out across the valley. I felt my carefully created world trembling and blurring around me, I felt again on the point of being catapulted into another level of comprehension, previously unexpected. I was afraid.

The vacvan's headlights flashed on and off, twice.

I found myself on the ground, hidden by the ropy shrubs. I had dragged the null down with me, without thinking about it, pinned him flat to the ground, arm over back. That had been the signal that Ren had received a call from the orbot, had given it the proper radio code reply to bring it down. I could imagine him grinning in the darkened cab as he worked the instruments.

I raised myself on an elbow, jerked the knife up, suspending it while I looked for the junction of spine and neck that would be the best place to strike. If I was going to kill him (*it*), I would have to kill him (*it!*) now. In quick succession, like a series of slides, like a computer equation running, I got: D'kotta—the cadet—Mason—the null. *It* and *him* tumbled in selection. Came up *him*. I lowered the knife. I couldn't do it. He was human. Everybody was.

For better or worse, I was changed. I was no longer the same person.

I looked up. Somewhere up there, hanging at the edge of the

atmosphere, was the tinsel collection of forces in opposition called a starship, delicately invulnerable as an iron butterfly. It would be phasing in and out of "reality" to hold its position above World, maintaining only the most tenuous of contacts with this continuum. It had launched an orbot, headed for a rendez-vous with the vacvan in this valley. The orbot was filled with the gene cultures that could be used to create hundreds of thousands of nonsentient clones who could be imprinted with behavior patterns and turned into computer-directed soldiers; crude but effective. The orbot was filled with millions of tiny metal blocks, kept under enormous compression: when released from tension, molecular memory would reshape them into a wide range of weapons needing only a power source to be functional. The orbot was carrying, in effect, a vast army and its combat equipment, in a form that could be transported in a five-hundred-foot vacvan and slipped into Urheim, where there were machines that could put it into use. It was the Combine's last chance, the second wind they needed in order to survive. It had been financed and arranged by various industrial firms in the Com-monwealth who had vested interests in the Combine's survival on World. The orbot's cargo had been assembled and sent off before D'kotta, when it had been calculated that the reinforce-ments would be significant in ensuring a Combine victory; now it was indispensable. D'kotta had made the Combine afraid that an attack on Urheim might be next, that the orbot might be intercepted by the Quaestors if the city was under siege when it tried to land. So the Combine had decided to land the orbot elsewhere and sneak the cargo in. The Blackfriars had been selected as a rendezvous, since it was unlikely the Quaestors would be on the alert for Combine activity in that area so soon after D'kotta, and even if stopped, the van might be taken for fleeing survivors and ignored. The starship had been contacted by esper en route, and the change in plan made.

Four men had died to learn of the original plan. Two more had died in order to learn of the new landing site and get the information to the Quaestors in time.

The orbot came down.

I watched it as in a dream, coming to my knees, head above

the shrubs. The null stirred under my hand, pushed against the ground, sat up.

The orbot was a speck, a dot, a ball, a toy. It was gliding silently in on gravs, directly overhead.

I could imagine Heynith readying the laser, Goth looking up and chewing his lip the way he always did in stress. I knew that my place should be with them, but I couldn't move. Fear and tension were still there, but they were under glass. I was already emotionally drained. I could sum up nothing else, even to face death.

The orbot had swelled into a huge, spherical mountain. It continued to settle toward the spot where we'd calculated it must land. Now it hung just over the valley center, nearly brushing the mountain walls on either side. The orbot filled the sky, and I leaned away from it instinctively. It dropped lower—

Heynith was the first to fire.

An intense beam of light erupted from the ground downslope, stabbed into the side of the orbot. Another followed from the opposite side of the valley, then the remaining two at once.

The orbot hung, transfixed by four steady, unbearably bright columns.

For a while, it seemed as if nothing was happening.

I could imagine the consternation aboard the orbot as the pilot tried to reverse gravs in time.

The boat's hull had become cherry red in four widening spots. Slowly, the spots turned white.

I could hear the null getting up beside me, near enough to touch. I had risen automatically, shading my eyes against glare.

The orbot exploded.

The reactor didn't go, of course; they're built so that can't happen. It was just the conventional auxiliary engines, used for steering and for powering internal systems. But that was enough.

Imagine a building humping itself into a giant stone fist, and bringing that fist down on you, *squash*. Pain so intense that it snuffs your consciousness before you can feel it.

Warned by instinct, I had time to do two things.

And I stepped in front of the null to shield him.

Then I was kicked into oblivion.

• • •

I awoke briefly to agony, the world a solid, blank red. Very, very
far away, I could hear someone screaming. It was me.

I awoke again. The pain had lessened. I could see. It was day,
and the night plants had died. The sun was dazzling on bare rock.
The null was standing over me, seeming to stretch up for miles
into the sky. I screamed in preternatural terror. The world
vanished.

The next time I opened my eyes, the sky was heavily overcast
and it was raining, one of those torrential southern downpours. A
Quaestor medic was doing something to my legs, and there was
a platvac nearby. The null was lying on his back a few feet away,
a bullet in his chest. His head was tilted up toward the scuttling
gray clouds. His eyes mirrored the rain.

That's what happened to my leg. So much nerve tissue destroyed
that they couldn't grow me a new one, and I had to put up with
this stiff prosthetic. But I got used to it. I considered it my tuition
fee.

I'd learned two things: that everybody is human, and that the
universe doesn't care one way or the other; only people do. The
universe just doesn't give a damn. Isn't that wonderful? Isn't that
a relief? It isn't out to get you, and it isn't going to help you
either. You're on your own. We all are, and we all have to answer
to ourselves. We make our own heavens and hells; we can't pass
the buck any further. How much easier when we could blame our
guilt or goodness on God.

Oh, I could read supernatural significance into it all—that I
was spared because I'd spared the null, that some benevolent
force was rewarding me—but what about Goth? Killed, and if
he hadn't balked in the first place, the null wouldn't have stayed
alive long enough for me to be entangled. What about the other
team members, all dead—wasn't there a man among them as
good as me and as much worth saving? No, there's a more direct
reason why I survived. Prompted by the knowledge of his
humanity, I had shielded him from the explosion. Three other
men survived that explosion, but they died from exposure in the

hours before the med team got there, baked to death by the sun. I didn't die because the null stood over me during the hours when the sun was rising and frying the rocks, *and his shadow shielded me from the sun.* I'm not saying that he consciously figured that out, deliberately shielded me (though who knows), but I had given him the only warmth he'd known in a long nightmare of pain, and so he remained by me when there was nothing stopping him from running away—and it came to the same result. You don't need intelligence or words to respond to empathy, it can be communicated through the touch of fingers—you know that if you've ever had a pet, ever been in love. So that's why I was spared, warmth for warmth, the same reason anything good ever happens in this life. When the med team arrived, they shot the null down because they thought it was trying to harm me. So much for supernatural rewards for the just.

So, empathy's the thing that binds life together; it's the flame we share against fear. Warmth's the only answer to the old cold questions.

So I went through life, boy; made mistakes, did a lot of things, got kicked around a lot more, loved a little, and ended up on Kos, waiting for evening.

But night's a relative thing. It always ends. It does; because even if you're not around to watch it, the sun always comes up, and someone'll be there to see.

It's a fine, beautiful morning.

It's always a beautiful morning somewhere, even on the day you die.

You're young—that doesn't comfort you yet.

But you'll learn.